❧ LA NOUVELLE HÉLOÏSE ❧

LA NOUVELLE HÉLOÏSE

JULIE, OR THE NEW ELOISE. LETTERS OF TWO LOVERS, INHABITANTS OF A SMALL TOWN AT THE FOOT OF THE ALPS.

❧ BY JEAN-JACQUES ROUSSEAU

Translated and Abridged by Judith H. McDowell

THE PENNSYLVANIA STATE UNIVERSITY PRESS

University Park, Pennsylvania

Paperback edition, 1987
ISBN 0-271-00602-1 (pbk.)
Third printing, 1993

❧ CONTENTS ❧

Introduction 1

A Note on this Translation 17

La Nouvelle Héloïse 23

Appendix 411

✤ INTRODUCTION ✤

THE FASCINATION of the intellectual, scientific, and social revolutions of eighteenth century France sometimes casts a shadow over one of the most interesting developments of that vigorous century: the rise of the novel. During the glorious age of Louis XIV, the novel had been a genre of minor importance, condemned by neo-classical writers, who preferred to cultivate tragedy and the epic, the more "noble" genres. But after the death of the Sun King, the once abused literary form began a gradual ascent to a position of eminence which by the end of the century was to eclipse that of the older, traditional modes of literary expression. The beginnings were tenuous and the progress was slow, but around the middle of the century the novel received an impetus which was to guarantee and to accelerate its development as a significant, valued literary form. This impetus was provided by the only extended work of fiction written by one of the most influential and prominent men of the century: Jean-Jacques Rousseau.

Between April, 1759, and January, 1760, Rousseau sent sections of a manuscript of an epistolary novel in six parts to Marc-Michel Rey, an Amsterdam printer, according to a previous agreement wherein Rey had consented to publish this book exactly as Rousseau had written it, incorporating even the manuscript errors. After a series of harsh letters between the author and the printer, the former criticizing the tardiness of the publication and the faultiness of the proofs and the latter defending himself as well as he could, the novel finally appeared in Paris in February, 1761, entitled *Julie, ou la Nouvelle Héloïse. Lettres de deux Amans, Habitans d'une petite Ville au pied des Alpes. Recueillies et publiées Par J. J. Rous-*

seau. The success of the book was immediate and overwhelming. Very shortly after its appearance, counterfeited editions were produced all over France, there being at that time no legal protection of foreign printers. In 1763, Rey put out a second authorized edition, one with numerous changes by the author, and he continued to republish the novel at intervals during Rousseau's lifetime. In all, seventy-two editions in French were put on sale between 1761 and 1800. With the exception of Voltaire's *Contes,* Le Sage's *Gil Blas,* and some of Prévost's novels, no other eighteenth century French fiction up to the time of Rousseau's death had even one-tenth this much circulation.

In his extremely thorough critical edition of *La Nouvelle Héloïse,* Daniel Mornet carefully traced the history of the French editions of the novel.[1] James H. Warner did the same for the eighteenth century English translation,[2] and found that the English version first appeared in April, 1761, testimony of the rapidity with which literary works crossed the channel in those days. This translation, entitled *Eloisa: or a series of original letters collected and published by J. J. Rousseau,* was done by William Kenrick, who for some inscrutable reason preferred to remain anonymous, and it was the basis for all subsequent editions of the English text up until this one. In all, according to Warner, there were ten English editions between 1761 and 1800.[3] *La Nouvelle Héloïse* had, then, an unusually large reading public in England and, subsequently, in America.

[1] J.-J. Rousseau, *La Nouvelle Héloïse,* ed. Daniel Mornet. Les Grands Écrivains de la France, 2nd Ser., 4 vols. (Paris, 1925).

[2] "Eighteenth Century English Reaction to *La Nouvelle Héloïse,*" *PMLA* (Sept., 1937), 803-19.

[3] *Ibid.,* p. 809. The dates of these editions were 1761 (three during that year), 1764, 1773-74 (in a collected works), 1773, 1776, 1784, 1794(?), and 1795. Contradicting Warner, however, is Frank Gees Black, who claims that there were fourteen English editions before 1800. ("The Epistolary Novel in the Late Eighteenth Century," *University of Oregon Studies in Literature and Philology,* No. 2 (April, 1940), p. 147.) Black may be including the Irish, Scottish, and American editions. There was one edition in Philadelphia in 1796, and some of the copies bear the marks of printers in Dublin and Edinburgh.

As for the English editions during the nineteenth century, I have been unable to locate any scholarly bibliographical investigations. I have learned of two editions, both in London, dated 1803 and 1810, and am reasonably sure that there has not been a printing of Kenrick's translation since 1810, because of Rousseau's decline in popularity in England after the Revolution. As Edmund Gosse pointed out (in "Rousseau in England in the Nineteenth Century," *Fortnightly Review,* XCVIII (1912), pp. 22-38), the first attacks upon Rousseau's influence in England, spearheaded by Burke, were directed against his political writings, but his novel also gradually fell into disfavor, among intellectuals at least. Although Shelley and Byron and even writers as late as Eliot and Ruskin

The setting of this remarkably successful book is in the country of Rousseau's youth, along the shores of the Lake of Geneva, with the main part of the action taking place in the small villages of Vevey and Clarens. By eighteenth century standards the plot is relatively simple and is one familiar to all literatures, that of the fallen and regenerated woman. The first three parts of the novel are devoted to the celebration of the passionate, mutual love of Saint-Preux and Julie; the last three praise Julie's return to virtue as a faithful wife and dedicated mother. Rousseau's moral point is implicitly but forcefully made: if she is carried away by true love, a woman may fall from innocence before she is married without leaving a stain upon her character, but after marriage such a lapse would be criminal. Fidelity between husband and wife is essential, for an honorable marriage is the true basis of society. Julie must learn to build a happy and productive domestic life on the ashes of her great love affair with Saint-Preux, and as long as she maintains the delusion that she has been cured of her passion for him she is successful.

The circumstances surrounding the composition of *La Nouvelle Héloïse* are interesting to examine for the light they throw upon the character of the author, as well as upon the novel itself. We know from the *Confessions* that Rousseau wrote the book between 1756 and 1758, mostly while at Madame d'Épinay's country home, the Hermitage, Rousseau's temporary sanctuary after his years in the Parisian salons. He had been accompanied to the Hermitage by Thérèse, a woman who was clearly no true companion to Jean-Jacques despite her obvious attachment to him, and he was living a difficult, solitary life. As usual, he took refuge in his imagination.

Despite his many adventures, Rousseau had never had a satisfactory love affair—satisfactory, that is, for a man who, like Rousseau, had been nurtured on the seventeenth century French romances of La Calprenède and others, from which by his own admission he had developed his sensibilities. As a release, therefore, from his frustrations as a lover, he invented an ideal woman, Julie d'Étange, and projected himself as the beloved of her heart, Saint-Preux. The process is described in Book IX of the *Confessions:*

The impossibility of attaining the real persons precipitated

---

were admittedly impressed by *La Nouvelle Héloïse,* the temper of the nineteenth century in England was not nearly as tuned to Rousseau as that of the eighteenth had been. As Gosse remarked, the Victorian sensibility was hostile to the dubious morals of Rousseau's hero and heroine, and by the middle of the nineteenth century both the novel and the *Confessions* were considered not only immoral, but dull in their immorality.

me into the land of chimeras; and seeing nothing that existed worthy of my exalted feelings, I fostered them in an ideal world which my creative imagination soon peopled with beings after my own heart. Never was this resource more opportune, and never did it prove more fertile. In my continual ecstasies I intoxicated myself with draughts of the most exquisite sentiments that have ever entered the heart of a man. Altogether ignoring the human race, I created for myself societies of perfect creatures celestial in their virtue and in their beauty, and of reliable, tender, and faithful friends such as I had never found here below. . . .

I imagined two women friends, rather than two of my own sex, since although examples of such friendships are rarer they are also more beautiful. I endowed them with analogous but different characters; with features if not perfect yet to my taste, and radiant with kindliness and sensibility. I made one dark, the other fair; one lively, the other gentle; one sensible, the other weak, but so touching in her weakness that virtue itself seemed to gain by it. I gave one of them a lover to whom the other was a tender friend and even something more; but I allowed of no rivalry or quarrels or jealousy because I find it hard to imagine any painful feelings, and I did not wish to discolour my charming picture with anything degrading to Nature. Being captivated by my two charming models, I identified myself as far as I could with the lover and friend. But I made him young and pleasant, whilst endowing him also with the virtues and faults that I felt in myself. . . .

I confined myself for a long time to so vague a plan because it was sufficient to fill my imagination with pleasant objects, and my heart with those feelings on which it loves to feed. This fiction, by constant repetition, finally assumed greater consistency and took a fixed and definite shape in my brain. It was then that the whim seized me to set down on paper some of the situations that it suggested to me and, by recalling all that I had felt in my youth, to give some sort of expression to my desire to love which I had never been able to satisfy, and which I now felt was devouring me.

At first I jotted down a few scattered letters, unrelated to one another and in no sequence; and when I made up my mind to connect them I was often in considerable trouble. What is almost incredible but is nevertheless a fact is that the first two parts were written almost entirely in this manner, without my having any well-formed plan or even foreseeing that one day I should be tempted to make a regular work of it.[4]

[4] All quotations from the *Confessions* have been taken from the translation by J. M. Cohen (Penguin Books, 1953).

So much for the composition of the first two parts, which tell of the lovers' passionate attraction, their intimacy, and, despite their separation, their hope of an eventual marriage. But in Part Three, a note of hopelessness is introduced. With Saint-Preux's renunciation of Julie, the novel reverses its emphasis and from celebrating indulged passion turns to the glorification of sacrifice and virtue. For the explanation of this reversal, we can again go to the *Confessions*.

At the end of January, 1757, after the composition of the first two parts of the novel, the Countess d'Houdetot visited Jean-Jacques at the Hermitage, a visit which by his own admission was the "beginning of a romance." At her second visit in the spring, Rousseau knew then that it was love, "the first and only love in all my life." Seeing her repeatedly, he began to look upon her as the realization of his ideal:

> I saw my Julie in Madame d'Houdetot, and soon I saw only Madame d'Houdetot, but endowed with all the perfections with which I had just embellished the idol of my heart. (Book IX)

But although Sophie d'Houdetot refused Jean-Jacques "nothing that the most tender friendship could grant," she nevertheless failed to imitate Julie in all particulars, for she had pledged herself to remain faithful to her first lover, Saint-Lambert. Rousseau managed to conquer his passion and respect the countess' scruples:

> If I had been young and attractive, and if subsequently Mme d'Houdetot had been weak, I should blame her conduct here; but as all this was not the case I cannot but applaud and admire her. The course she adopted displayed generosity and prudence alike. She could not leave me suddenly without telling Saint-Lambert the reason, which would have compelled him to visit me. That would have meant risking a break between two friends, and perhaps a scandal, which she was anxious to avoid. For me she felt both respect and good-will. She was sorry for my foolishness; without flattering it she deplored it, and tried to cure me of it. She was glad to preserve a friend whom she valued both for her lover and herself, and talked to me about nothing with so much pleasure as about the intimate and delightful trio we could form together once I had returned to my senses. But she did not always confine herself to these friendly exhortations, and did not spare me, when necessary, the harsher reproaches I thoroughly deserved.
>
> I was still less sparing of them myself. Once I was alone I came to my senses, and I was calmer for having spoken. A love

known to the person who inspires it becomes more bearable. The violence with which I reproached myself for my passion should have cured me, if a cure had been possible. What powerful arguments did I not call to my aid in order to stifle it! My moral sense, my belief, my principles, the shame, the faithlessness, the crime, the abuse of a trust I owed to friendship and, last of all, the absurdity of being consumed at my age by the most extravagant of passions for an object whose heart was already engaged, and could neither make me any return nor afford me any hope: by a passion indeed which far from having anything to gain by constancy became less bearable every day. . . .

But I am wrong to speak of an unrequited love, for mine was in a sense returned. There was equal love on both sides, although it was never mutual. We were both intoxicated with love,—hers for her lover, and mine for her; our sighs and our delicious tears mingled together. We confided tenderly in one another, and our feelings were so closely in tune that it was impossible for them not to have united in something. Yet even when our intoxication was at its most dangerous height she never forgot herself for a moment. As for myself, I protest, I swear, that if ever I was betrayed by my senses and tried to make her unfaithful, I never truly desired it. The vehemence of my passion of itself kept it within bounds. The duty of self-denial had exalted my soul. The light of every virtue adorned in my eyes the idol of my heart; to have soiled that divine image would have been to destroy it. I might have been able to commit the crime; a hundred times it has been committed in my heart. But to dishonour my Sophie! Could that ever be possible? No, no! I told her a hundred times that, if it had been in my power to gratify myself, if she had put herself at my mercy of her own free will, except in a few short moments of madness I should have refused to purchase my own happiness at such a price. I loved her too well to wish to possess her. (Book IX)

In a similar way, as we see in *La Nouvelle Héloïse,* Saint-Preux manages to respect Julie's scruples and schools himself to live in relative tranquillity with Julie and her husband, Wolmar, though this *ménage à trois* may seem not a little unusual to modern readers. The novel, then, abruptly turns from the theme of requited passion to that of virtuous sacrifice at a point corresponding to the time that Jean-Jacques was forced to stifle his passion for Sophie d'Houdetot.[5]

[5] However, Daniel Mornet, in his investigation into the chronology of the composition of *La Nouvelle Héloïse,* found that Rousseau had conceived the char-

That Rousseau projected Julie from Madame d'Houdetot and Saint-Preux from himself in the last three parts of *La Nouvelle Héloïse* is even more evident when one examines some of the correspondence between the novelist and the countess, for they write to each other in the same effusive style and sentimental vein as do Saint-Preux and Julie. Here, for example, are some excerpts from Madame d'Houdetot's letters to Rousseau:

> Oh love! Oh friendship! As long as you will exist for me, you will embellish my life and you will make it dear to me. Do you not ask me what my life consists of? Indifferently, I perform the duties of society, to which I only lend myself; I go to plays for my amusement and my diversion. But my most beloved, most continual, most delightful occupation is to give myself up to the sentiments of my heart, to contemplate them, to be nourished by them, to express them to the one who inspires them in me. That is what my true life consists of, and what makes me feel the pleasures of existence. . . .
>
> Let us not, my friend, scorn a sentiment which elevates the soul as much as love does and which is capable of giving so much vitality to the virtues. Love, such as we conceive of it, cannot exist in a mediocre soul, and it can never debase the one in which it dwells nor inspire in it anything for which it may be ashamed.[6]

And here is a typical letter from Jean-Jacques to Sophie:

> To whom can I sooner speak of the delights of these memories than to her who has made me enjoy them so well once more? It is you whose duty it is to make dear to me the memory of my last errors by that of the virtues which have reclaimed me from them. You have made me too ashamed of my faults for me to be able to be ashamed of them now; and I do not know what makes me prouder, the victories won over myself or the assistance which has made me win them. If I had listened only to a criminal passion, if I had been base for one moment, and if I

---

acter of Wolmar and had even planned out the scene of the visit to Meillerie, with which Part Four concludes, before Madame d'Houdetot's second visit in the spring of 1757. As one easily surmises, the *Confessions* are not always to be trusted as a reliable record of Rousseau's life. Nevertheless, it seems very clear that the heavily moralistic tone of the last three parts of the novel was directly inspired by Rousseau's own sacrifice of Sophie to Saint-Lambert, even though he may have conceived of Saint-Preux's similar sacrifice somewhat earlier.

[6] Quoted in Hippolyte Buffenoir, *La Comtesse d'Houdetot, Une Amie de J.-J. Rousseau* (Paris, 1901), pp. 133, 135-36. Translation mine.

had found you weak, how dear I would be paying today for
the ecstasies which would have seemed so sweet! Deprived of all
the sentiments which have united us, we would have ceased to
be united; shame and remorse would have made us odious to
each other. I would hate you for having loved you too much,
and what intoxication of voluptuousness might ever have been
able to recompense my heart for so pure and so tender an attachment? Would you be as dear to me, after having gratified
my desires, as you are after having made me virtuous? [7]

One need only turn, almost at random, to the pages of Rousseau's
novel to find these sentiments and this language duplicated.

La Nouvelle Héloïse, then, is clearly a *roman vécu* in many respects and as such deserves study for the insight it provides into the
character of the author. But, of course, Rousseau did not compose
his novel purely from his personal experience and recollected emotions. He was working, moreover, within the established literary
tradition of the sentimental novel. With customary thoroughness,
Daniel Mornet investigated the history of prose fiction in France,
as it relates to the appearance of La Nouvelle Héloïse,[8] and concluded that Rousseau's novel was less original than even the author
himself thought. By the time of its composition, French taste was
veering away from the novel of intrigue and adventure and toward
that of morality and sentiment. The vogue of the *comédie larmoy-
ante* in the mid-eighteenth century illustrates that well before La
Nouvelle Héloïse the French public took pleasure in pouring forth
tears and pious platitudes at prodigious rates. But it was, of course,
the English novel of sentiment to which Rousseau was most indebted.

Long before Jean-Jacques entered his land of chimeras, a vigorous anglomania had begun to undermine the neoclassical literary
traditions of the French. The most influential single author in this
English vogue was Richardson, whose *Pamela* and *Clarissa Harlowe*, translated by Prévost in 1751, made a singular impression
upon French novelists. Certainly Rousseau was influenced by Richardson, especially by *Clarissa Harlowe*, which in his *Letter to
d'Alembert* he praised enthusiastically and extravagantly. There
are some noticeable similarities between *Clarissa Harlowe* and *La
Nouvelle Héloïse*, particularly in the epistolary technique and the

[7] *Ibid.*, pp. 154-55. Translation mine.
[8] *Op. cit.*, Vol. I, pp. 7-60.

constant eulogizing of simplicity and virtue. We also find some resemblances in the plots of the two novels: Clarissa has a confidant in Miss Howe, just as Julie has one in Claire; Clarissa's cousin Morden acts in some ways much like Lord Bomston; Clarissa's father, in attempting to force her to marry Solmes, resembles the Baron d'Étange in his efforts to unite Julie and Wolmar; both Clarissa and Julie are horrified at the prospects of a duel and endeavor to prevent it; and Lovelace and Saint-Preux are both haunted by a fatal dream. But these resemblances must not be pushed too far.[9] Mornet urges us to believe that even though the novels of Richardson may have created the atmosphere in which Julie and Saint-Preux breathed, their blood and soul were Rousseau's alone.

Perhaps more important than the literary sources upon which Rousseau drew for *La Nouvelle Héloïse* are those compositions subsequently inspired by it. Even though Voltaire called the success of the novel one of the infamies of the century, *La Nouvelle Héloïse* became one of the seminal books of the preromantic period. Of course, it is unrealistic to believe that Rousseau's novel created romanticism, as it is sometimes claimed, or that it even created romantics. As Daniel Mornet found in his investigation of all the novels published in France between 1761 and 1780, only fifty out of more than nine hundred books were clearly imitations of *La Nouvelle Héloïse* in one way or another, and it must be remembered that even when the imitators cited Rousseau as their inspiration, they were also disciples of Richardson and Prévost.[10] And even though there were seventy-two editions of Rousseau's novel before 1800, between 1759 and the Revolution there were also at least fifty editions of *Candide*. But despite the relatively small quantitative influence of *La Nouvelle Héloïse*, it cannot be denied that the novel created for Rousseau a place beside Voltaire as a director of European thought.

Moreover, besides the influence of *La Nouvelle Héloïse* upon the taste and morality of the eighteenth century reading public, the novel had considerable indirect literary repercussions. For one thing, as Mornet found, before *La Nouvelle Héloïse* outside nature

---

[9] Joseph Texte points out a great many more parallels in *Jean-Jacques Rousseau and the Cosmopolitan Spirit in Literature*, trans. J. W. Matthews (London, 1899), pp. 233-49.

[10] See Mornet, *op. cit.*, Vol. I, Ch. 4, pp. 237-305 ("L'Influence de *La Nouvelle Héloïse*"). Mornet also appends to his critical notice a lengthy bibliography of eighteenth century novels, classified according to type.

played only a small role in the eighteenth century novel; after 1761 nature is extremely important in fiction.[11] Furthermore, after Rousseau the prestige of the adventure and historical novel declined, not to be completely revived until Sir Walter Scott, and that of the sentimental and moralistic novel increased. The *roman personnel* also came into favor for the first time, as M. H. Abrams notes, when *La Nouvelle Héloïse* invited the reader to identify the hero with his creator and thus blazed the trail for Goethe's *Werther*, Friedrich Schlegel's *Lucinde*, Tieck's *William Lovell*, and Chateaubriand's *Réné*.[12] Finally, the success of Rousseau's book possibly had even a significant negative result, in the formulation of the appeal and influence of the Marquis de Sade. In one sense, as Mario Praz has pointed out, de Sade's books are a reaction to the exaggerated sentiment of Richardson and Rousseau: "*Justine* is a reversal of the *Nouvelle Héloïse*." [13]

That *La Nouvelle Héloïse* had the enormous success that it did, and that Rousseau's characters subsequently became at least the spiritual parents of countless romantic fictions, can perhaps best be explained by the particular quality and appeal of Jean-Jacques' sentimentalism. But before we attempt to analyze the nature of this sentimentalism, let us first define the term as it applies to Rousseau and to the sentimentalists who preceded him. Actually, the word "sentimentalism" may be used in two relatively distinct senses, the first referring to the optimistic emphasis upon the goodness of the human being. This line of thought had for its source the deism and humanitarianism of the early part of the eighteenth century and represented, in part, a reaction against orthodox Calvinistic theology with its doctrine of the depravity of man. Such optimistic emphasis upon human perfectibility is connected closely to the primitivistic doctrine that the savage, who has remained closer to nature and who has been less subject to the corrupting influence of society, is thus nobler and more nearly perfect than civilized man. The result of this emphasis was, quite naturally, a reliance upon the feelings, as opposed to reason and law, as guides to truth and conduct. This sort of sentimentalism we may call "sensibility," in order to distinguish it from the other sense of the term "sentimentalism"

[11] See Mornet's *Le Sentiment de la nature de Jean-Jacques Rousseau à Bernardin de Saint-Pierre* (Paris, 1907).

[12] *The Mirror and the Lamp* (New York, 1958), p. 98. Benjamin Constant's *Adolphe* might be added to this list.

[13] *The Romantic Agony* (New York, 1956), p. 436.

—namely, the pure and directionless indulgence in emotion, often preceded by a direct and conscious effort to induce emotion, and the failure to restrain or evaluate emotion through the exercise of the judgment. The earmarks of the first sort of sentimentalism, or sensibility, are a contempt for urban life and the conventions of civilized society, such as its business and legal activities and its aesthetic tastes, and a love for the simplicity of rural life and the solitude and beauty of the countryside. The obvious manifestations of sentimentalism in the second sense are the copious tears of the sentimental heroes and heroines, the numerous sighs and palpitations, the ecstasies, the thrills, and the swoons which abound in sentimental fiction.

La Nouvelle Héloïse and the sentimental novels which preceded it clearly illustrate sentimentalism in both these senses. But to understand why sentimentalism caught on so rapidly and so securely after the publication of La Nouvelle Héloïse, we must observe Rousseau's peculiar treatment of the sentiments. We must note the particular quality of sublimity which he gave to them, and which thus strengthened their position in the "age of reason" as a source of personal enjoyment which would eventually undermine the traditionally accepted sources and lead to the romanticism of the nineteenth century. To do this, let us analyze certain sentimental attitudes and moods which are apparent in the novel.

The first of these attitudes is that toward nature. Now, "nature" is an extremely ambiguous term in La Nouvelle Héloïse. Of course, there are many fine and eloquent passages of description of the country around the Lake of Geneva, description of what Saint-Preux calls "the savage places which constitute in my eyes the charms of this country." (Part One, Letter XVIII.) There is the description, too, of Julie's Elysium at Clarens, which is "without order and without symmetry." (Part Four, Letter XI.) These sentimental descriptions reflect the author's sensibility, his preference for the wild and uncultivated places; for, as Saint-Preux writes, "It is on the summits of mountains, in the depths of forests, on desert islands," that nature "displays its most affecting charms." (Part Four, Letter XI.) But "nature" in the novel is far more than the wild beauties of the Swiss countryside, the opposite of the formal and artificial gardens of the neoclassicists. It is, in effect, a reflection of, or response to, the emotional state of the man of feeling, the "sensitive soul," for whom alone natural beauties exist. When, for example, Saint-Preux believes himself permanently separated from Julie at Meillerie, he writes to her that

One sees nothing green any more, the grass is yellow and withered, the trees are bare, the dry and cold north-east wind heaps up the snow and ice, and all nature is dead in my eyes, like the hope in the bottom of my heart. (Part One, Letter XXVI)

On the other hand, when he eagerly anticipates the proposed rendezvous with his mistress in the isolated chalet near the source of the Vevaise, he writes,

I find the country more gay, the green more fresh and vivid, the air more pure, the sky more serene. The song of the birds seems to be more tender and voluptuous; the murmur of the brooks evokes a more amorous languor; from afar the blooming vine exudes the sweetest perfumes; a secret charm either embellishes or fascinates my senses. One would say that the earth adorns itself to make for your happy lover a nuptial bed worthy of the beauty he adores and of the passion which consumes him. (Part One, Letter XXXVIII)

Moreover, "nature" is also used in *La Nouvelle Héloïse* to refer to the simplicity of the rustic life in the country, as opposed to the artificial and corrupt "civilized" life at Paris. Whereas the urban environment evokes only contempt, "nature" in this sense touches the purer sentiments of the "sensitive soul"; the appeal of this "nature," however, is extremely indefinite.

But "nature" in *La Nouvelle Héloïse* has still a further significance, distinct from the above mentioned aspects of sentimentalism and sensibility. It is in this further sense that it is closely connected with the second sentimental attitude, namely, the moral attitude. Rousseau believes that though most men have been perverted by society, there remain a few, the "sensitive souls," in whom "nature" still persists. Saint-Preux and Julie, of course, belong to this group. Julie, despite her fall from innocence, is referred to in glowing terms, and for her moral character she is given praise which formerly had been reserved for canonized saints at least. And why? Because the voice of "nature" is strong in her. Because, we are told, she uses her heart for her guide, not the "absurd maxims" of society, and therefore her conduct is undeniably right. Though in the eyes of conventional society or conventional religion she may be "guilty," to Saint-Preux and other "sensitive souls" she is completely virtuous.

This sentimental attitude toward virtue is extremely interesting, for it constitutes one of the central themes of the novel. Rousseau warns the reader in a preface that in his book "all the sentiments will be unnatural for those who do not believe in virtue." And so, even though the plot of the novel revolves around the theme of the fallen woman, the theme of virtue is developed to an extreme degree. All the characters emit seemingly interminable discourses on the subject of virtue, despite the fact that the central ones, at the beginning of the novel at least, do not have the strength of will to practice the restraint which virtue imposes. The truth of the matter is that in *La Nouvelle Héloïse* virtue is not connected with action or conduct. Rather, it is a sentiment. Indeed, it is a passion, and, moreover, the strongest of them all. We are told this quite explicitly by Wolmar, as Julie reports in a letter to Claire:

> . . . we triumph over passions only by opposing one to another. When the passion of virtue comes to the fore, it alone dominates and keeps all the rest in a state of equilibrium. (Part Four, Letter XII)

Thus it is that the "sensitive soul," no matter what his actual conduct may be, will be judged virtuous as long as he has a passion for virtue. Lord Bomston may therefore say of Saint-Preux and Julie,

> Your two souls are so extraordinary that they cannot be judged by common rules. . . . Joined to your love is an emulation of virtue which elevates you, and you would both be less worthy if you were not in love. (Part One, Letter LX)

This attitude toward the passion of virtue and those toward other passions as well, are another interesting sentimental aspect of *La Nouvelle Héloïse*. For the possession of passions, the stronger the better, is a proof of the excellent character of the passionate "sensitive soul." Lord Bomston thus says in a letter to Claire, describing the suffering Saint-Preux, who has been forcibly separated from his mistress,

> An ardent and unhappy passion is for a time, for always perhaps, capable of smothering some of his faculties, but it is itself a proof of their excellence and of the use he could make of them in cultivating wisdom; for the highest reason is only attained through the same power of the soul which gives rise to great passions, and we serve philosophy worthily only with the same ardor that we feel for a mistress. (Part Two, Letter II)

The passionate "sensitive soul," thus, has this advantage over the common herd. There is still a further advantage in that, though he may be a victim of the prejudices of society, he may console himself by expressing his passions. As Rousseau tells us in a preface to the novel,

> Passion, overflowing, expresses itself more effusively than force-fully. It does not even think of being persuasive; it does not suspect that anyone may question it. When it expresses what it feels, it is less to expose its feelings to others than to comfort itself.

And the proper method of this expression, characteristically, is vague and directionless, disordered and repetitious. The eloquence of a passionate love letter is in its very disorder, Rousseau tells us, again in a preface, and in reading such a letter, "one feels oneself moved without knowing why."

Besides these various sentimental attitudes toward nature, virtue, and passion in *La Nouvelle Héloïse*, there are certain observable moods of feeling in the novel which, though distinct, are closely connected and seem to bring about relatively similar results. As we have observed in the definition of the second sort of sentimentalism, there is in Rousseau—and in preceding sentimentalists, to be sure —an intense delight in the subjective emotional state, an enjoyment of sentiment and emotional thrills. The distinctive feature of *La Nouvelle Héloïse*, it would appear, is that this enjoyment is carried to the point of sublimity and thus subverts the common sense rationalism which is observable in earlier sentimentalists such as Prévost. For example, Saint-Preux describes to Claire in the following manner the days he spent with Julie :

> Days of pleasure and glory, no, they were not those of a mortal! They were too beautiful to have perished. A gentle ecstasy filled their whole duration, and converged them like eternity into a point. There was neither past nor future for me, and I tasted the delights of a thousand centuries at once. (Part Three, Letter VI)

One would suspect that this description of a period of intense emotion is simply a matter of the jargon of the sentimentalist, were it not for the fact that there are so many such expressions throughout the novel. Saint-Preux seems to live spasmodically in sublime raptures, to seek constantly to experience the sensation-packed, sublime moment. And this experience is not always connected with his passion for Julie; often it ties in with his affinity to nature.

But, of course, the sublime moments of intense emotional thrill are transitory, and sometimes, no matter how earnestly the "sensitive soul" seeks to experience them, they are not to be had. Here lies the source of a second sentimental mood of the novel: melancholy. The numerous laments and threats of suicide which Saint-Preux utters whenever he feels himself cut off from the object of his heart's desire, are an ample indication of the intensity of this melancholy. And even when his desires have been satisfied, he is incapable of any mood but one of melancholy, for the sublime moment has passed. As he writes to Julie, just after returning from a night of love,

> Oh let us die, my sweet friend! Let us die, beloved of my heart! What shall we do henceforward with an insipid youth, now that we have exhausted all its delights? (Part One, Letter LV)

Such melancholy, however, is not unbearable, for the "sensitive souls" are never drawn to the point of actual suicide.[14] Moreover, they obviously derive a certain exquisite delight from their suffering. This somewhat masochistic pleasure is made explicit by Saint-Preux in a letter to Julie during one of their separations:

> But nevertheless, do you not feel that our excessive misery is not without compensation, and that if they [Claire and Monsieur d'Orbe] have pleasures which we are deprived of, we have some also which they cannot know? Yes, my sweet friend, in spite of absence, privations, alarms, in spite of despair itself, the powerful exertion of two hearts toward each other is always attended by a secret pleasure unknown to tranquil souls. It is one of the miracles of love to make us find pleasure in suffering, and we should regard as the worst of misfortunes a state of indifference and oblivion which would take all the feeling of our misery from us. Let us lament our fate, oh Julie! But let us not envy anyone. (Part Two, Letter XVI)

And so, though melancholy is characterized by despair and despondency, it is not without its recompenses, for the "sensitive soul" in a melancholic mood can have feelings of pleasure somewhat akin to (though not, of course, so intense as) those which are produced by moments of sublimity.

[14] However, after Goethe's *Werther* (1774) they went to such lengths.

Rousseau's treatment of the sentiments, then, is distinct from that of his predecessors in sentimental fiction, though, to be sure, both had certain general features in common. His is not the simple analysis, relatively speaking, of the sentiments that we find in Marivaux, for example. Nor does Rousseau make an appeal to the reader's pity, as Prévost does, for the plight of the sentimental hero trapped in a web created by his feelings. Nor is Rousseau's tone so somber or moralistic as that of Richardson. Rather, in *La Nouvelle Héloïse* we find a glorification of the sentiments, an assertion of the superiority and importance of individual feelings. The intense delight in subjective emotional states is further enhanced because of this glorification and because, as Rousseau emphasizes throughout the novel, such states are revelatory of new truths, always vague but significant.

That Rousseau thus made of the sentiments a singular source of intense and glorified pleasure is an important reason, no doubt, for the immense success of his novel and for its influence. To Rousseau's generation, witnessing the wearisome decadence of the neo-classical tradition, with all its artificial restraint and decorum, this doctrine of the emancipation of the emotions had a great and wide appeal. And in the subsequent romantic period, it had far-reaching and well-known consequences.

❖ A NOTE ON THIS TRANSLATION ❖

IN MY TRANSLATION of *La Nouvelle Héloïse* I have been concerned not solely with literal exactness but also, and perhaps more importantly, with conveying to the reader the distinctive flavor of Rousseau's prose, with capturing not only the novelist's meaning but the texture of his style as well. To illustrate more thoroughly what I have attempted to do, I should first like to point out some of the qualities of the French text.

In a dialogue written as a preface to *La Nouvelle Héloïse*, Rousseau has the participants, himself and an unnamed critic, engage in a discussion of the style of the letters which comprise the novel. At one point, the author contends to his disbelieving critic that the faultiness of one's language gives evidence of the intensity of one's feelings. He argues:

> Read a love letter written by someone in his study, by a wit who wants to appear brilliant; in spite of the paucity of fire he may have in his head, his pen will burn up the paper, as they say, but the warmth he inspires will not go any further. You will be charmed, even perhaps stirred, but it will be merely a short-lived, sterile emotion which will leave you only words to remember it by. On the other hand, a letter that love has truly dictated, a letter from an honestly impassioned lover will be loosely written, verbose, drawn out to great lengths, disorderly, repetitious. The lover's heart, full of overflowing emotion, keeps saying the same thing over and over and never finishes saying it, like a living spring which endlessly gushes forth and is never exhausted. There is no wit, nothing remarkable in it; you don't remember any words or turns of phrase. You admire nothing; you are struck by nothing. However, you feel your soul touched; you feel moved without understanding why.

The effusive style of the impassioned love letter described above is, for the most part, Rousseau's own. With little reticence, Jean-Jacques writes as the whim seizes him, as he admits in Book IX of the *Confessions*. However, it must be remembered that Rousseau was a musician. The disorder, the repetition, and the gushing quality of his prose do not keep it from having a certain rhythm and balance.

I should like to illustrate Rousseau's style by analyzing a representative passage from *La Nouvelle Héloïse*. The following is the beginning of Letter XXVI of Part One, written by Saint-Preux to Julie during their first separation as he keeps watch on her house from the crags of Meillerie:

[1] Que mon état est changé dans peu de jours! [2] Que d'amertumes se mêlent à la douceur de me rapprocher de vous! [3] Que de tristes réflexions m'assiègent! [4] Que de traverses mes craintes me font prévoir! [5] O Julie, que c'est un fatal présent du ciel qu'une âme sensible! [6] Celui qui l'a reçu s'attendre à n'avoir que peine et douleur sur la terre. [7] Vil jouet de l'air et des saisons, le soleil ou les brouillards, l'air couvert ou serein régleront sa destinée, et il sera content ou triste au gré des vents. [8] Victime des préjugés, il trouvera dans d'absurdes maximes un obstacle invincible aux justes voeux de son coeur. [9] Les hommes le puniront d'avoir des sentiments droits de chaque chose, et d'en juger par ce qui est véritable plutôt que par ce qui est de convention. [10] Seul il suffiroit pour faire sa propre misère, en se livrant indiscrètement aux attraits divins de l'honnête et du beau, tandis que les pesantes chaînes de la nécessité l'attachent à l'ignominie. [11] Il cherchera la félicité suprême sans se souvenir qu'il est homme: son coeur et sa raison seront incessamment en guerre, et des désirs sans bornes lui prépareront d'éternelles privations.

[12] Telle est la situation cruelle où me plongent, le sort qui m'accable, et mes sentiments qui m'élèvent, et ton père qui me méprise, et toi qui fais le charme et le tourment de ma vie. [13] Sans toi, Beauté fatale! je n'aurois jamais senti ce contraste insupportable de grandeur au fond de mon âme et de bassesse dans ma fortune. [14] J'aurois vécu tranquille et serois mort content, sans daigner remarquer quel rang j'avois occupé sur la terre. [15] Mais t'avoir vue et ne pouvoir te posséder, t'adorer et n'être qu'un homme! être aimé et ne pouvoir être heureux! habiter les mêmes lieux et ne pouvoir vivre ensemble! [16] O Julie à qui je ne puis renoncer! [17] O destinée que je ne puis vaincre! [18] Quels combats affreux vous excités en moi, sans pouvoir jamais surmonter mes désirs ni mon impuissance!

A reader's attention to this passage is captured immediately by the rhetorical formulas of the sentimentalist—"O Julie . . . Beauté fatale!"—and by the liberal use of the exclamation point to express the generally disturbed state of affairs. But upon reading the passage more closely, the reader is impressed by the rhythmical patterns which establish themselves. Observe the climactic arrangement of the sentences of the first paragraph: the first four are very short; [5] and [6] are somewhat longer; [7] and [8] are about the length of an average sentence; and [9], [10], and [11] are rather long. This short-long-longer sentence pattern, with its corresponding lengthening of cadence, and the converse of this pattern, with its shortening, can be found in many of Rousseau's paragraphs throughout the novel. Just as in his musical compositions, in his prose Jean-Jacques knew how to quicken and retard tempo for the sake of emphasis and variety.

Another striking feature of the quoted passage is the balance of the elements. After the emphatic parallelism of the opening four sentences, Rousseau begins pairing terms: in [6], the nouns "peine et douleur"; in [7], the prepositional phrases "de l'air et des saisons," the nouns "le soleil ou les brouillards," and the adjectives "couvert ou serein" and "content ou triste"; in [9], the infinitives "d'avoir . . . et d'en juger" and the clauses "ce qui est véritable . . . ce qui est de convention"; in [10], the prepositional phrases "de l'honnête et du beau"; and in [11], the two independent clauses of the compound sentence. In sentence [12], the pattern is doubled, with the paralleling of four nouns and their modifying clauses. In [13] and [14], we again find the pairing of prepositional phrases, "de grandeur au fond de mon âme et de bassesse dans ma fortune," and of predicates "aurois vécu tranquille et serois mort content"; and in [15] we again see the double pattern in the series of infinitive phrases. Sentences [16] and [17] are pairs themselves, and [18] ends with the balanced nouns "mes désirs" and "mon impuissance." Thus, although the passage is in some ways "loosely written, verbose, drawn out to great lengths, disorderly, repetitious," it nevertheless has a formal balanced structure, with repeated rhythmical patterns to tie the whole subtly together.

My chief problem as a translator has been to convey this sense of rhythm and balance in Rousseau's prose. In general, I have solved it by translating as simply and as literally as possible, but attempting as much as I could to capture the rhythmic patterns of Rousseau's sentences without creating an awkward word order in English. However, sometimes a literal translation was impossible, as in

several instances where Rousseau's narrative shifts suddenly and
sporadically from the past tense to the historical present. The author's obvious intention was to convey a sense of excitement, but
such an abrupt shift of tense in English is merely awkward, and
therefore I have kept the past tense throughout these narrative
portions, allowing the short, breathless sentences to provide the
sense of excitement. Another change I have often made in the text is
in the matter of punctuation. By English standards, even modern
French punctuation is somewhat chaotic, and Rousseau seemed to
have little logic behind his use of commas, colons, semicolons, or
periods. I have therefore taken considerable liberties for the sake
of clarity, and the novel has been punctuated in accordance with
formal English rules. However, I have almost always left in the ubi-
quitous exclamation point, as well as the ellipses, wherever I found
them. Finally, I have made no distinction between *tu* and *vous* in
my translation. My reason was not simply that *thee, thou,* and *thy*
seem overly archaic these days, but also that Rousseau himself often
uses *vous* where one might reasonably expect to find the familiar
form.[15] Consequently, since there is a conspicuous lack of consistency in this matter, I have resolved it by translating both the
French forms as *you.*

In no way have I attempted to use the conventional style of the
eighteenth century English novel of sentiment to approximate the
prose of *La Nouvelle Héloïse,* for such would obviously give a thoroughly inaccurate impression of Rousseau's intentions. The first
translator, William Kenrick, committed this fault, for he failed to
see that Rousseau's eighteenth century sensibilities are conveyed
less by the convolutions of style and formality of vocabulary, as is
the case with many English novels, than by the content of the book.
For example, Kenrick substitutes for Saint-Preux's complaint to
Julie, "Mon coeur a plus qu'il n'esperoit, et n'est pas content," the
following stilted sentence: "My present felicity seems far to exceed
my most sanguine expectations, and yet I am discontented." [16] Such
palpable absurdities are typical of Kenrick's version.[17] Although

---

[15] Mornet noted that in Rousseau's day the *vous* was frequently used even between lovers. (J.-J. Rousseau, *La Nouvelle Héloïse,* ed. Daniel Mornet. Les Grands
Ecrivains de la France, 2nd Ser. Vol. II, p. 16, nl. Paris, 1925.)

[16] My translation: "My heart has more than it hoped for, and yet is not content."

[17] James H. Warner examined the whole of Kenrick's translation, comparing it
to the original in an attempt to discover in exactly what form Rousseau was
presented to the eighteenth century English readers. He came to the following
conclusion about Kenrick's work:

for many years the critics applauded it, it is clearly a gross misrepresentation of the original.

To remain faithful to Rousseau and at the same time to bring *La Nouvelle Héloïse* within the interest range of the twentieth century reader—this has been my aim both in the translation and in the abridgment of the novel. Although not long by the standards of an eighteenth century reading public conditioned by the virtually interminable tribulations of Clarissa Harlowe, Rousseau's book seems unnecessarily protracted to modern taste. Rousseau is often repetitious, describing an event sometimes from three or four points of view, breaking into his narrative to recapitulate the plot, and restating an opinion or a moral dictum several times. These repetitious elements can be deleted without serious harm to the plot or to the characterizations of the novel. Moreover, like many eighteenth century novelists, Rousseau delighted in digressions on moral, social, and political topics. A great many of these digressions are to be found in essence, sometimes in almost the same form, in such works as *Emile*, the *Discourses*, and the *Social Contract* (all available in good, modern translations), and I have felt justified in deleting them when they serve to impede the progress of the book. By far the greatest number of my deletions has come in the last three parts, where the moralistic tone becomes heavier and the digressions lengthier. Conversely, I have translated the first two parts almost in their entirety, for these opening sections contain the greater part of the book's action and fewer digressions to weaken a reader's interest. Only in few cases have I removed merely a single sentence or a short paragraph. Almost all the deletions have consisted at least of a lengthy paragraph, and most frequently I have cut out substan-

---

"As one would anticipate from these alterations, the translation is inaccurate and inferior to the original in almost every respect. The transfer into an English idiom resulted almost invariably in longer word-groups, and hence in more infrequent, though not less numerous, pauses. The translator lengthened many phrases, apparently to provide greater smoothness. . . . Weakness also resulted from the omission and alteration of vigorous, realistic figures, and from the loss of occasional assonance. In other words, the English version exemplifies a relatively smooth and restrained type of prose which is particularly unsuited to the prevailingly impassioned tone of the original.

"Consequently Kenrick failed to accomplish his expressed desires. In no sense was his translation less diffuse than the original; it was more so. His substitutions of general for concrete expressions certainly did not improve any alleged vagueness or lack of accuracy. The changes which, according to the translator, were to atone for certain deficiencies in 'propriety' may also be questioned. In short, Kenrick succeeded only in his resolution not to be literal or 'servile,' and in his determination to confine himself to the English idiom." ("Eighteenth Century English Reaction to *La Nouvelle Héloïse*," *PMLA* (Sept., 1937), p. 808.)

tial portions of the text, sometimes even an entire letter. The length of the complete novel is about 315,000 words; I have cut it to approximately 180,000. I have marked each cut by an arabic numeral —[1], [2], and so on—and summarized the deleted portion in an appendix, citing wherever applicable other works by Rousseau which contain similar or relevant material.

The text I have used as a basis for this translation, as I have previously noted, is the definitive critical edition of *La Nouvelle Héloïse* done by the French scholar, Daniel Mornet. One of the many ways in which this excellent and copiously footnoted edition has facilitated my task as translator is by providing, wherever possible, modern French equivalents of eighteenth century terms now out of memory's reach and of the Swiss provincial terms which Rousseau occasionally used. I am also indebted to Mornet's edition for most of the translator's notes which I have from time to time felt necessary to include for the sake of perfect clarity. I am further indebted to Dr. Harold M. Priest, Professor of English at the University of Denver, for reading the manuscript and for obligingly supplying the translations of the Italian passages. Finally, I wish to acknowledge the invaluable assistance of my husband, Dr. Robert E. Mc-Dowell.

Summer, 1967   J.H.M.

PART I

❦ LETTER I ❦

To Julie

I MUST FLY from you, Mademoiselle, I know I must. I should not have waited so long, or rather, I should never have seen you. But what can I do now? How shall I begin? You have promised me your friendship; consider my difficulties and advise me.

You know that I entered your home only at the invitation of your mother. Knowing that I had cultivated some acceptable talents, she thought that, here in a place where teachers are not available, I would be of some use in the education of a daughter whom she adores. In turn, proud to be instrumental in adding any embellishment to such a beautiful character, I dared to take this dangerous task upon myself without foreseeing the peril of it, or at least without dreading it. I shall not tell you that I am beginning to pay for my presumption. I hope that I shall never forget myself to the point of saying things to you which are not proper for you to hear, or of failing in the respect I owe to your virtue even more than to your noble birth and to your personal charms. If I must suffer, at least I have the consolation of suffering alone, and I would not wish for a happiness which might cost you yours.

However, I see you every day, and I notice that without knowing it you are innocently aggravating torments with which you cannot sympathize and of which you must be ignorant. Indeed, I know the course prudence, for want of hope, prescribes in cases like this, and I would endeavor to follow it, if I could in this case reconcile prudence with courtesy; but how can I decently leave a house whose mistress has herself bidden me enter, in which she overwhelms me with kindnesses, in which she believes me to be of some use to her whom she holds most dear in the world? How can I deprive this affectionate mother of the pleasure of one day surprising her husband with your progress in the studies which she keeps hidden from him for this very purpose? Must I leave impolitely, without saying anything? Must I declare to her the reason for my leaving? And will not even this declaration be offensive to her, coming from a man whose birth and fortune cannot permit him to hope for your hand?

I see, Mademoiselle, only one way of getting out of the predicament in which I find myself. It is if the hand that plunged me into it extricates me, if my punishment as well as my fault comes from you, and if at least through pity for me you deign to refuse me your presence. Show my letter to your parents; have your door denied to me; spurn me in whatever manner you please. I can endure everything from you, but I cannot fly from you of my own accord.

You, to spurn me! I, to fly from you! And why? Why then is it a crime to be sensible of merit, and to love one whom I must necessarily honor? No, lovely Julie, your physical charms might have dazzled my eyes, but they might never have led my heart astray without the more powerful attraction that animates them. It is that touching combination of a lively sensibility and an invariably sweet disposition, it is that tender pity for all the misfortunes of others, it is that justness of spirit and that exquisite taste which derive their excellence from the purity of your soul—these are, in short, the charms of your sentiments which, much more than those of your person, I adore. I confess that you may be imagined still more beautiful, but more lovable and more worthy of the heart of an honorable man—no Julie, it is not possible.

Sometimes I dare to flatter myself that heaven has brought about a secret sympathy in our affections, as well as in our tastes and our ages. Being still so young, we are impaired by nothing in our natural tendencies, and all our inclinations seem to agree. Before having acquired the standard prejudices of the world, we have some similar ways of feeling and seeing, and why should I not dare to imagine in our hearts the same agreement that I perceive in our judgments? Sometimes our eyes meet; a few sighs escape us at the same time; a few furtive tears . . . oh Julie! If this accord came from far . . . if heaven had destined . . . all human power . . . ah, pardon me! I am mistaken. I dare to take my wishes for hope; the ardor of my desires lends to their realization the possibility which it lacks.

With dread I see what torment my heart prepares for itself. I am not seeking to indulge my weakness; I should like to hate it, if that were possible. Judge for yourself whether my sentiments are pure by the kind of favor I have just asked of you. Destroy, if it can be done, the source of the poison which both nourishes and kills me. I wish only to be cured or to die, and I beg for your severity as a lover would beg for your kindness.

Yes, I promise, I swear on my part to do all I can to recover my reason, or to hide in the bottom of my soul the anxiety which I feel taking form there; but for pity's sake, turn away from me those soft eyes which deal death to me; conceal from my sight your features, your expression, your arms, your hands, your blond hair, your gestures; avoid the eager imprudence of my glances; hold back that touching voice which I never hear without emotion. Be, alas, other than yourself, in order that my heart may be able to return to itself.

Shall I speak to you straightforwardly? In these games that the idleness of the evening gives rise to, you allow yourself some cruel liberties in front of everyone. You have no more reserve with me than with anyone else. Even yesterday, when as a forfeit you almost had to let me take a kiss, you resisted only feebly. Fortunately, I took care not to persist. I felt in my increasing turmoil that I was going to lose control, and I checked myself. Ah! If at least I had been able to enjoy that kiss to my liking, it would have been accompanied by my last breath, and I should have died the happiest of men.

For mercy's sake, let us leave off these games which can have distressing consequences. No, there is not one of them which may not be dangerous, not even the most childish one of all. I always tremble as I take your hand when we play them, and I don't know how it happens that I always must take it. Scarcely is it in mine when a thrill seizes me. The game gives me a fever, or rather, a delirium. I no longer see, I no longer feel anything; and in this moment of mental derangement, what shall I say, what do, where conceal myself, how account for myself?

During our lessons, there is another dangerous consequence. If I see you for one instant without your mother or without your cousin present, you suddenly change your demeanor. You take on such a serious expression, so cold, so chilling, that my respect and fear of displeasing you destroy my presence of mind and my judgment, and for trembling I can hardly stammer out a few words of a lesson that even with all your talents you can follow only with difficulty. Thus, your affected change at once becomes a disadvantage for us both; you grieve me and learn nothing at all, while I am at a loss to imagine what motive can thus change the temperament of so reasonable a person. I venture to ask how you can be so gay in public and so reserved when we are by ourselves. I thought that it should be just the contrary and that it was necessary to restrain one's conduct in proportion to the number of spectators. Instead of that, I observe in you, always with the same perplexity on my part, the ceremonious tone in private, the intimate tone in front of everyone. Deign to be more consistent, and perhaps I shall be less tormented.

If compassion, natural in well-born souls, can cause you to be moved by the pains of an unfortunate man for whom you have shown some esteem, some slight changes in your conduct will make his situation less troublesome and will make him able to bear both his silence and his misfortunes more peacefully. If his condition does not move you, and if you wish to use your power to get rid of him, you can do it without a murmur from him; he still prefers to be destroyed by your order rather than by an indiscreet, vehement emotion which might make him guilty in your eyes. Finally, whatever you may prescribe as my lot, at least I shall not have to reproach myself for having indulged in a rash hope; and if you have read this letter, you have done all that I would dare ask of you, even had I no refusal to fear.

❧ LETTER II ❧

To Julie

HOW MISTAKEN I was, Mademoiselle, in my first letter! Instead of alleviating my pains, I have only increased them by exposing myself to your displeasure, for I feel that the worst thing of all is to displease you. Your silence, your cold and reserved attitude declares my doom only too well. You have granted my request in part but thus only punish me more for it.

> E poi ch' amor di me vi fece accorta
> Fur i biondi capelli allor velati,
> E l'amoroso sguardo in se raccolto.
> PETRARCH

> Since love made you aware of me
> The blond tresses have been covered
> And the amorous glance withheld.

You suppress the innocent familiarity in public about which I was so foolish to complain; but you are only more severe in private, and thus your ingenious cruelty exerts itself both in your obliging-ness and in your refusals.

How can you not realize how cruel this coldness is to me! You should find me punished too much. With what earnestness would I alter the past so that you might not have seen that fatal letter! No, for fear of offending you again, I would not even write this one, if I had not written the first. I do not wish to increase my error but to atone for it. To appease you, must I say that I was mistaken? Must I protest that it was not love which I felt for you? . . . I, *I* should pronounce that odious perjury! Is this vile lie worthy of a heart in which you reign supreme? Ah! How unhappy I am doomed to be, for though I have been rash, I shall not be a liar nor a coward, and the crime that my heart committed my pen cannot disown.

I feel in advance the weight of your indignation, and I await its final consequence, as a favor you owe me for want of any other, for the passion which consumes me deserves to be punished but not scorned. For pity's sake, do not leave me to myself; condescend at least to settle my fate; tell me your pleasure. Whatever you com-mand, I shall obey implicitly. Will you impose an eternal silence upon me? I shall restrain myself and keep it. Will you banish me from your presence? I swear that you will see me no more. Will you command me to die? Ah! That will not be the most difficult to obey. There is no command to which I do not consent, except the one to love you no longer. Yet I would even obey that one, if it were pos-sible.

A hundred times a day I am tempted to throw myself at your feet, to bathe them with my tears, to obtain there my death or my par-don. But always a deadly fear strikes a chill into my courage, my knees tremble and dare not bend, words expire on my lips, and my soul finds no assurance against the dread of angering you. Is there in the world a condition more horrible than mine? My heart knows too well how guilty it is and yet could not cease being so. My crime and my remorse trouble it simultaneously, and without knowing what my fate shall be, I waver in an unbearable doubt between the hope for compassion and the fear of punishment.

But no, I hope for nothing. I do not have the right to hope. The only favor that I may expect from you is to hasten my punish-ment. Let your just revenge be satisfied. Am I not miserable enough to be reduced to begging for it myself? Punish me, you must. But if you are not pitiless, abandon this cold and displeased attitude

which drives me to despair. When a guilty man is sent to his
death, one no longer shows resentment toward him.

⚜ LETTER III ⚜

To Julie

DO NOT lose your patience, Mademoiselle; this is the last importunity you will receive from me.

When I began loving you, how far I was from seeing all the misfortunes I was preparing for myself! At first I foresaw only the unhappiness of a hopeless passion that reason might overcome in
time; next I became acquainted with a greater sorrow in the pain of
displeasing you; and now I am experiencing the most cruel anguish
of all in the discovery of your own misery. Oh Julie! With bitterness
I see it, my complaints are disturbing your tranquillity. You keep
an invincible silence, but everything reveals your hidden agitation
to my attentive heart. Your eyes become melancholy, pensive, fixed
upon the ground; a few distracted looks steal toward me; your
bloom fades; an unusual pallor covers your cheeks; your gaiety
leaves you; a mortal sadness overcomes you; and it is only the un-
alterable sweetness of your soul which preserves your good humor.

Be it sensibility, be it disdain, be it pity for my distress, you are
affected, I see. I fear I am adding to your unhappiness, and this
fear grieves me much more than the hope which could be construed from it can please me, for if I know myself, your happiness
is dearer to me than my own.

As for me, however, I am now beginning to understand how
much I misjudged my own heart, and I see too late that what I first
took for a passing delirium shall constitute my future destiny. It is
your recent sadness which has made me feel my own despair. Never,
no, never might the luster of your eyes, the glow of your complexion, the excellence of your intellect, and all the charm of your former gaiety have produced an effect like that of your despondency.
Do not doubt, divine Julie, that if you could see what an intolerable
flame this week of your languor has kindled in my soul, you yourself would suffer from the pains you cause me. There is now no

remedy for them, and with despair I feel that the fire which consumes me will be extinguished only in the tomb.

Be it so. Whoever cannot make himself happy can at least deserve to be so, and I shall compel you to esteem a man to whom you have not deigned to make the slightest response. I am young and can one day merit the consideration of which I am not now worthy. In the meantime, I must give you back the tranquillity which I have lost forever and which I have taken from you in spite of myself. It is fair that I alone bear the punishment for the crime of which I alone am guilty. Adieu, too beautiful Julie, live tranquilly and recover your happiness; after tomorrow you shall see me no longer. But rest assured that the ardent and pure love with which I have burned for you will not be extinguished in my lifetime, that my heart full of so worthy an object would never debase itself by loving another, that it shall divide all its future homage between you and virtue, and that no other fires shall ever profane the altar at which Julie was adored.

Note from Julie

Do not go away with the idea that your leaving has been made necessary. A virtuous heart would subdue its feelings or keep silent, and perhaps then become formidable in silence. But you . . . you may stay.

Answer

I have kept silent a long time; your coldness has finally made me speak. Even if one can conquer his passions for the sake of virtue, he cannot bear the scorn of her whom he loves. I must leave.

Second Note from Julie

No, Monsieur, after what you have seemed to feel, after what you have dared to tell me, a man such as you have pretended to be does not leave; he does more.

Answer

I have pretended nothing except to have a moderate passion in a heart which actually is in despair. Tomorrow you shall be content, and whatever you may say then, I shall have done less than leaving you.

Third Note from Julie

Madman! If my life is dear to you, be fearful of taking yours. I am beset and can neither speak nor write to you until tomorrow. Wait.

❖ LETTER IV ❖

From Julie

MUST I THEN finally confess this fatal, too poorly concealed secret! How many times have I sworn that it would not leave my heart except with my life! But the danger to your life tears it from me. The secret is out, and my honor also is lost. Alas! I have kept my word too well. Is there a death more cruel than to survive one's honor?

What shall I say, how shall I break such a painful silence? Or rather, have I not already said everything, and have you not understood me only too well? Ah! You have seen too much of it not to guess the rest! Led imperceptibly into the snares of the vile seducer, I see, without being able to stop myself, the horrible precipice toward which I am running. Artful man, it is my love much more than yours which causes your boldness. You see the disorder in my heart; you take advantage of it in order to ruin me. And now that you have made me despicable, the worst of my misfortune is to be forced to despise you. Ah, wretch! I esteem you, and you bring me to shame! Believe me, if your heart was capable of enjoying this triumph peacefully, it would never have obtained it.

You know that your remorse will increase, because my soul had no inclinations toward vice. Modesty and virtue were dear to me; I hoped to cherish them in a life of simplicity and industry. But to what purpose were my efforts which Heaven rejected? Since the first day that I had the misfortune to see you, I have felt the poison which destroys my sense and my reason; I felt it from the first instant. Your eyes, your sentiments, your speech, and your criminal pen make it each day more deadly.

I have neglected nothing in the attempt to arrest the progress of this fatal passion. Powerless to resist it, I would have liked to defend myself from being overcome, but your eagerness has outwitted my vain precaution. A hundred times I have wanted to throw myself at my parents' feet; a hundred times I have wanted to open my guilty heart to them. But they cannot know what is taking place there; they would apply common remedies to a desperate disease. My mother is weak and without authority, I know the inflexible severity of my father, and if I told them I would only ruin and dishonor myself, my family, and you. My friend Claire is absent; my brother is dead. I can find no one in the world to protect me against the enemy which haunts me. I beg Heaven in vain; Heaven is deaf to the prayers of irresolute souls. Everything feeds the ardor with which I am devoured; everything gives me up to myself, or rather, everything gives me up to you. The whole of nature seems to be your accomplice. All my efforts are vain; I adore you in spite of myself. How could my heart, which has not been able to resist with its full force, now surrender only halfway? How could this heart, which knows nothing about dissimulation, hide from you the rest of its weakness? Ah! The first step, which costs the most, was the one which should not have been taken; how shall I stop myself from taking the rest? No, since this first step I feel myself drawn into the abyss, and you can now make me as unhappy as you shall wish.

Such is the frightful situation in which I see myself, in which I can no longer get help from anyone but him who has reduced me to seeking it, and in which in order to defend me from ruin you must be my only protector against yourself. I could, I know, postpone this confession of my despair. I could for some time have disguised my shameful weakness and by yielding to it gradually have thus deceived even myself—a vain dissimulation which could flatter my pride and not save my virtue. Ah, I see too well, I feel too well where the first misstep is leading, and I was not seeking to make way for my ruin but to avoid it.

Yet, if you are not the lowest of men, if some spark of virtue shines in your soul, if there still remains some trace of the sentiments of honor with which you seemed to be imbued, can I believe you vile enough to abuse the fatal confession which my delirium tears from me? No, I know you well: you will sustain me in my weakness, you will become my defender, you will protect me against my own heart. Your virtues are the last refuge of my innocence; my honor dares to confide itself in yours; you cannot preserve the one without the other. Generous soul, ah! preserve them both, and, for your own sake at least, take pity on me.

Oh God! Have I been sufficiently humiliated? I am on my knees writing to you; I bathe my paper with my tears; I raise to you my timid supplications. And yet do not think that I am ignorant of the fact that it was for me to receive them from you, and that in order to be obeyed, I had only with artifice to be scornful. Dear friend, disregard that frivolous convention but leave me my innocence. I prefer to be your slave and live virtuously than to buy your obedience at the price of my honor. If you deign to hear me, what love, what gratitude are you to expect from her who shall owe you her return to sanity! How charming is the sweet union of two pure souls! Your conquered desires will be the source of your happiness, and the pleasures which you shall enjoy will be worthy of Heaven itself.

I believe, I hope that a heart which has seemed to me to deserve all the affection of mine will not belie the generosity which I expect from it. I hope, moreover, that if it were cowardly enough to take advantage of my bewilderment and the confessions it tears from me, scorn and indignation would return to me the power of reason which I have lost; and I hope also that I should not be so cowardly myself as to fear a lover of whom I should have to be ashamed. You will be virtuous or be scorned; I shall be respected or cured of my passion. This is the only hope, besides that of dying, which is left for me.

❧ LETTER V ❧

To Julie

HEAVENLY POWERS! I had one soul for sorrow, give me another for happiness. Love, spirit of my existence, come sustain me as I grow faint. How inexpressible is the charm of virtue, how invincible the power of the loved one's voice! Happiness, pleasures, ecstasies, how poignant your impressions are! Who can withstand them? Oh, how shall I be equal to the torrent of delights which has just flooded my heart! How shall I dispel the apprehension of a fearful girl? Julie

. . . no, not my Julie on her knees! My Julie shedding tears! . . .
She, to whom the universe should pay its respects, begging a man
who adores her not to insult her, not to dishonor himself! If I could
become indignant with you, I would, because of your fears which
debase us. Pure and celestial beauty, be a better judge of the nature of your conquest! Oh! If I adore your physical charms, is it not
above all for the imprint of that spotless soul which animates them,
the divine mark of which is evident in all your features? Do you
fear succumbing to my designs? But what designs can she dread who
stamps all the feelings she inspires with respect and with honor? Is
there in the world a man vile enough to dare be bold with you?

Permit, permit me to savor the unexpected happiness of being
loved . . . loved by her . . . kings of the world, how I now look
down upon you! Let me read a thousand times that enchanting letter, in which your love and your feelings are written in glowing
colors, in which, in spite of all the violent agitation of your soul, I
see with ecstasy how the most lively passions retain in a chaste soul
the holy character of virtue. What monster, after having read that
touching letter, could take advantage of your condition and show
by that most criminal act his profound contempt for himself? No,
dear love, have confidence in a faithful friend who is wholly incapable of deceiving you. Although my reason may be forever lost,
although the agitation of my senses increases each instant, your
person is henceforward for me not only the most attractive but the
most sacred treasure with which a mortal was ever entrusted. My
ardor and its object will together preserve an inalterable purity. I
should shudder more to lay a hand upon your chaste form than to
commit the most vile incest, and you are not more inviolably safe
with your father than with your lover. Oh, if ever that happy
lover forgets himself for one moment in your presence . . . but
could Julie's lover be a base soul! No, when I shall cease to love
virtue, I shall no longer love you; at my first base action, I wish no
longer for you to love me.

Be reassured then, I implore you in the name of the tender and
pure love which unites us. This love is to be for you the guarantee
of my self-control and my respect; this love is to answer to you for
itself. And why should your fears exceed my desires? To what
other happiness would wish to aspire, if my whole heart can
scarcely be adequate to that which it now enjoys? We are both
young, it is true, we are in love for the first and only time in our
lives, and we have no experience with passion. But is the honor
which conducts us a deceitful guide? Is there ever need for experi-

ence which is acquired only through vice? I am deceiving myself if
the right feelings are not all in the bottom of my heart. I am not a
vile seducer, as you called me in your despair, but a simple and sensitive man who readily shows what he feels and feels nothing for
which he must be ashamed. To say it all in a few words, I abhor a
criminal act more than I love Julie. I don't know, no, I doubt if the
nature of the love which you inspire is even compatible with vice
and if anyone besides a chaste soul could be sufficiently sensible of
all your charms. As for me, the more I am affected by them, the
more elevated are my sentiments. What good act that I should not
have done for itself would I not do now to make myself worthy of
you? Ah! Trust in the fires that you inspire in me and that you
know so well how to purify. Believe that it is enough that I adore
you in order to respect forever the precious treasure with which
you have entrusted me. Oh what a heart I will possess! True
happiness, the homage of the loved one, the victory of an honorable
love—how much more valuable are these than all its pleasures!

✤ LETTER VI ✤

From Julie to Claire

ARE YOU RESOLVED, my cousin, to spend your life mourning poor
Chaillot, and must the dead make you forget the living? Your grief
is just, and I share it with you, but is it to be eternal? Since the
death of your mother, Chaillot had reared you with the greatest
care; she had been your friend rather than your governess. She
loved you tenderly and loved me because you love me; her memory
will ever inspire us only with principles of wisdom and honor. I
know all this, my dear, and I acknowledge it gratefully. But you
must acknowledge also that the good woman was scarcely prudent
with us; that she told us, unnecessarily, the most indiscreet secrets;
that she entertained us endlessly with the maxims of gallantry, with
the adventures of her youth, with the intrigues of lovers; and that
in order to secure us against the snares of men, though she did not
teach us to set them ourselves, she at least instructed us in a thousand things that young girls would well do without. Console your-

self, then, for her death as for a misfortune which is not without some compensations. At our age, her lessons were beginning to become dangerous, and Heaven has perhaps withdrawn her from us at the moment when it was not good for her to stay with us any longer. Do you remember all you said to me when I lost the best of brothers? Was Chaillot more dear to you? Have you more cause to grieve for her?

Return, my dear, she has need of you no longer. Alas! While you waste your time in superfluous grief, do you not fear that your absence may be causing another misfortune? How can you not fear, you who know the state of my heart, to abandon your friend to the dangers which your presence would have prevented? Oh, what things have happened since your departure! You will shudder in learning what risks I have run through my imprudence. I hope I have been rescued from them, but I am as it were at the mercy of another. It is for you to restore me to myself; hurry then to return. I have said nothing so much as that your attentions were useful to your poor governess; I should have been the first to exhort you to give them to her. But since she is dead, it is to her family that you are obligated. We shall fulfill those obligations better here together than you could alone in the country; and you will perform the duties of gratitude without neglecting those of friendship.

Since my father left, we have resumed our former manner of living, and my mother leaves me alone less frequently. But that is through habit more than through mistrust. Her visits take up less time than we need for my little lessons, and Babi fills her place rather negligently. Although I do not find my good mother sufficiently watchful, I cannot resolve to tell her so. I would willingly provide for my own security without losing her esteem, and it is you alone who can bring about all that. Return, my Claire, return without delay. I regret the lessons I am taking without you, and I am afraid of becoming too learned. Our tutor is not only a man of merit; he is virtuous and therefore more dangerous. I am too pleased with him to be so with myself. At our ages, with a charming man, be he ever so virtuous, two young girls are preferable to one.

❖ LETTER VII ❖

Answer

I UNDERSTAND, and I tremble for you. Not that I believe the danger as pressing as you imagine it. Your fear makes me less apprehensive for the present, but the future frightens me, and if you cannot conquer your passions, I foresee nothing but misfortune. Alas! How many times has poor Chaillot predicted to me that the first sigh from your heart would determine your future! Ah cousin, you are still so young, and already your destiny is fulfilled! How we are going to miss her, that knowing woman whom you think it was advantageous for us to lose! Perhaps we ought to have first fallen into safer hands, but we are too educated in leaving hers to allow ourselves to be governed by others and not educated enough to govern ourselves. She alone could shield us against the dangers to which she had exposed us. She taught us a great deal, and, it seems to me, we have ourselves thought a great deal for our age. The lively and tender friendship which has united us almost since the cradle has informed our hearts prematurely, so to speak, about all the passions. We know their signs and their effects well enough; we lack only the art of repressing them. God grant that your young philosopher may be acquainted with this art better than we!

When I say *we*, you understand me; it is you above all of whom I speak. As for me, the governess always told me that my giddiness instead of my reason would be my security, that I should never have the wit to be in love, and that I was too foolish ever to be guilty of follies. My Julie, take care; the better she thought your reason, the more she feared for your heart. Be of good courage, however; I know that your soul will do all that wisdom and honor can, and in its turn mine will do, doubt not, all that friendship can. If we know too much for our age, at least this study has cost our morals nothing. Believe me, my dear, there are many girls more ignorant than we who are less virtuous. We are so because we wish to be, and whatever one may say of it, that is the way of being so most surely.

Nevertheless, from what you tell me, I shall not have a moment's rest until I am near you, for if you are afraid of danger, it is not

completely imaginary. It is true that the preventive measure is easy;
a word to your mother and everything is finished. But I understand
you: you do not want a conclusive expedient; you would willingly
remove the possibility of succumbing but not the honor of resisting.
Oh poor cousin! . . . yet if the slightest glimmer . . . if Baron *family*
d'Étange might consent to give his daughter, his only child, to the
son of an inconsiderable bourgeois without fortune! Do you hope
he will? Or what, then, are you hoping for? What do you want?
. . . Poor, poor cousin! . . . Yet fear nothing from me. Your friend
will keep your secret. Many people would find it more honest to
reveal it; perhaps they are right. As for me, I, who am not a great
rationalizer, I want no honesty which betrays friendship, faith, or
confidence. I suppose that each relationship, each age has its maxims, its duties, its virtues; that what would be prudence to others
would be perfidy to me; and that to confuse these things would
make us wicked instead of wise and happy. If your love is weak, we
shall conquer it; if it is extreme, it would be to expose it to tragedy
to attack it with violent measures, and friendship will not attempt
those for which it cannot be answerable. But in return you have
to conduct yourself properly when you are under my protection.
You will see, you will see what it is to have an eighteen year old
duenna!

I am not absent, as you know, for my own pleasure, and spring
is not so agreeable in the country as you think. We suffer here from
the cold and the heat at the same time; there is no shade at all for
walks, and we need a fire in the house. My father, for his part, begins to notice, in the midst of his projects, that the newspapers are
later arriving here than in town. Thus everyone asks for nothing
better than to return, and you will embrace me, I hope, in four or
five days. But what disturbs me is that four or five days make I don't
know how many hours, several of which are destined for the philosopher. For the *philosopher*, do you hear, cousin? Remember that
the clock strikes those hours only for him.

Do not blush here and lower your eyes. To take on a serious air
is impossible for you; your features will not agree to it. You well
know that I could not cry without laughing, and yet I have no less
sensibility than others; I do not feel our separation less severely, nor
do I grieve less for good Chaillot. I am infinitely grateful to you for
wishing to share with me the care of her family. I shall never abandon them, but you would no longer be yourself if you neglected any
opportunity to do good. I agree that poor Chaillot was talkative,
rather free in her ordinary conversation, hardly discreet with

young girls, and fond of speaking of her former life. Also, it is not so much the qualities of her mind which I regret losing, although she had excellent ones among the bad. The loss I mourn is of her good heart, of her perfect affection which gave her the tenderness of a mother together with the confidence of a sister. She took the place of all my family for me. I scarcely knew my mother, my father loves me only as much as he is capable of loving, we lost your amiable brother, and I see mine almost never. Here I am, like a forsaken orphan. My child, you alone are left for me, for you are like a kind mother. Still, you are right. You are left for me. I was mourning! I was foolish then; what had I to mourn?

P.S. For fear of an accident, I am addressing this letter to our teacher in order that it may reach you more safely.

✤ LETTER VIII* ✤

To Julie

HOW CURIOUS are the caprices of love, beautiful Julie! My heart has more than it hoped for and yet is not content. You love me, you tell me so, and still I sigh. This unjust heart dares to keep desiring when there is no longer anything to desire; it punishes me with its fancies and makes me uneasy in the very midst of happiness. Do not think that I have forgotten the rules imposed upon me nor lost the will to observe them. No, but a secret resentment disturbs me in seeing that these laws are painful only to me, that you who once pretended to be so weak are so strong at present, and that I have so few struggles to make against myself, so careful are you to prevent them.

How changed you are since two months ago, and you alone have changed! Your languor has disappeared; there is no more mortification or despondency; all your graces have returned to their posts;

---

* A gap is apparent here and often will be found in the rest of this correspondence. Several letters have been lost; others have been suppressed; still others have undergone abridgment. But nothing essential is missing which may not be easily filled in with the help of what remains. [*Rousseau*]

all your charms are reanimated; the newly opened rose is not more
fresh than you; the flashes of sprightliness have begun again; you
are witty with everyone; you are playful, even with me, just as before; and, what unsettles me more than all the rest, you swear an
eternal love for me with an air as gay as if you were saying the most
amusing thing in the world.

Tell me, tell me, you inconstant creature, is this the character
of a violent, ungovernable passion? And if you had the slightest
desire to conquer it, would not the constraint at least stifle your
playfulness? Oh, how much more amiable you were when you were
less beautiful! How I miss that touching pallor, the precious assurance of the lover's happiness, and how I hate the indiscreet
health you have recovered at the expense of my tranquillity! Yes,
I should prefer to see you still ill rather than see this contented air,
these brilliant eyes, this blooming complexion which outrages me.
Have you so soon forgotten that you were not like this when you
were begging for my mercy? Julie, Julie, in such a short time how
tranquil this violent love has become!

But what offends me even more is that, after having committed
yourself to my honor, you seem to be mistrustful of it and that you
flee from dangers as if there remained any for you to fear. Is it thus
that you give credit to my discretion, and did my inviolable respect
deserve this affront from you? The absence of your father is far
from leaving us more freedom; one can scarcely see you alone. Your
inseparable cousin no longer leaves your side. Insensibly, we are
resuming our former way of living and our former circumspection,
with this difference only: that then it was irksome to you and now
it pleases you.

What then shall be the reward of such pure veneration, if it is
not your esteem? And of what avail to me is this eternal and voluntary abstinence from the sweetest thing in the world, if she who
demands it is not at all grateful? Indeed, I am tired of suffering
uselessly and of condemning myself to the hardest privations without being given credit for them. What! Must you grow more beautiful with impunity while you are treating me contemptuously!
Must my eyes ceaselessly devour the delights which my lips never
dare approach! Must I finally relinquish all hope, without at least
being able to acquire honor from so rigorous a sacrifice! No, since
you do not put your trust in my faithfulness, I no longer wish to
leave it vainly pledged. It is an unfair security which you extract
from my word and from your own precaution at the same time. You
are too ungrateful, or I am too scrupulous, and I am resolved not

to refuse the opportunities which fortune, in spite of you, may throw my way. Finally, whatever may happen to me, I feel that I have undertaken a charge above my powers. Julie, be on your guard again; I am returning to you a treasure too dangerous for the faith of the guardian, and its defense will cost your heart less than you have pretended to fear.

I am speaking seriously. Rely upon yourself, or drive me away, that is to say, deprive me of my life. I have given a rash pledge. I am amazed that I have kept it so long; I know that I ought to keep it always, but I feel that is impossible. One deserves to fail when he imposes upon himself such perilous trials. Have faith in me, dear and tender Julie; believe in this sensitive heart which lives only for you. You will always be respected, but I may lose my reason for one moment, and the intoxication of the senses may inspire a crime which would be horrible in a state of composure. Happy for not having deceived your expectation, I have conquered my passions for two months, and you owe me the reward for two centuries of suffering.

✤ LETTER IX ✤

From Julie

I UNDERSTAND: the pleasures of vice and the honor of virtue constitute a combination you would find enjoyable. Is that your morality? . . . Ah! My good friend, you grow tired of being honorable quite quickly! Is your honor, then, only a ruse? A curious sign of affection it is to complain of my health! Could it be that you were hoping to see it destroyed by my foolish love and that you were expecting me at that moment to beg you for my life? Or else were you counting on respecting me as long as I should be formidable and recanting when I should become lenient? I see no assertable merit in such sacrifices.

With equal justice you reproach me for the care I take in sparing you from painful combats with yourself, as if you should not rather thank me for it. Then you withdraw yourself from the pledge you have taken, as from a duty too burdensome, so that in the same letter you complain that you have too much misery and that you do not have enough. Consider the matter better and try to be consistent, in order to give your pretended griefs a less frivolous appearance. Or rather, abandon altogether this dissimulation which is inconsistent with your character. Whatever you might say, your heart is more content with mine than it pretends to be. Ungrateful man, you know too well that it will never do you harm! Your letter contradicts you by its sprightly style, for you would not be so witty if you were less tranquil. But so much for the vain reproaches which regard you; let us turn to those which concern me and which seem at first to be better founded.

I know very well that the serene and gentle life which we have been leading for the past two months is not in accord with my earlier declaration, and I confess that you have cause to be surprised by this contrast. You first saw me in despair, and you find me at present too peaceful; thus you accuse my feelings of inconstancy and my heart of capriciousness. Ah, my friend! Are you not judging my heart too severely? You need more than a day to know it. Wait, and you shall find, perhaps, that this heart which loves you is not unworthy of yours.

If you could understand with what fright I experienced the first touches of the sentiment which unites us, you could form an idea of the suffering that it was to cause me. I had been reared under such strict rules that even the most pure love seemed to me the height of dishonor. Everyone taught me or made me believe that a sensible girl was ruined at the first tender word which escaped her lips. My disordered imagination confounded the crime with the declaration of passion, and I had conceived such a frightful idea of this first step that I scarcely saw any interval between it and the last. An excessive self-distrust augmented my alarm. The battles of modesty seemed to me those of chastity; I mistook the torture of silence for the transport of desire. I believed that I should be lost as soon as I had spoken, and yet it was necessary to speak or else lose you. Thus, no longer able to disguise my feelings, I tried to call forth the nobility of yours, and entrusting myself more to you than to myself, I wanted, by engaging your honor in my defense, to rely upon the resources of which I believed myself already deprived.

I have discovered that I was mistaken. I had no sooner spoken when I was relieved, you had no sooner answered when I felt completely calm, and two months of experience have taught me that my excessively tender heart needs love but that my senses have no need of a lover. Judge, you who love virtue, with what joy I made this happy discovery. Having emerged from that profound shame into which my fears had plunged me, I am now enjoying the delicious pleasure of a guiltless passion. This constitutes the happiness of my life; my disposition and my health feel the effects of it; I can scarcely conceive of anything more sweet; and the union of love and innocence seems to me to be paradise on earth.

Since then I have feared you no longer, and when I took care to avoid being alone with you, it was as much for your sake as for mine, for your eyes and your sighs revealed more passion than wisdom, and if you had forgotten the bounds you yourself have prescribed, I should not have forgotten them.

Ah! My friend, I wish I might communicate to your soul the feeling of happiness and peace which reigns in the depths of mine! Would that I could teach you to enjoy tranquilly the most delicious state in life! The charms of the union of hearts join with those of innocence; no fear, no shame disturbs our felicity. In the midst of the true pleasures of love, we can speak of virtue without blushing:

E v'è il piacer con l'onesta de accanto.
METASTASIO

And pleasure is there side by side with honor.

Yet, an indefinable, sad presentiment arises in my breast and cries out that we are now enjoying the only happy time that heaven has allotted us. I foresee only absence, anxiety, troubles, obstacles. The slightest change in our present condition could only seem to me an evil one. No, even were we united forever by a sweeter bond, I doubt whether our happiness would not soon be destroyed by its excess. The moment of possession is a crisis in love, and all change is dangerous to ours. We can do nothing worse than to destroy it.

I implore you, my tender and only friend, try to calm the turbulence of those vain desires which are always followed by regret, repentance, and sorrow. Let us peacefully enjoy our present situation. You take pleasure in giving me lessons, and you know only too well how I take pleasure in receiving them. Let the lessons be still more frequent; let us part only as much as it is necessary for propriety's sake. Let us use the moments which we cannot spend together in writing each other, and let us profit by this precious time, after which we shall long one day, perhaps. Ah! May our present happiness last as long as our lives! The mind is adorned, the reason becomes enlightened, the soul is strengthened, and the heart joys. What does our happiness lack?

✤ LETTER X ✤

To Julie

HOW RIGHT you are, my Julie, to say that I do not yet know you! I always think I know all the treasures of your beautiful soul, and always I discover new ones. What woman ever joined tenderness to virtue as you do, and tempering one with the other, made both more charming? I find something indescribably lovable and charming in your wisdom, which also makes me desolate, and you gild with so much grace the privations you impose upon me that you nearly make them dear to me.

I feel more every day that the greatest good is to be loved by you. There is no other, there can be no other which equals it, and if it were necessary to choose between your heart and the possession of your person, no, charming Julie, I would not hesitate for an instant. But why this bitter alternative? And why make incompatible what nature has united? Our time is precious, you say; let us be wise enough to enjoy it as it is, and let us keep from disturbing its peaceful course by our impatience. Ah! May it be so and may it be happy! But to profit from a pleasant condition, should one neglect a better one, and prefer moderate happiness to a supreme felicity? Is not all that time lost which might have been better employed? Ah! If it were possible for us to live a thousand years in a quarter of an hour, what good would it be for us sadly to tell over the days as we will have lived them?

All that you say of the happiness of our present situation is incontestable. I feel that we ought to be happy, and yet I am not. Your lips speak wisdom beautifully, but the voice of nature is stronger. What means of resisting it are there when it agrees with the voice of the heart! Besides you alone, I see nothing under the sun which is worthy of taking possession of my soul and my senses. No, without you, even nature no longer means anything to me; but its realm is in your eyes, and there it is invincible.

You feel nothing of this, heavenly Julie. You are content in ravishing my senses and are not at war with your own. It seems that
human passions are beneath such a sublime soul, and just as you
have the beauty of angels, so also do you have their purity. Oh,
the purity which I respect in murmuring that I might either draw
you down or else elevate myself to your level! But no, I shall always
creep on the ground and shall see you always shining in the heavens. Ah! Be happy at the expense of my tranquillity, enjoy all
your virtues, and may the wicked mortal perish who shall ever try
to defile one of them. Be happy, I shall try to forget how much I am
to be pitied, and I shall draw from your happiness even the consolation for my misery. Yes, dear heart, it seems to me that my love is as
pure as its adorable object; all the desires inflamed by your charms
are extinguished in the perfections of your soul. I see that soul so
peaceful that I do not dare disturb it. Each time I am tempted to
steal the least caress from you, even if the danger of offending you
prevents me, my heart prevents me still more by the fear of altering
so pure a felicity. In the price of the happiness to which I aspire, I
no longer see anything but what it can cost you; and finding my
happiness incompatible with yours—judge now how much I love
you!—it is mine that I renounce.

What inexplicable contradictions are in the sentiments you inspire in me. I am at the same time submissive and bold, impetuous
and restrained. I cannot look at you without experiencing struggles
inside. Your glances, your voice lovingly reveal to the heart the
touching charm of innocence; it is a divine charm that one would
regret to destroy. If I now dare indulge a wishful idea, it is only in
your absence. My desires dare only go as far as addressing you in
my imagination, and it is there that I avenge myself for the respect
I am constrained to have for you.

Yet, I languish and waste away. The fire runs in my veins, nothing could extinguish nor calm it, and I only aggravate it by wishing
to restrain it. I ought to be happy, and I am, I agree; I do not complain of my lot. Such as it is, I would not exchange it with that of
the kings of the earth. Yet a real pain tortures me, which I seek
vainly to avoid. I should not wish to die, and yet I am dying; I wish
to live for you, and it is you who are depriving me of my life.

✤ LETTER XI ✤

From Julie

MY FRIEND, I feel that each day I am becoming more attached to you. I can no longer be parted from you, the least absence is unbearable, and I must see you or write you, to occupy myself ceaselessly with thoughts of you.

Thus my love keeps pace with yours. For now I know how much you love me, by the real fear you have of displeasing me, whereas your first fears were merely assumed in order to advance your cause better. I know very well how to distinguish the dictates of your heart from the delirium of your heated imagination, and I see a hundred times more affection in your present restraint than in your first ecstasies. I also know that your situation, troublesome as it is, is not without pleasures. It is sweet for a true lover to make sacrifices, all of which are credited to him and none of which is forgotten in the heart of her whom he loves. Who knows even if, knowing my sensibility, you are not using a deeper plot to seduce me? But no, I am unfair, and you are incapable of deceiving me. Yet, if I am wise, I shall distrust compassion even more than love. I feel myself a thousand times more touched by your respects than by your ecstasies, and I indeed fear that in taking the most honest course you may have in the long run taken the most dangerous.

In the overflowing of my heart, I must tell you a truth which it feels strongly and of which your own heart cannot fail to convince you. It is that in spite of fortune, of parents, and of ourselves, our destinies are forever united, and that we can no longer be happy or unhappy except together. Our souls touch, so to speak, at all points, and we feel an entire coherence. (Correct me, my friend, if I am poorly applying your lessons in physics.) Fate may indeed separate us, but not disunite us. We shall henceforward have only mutual pleasures and mutual pains; and like those magnets of which you were telling me that have, it is said, the same movements in different places, we should have the same sensations though we were at the two poles of the earth.

Rid yourself then of the hope, if you ever had it, of having an

exclusive happiness for yourself and of buying it at the expense of
mine. Do not hope to be happy if I were dishonored or to contemplate my shame and my tears with a satisfied eye. Believe me, my
friend, I know your heart better than you know it. A love so tender and so true must be capable of mastering desires; you have too
many of them to consummate without destroying yourself, and you
can no longer complete my ruin without bringing on your own.

I would like you to feel how important it is to both of us for you
to entrust me with the care of our common destiny. Do you doubt
that you are as dear to me as myself, and do you think that any happiness could exist for me which you would not share? No, my friend,
I have the same interests as you have and a little more reason with
which to manage them. I confess that I am the younger, but have
you never noticed that if reason ordinarily is weaker and more
quickly extinguished in women, it is also formed earlier, just as a
frail sunflower grows and dies sooner than an oak? From an early
age, we find ourselves charged with such a dangerous treasure that
the care of preserving it soon awakens the judgment, and an excellent way of foreseeing the consequences of things is to sense
keenly all the risks they make us run. As for me, the more I think
about our situation, the more I find that reason demands of you
exactly what I demand in the name of love. Be submissive, then,
to its sweet voice, and let yourself be led by one, alas, who is also
blind but who at least has some support.

I do not know, my friend, if our hearts will be fortunate enough
to understand each other, or if in reading this letter you will share
the tender emotion which dictated it. Nor do I know if in certain
things we will ever be able to reach the same agreement in opinion
as we have in sentiment. But I am certain that the judgment of the
one who least separates his happiness from that of the other is the
judgment we must follow.

❖ LETTER XII ❖

To Julie

MY JULIE, how touching is the simplicity of your letter! How
clearly I see in it the serenity of an innocent soul and the tender

solicitude of love! Your thoughts are expressed artlessly and with-out difficulty; they make a delicate impression on my heart which an affected style does not produce at all. You urge invincible rea-sons with so simple an air that it is necessary to reflect on them to feel their force, and sublime sentiments are so natural to you that one is tempted to take them for common thoughts. Ah yes, with-out a doubt, it is for you to control our destiny. It is not a right which I allow you, it is a duty which I require of you and a justice which I ask of you, for your reason must make amends for the harm you have done mine. From this instant I give you lifelong control of my will; dispose of me as of a man who has no interest of his own and whose whole being has no connection except with you. Do not doubt that I shall keep the pledge I am taking, no matter what you command. I shall be more worthy, you will be happier, and I see above all the certain reward for my obedience. Therefore, I re-linquish to you, without reservation, the care of our common hap-piness; secure your own, and all is done. As for me, who can neither forget you for an instant nor think of you without the ecstasies which I must overcome, I intend to busy myself solely with the duties you have imposed upon me.

In the year that we have been studying together, we have scarcely done any but disordered and almost random reading, the more to consult your taste than to improve it. Besides, so much disturbance in our souls hardly left our minds free. Our eyes were poorly fixed on the book, our mouths pronounced only the words, and our at-tention was always deficient. Your little cousin, who was not so pre-occupied, reproached us for our infrequent comprehension and did herself an easy honor by outstripping us. Insensibly, she has be-come more learned than the teacher, and however we might have sometimes laughed at her pretentions, she is, really, the only one of the three who remembers anything from all that we have studied.

In order, then, to regain the lost time (Ah, Julie, was it ever bet-ter spent?), I have formed a kind of plan which may be able to re-pair methodically the harm that our distractions have done to our learning. I am sending it; we shall read it together presently. [1]

Out of regard for your inseparable cousin, I have allowed a few books of light literature that I should not have allowed for you. Outside of Petrarch, Tasso, Metastasio, and the masters of the French drama, I have included neither poetry nor books about love, contrary to the usual reading designed for your sex. What should we learn of love in these books? Ah Julie, our hearts tell us more about it than they, and language borrowed from books is indeed

cold for anyone who is himself impassioned! Besides, these studies
enervate the soul, throw it into indolence, and take from it all its
strength. On the contrary, real love is a devouring fire which in-
stills its ardor in all other sentiments and enlivens them with new
vigor. Thus it is said that love created heroes. How fortunate is he
whom fate has disposed to become one and who has Julie to love!

✤ LETTER XIII ✤

From Julie

INDEED, I told you we were happy; nothing proves it better than
the uneasiness I experience at the slightest change in our situation.
If we had had truly violent anguish before, could an absence of
two days create so much for us? I say *us*, for I know that my friend
shares my impatience; he shares it because I feel it, and he feels it
also on his own account. I no longer need for him to tell me these
things.

We have been in the country only since last night, it is not yet
the hour at which I should see you if I were in town, and yet the
distance between us already makes your absence more unbearable.
If you had not forbidden me geometry, I should tell you that my
uneasiness increases in a compound ratio of the intervals of time
and space, so much do I find that distance adds to the pain of absence.

I have brought along your letter and your study plan, to reflect
on both, and I have read the first twice already. The conclusion
touches me extremely. I see, my friend, that you feel real love, since
you have preserved your sense of honor and since you still know in
the tenderest part of your heart how to make sacrifices to virtue.
Surely, to make use of the means of education to corrupt a woman
is of all seductions the most damnable, and to wish to soften a mistress with the aid of novels is indeed to have few resources of one's
own. If you had used philosophy to forward your designs, if you had
tried to establish maxims favorable to your interest, those very
methods of deceit would soon have undeceived me, but the most
dangerous of your seductions is not to use these methods at all. At

the moment when the desire to love took hold of my heart and when I felt the need for an eternal attachment, I did not ask Heaven to unite me to a charming man but to a man who had a beautiful soul; for I felt that such a soul was, of all the attributes one can have, least subject to future aversion, and that integrity and honor adorn all the sentiments that accompany them. For having chosen properly, like Solomon, I have obtained not only what I asked for but also what I did not ask. I look upon this as a good omen for my other plans, and I do not despair, my friend, of one day being able to make you as happy as you deserve to be. The means are slow, difficult, and uncertain; the obstacles are terrible. I dare promise nothing, but be assured that nothing that patience and love can do will be forgotten. Meanwhile, continue to humor my mother in everything, and prepare yourself at the return of my father, who is finally retiring completely after thirty years of service, to endure the haughtiness of a blunt but very honorable old gentleman, who will love you without showing it and esteem you without saying so.

I interrupted my letter to take a walk in the grove which is near our house. Oh, my sweet friend! I took you there with me, or rather, I carried you there in my heart. I sought those places where I thought we should have wandered together; I marked the retreats which seem worthy to shelter us. Our hearts overflowed in advance in these delightful arbors, which added to the pleasure we enjoyed in being together; they received in their turn a new value as the shelter of two true lovers, and I was astonished that alone I had not noticed the beauties I found there with you.

Among the natural arbors which make up this charming place, there is one more charming than the rest, with which I am most delighted and in which, for that reason, I am reserving a little surprise for my friend. It shall not be said that he will always be respectful but I never generous. It is there that I wish to make him feel, in spite of common opinions, how much more valuable is that which the heart gives than that which importunity snatches. Yet, for fear that your vivid imagination may lead you too far, I must warn you that we shall not go together into the arbor without the inseparable cousin.

With respect to her, it is decided that, if it does not displease you too much, you will come with her to see us on Monday. My mother will send her carriage to my cousin, you will appear at her house at ten o'clock, she will bring you here, you will spend the day with us, and we shall all return together the next day after dinner.

veris.

I was at this point in my letter when I reflected that I did not have the same opportunities for sending it to you as in town. I had first thought of sending you one of your books through Gustin, the gardener's son, and of putting on it a paper cover in which I should have inserted my letter. But besides the fact that it is not certain you might think of looking for it, it would be impardonably imprudent to expose our destiny to such hazards. I must be satisfied, then, with simply telling you of the Monday rendez-vous by a note, and I shall keep this letter to give you personally. Besides, I was a little apprehensive that you might comment too freely on the mystery of the arbor.

❧ LETTER XIV ❧

To Julie

WHAT HAVE YOU DONE, ah! what have you done, my Julie? You wanted to reward me and you have destroyed me. I am drunk, or rather, I am insane. My senses are disordered; all my faculties are disturbed by that fatal kiss. You wished to ease my pain? Cruel one, you sharpened it. It was poison that I gathered from your lips. It is seething within me, it inflames my blood, it is killing me, and thus your compassion has caused my death.

Oh, never will the immortal memory of that moment of illusion, of delirium, and of enchantment be effaced from my soul. As long as Julie's charms are impressed there, as long as my agitated heart feels and sighs, this memory will constitute the torment and the happiness of my life!

Alas! I enjoyed only an apparent tranquillity. Having submitted to your supreme will, I was no longer complaining of a fate over which you condescended to preside. I had subdued the passionate fits of a rash imagination, I had veiled my eyes and fettered my heart, I but half expressed my desires, and I was as happy as possible. Then I received your letter. I flew to your cousin. We went to Clarens, I caught sight of you, and my heart beat quickly. The sweet sound of your voice disturbed it anew, I approached you as if transported, and I had great need of the diversion your cousin pro-

vided to hide my disturbance from your mother. We walked through
the garden, we dined calmly, and you secretly gave me your letter
which I did not dare read before that formidable witness. The sun
began to set, all three of us eluded the last of its rays in the woods,
and my peaceful simplicity did not even imagine a sweeter state.

Approaching the arbor, I perceived, not without a secret emotion,
your significant signs, your mutual smiles, and the increasing glow
in your cheeks. As soon as we entered, I was surprised to see your
cousin approach me and, with an amused, beseeching air, ask me for
a kiss. Without understanding anything of this mystery, I kissed our
charming friend, and as completely amiable, completely delightful
as she is, I never had better proof that sensations are nothing but
what the heart makes them. But when I guessed a moment later,
when I felt . . . my hand trembled . . . a gentle quiver . . . your
rosy lips . . . Julie's lips . . . placed on, pressed against mine, and
my body clasped in your arms! No, lightning is no more fiery nor
quick than the fire which instantly inflamed me. I was sensible
all over of that delicious touch. From our burning lips, fire breathed
forth with our sighs, and my heart was at the point of death under
the weight of sensual pleasure, when suddenly I saw you grow pale,
close your beautiful eyes, lean upon your cousin, and fall into a faint.
Thus my fright extinguished my pleasure, and my happiness was
soon gone like a flash of lightning.

I have scarcely known what has happened to me since that fatal
moment. The deep impression that it made cannot be effaced. A
favor? . . . It is a horrible torment . . . No, keep your kisses, I
cannot bear them . . . They are too painful, too penetrating; they
pierce, they burn to the quick . . . They would drive me insane.
One, one only has thrown me into a frenzy from which I cannot recover. I am no longer myself, and you are no longer the same to me.
I do not see you restrained and severe as you were formerly, but I
see and feel you forever pressed to my breast as you were for an instant. Oh Julie! Whatever the consequence of my ungovernable passion may be, whatever treatment your severity may determine for
me, I can no longer live in my present condition, and I feel that I
must at last die at your feet . . . or in your arms.

❧ LETTER XV ❧

From Julie

IT IS IMPORTANT, my friend, that we part for a little while, and here
is the first test of the obedience you have promised me. If I demand
it on this occasion, be assured that I have a very forceful reason for
it. I must have one, as you well know, to be resolved to send you
away. As for you, you need no other than that I wish it.

For a long time you have talked of taking a trip to the Valais.
I should like you to go now, before winter comes. Although the autumn is still pleasant here, you can see the peak of the Dent-de-
Jamant * already white with snow, and in six weeks I would not permit you to take a trip in such rough country. Try, then, to leave tomorrow. You can write me at the address I am sending you, and you
can send me yours when you have arrived at Sion.

You have never wished to speak to me of the state of your finances,
but you are not in your own part of the country, and I know that
even there your fortune is small and that you only diminish it here,
where you stay merely because of me. I therefore suppose that part
of your fortune is in my purse, and thus I am sending you a small
amount in this box, which you must not open before the porter. I
do not intend to protest against objections, and I esteem you too
much to believe you capable of raising any.

I forbid you not only to return without my order, but also to come
to take leave of us. You can write to my mother or to me, simply to
inform us that you are forced to leave immediately on unexpected
business, and to give me, if you wish, some directions for my reading
until your return. All that must be done in a natural way and without any appearance of mystery. Adieu, my friend, do not forget that
you take with you Julie's heart and tranquillity both.

* High mountain in the Vaud region. [*Rousseau*]

✤ LETTER XVI ✤

Answer

I READ your terrible letter, and I shudder at each line. Yet I will obey; I have promised; I must, I will obey. But you do not know, no, cruel one, you will never know what such a sacrifice costs my heart. Ah, you did not need the test of the arbor to make me aware of it! That was a merciless refinement of inhumanity, and I can at least defy you to make me more unhappy.

You will receive your box in the same condition as you sent it. To add ignominy to cruelty is too much. I have allowed you to become mistress of my fate but not arbiter of my honor. That is a sacred treasure (the only one, alas, which I have left!) with which no one but myself will be charged as long as I live.

✤ LETTER XVII ✤

Reply

YOUR LETTER is to be pitied. It is the only characterless thing you have ever written.

So I offend your honor, for which I would give my life a thousand times? I offend *your* honor, ungrateful one! you who have seen me ready to abandon mine to you? But where is it, this honor that I offend? Tell me, you servile heart, you indelicate soul. Ah! How contemptible you are, if you only have an honor that Julie may not know! To think that those who wish to share their destiny dare not share also their goods, and he who professes to be mine considers himself insulted by my gifts! And since when has it been vile to receive things from her whom one loves? Since when have the gifts of the heart dishonored the heart who accepts them? But, you say, a man who receives things from another is scorned; he whose needs surpass his fortune is despised. But who despises him? The abject souls who place honor in wealth and estimate their virtue by the weight of their gold. Are these base precepts the honor of a good man? And then is not even reason in favor of the poor?

Without a doubt, an honest man cannot accept vile gifts, but you should learn that these do more dishonor to the hand which offers them, and a gift honorably offered is always honorably received. Now, surely my heart cannot reproach me for offering this one; it glories in the motive of it.* I know nothing more contemptible than a man whose heart and attentions are bought, except the woman who purchases them. But between two united hearts, it is just and obligatory that their fortunes should be held in common, and if I find I have reserved more than my share, I keep without scruple what I intended for myself, and I owe you what I did not first give you. Ah! If love's gifts are rejected, how can a heart ever be grateful?

Do you suppose that I am inattentive to my own needs by providing for yours? I shall give you an indisputable proof to the contrary. The purse I am sending back contains double what it did the first time, and I could have doubled it again if I had wanted. My father gives me an allowance for my needs, a moderate one, to be sure, but I never need to touch it, so attentive is my mother in providing for everything. Besides, my own embroidery and my lace are sufficient for my personal use. It is true that I was not always so rich, but my attention to a fatal passion has for a long time made me neglect certain charitable duties which used to require my superfluous money. That is one more reason to dispose of it as I am doing; you must be humbled for the evil you have caused so that love may expiate the crimes that it perpetrates.

But let us come to the point. You say that honor forbids you to accept my gifts. If that is so, I have nothing more to say, and I agree with you that you must not be careless in such a matter. If, therefore, you can prove this to be the case, do so clearly, incontestably, and without evasion, for you know that I hate sophistry. Then you may return the purse, I shall take it back without complaining, and no more will be said.

But since I like neither punctiliously affected people nor false points of honor, if you send the box back once again without jus-

* She is right. In the secret motive behind this voyage, the reader will see that money was never more honestly employed. It is a great pity that it was not more successful. [Rousseau]

tification, or if your justification is unsatisfactory, we must see each other no more. Adieu. Consider this well.

❖ LETTER XVIII ❖

To Julie

I HAVE taken your gifts, I have left without seeing you, and here I am at a considerable distance from you. Is your tyranny satisfied, and have I obeyed you well enough?

I cannot tell you of my trip, scarcely do I know how I made it. I took three days to travel twenty leagues. Each step which put me farther from you tore my body from my soul and gave me a foretaste of the feeling of death. I intended to describe to you what I should see. Vain project! I saw nothing but you and can describe for you only Julie. The powerful emotions which I have just experienced one after another have thrown me into continual distraction. I imagined myself constantly where I was not, I had scarcely enough presence of mind to ask and follow my road, and I have arrived at Sion without ever leaving Vevey.

Thus I have discovered the secret of eluding your strictness and of seeing you without disobeying you. Yes, cruel one, whatever you might do, you cannot keep me from you completely. I have dragged into exile only the most inconsiderable part of myself; all that is truly alive in me dwells forever near you. My soul roams with impunity over your eyes, over your lips, over your breast, over all your charms. It penetrates everywhere like a subtle vapor, and I am happier despite you than I ever was with your permission.

I have some persons to see here, some business affairs to transact; that is why I am desolate. I am not to be pitied in my solitude, where I can occupy myself with thoughts of you and transport myself imaginatively to wherever you are. Only active employment which calls me back to myself is unbearable. I am going to transact my affairs badly and quickly, in order to be free soon and to be able to wander at my leisure through the savage places which constitute in my eyes the charms of this country. I must shun everyone and live alone in the world, if I cannot live in it with you.

✤ LETTER XIX ✤

To Julie

NOTHING but your command detains me any longer. The five days I have spent here have been more than sufficient for my concerns, if things in which the heart has no interest may be so called. At last you have no more pretexts and can keep me away from you only to torture me.

I am beginning to be very uneasy over the fate of my first letter. It was written and posted immediately upon my arrival, the address on it was faithfully copied from the one you sent me, I sent you mine with equal care, and if you had answered promptly, your letter should have reached me by now. Yet, your answer does not come, and there is no possible or disastrous reason for its delay that my troubled mind has not imagined. Oh my Julie! In one week what unforeseen catastrophes can forever break the sweetest bonds in the world! I shudder to think that there is only one way to make me happy and millions to make me miserable. Julie, could you have forgotten me? Ah! That is the most frightful of my fears! I can prepare myself for other misfortunes, but all the strength of my soul fails at the mere suspicion of that one.

I see the slight basis for my alarm, and yet I cannot allay it. Away from you, the consciousness of my misfortunes increases endlessly, and as if I did not have enough to dishearten me, I invent imaginary ones to add weight to all the others. At first my uneasiness was more tolerable. The confusion of a sudden departure, the difficulty of the trip dissipated my grief. But it is sharpened in this tranquil solitude. Alas! I was struggling, and a deadly sword pierced my heart, but I did not feel the pain until a long time after the wound.

A hundred times, reading novels, I have laughed at the lovers' cold complaints over absence. Ah! I did not know then how unbearable yours one day would be for me! Now I feel how improper it is for a tranquil soul to pass judgment on passion, how senseless it is to laugh at sentiments which have not been experienced. Yet, shall I confess to you? An indefinably sweet and consoling idea eases my suffering in being far from you, when I think that you have commanded it. The pain you cause me is less cruel than if fortune had sent it. If it serves to make you happy, I would be sorry not to have felt it. It is the guarantee of its reward, for I know your soul too well to believe you capable of cruelty for its own sake.

If you wish to test me, I will complain no more. It is fair that you should know whether I am constant, patient, submissive—in a word, deserving of the blessings you are reserving for me. Gods! If that were your idea, I should complain of suffering too little. Ah, no! In order to support such a sweet hope in my heart, invent if you can some torment better proportioned to its reward.

❧ LETTER XX ❧

From Julie

I RECEIVED both your letters at once, and I see, by the uneasiness which you indicate in the second over the fate of the first, that when imagination takes the lead of reason, the latter does not hurry to follow and often lets the former proceed alone. Did you think when you reached Sion that the postman was all ready, waiting only for your letter to leave, that this letter would be delivered to me on the instant of its arrival, and that my answer would be treated with equal dispatch? Things are not like that, my good friend. Your two letters reached me together, because the postman, who comes but once a week,* left only after you mailed the second. Some time is required to distribute the letters, more is needed for my messenger to give me mine in secret, and the postman does not leave here until two days later. Thus, all things calculated, it takes us a week, when we choose the proper day to post our letters, to receive answers from one another. I explain this to you, in order to calm your impatience once and for all. While you are exclaiming against fortune and my negligence, you see that I am skillfully obtaining information about everything that can assure our correspondence and prevent our anxieties. I let you decide from what quarter comes the most loving care.

Let us speak no more of pain, my good friend. Ah, rather respect

* At present he comes twice. [*Rousseau*]

and share the pleasure I feel in seeing the best of fathers again after an eight months' absence! He arrived Thursday evening, and I have thought only of him since that happy moment.* Oh, you whom next to my parents I love most in the world, why must your letters, your scolding come to vex my soul and disturb the first joys of a re-united family? You would prefer my heart to occupy itself continu-ally with you, but tell me if yours could love an unnatural daughter whose passions could make her forget the claims of her family and whose lover's complaints would make her insensible to her father's caresses? No, my worthy friend, do not with unfair reproaches poison the innocent joy that such a sweet sentiment inspires in me. You whose soul is so tender and so sensitive, can you not understand what delight it is to feel the joyously throbbing bosom of a father against that of his daughter in a pure and sacred embrace? Ah! Do you think that at that moment the affections may be divided and nothing stolen from nature?

> Sol che son figlia io mi rammento adesso.
> METASTASIO

Only that I am a daughter I bear in mind at present.

Yet do not think that I can forget you. Can we ever forget those we have once loved? No, the most vivid impressions of a single mo-ment certainly do not efface the others. With chagrin I saw you leave, and with pleasure I shall see you return. But . . . be patient like me, because you must, and ask no more. Be assured that I shall call you back as soon as possible, and remember that often those who complain quite loudly of absence do not suffer the most from it.

✣ LETTER XXI ✣

To Julie

HOW I SUFFERED in receiving that letter I longed for so eagerly! I waited for the postman at the post office. He had scarcely opened his

---

* The preceding paragraph proves that she is not telling the whole truth. [Rous-seau]

packet when I gave my name. I made myself importunate. I was told
that there was a letter for me, I felt a thrill, and I asked for it, disturbed by a mortal impatience. Finally I received it. Julie, I saw the
lines written by your adored hand! Mine trembled as I went forward
to receive this precious treasure. I would have liked to kiss those
sacred letters a thousand times. Oh, the circumspection of a fearful love! I dared not bring the letter to my lips nor open it before so
many witnesses. Immediately, I stole away. My knees were trembling under me, and my growing emotion scarcely let me see my
road. I opened the letter at the first turn. I read through it, I devoured it, and hardly had I come to those lines in which you so well
described the pleasures of your heart in embracing your venerable
father when I burst into tears. People looked at me, and I went into
a passage-way to escape them. There I shared your tenderness, with
ecstasy I embraced that happy father whom I hardly know, and the
voice of nature reminding me of my own, I shed new tears to his
honored memory.

And what did you intend to learn, incomparable daughter, from
my vain and sorry knowledge? Ah, it is from you that one must learn
all the goodness, all the probity possible in a human soul, and, most
of all, that divine union of virtue, love, and nature, which never
existed except in you! No, there is no virtuous affection which does
not have its place in your heart, which is not distinguished there by
your particular sensibility. And for the better regulation of my own,
just as I have often deferred all my actions to your will, I am convinced that all my sentiments must also be determined by yours.

Yet what a difference there is between your situation and mine,
condescend to notice it! I am not speaking of rank and fortune;
honor and love suffice for want of all that. But you are surrounded
by people whom you cherish and who adore you. The attentions
of a tender mother and of a father for whom you are the only hope,
the friendship of a cousin who seems to live only for your sake, a
whole family for whom you constitute the ornament, an entire town
proud of your having been born there—all these engage and divide your affection, and what is left for love is only slight compared to what the claims of family and friendship take from it. But
I, Julie, alas! Wandering, without a family and almost without a
country, I have no one on this earth but you. Love alone is all I
possess. Therefore, do not be surprised if, though your soul may be
the most sensitive, mine best knows how to love, and if, though I
yield to you in so many things, I win the prize of love at least in this
respect.

Yet do not fear that I will trouble you any more with my indiscreet complaints. No, I shall respect the pure joy you feel, both for its own sake and for yours. I shall imagine the touching sight of your pleasures, I shall share them from afar, and having no happiness of my own, I shall enjoy yours. Whatever your reasons for keeping us apart, I respect them. What use would it be to me to know them, if, when I must disapprove of them, I should still have to obey your will? Could it be more painful to keep silent than to leave you? Always remember, oh Julie, that your soul has two bodies to govern, and that the one which it animates by choice will always be the most faithful.

nodo più forte:
Fabricato da noi, non dalla sorte.
METASTASIO

a stronger knot
Formed by us, not by fate.

I will keep silent, then, and until it pleases you to end my exile, I will try to lessen the tedium of it by exploring the mountains of the Valais while they are still practicable. I am discovering that this unknown country deserves notice, and that to be admired it needs only perceptive spectators. I shall try to make some observations worthy of pleasing you. To amuse a fashionable woman, one must describe a witty and gallant people. But you, my Julie, ah, I know well that the picture of a happy and simple people is the one I must paint for your heart.

❖ LETTER XXII ❖

From Julie

AT LAST the first step is taken, and you have been mentioned to my father. In spite of your scornful opinion of my learning, he has been surprised by it, nor did he less admire my progress in music and in drawing,* and, to the great astonishment of my mother, who is prejudiced by your calumnies,† he has been very content with my skill in everything, except heraldry, which he thinks I have neglected. But this skill was not acquired without a teacher. I was compelled to name mine, and I did so with a pompous enumeration of all the skills you proposed to teach me, except one. My father remembered having seen you several times during his last trip home, and he seemed not to have kept an unfavorable impression of you.

Next he asked about your fortune—he was told that it was mediocre; about your birth—he was told that it was honest. This word *honest* is very equivocal in the ear of nobility, and it aroused suspicions which were confirmed in the explanation. As soon as he knew your birth was not noble, he asked what you were paid each month. My mother, having her turn to talk, said that such an arrangement could not even be proposed and that, on the contrary, you had constantly refused even the most inconsiderable presents of necessary articles that she had tried to give you. But your pride only inflamed his own, and how was he to bear the idea of being indebted to a man who was meanly born? He has decided, therefore, that you should be offered payment, and in case you refuse it, notwithstanding your merit, which he admits, you will be dismissed. There, my friend, is the résumé of a conversation concerning my most honored teacher, during which his humble pupil was not very much at ease. I thought I could not hurry too much to give you this information, so as to leave you time to consider it. As soon as you have made up your mind, do not fail to let me know it, for this is a matter entirely within your own jurisdiction, and my rights do not go that far.

I learn of your trips in the mountains with uneasiness, not because I think you will not find a pleasant diversion there or because your detailed account of what you see will not give me pleasure, but I am afraid that you are hardly in condition to endure the fatigue of such journeys. Besides, the season is very advanced. From one day to the next, everything can be covered with snow, and possibly you will suffer even more from cold than from fatigue. If you fell sick in that distant country, I should never be consoled. Therefore, come back,

---

* Here, it seems to me, is a twenty year old scholar who is prodigiously learned! At thirty, it is true, Julie congratulates him for being no longer so erudite. [*Rousseau*]

† This has reference to a letter to the mother, written in a doubtful tone, which has been suppressed. [*Rousseau*]

my good friend, closer to me. It is not yet time to return to Vevey,
but I wish that you were in a less savage place and that we could
correspond more easily. I leave the choice of the place to you. Try
only to keep it secret from anyone here, and be discreet without being mysterious. I shall advise you no further on this subject. I depend upon you to be prudent for your own interest, and even more
for mine.

Adieu, my friend. I can no longer spend a long time with you.
You know what precautions I am obliged to take to write you. That
is not all: my father has brought with him a venerable stranger, his
old friend, who once saved his life in the war. Imagine the reception we are endeavoring to give him! He leaves tomorrow, and we
are impatient to procure him today every sort of entertainment that
can express our gratitude to such a benefactor. I am called. I must
conclude. Adieu once more.

❧ LETTER XXIII ❧

To Julie

I HAVE spent only a week in traveling through a country which
would require years of observation, but besides the fact that I was
driven back by the snow, I wanted to return to meet the postman,
who may bring, I hope, one of your letters. Waiting for it, I begin
this one, and I shall write another afterwards to answer yours, if it
is necessary.

I shall not give you here a detailed account of my trip and observations. I have written a report of it all which I intend to bring you.
Our correspondence must be reserved for things which touch us
more closely. I shall content myself with telling you of the state of
my soul, for it is only fair that I should render you an account of the
use being made of your property.

I left, dejected by my suffering but consoled by your joy, which
kept me in a certain languid state that is not without charm for a
sensitive heart. On foot, I slowly ascended the mountains along
rather rugged trails, led by a man I had employed as my guide but in
whom during the whole trip I found a friend rather than a hired as-

romantic landscape (handwritten)

sistant. I wished to meditate but I was always distracted by some unexpected sight. Sometimes immense rocks hung ruinous over my
head. Sometimes high and clamorous waterfalls deluged me with
their heavy mist. Sometimes a perpetual torrent at my side would
open an abyss which my eyes dared not fathom. Sometimes I was
lost in the obscurity of a luxurious forest. Sometimes as I emerged
from a gorge a pleasant meadow suddenly gladdened my eyes.[2] *up on mtn* (handwritten)

During the first day, I attributed the serenity that I felt again in
my soul to pleasures of that sort. I wondered at the control that the
most inanimate creations have over our most lively passions, and I
scorned philosophy for having less power over the soul than a succession of lifeless objects. But finding that this peaceful state lasted
the night and increased the next day, I did not hesitate to decide
that there was still some other cause which I had not discovered.
That day I reached the lowest mountains, and passing over their
rugged tops, I arrived at the highest summit I could attain. After
walking in the clouds, I came to a more serene place, from which, in
the proper season, one may see the thunder and the storm gathering
below him—the too flattering picture of human wisdom, the original
of which never existed, or exists only in the places from which the
emblem has been taken.

It was there, in the purity of that air, that I plainly discerned the
true cause of my change of humor and of the return of this interior
peace which I had lost so long ago. In fact, this is a general impression that all men experience, although they all do not observe it, for
in the high mountains where the air is pure and thin, one breathes
more easily, his body is lighter and his mind more serene. Pleasures
are less ardent there, the passions more moderate. Meditations take
on an indescribably grand and sublime character, in proportion to
the grandeur of the surrounding objects, and an indefinable, tranquil voluptuousness which has nothing of the pungent and sensual.
It seems that in being lifted above human society, one leaves below all base and terrestial sentiments, and that as he approaches the
ethereal regions, his soul acquires something of their eternal purity.
One is serious there but not melancholy, peaceful but not indolent,
content to exist and to think. All overly vivid desires become dulled.
They lose that sharpness which makes them painful, they leave only
a light and sweet emotion in the bottom of the heart, and it is thus
that a pleasing climate causes the passions, which elsewhere constitute man's torment, to contribute to his happiness. I doubt
whether any violent agitation or any vapor sickness could withstand
a prolonged stay in the mountains, and I am surprised that baths of

salutary and beneficial mountain air are not one of the great remedies of medicine and morality.[3]

I would have spent my whole trip under the spell of the countryside, if I had not found an even more enchanting one in meeting
the inhabitants. In my report you will find a short sketch of their
manners, their simplicity, their evenness of temper, and that peaceful tranquillity which makes them happy by an exemption from misery rather than by the enjoyment of pleasures. But what I have not
been able to describe for you, and what one can hardly imagine,
is their disinterested humanity and their hospitable zeal toward all
strangers that chance or curiosity leads among them.[4]

While I was delightedly traveling in these places, so little known
and so worthy of admiration, what were you doing in the meantime, my Julie? Did your friend forget you? Julie forgotten? Should I
not rather forget myself? And how could I be alone for a single moment, I who exist only for you? I never noticed more readily how I
instinctively find a place for our inseparable souls in various places
according to the state of my mind. When I am sad, my soul takes
refuge near yours and seeks consolation wherever you are. That
was the case when I left you. When I am happy, I cannot enjoy anything alone, and then in order to share it I call you wherever I am.
That was the case during this whole trip, where, the variety of scenes
forever calling me back to my own situation, I led you everywhere
with me. I did not take a step without you. I did not admire a view
without hurrying to show it to you. All the trees that I encountered
lent you their shade; all the grassy banks served you as a bench.
Sometimes, seated at your side, I gazed with you at the scene before
us; sometimes, at your knee, I surveyed one more worthy of the contemplation of a sensible man. Did I come to a difficult pass? I saw
you leap over it with the agility of a fawn bounding after its mother.
Was it necessary to cross a stream? I dared to press such a light burden into my arms. I walked through the stream slowly, delightedly,
and was sorry to reach the opposite path. Everything in this peaceful
place reminded me of you. The striking natural beauty, the invari-
able purity of the air, the simple manners of the people, their constant and sure wisdom, the amiable modesty of the women and
their innocent graces—in short, all that gave pleasure to my eye
and my heart reminded them only of her whom they constantly seek.

Oh my Julie! I kept saying tenderly, would that I could spend my
days with you in these unknown places, fortunate in our happiness
and unknown to the world! Would that I could here collect my
whole soul in you alone and become in turn the universe to

you! Then your adored charms would enjoy the homage they deserve! Then our hearts would forever savor the delights of love! A long and sweet intoxication would let us forget the passage of time, and when age at last had calmed our first passions, the habit of thinking and feeling together would have begotten a friendship no less tender to succeed their transports. All the honest sentiments, nourished in our youth with those of love, would fill one day its vacant place. We would fulfill all the duties of humanity in the midst of and by the example of this happy people. Ceaselessly we should unite in acts of benevolence, and we should not die without having lived.

The mail is arriving. I must finish my letter and run to receive yours. How my heart will beat until that moment! Alas! I was happy in my reverie. My happiness flies with it. What will I be in reality?

✣ LETTER XXIV ✣

To Julie

I CAN immediately answer the article in your letter which regards payment, for I have no need, thank God, to reflect on it. These, my Julie, are my sentiments on this point.

In what people call honor, I distinguish between that which is founded on public opinion and that which is derived from self-esteem. The first consists in vain prejudices no more stable than a ruffled wave, but the second has its basis in the eternal truths of morality. The honor of public opinion can be advantageous with regard to fortune, but it does not reach the soul and thus has no influence on real happiness. True honor, on the contrary, is the essence of happiness, because it alone inspires that permanent feeling of interior satisfaction which constitutes the happiness of a rational being. Let us, my Julie, apply these principles to your question and the answer will soon be decided.

To set myself up as a teacher of philosophy and, like the fool in the fable,* take money for teaching wisdom will seem base in the eyes of the world, and I confess that there is something ridiculous

* La Fontaine's fable, "Le Fou Qui Vend La Sagesse." [*Translator's note*]

in it. However, since no man can subsist merely of himself, and since he almost always can manage only by his work, we shall put this scornful opinion in the class of the most dangerous prejudices. We shall not be so foolish as to sacrifice our happiness to this senseless idea. You will not esteem me less on this account, nor shall I deserve any more pity for living by the talents I have cultivated.

But here, my Julie, we have other considerations. Let us leave the multitude and look into ourselves. What would I really be to your father by taking a salary from him for the lessons I give you and thus selling him part of my time, that is to say, part of my person? A mercenary, his hireling, a kind of servant. And as a guarantee of his confidence and of the safety of his possessions, he will have my tacit faith, the same as from the meanest of his domestics.

Now, what more precious possession can a father have than his only daughter, even were it another than Julie? What then will he do who sold that father his services? Will he stifle his feelings for the daughter? Ah! You know that is impossible! Or else, unscrupulously giving in to his heart's inclination, will he wound in the most tender place the man to whom he has pledged his faith? In this case I see such a teacher only as a perfidious man who tramples underfoot the most sacred trust,* a traitor, a seducer-servant whom the law very justly condemns to death. I hope that she to whom I am speaking understands me; it is not death that I fear, but the ignominy of deserving it and my own self-contempt.

When the letters of Eloise and Abelard fell into your hands, you remember what I said to you about reading them and about the conduct of that priest. I have always pitied Eloise. She had a heart made for love, but Abelard has ever seemed to me only a miserable creature who deserved his fate and who was a stranger as much to love as to virtue. After having passed this judgment on him, ought I to imitate him? What wretch dares preach a morality which he will not practice! Whoever is blinded by his passion to that point is soon punished and loses the power to enjoy the sensations to which he has sacrificed his honor. Love is deprived of its greatest charm when honesty abandons it. To feel its whole value, the heart

* Unfortunate young man! He does not see that in allowing himself to be paid in gratitude what he refuses in money, he is violating a still more sacred trust. Instead of teaching Julie he corrupts her; instead of nourishing he poisons her. He is thanked by a deceived mother for the ruin of her child. One feels, however, that he has a sincere love of virtue, but his passion leads him astray; and if his extreme youth did not excuse him, with all his fine speeches he would be only a scoundrel. The two lovers are to be pitied; only the mother is inexcusable. [*Rousseau*]

must delight in it, and it must ennoble us by ennobling the one we love. Take away the idea of perfection, and you take away enthusiasm; take away esteem, and love is nothing. How could a woman honor a man who dishonors himself? How could he adore a woman who has no fear of abandoning herself to a vile seducer? This way, mutual contempt soon results, love is nothing for them but a shameful relationship, and they lose honor without finding happiness.

It is different, my Julie, with two lovers of the same age, both seized with the same passion, united by a mutual attachment, under no particular engagements, both enjoying their original liberty, and forbidden by no law to pledge themselves to each other. The most severe laws can impose upon them no other hardship than the natural consequence of their love. Their only punishment for their love is the obligation to love one another forever; and if there is some unhappy region in the world where a cruel authority may break these innocent bonds, it is punished, no doubt, by the crimes that this coercion engenders.

These are my reasons, wise and virtuous Julie. This is only a cold commentary on those which you urged with so much energy and spirit in one of your letters, but it is enough to show you how much I am of your opinion. You remember that I did not insist on refusing your gifts, and that, in spite of my prejudiced aversion, I accepted them in silence, indeed not finding in true honor any substantial reason for refusing them. But in this case, duty, reason, even love, all speak too plainly to be disregarded. If I must choose between honor and you, my heart is prepared to lose you. It loves you too much, oh Julie, to keep you at that price.

❧ LETTER XXV ❧

From Julie

THE ACCOUNT of your voyage is charming, my good friend. It would make me love its author, even were he a stranger to me.[5] But I am too busy with your second letter to answer the first in detail. Thus, my friend, let us leave the Valais for another time, and let us limit ourselves now to our private concerns. We shall be busy enough with them.

I knew the resolution you would take. We know each other too well to be still uncertain of each other's minds. If virtue ever forsakes us, be assured that it will never be in those occasions which require courage and sacrifices.* The first move when the attack is violent is to resist, and we shall be victorious, I hope, as long as we are forewarned by our enemy to take up arms. It is in the middle of a sleep, it is in the midst of a sweet repose that surprises must be feared; but above all it is continual hardship that is an intolerable burden, and the soul resists sharp pain much more easily than prolonged misery. That, my friend, is the harsh kind of struggle which we shall henceforth have to undergo. Duty does not demand heroic actions of us but an even more heroic resistance to relentless grief.

I foresaw too well that the time of happiness would pass like a flash of lightning. The time of misfortune is beginning with no end in sight. Everything alarms and discourages me, a mortal languor has taken hold of my soul, and for no immediate reason, involuntary tears steal from my eyes. I do not see inevitable hardships for us in the future, but I had been cultivating a hope and now see it fading every day. What use is there, alas, to water the leaves when the tree is cut at the root?

I feel, my friend, that the weight of your absence is crushing me. I cannot live without you, I know, and this frightens me most. A hundred times a day, I walk through the places where we used to be together, but I never find you there. I wait for you at your usual hour, but the hour comes and goes and you do not appear. Everything I see reminds me of you, only to inform me that I have lost you. You do not have this frightful torment. Your heart says only that you miss me. Ah, if you knew what a worse torture it is to remain at home when we are parted, how you would prefer your state to mine!

Yet, if I dared to grieve! If I dared to speak of my sorrow, I should be comforted for the misfortunes of which I complain. But except for a few secret sighs breathed into my cousin's bosom, I must stifle all the rest. I must contain my tears. I must smile though I am dying.

> Sentirsi, oh Dei, morir;
> E non poter mai dir:
> Morir me sento!
> METASTASIO

* It will soon be seen that this assertion cannot be further from the truth. [*Rousseau*]

> To feel oneself, oh gods, dying;
> And not to be able to say:
> I feel myself dying!

The worst is that all these misfortunes endlessly aggravate my greatest pain, and that the more desolate your memory makes me the more I love to think of you. Tell me, my friend, my sweet friend! Are you feeling how tender a languishing heart is and how sadness increases love?

I have a thousand things to say to you, but besides the fact that it is better to wait to know positively where you are, I cannot continue this letter in my present state. Adieu, my friend. I forsake my pen, but be assured that I shall never forsake you.

Note to Julie

I am sending this note to the usual address, through a boatman who is a stranger to me, to inform you that I have taken refuge at Meillerie, on the shore opposite from you, in order to enjoy at least the sight of the place which I dare not come near.

❧ LETTER XXVI ❧

To Julie

HOW MY CONDITION has changed in so short a time! What bitterness is mixed with the sweetness of coming close to you again! What sad reflections beset me! What obstacles my fears make me foresee! Oh Julie, what a fatal gift from Heaven is a sensitive soul! He who receives it must expect to have only pain and sorrow on this earth. The plaything of the air and the seasons, his fate is determined by sunlight or mists, cloudy or clear weather, and he will be content or sad as the winds blow. A victim of prejudices, he will find in society's absurd precepts an invincible obstacle to the just desires of his heart. Men will punish him for having sincere sentiments in every affair and for passing judgment on it according to that which is true rather than that which is conventional. But he alone is enough to create his own misery by indiscreetly giving himself up to the divine allure of the good and the beautiful while the heavy chains of necessity attach him to ignominy. He seeks supreme happiness without remembering that he is only mortal. His heart and his reason are incessantly at war, and his limitless desires prepare eternal privations for him.

Such is the cruel situation into which I am plunged by the fate which crushes me, my sentiments which elevate me, your father who scorns me, and you who constitute the delight and the torment of my life. Without you, fatal beauty! I should never have felt this unbearable contrast between the grandeur of my soul and the meanness of my fortune. I should have lived quietly and died content, without condescending to notice what rank I held on earth. But to have seen you and not be able to possess you, to adore you and be only an obscure man! To be loved and not be able to be happy! To live in the same places and not be able to live together! Oh Julie whom I cannot renounce! Oh destiny which I cannot surmount! What frightful struggles I undergo, and yet I can never overcome my desires nor rise above my powerlessness!

What a bizarre and inconceivable consequence! Since I have come back near you, my mind dwells only on distressing thoughts. Perhaps the place where I am contributes to this melancholy. It is sad and dreadful. But it is thus more suited to the state of my soul, and so I stay more patiently here than I would in a more pleasant place. A ridge of bleak rocks borders the coast and surrounds my lodging, which is made still more dismal by the winter season. Ah! I feel, my Julie, that if I had to give you up, I should have no other place, no other season.

In the violent disturbance which distracts me, I cannot stay in one place. I run, I climb eagerly, I leap over the crags. Taking long strides, I walk through all the surrounding area, and I find in everything the same horror which reigns inside me. One sees nothing green any more, the grass is yellow and withered, the trees are bare, the dry and cold north-east wind heaps up the snow and ice, and all nature is dead in my eyes, like the hope in the bottom of my heart.

Among the crags on this side, I have found a little ledge in a lonely cleft from which I have a distinct view of the fortunate town in which you live. Judge with what eagerness my eyes flew towards that cherished place. The first day I made a thousand efforts to distinguish your house, but because of the extreme distance they were useless, and I perceived that my imagination was deceiving my tired eyes. I ran to the curate's to borrow a telescope, with which I saw or thought I saw your house, and since that time I have spent entire days in that cleft contemplating the lucky walls which enclose the source of my life. In spite of the season, I go there at daybreak and do not return until night. I make a fire from leaves and some dry wood, which with my running serves to protect me from the excessive cold. I have taken such a liking to this wild place that I even bring ink and paper here, and I am now writing this letter on a slab of rock that the ice has detached from a nearby crag.

Here, my Julie, your unfortunate lover manages to enjoy the last pleasures which perhaps will ever delight him in this world. From this place he secretly dares to penetrate through open spaces and walls into your very room. Your charming features dazzle him again; your tender looks revive his dying heart. He hears the sound of your sweet voice; he dares seek again in your arms that delirium which he experienced in the arbor. But this is the idle phantom of a disturbed soul which is lost among his desires! Soon forced to return to reality, even then I contemplate you at least in the daily conduct of your innocent life. From afar, I follow your various daily occupations, and I imagine them at the times when and in the places where I once so fortunately witnessed them. I see you ever attentive to duties which make you more estimable, and my heart grows tender with delight over the inexhaustible goodness of yours. In the morning, I say to myself, she is now awaking from a peaceful sleep, her complexion has the freshness of a rose, and her soul enjoys a sweet calm. To her creator, she dedicates a day which will not be lost to virtue. Now she goes to her mother. The tender affections of her heart spill over when she is with her parents, and she helps them with the domestic cares of the house. She perhaps calms an imprudent servant; she perhaps pleads with him in secret; she perhaps asks a favor for another. At another time, she busies herself tirelessly with the duties of her sex. She embellishes her soul with useful knowledge. She adds the refinements of the fine arts to her exquisite manners and those of the dance to her natural agility. Sometimes I see her in an elegant but simple dress which needlessly sets off her charms. I see her here consulting a venerable pastor about the ignored misery of an indigent family, there aiding or consoling a sad widow and helpless orphan. Sometimes she entertains an honest group with her sensible and modest conversation; sometimes, in laughing with her companions, she tempers her tone of wisdom and discretion with a playful youthfulness. Sometimes, ah forgive me! I

dare even to see you busying yourself with me. I see your soft eyes
running over one of my letters. I read in their sweet languor that
you are writing to your lucky lover. I see you speaking to your cousin
of him with tender emotion. Oh Julie! Oh Julie! Shall we never be
united? Shall we never spend our days together? Could we be parted
forever? No, may that frightful idea be far from my mind! But because of it, my tenderness is suddenly changed into furor. Rage
makes me run from crag to crag. I utter involuntary moans and
cries. I roar like an incensed lion. I am capable of everything, except
giving you up, and there is nothing, no, nothing that I may not do
in order to possess you or to die.

I was at this point in my letter and was only waiting for a safe
opportunity to send it to you, when I received from Sion the last
one you wrote me there. How the sadness it expresses has allayed
mine! What a striking proof I see in it of what you once told me concerning the sympathy between our souls even in distant places! Your
sorrow, I confess, is calmer. Mine is more unmanageable, but the
same sentiment must take its color from the natures which feel it,
and it is quite natural that the greatest losses cause the greatest sorrows. What am I saying, losses? Ah! Who could bear them? No, be
assured at last, my Julie, that an eternal decree from Heaven destined us for each other; that is the first law we must obey. It is the
first duty in life to unite ourselves to the person who is to make it
sweet for us. I see and I regret that your projects are misleading and
vain. You want to break down insurmountable barriers, and you
neglect the only possible means. Enthusiasm for chastity takes away
your reason, and your virtue is no more than a delirium.

Ah! If you could remain always as young and brilliant as you are
now, I should ask Heaven only to know of your eternal happiness,
to see you once every year of my life, only once, and to spend the
rest of my time contemplating your home from afar, adoring you
from the midst of these crags. But alas! Behold the speed of that star
which never stops. It flies and time passes. Opportunity slips away.
Your beauty, even your beauty will have its end. It must fade and
one day die like a flower which falls before it is gathered, and meanwhile I sigh, I suffer, my youth is consumed in tears and withers in
sorrow. Think, think, Julie, that we are already counting years lost
for pleasure. Think that they will never return, that those left for us
will be the same if we let them escape again. Oh my blind love!
You are seeking an imaginary happiness for a future which we shall
never have. You are intent upon a distant time, and you do not see
that meanwhile we are continually wasting away, and that our souls,

overwhelmed by love and sorrow, are melting like the snow. Awake, there is still time. Awake, my Julie, from this disastrous delusion. Abandon your projects, and be happy. Come, oh my soul, into your lover's arms to reunite the two halves of our single being. Come before Heaven, the guide of our flight and witness to our vows, and let us swear to live and die for each other. I need not reassure you, I know, against the fear of poverty. Let us be happy, and though poor, ah, what treasure we shall have acquired! But let us not affront humanity by thinking that there is no refuge left in the whole world for two unfortunate lovers. I have arms, I am strong. The bread earned by my work will seem more delicious to you than banquet dishes. Can a meal prepared with love ever be tasteless? Ah, my tender and dear love, if our happiness were only for a single day, could you wish to leave this short life without having tasted it?

I have only one word more to say to you, oh Julie! You know the ancient use of the rock of Leucadia, the last refuge of so many unhappy lovers. This place resembles it in many respects. The cliff is steep, the water is deep, and I am in despair.

✤ LETTER XXVII ✤

From Claire

MY SORROW scarcely leaves me the strength to write you. Your misfortunes and mine are at their crisis. The lovely Julie is at the brink of death and has not perhaps two days left. The effort she made in parting from you began to affect her health. The first conversation she had with her father about you brought on new attacks. Other more recent griefs have increased her disorder, and your last letter has done the rest. She was so acutely affected by it that after having spent a night in frightful agony, she was seized yesterday with an intense fever which has increased continually and has at last made her delirious. In this condition, she calls your name at every moment, and speaks of you with a vehemence that shows her preoccupation with you. Her father is kept away as much as possible; that sufficiently proves that my aunt suspects the truth. She has even anxiously asked me if you were on your way back, and I see that, her daughter's danger for the moment outweighing all other considerations, she would not be sorry to see you here.

Come then without delay. I have hired the boat expressly to bring you this letter. It is at your command, use it for your return, and above all do not lose a moment, if you wish to see once again the most tender and loving person that ever lived.

✤ LETTER XXVIII ✤

From Julie to Claire

HOW BITTER the life you have restored to me is made by your absence! What a convalescence! A passion more terrible than fever and delirium sweeps me away to my ruin. Cruel one! You leave me just when I need you most. You have left me for a week; perhaps you will never see me again. Oh, if you knew what the madman dares to propose to me! . . . and in what manner! . . . to elope! to follow him! to be carried off! . . . the wretch! . . . But of whom am I complaining? My heart, my unworthy heart tells me a hundred times more than he . . . great God! What would it be, if he knew all? . . . He would become frenzied, I would be swept away, I would be forced to leave . . . I shudder . . .

But then has my father sold me? He considers his daughter as property, as a slave; he acquits himself at my expense! He purchases his life with mine! . . . for I see too well that I shall never live through it . . . cruel and unnatural father! Does he deserve . . . what! deserve? He is the best of fathers. He wants to marry his daughter to his friend, that is his crime. But my mother, my tender mother! What evil has she done me? . . . Ah, a great deal! She has loved me too much; she has ruined me.

Claire, what shall I do? What shall become of me? Hans has not come. I do not know how to send you this letter. Before you receive it . . . before you return . . . who knows . . . fleeing, wandering, dishonored . . . it is all over, it is all over, the crisis has come. One day, one hour, perhaps one moment . . . who may sidestep his fate? . . . Oh, wherever I live and die, into whatever obscure retreat I drag my shame and my despair, Claire, remember your friend . . . Alas! Misery and shame change one's heart . . . Ah, if ever mine forgets you, it shall have changed a great deal!

❧ LETTER XXIX ❧

From Julie to Claire

STAY, AH STAY! Never return. You would only come too late. I must never see you again. How should I bear to have you look upon me?

Where were you, my sweet friend, my protector, my guardian angel? You abandoned me, and I was ruined. What, was this fatal trip so necessary or so urgent? How could you have left me alone at the most dangerous moment of my life? What remorse you have caused yourself through this criminal negligence! It will be as eternal as my tears. Your loss is as irretrievable as mine, for it is as difficult to gain another friend equal to you as it is impossible to recover my innocence.

What have I said, wretch that I am? I can neither tell nor keep my secret. What use is secrecy when remorse cries out? Does not the whole universe reproach me for my error? Is not my disgrace written on every object? If I do not pour out my heart to you, it will burst. And you, do you not reproach yourself for anything, my compliant and over-confident friend? Ah! Did you not betray me? It is your trust, your blind friendship, it is your fatal indulgence which has ruined me.

What demon inspired you to call him back, that cruel creature who has caused my disgrace? Was his perfidious care to restore me to life only for the purpose of making it insupportable? May he go away forever, the barbarous one! May a vestige of pity touch him; may he come no longer to redouble my torments by his presence; may he deny himself the savage pleasure of witnessing my tears. But what am I saying, alas? He is not guilty. Only I am. All my misfortunes are of my own doing, and I have no one to reproach but myself. But vice has already corrupted my soul; its first effect is to make us accuse others of our crimes.

No, no, he was never capable of being false to his vows. His vir-

tuous heart does not know the abject art of injuring the one he
loves. Ah! Without a doubt, he knows how to love better than I,
since he knows how to conquer his passions better. A hundred times
I witnessed his struggles and his victory. His eyes would sparkle with
the fire of his desires. He would rush toward me in the impetuous-
ness of a blind passion. But he would stop himself suddenly; an insurmountable barrier seemed to have surrounded me, never to be
overcome by his impetuous but chaste love. I dared watch this dangerous spectacle too much. I myself was troubled by his fits of passion. His sighs oppressed my heart. I shared his torments when I
thought I was only pitying them. I saw him trembling with emotion,
ready to lose consciousness at my feet. Perhaps love alone would
have saved me; oh my cousin, it is pity that destroyed me.

My disastrous passion seems to have tried to disguise itself with
an all-virtuous mask in order to deceive me. That very day he
urged me even more ardently to elope with him. That would have
distressed the best of fathers; that would have plunged a dagger into
my mother's heart. I resisted, I rejected the proposal with horror.
But the impossibility of ever realizing our hopes, the necessity for
concealing this impossibility from him, the regret I felt for deceiving
so submissive and so tender a lover after having flattered his expectation—all these were battering down my courage, all were augmenting my weakness, all were disordering my reason. I had to destroy my parents, my lover, or myself. Without knowing what I was
doing, I chose my own destruction. I forgot everything but love.
Thus, one unguarded moment has ruined me forever. I have fallen
into the abyss of shame from which a girl never returns, and if I
live, it is only to be more wretched.

Sighing, I search for some vestige of consolation on this earth. I
see only you, my loving friend. Do not deprive me of such an appealing resource, I implore you; do not take from me the sweetness
of your friendship. I have lost the right to claim it, but never have
I needed it so much. Let your pity replace your esteem. Come, my
dear, open your heart to my remorse. Come to receive your friend's
tears. Shield me, if you can, from my self-contempt, and convince
me that I have not lost everything, since I still have your heart.

❖ LETTER XXX ❖

Answer

WRETCHED GIRL! Alas, what have you done? My God! You so deserved to remain virtuous! What shall I say to you in the horror of your situation and in the despondency into which it plunges you? Shall I finish crushing your poor heart, or shall I offer you consolations which I myself need? Shall I point out to you things as they are or as it is proper for you to see them? Holy and pure friendship! Bring to my soul your sweet illusions, and in the tender pity which you inspire, first deceive me about the wrongs which you can no longer make right.

I feared, you know, the misfortune for which you are remorseful. How many times have I predicted it and been disregarded! . . . It is the result of my rash confidence, you say . . . Ah! There is no question of that any more. I should have betrayed your secret, no doubt, if I could have saved you that way. But I read your oversensitive heart better than you; I saw it consuming itself with a devouring fire that nothing could extinguish. I perceived that this heart palpitating with love had to be happy or it would die, and when your fear of succumbing made you banish your lover so tearfully, I decided that soon either you would be dead or he would be recalled. But how frightened I was when I saw you determined against living and so close to death! Do not therefore accuse your lover or yourself of a crime for which I am the most guilty, since I foresaw it without preventing it.

It is true that I left against my will, but you saw that I had to obey. Yet, if I had thought you so near your undoing, they should have sooner torn me to pieces than made me leave you. I was mistaken about the moment of danger. Weak and still languishing, you seemed to me secure against so short an absence. I did not foresee the dangerous dilemma you were soon to face; I forgot that your weakness left your dejected heart more defenceless against itself. I ask pardon for mine, but I can hardly repent a mistake which saved your life. I do not have that unfeeling courage which made you renounce me, I could not have lost you without a fatal despair, and I still prefer you alive though remorseful.

But why so many tears, dear and sweet friend? Why this remorse greater than your error and this undeserved self-contempt? Will one moment of weakness efface so many sacrifices, and is not the very illness you are recovering from a proof of your virtue? You think only of your defeat and you forget all the painful victories which have preceded it. Since you have been tried more than those who resist, have you not done more for the sake of honor than they? If nothing can justify you to yourself, think at least of that which excuses you. I scarcely know what it is that people call love. I shall always be able to resist the ecstasies it inspires, but I should have resisted a love like yours much less than you did, and thus without having surrendered, I am less chaste than you.

These words will shock you, but your greatest misfortune is having made them necessary. I would give my life if they could not be applied to you, for I hate evil precepts even more than evil actions.* If the mistake were still to be committed, if I were base enough to speak to you this way, and if you were to listen to me, we should both be the lowest of creatures. But now, my dear, I must speak this way to you and you must listen to me or you are lost; for you still possess a thousand charming qualities which only self-esteem can preserve, which excessive shame and the humiliation that follows it would infallibly destroy, and this esteem is based more on your opinion of yourself than on your real worth.

Do not give way, then, to a dangerous dejection which would debase you more than your frailty. Is true love degrading to the soul? Do not let one error committed through love take from you that noble enthusiasm for the honest and the beautiful which always raised you above yourself. Is one spot visible in the sunlight? How many virtues do you have left in place of the one which is impaired? Will you now be less sweet, less sincere, less modest, less charitable? Will you be less deserving, in a word, of all our homage? Will honor, humanity, friendship, or pure love be less dear to your heart? Will you cherish any less even that virtue which you no longer have? No, dear and good Julie, your Claire pities and adores you; she knows, she feels that nothing but good can still come from your soul. Ah! Believe me, you have much yet to lose before any other woman, even one more chaste, could ever be as good as you!

---

* This sentiment is just and sound. Unruly passions inspire evil actions, but evil precepts corrupt the reason itself and cut off the possibility of a return to virtue. [Rousseau]

After all, I still have you. I can be consoled for anything except for losing you. Your first letter made me tremble. It might have almost made me desire the second, if I had not received it at the same time. To wish to forsake your friend! To plan to fly without me! You do not speak at all of that, which is your greatest crime. You should have been ashamed of that a hundred times more than of the other. But you, ungrateful creature, thought only of your love . . . I should have been wounded to the core.

With a mortal impatience I count the moments that I am forced to spend far from you. They are cruelly prolonged. We are to stay at Lausanne for six more days, after which I shall fly to my only friend. I shall console her or grieve with her, wipe away or share her tears. In your sorrow I shall speak more tender friendship than inflexible reason. Dear cousin, we must grieve, love each other, keep silent, and if we can, efface by dint of future virtues one error that cannot be blotted out with tears. Ah! My poor Chaillot!

❧ LETTER XXXI ❧

To Julie

WHAT PRODIGY of Heaven are you then, inconceivable Julie? And by what art, known to you alone, can you assemble so many incompatible impulses in one heart? Drunk with love and sensual pleasure, mine is overwhelmed by sadness. I suffer and languish in the midst of the supreme happiness, and I reproach myself for my excessive good fortune as if for a crime. God! What frightful torment it is not to dare give oneself up completely to any sentiment but to have them incessantly warring against each other and always to combine bitterness with pleasure! It would be a hundred times more preferable merely to be miserable.

What use is it to me, alas, to be happy? I no longer feel my own anxiety, but yours instead, and it only torments me more sensibly. Vainly you wish to hide your distress from me; I read it in spite of you in your languor and the lowering of your eyes. Can those expressive eyes conceal any secret from love? I see, I see the hidden chagrin which besets you under an apparent serenity, and your melancholy, veiled by a sweet smile, only affects my heart more bitterly.

This is not the time to hide anything from me. Yesterday I was in your mother's room, she left for a moment, and I heard sighs which pierced my soul. With that, how could I fail to recognize their source? I drew near the place from which they seemed to come. I entered your rooms; I got as far as your dressing room. What did I think when, opening the door a little, I perceived her who ought to be on the throne of the universe seated on the floor, her head leaning on a chair which was dampened by her tears? Ah, if it had been my blood, I should have suffered less! With what remorse was I stung at that instant! My bliss became my torment, I no longer felt anything but your distress, and I would have atoned for your tears and all my pleasure with my life. I wished to hurl myself at your feet; I wished to wipe those precious tears away with my lips, to bury them in the bottom of my heart, to die or to dry them up forever; but I heard your mother coming back, and I had to return abruptly to my place. I carried away all your sorrow and the remorse which will never end except with it.

How humiliated I am, how debased I am by your repentance! I am very despicable, then, if our union makes you despise yourself and if the delight of my life is the torment of yours. Be more just to yourself, my Julie; look with a less prejudiced eye upon the holy bonds your heart has formed. Have you not obeyed the purest laws of nature? Have you not freely entered into the holiest of engagements? What have you done that both divine and human laws can and must not authorize? What does the tie that joins us lack except a public declaration? Consent to be mine, and you are no longer sinful. Oh my wife! Oh my worthy and chaste companion! Oh delight and happiness of my life! No, it is not what your love has done that can be a crime, but what you would like to rob from it; only by accepting another husband can you offend honor. Belong forever to the friend of your heart if you wish to remain innocent. The tie which unites us is legitimate; only an infidelity which would break it would be reproachful, and from now on it is for your love to be the guardian of your virtue.

But if your sorrow were reasonable, if your remorse were well-founded, why keep my share of it from me? Why do my eyes not shed half your tears? You have no grief that I ought not feel, no sentiment that I ought not share, and my justly jealous heart reproaches you for all the tears which you do not pour out into my bosom. Tell me, cold and dissembling lover, is not everything that your soul does not communicate to mine stolen from my love? Must not everything be in common between us? Do you no longer remember having said so? Ah! If you loved as I do, my happiness would console you as much as your grief afflicts me, and you would feel my pleasure as I feel your sorrow.

But I see that you scorn me as a madman because my reason goes astray in the midst of delights. My ecstasies frighten you, my delirium makes you pity me, and you do not consider that the utmost human strength cannot be equal to limitless pleasure. Do you think that a sensitive soul may enjoy infinite bliss moderately? Do you think that he can withstand so many kinds of raptures all at once without losing his bearing? Do you not know that there is a time when no one's reason resists any longer, and that there is no man in the world whose good sense may then prevail? Therefore, pity the distraction into which you have thrown me, and do not be contemptuous of errors which you occasion. I am no longer master of myself, I confess; my estranged soul is wholly absorbed in yours. Thus, I am more fit to feel your sorrows and more worthy to share them. Oh Julie, do not conceal them from your other self.

❖ LETTER XXXII ❖

Response

THERE WAS A TIME, my dear friend, when our letters were easy and delightful. The sentiment which dictated them poured out with an elegant simplicity. They needed neither art nor coloring, and their purity constituted all their eloquence. That happy time is no more. Alas! It cannot return, and as the first consequence of so cruel a change, our hearts have already ceased to understand each other.

Your eyes have seen my sorrows. You think you have fathomed the source of them, you wish to console me by vain words, and while you think you are deluding me, it is yourself, my friend, whom you delude. Believe me, believe in the tender heart of your Julie; my remorse is much less for having given too much to love than for having deprived it of its greatest charm. That sweet enchantment of virtue is vanished like a dream. Our passions have lost that divine ardor which gave vigor to them by purifying them. We have sought pleasure, and happiness has fled us. Recall once more those delightful moments in which our hearts fused the more we respected each other, in which our passion drew from its own excess the strength to conquer itself, in which our innocence consoled us for our restraint, in which the homage paid to honor turned everything to the profit of love. Compare such a charming time to our present situation. What disturbances! What fright! What mortal alarms! How our immoderate sentiments have lost their first sweetness! What has become of that zeal for prudence and honesty, the love of which used to inspire all our actions and which in turn made love more delightful? Our enjoyments used to be peaceful and lasting; we now have nothing but fits of passion. This mad joy is more like attacks of frenzy than tender caresses. A pure and holy flame used to burn our hearts; now, given up to the delusions of the senses, we are nothing but common lovers, sufficiently happy if jealous love still condescends to preside over the pleasures which even the most brutish mortal can enjoy.

There, my friend, are the losses which we share, and which I do not regret less for you than for myself. I say nothing concerning the one more immediately mine; your heart is capable of feeling it. Look at my shame, and grieve if you know how to love. My mistake is irreparable; my tears will never dry. Oh you who caused them to flow, be fearful of attempting to end such just sorrows; my whole hope is for them to be made eternal. The worst of my crimes would be to be comforted for them, and the ultimate disgrace is to lose, along with innocence, the sentiment which makes us love it.

I know my fate, I sense the horror of it, and yet one consolation is left me in my despair. It is the only one, but it is sweet. It is from you that I expect it, my dear friend. Since I no longer dare think of myself, I think with more pleasure of the one I love. I give you all the esteem that you have taken from me, and you become only more dear to me by compelling me to despise myself. Love, this fatal love which destroys me, gives you new value; you are elevated while I am degraded, and your soul seems to have profited from all the debasement of mine. Therefore, from now on be my only hope. It is for you to justify my crime, if you can, cover it with the honesty of your sentiments, let your merit efface my shame, and excuse with the strength of your virtues the loss of mine that you occasioned. Be my whole being, now that I am nothing. The only honor I have left is wholly in you, and as long as you are worthy of respect, I shall not be completely contemptible.

Though I regret the return of my health, I cannot conceal it any longer. My face belies my speech and my pretended convalescence can no longer deceive anyone. Hurry then, before I am forced to resume my ordinary duties, to take the step upon which we have agreed. I see clearly that my mother has conceived some suspicions and that she is watching us. My father seems to know nothing, I confess; that proud gentleman does not even imagine that a man not nobly born may be in love with his daughter. But after all, you know his resolution. He will send you away if you do not prevent him, and in order, then, to keep your access to our house, you must banish yourself from it completely. Believe me, speak to my mother while there is still time. Pretend to have some business affairs which keep you from continuing to tutor me, and let us give up our frequent meetings so that we may meet at least sometimes; for if the door is closed to you, you can present yourself at it no longer, but if you close it yourself, your visits will be, in a way, at your discretion, and with a little ingenuity and management, you will be able to pay them more frequently afterwards without anyone noticing or finding it amiss. I shall tell you this evening the means that I am inventing for other opportunities to meet, and you will agree that my inseparable cousin, who formerly occasioned so many complaints, will not now be useless to two lovers, whom, indeed, she should never have left alone.

❧ LETTER XXXIII ❧

From Julie

AH, MY FRIEND, what a poor refuge for two lovers a social gathering is! What torment to meet and have to restrain ourselves! It would be a hundred times better not to see each other at all. How can we be calm with so many emotions? How can we be so different from ourselves? How can we think of so many things when one alone preoccupies us? How can we control our gestures and eyes when our hearts are soaring? I never in my life felt an anxiety equal to the one I experienced yesterday when you were announced at the home of Madame d'Hervart. When your name was pronounced, I thought it was a reproach addressed to me; I imagined that the whole group was watching me. I no longer knew what I was doing, and when you came in, I blushed so excessively that my cousin, who was watching over me, was obliged to hold her fan up in front of me, as if whispering in my ear. I feared that even that artifice might create a poor impression and that people might look for a mystery in that whispering. In short, in everything I found new reasons for alarms, and I never felt more fully how a guilty conscience needs no accuser.

Claire pretended to observe that you were not presenting a better figure. You seemed to her to be embarrassed, uncertain what to do, not daring to advance or retire, to approach me or withdraw, and looking all around the room in order to have, she said, a pretence for looking at us. A little recovered from my confusion, I thought I perceived yours, when young Madame Belon spoke to you and you sat chatting with her, becoming calmer at her side.

I feel, my friend, that this manner of living, which affords so much constraint and so little pleasure, is not good for us. Our love is too great for such restraint. These public assemblies are only fit for people who, not being in love, are nevertheless on good terms, or people who can dispense with secrecy. My anxiety is too disquieting, your indiscretions too dangerous, and I cannot always keep a Madame Belon at my side to create a diversion in case one is needed.

Let us return, let us return to that solitary and peaceful life, from which I drew you so inadvertently. That life gave rise to and nourished our passions; perhaps they would be weakened by this more dissipated manner of living. All the great passions are formed in solitude. There is nothing like them among society, where there is no time for a single object to make a profound impression and where the variety of pleasures enervates the strength of the sentiments. Solitude is also more suited to my melancholy; it is sustained by the same food as my love. Your dear image nourishes both, and I prefer to see you tender and sensible in my heart than constrained and distracted in an assembly.

Besides, there may come a time when I should be forced into a greater seclusion. Would that it had already come, this desired time! Prudence as well as my own inclination require that I accustom myself beforehand to habits which necessity may demand. Ah! If from my error could spring the means of amending it! The sweet hope of one day being . . . but inadvertently I say more than I wish about the design which preoccupies me. Forgive me this mystery, my dearest friend; my heart shall never keep any secret which would be sweet for you to know. You must nevertheless be ignorant of this one, and all that I can tell you at present is that love, which occasioned our misfortunes, is to bring us relief from them. Consider, comment to yourself, if you want, but I forbid you to question me.

❧ LETTER XXXIV ❧

Response

HOW INDEBTED I am to that pretty Madam Belon, for the pleasure she provided me! Forgive me, divine Julie, but I dared enjoy for a moment your tender fears, and that moment was one of the sweetest of my life. How charming were those uneasy and curious glances which you stole toward me and which were immediately lowered to avoid mine! What was your happy lover doing then? Was he chatting with Madame Belon? Ah, my Julie, can you think so? No, no, incomparable girl, he was more worthily occupied. With what delight was his heart following the emotions of yours! With what avid impatience were his eyes devouring your features! Your love, your beauty filled, ravished his soul; it was scarcely equal to so many delightful sentiments. My only regret is that I was enjoying at your expense pleasures which you did not share. Do I know what Madame Belon said to me during that whole time? Do I know what I answered her? Did I even know it at the time of our conversation? Could she tell it, and could she understand the slightest thing in the discourse of a man who was speaking without thinking and answering without listening?

> Com' huom, che par ch' ascolti, e nulla intende.
>
> [?]
>
> Like a man who seems to listen and yet hears nothing.

And she has conceived the most perfect contempt for me. She has said to everyone, to you perhaps, that I have no common sense, or what is worse, not the slightest wit, and that I am completely as foolish as my books. But what does it matter to me what she says and thinks? Does not my Julie alone determine my fate and the position I hold? Let the rest of the world think of me as it likes; my whole worth is in your esteem.

Ah, do not think that Madame Belon or any superior beauty is privileged to create the diversion you speak of and to keep my heart and my eyes from you for a moment! If you doubt my sincerity, if you could do this mortal injury to my love and to your charms, tell me, how could I have taken account of all that took place around you? Did I not see you shining among the beautiful young women like the sun among the stars which it eclipses? Did I not see the *cavaliers** gather around your chair? Did I not see the admiration they singled you out for, in spite of your companions? Did I not notice their assiduous attentions, their compliments and their gallantry? Did I not see you receive everything with that air of modesty and indifference that is more affecting than pride? When you took off your glove for the refreshments, did I not see the effect which that uncovered arm produced among the spectators? Did I not see the young stranger who picked up your glove tempted to kiss the charming hand which took it? Did I not see a bolder stranger whose ardent stare drained my life's blood and obliged you, when you saw it, to add a pin to your shawl? I was not so distracted as you think. I saw all this, Julie, and yet was not jealous, for I know your heart. It is not, I am convinced, one of those which can be twice in love. Will you accuse mine of being so?

Then let us return to that solitary life which I left only with regret. No, my heart finds no satisfaction in the hubbub of society. False pleasures make the privation from true ones more bitter, and I prefer my suffering to empty compensations. But, my Julie, there is, there perhaps can be more substantial satisfaction in any situation other than our present constraint, and you seem to forget it! What, to spend two whole weeks so close to one another, without meeting or speaking! Ah, what do you want a heart burning with love to do during so many centuries? Even separation would be less cruel. What use is an excess of prudence which does us more harm than it prevents? What use is it to prolong a life in torment? Would it not be a hundred times more preferable to meet for a single instant and then die?

I own freely, my sweet friend, that I should like to discover the pleasant secret which you are hiding from me. There never was any that could interest us more, but I am needlessly attempting to

---

* *Cavaliers:* an old word which is no longer used. One says *gentlemen*. I am indebted to the provincials for this important remark and for being thus useful to the public at least once. [*Rousseau*]

know it. I shall nevertheless keep the silence you impose and repress an indiscreet curiosity, but in respecting so sweet a mystery,
may I not at least be assured of soon being satisfied? Who knows,
who yet knows if your projects are not vain fancies? Dear soul of my
life, ah! At least let us begin to make them realities.

P.S. I neglected to tell you that Monsieur Roguin has offered me
a company in the regiment he is raising for the king of Sardinia. I
have been sensibly moved by the esteem of this brave officer. Thank-
ing him, I told him that I was too short-sighted for the service and
that my passion for study unfitted me for so active a life. In this, I
have not made a sacrifice to love. I think that everyone owes his life
and blood to his country and that he is not permitted to part with
it for princes to whom he is in no way indebted, still less to sell himself and turn the most noble profession in the world into that of a
vile mercenary. These precepts were those of my father, whom
I should be very happy to imitate in his love for his duty and for
his country. He never would enter the service of any foreign prince,
but in the war of 1712 he bore arms honorably for his own country.
He was in several battles, in one of which he was wounded, and
in the battle of Wilmerghen he had the good fortune to capture an
enemy flag under the eyes of General de Sacconex.

❧ LETTER XXXV ❧

From Julie

I DO NOT FIND, my friend, that the few words I said laughingly about
Madame Belon were worth so serious an explanation. Taking so
much trouble to justify oneself sometimes produces a contrary result, and it is only the attention given to trifles which makes them
important. That surely will never happen between us, for well-oc-
cupied hearts are hardly punctilious, and lovers' disputes over nothing almost always have a much deeper foundation than they think.
    I am glad, however, that this trifle may furnish us an opportu-
nity to discuss jealousy, a subject unfortunately too important for
me.

I see, my friend, by the temper of our souls and by the agreement of our dispositions, that love will be the great business of our lives. Whenever love has once made the deep impression that we have felt, it must extinguish or absorb every other passion. The slightest cooling of our passion would soon be the languor of death for us; an invincible apathy, an eternal indifference would replace our extinguished love, and we could not live for very long after having ceased to love. As for me, you well know that only the delirium of passion blinds me to the horror of my present situation, and that I must love extravagantly or die of sorrow. See, then, if I am justified in seriously discussing a point on which depends the happiness or the misery of my life.

As far as I can know myself, it seems to me that though I am often too emotional, I am nevertheless little inclined to anger. My annoyances would have to ferment a long time within me before I would dare reveal their source to their author, and since I am persuaded that one cannot do offence without intending to, I would rather submit to a hundred subjects of complaint than ever come to an explanation. Such a disposition must go to extremes with ever so little a penchant for jealousy, and I am much afraid of feeling this dangerous penchant in my own heart. It is not that I am not convinced that your heart is made for mine and no other, but one can be deceived, mistake a passing fancy for a real passion, and do as many things because of his imagination as he might perhaps have done because of love. Now, if you can believe yourself inconstant without really being so, I could falsely accuse you of infidelity. This frightful doubt would poison my life, however; I would suffer without complaining and die inconsolable without having ceased to be loved.

I implore you, let us prevent this misfortune, the mere idea of which makes me shudder. Therefore, my sweet friend, swear to me —not by love, an oath which is kept only when it is superfluous, but by the holy name of honor which you so respect—that I shall ever be the confidante of your heart, and that it will have no unexpected change of which I shall not be the first one told. Do not plead that you never will have anything to tell me; I believe, I hope so, but prevent my foolish alarms and pledge to secure my present peace eternally against a future which could never be. I should be less pitiable learning my real misfortunes from you than suffering ceaselessly from imaginary ones; at least I should enjoy your remorse, for if you no longer shared my passion, you would still share my pain, and thus I should find the tears that I would shed into your bosom less bitter.

It is on this account, my friend, that I am doubly pleased in my choice, both in the sweet bond which unites us, and in the honor which assures it. With us, the dictates of principle are followed in matters of pure sentiment; with us, strict virtue can dispel the problems of tender love. If I had a lover without principle, even were he to love me eternally, where should I find the guarantee of this constancy? What means should I have to silence my continual misgivings, and how could I assure myself of not being deceived either by his pretense or by my own credulity? But you, my worthy and respectable friend, you who are incapable of artifice or of dissembling, you will, I know, preserve the honesty you have promised me. The shame of confessing an infidelity will not outweigh the duty of your upright soul to keep your word, and if you could no longer love your Julie, you would say to her, . . . yes, you could say to her, "Oh Julie, I do not. . . ." My friend, never shall I write those words.

What do you think of my device? It is the only one, I am sure, which could root out all my feeling of jealousy. There is an indefinable enchantment in entrusting your love to your good faith, thus removing my ability to believe you unfaithful when you would not first inform me yourself. That, my dear, is the certain effect of the promise I am exacting from you, for I could believe you an inconstant lover but not a deceiving friend, and even if I should doubt your heart, I could never doubt your faith. What pleasure I enjoy in taking useless precautions in this matter, in anticipating a change of heart, the impossibility of which I feel so well! What delight it is to speak of jealousy with so faithful a lover! Ah, if you were capable of inconstancy, do not believe that I could speak to you in this way! My poor heart would not be so clever in that case, and the slightest real distrust would soon deprive me of my desire to secure myself against it.

There, my very honored teacher, is matter for discussion for this evening, for your two humble pupils will have the honor of supping with you at the home of my uncle. Your learned comments on the gazette have raised you so high in his eyes that no great artifice was needed to get you invited. My cousin has had her harpsichord tuned, my uncle has leafed through Lamberti's book, and I shall perhaps repeat the lesson of the arbor at Clarens. Oh, you doctor of all sciences, you must adapt your knowledge to all of us. Mon-

sieur d'Orbe, who you may be sure is invited, has been told to begin
a learned dissertation on the future homage to the king of Naples,
during which we shall all three go into my cousin's room. There,
my loyal vassal, on your knees before your lady and mistress, your
hand in hers, and in the presence of her chancellor, you will swear
faith to her and loyalty on every occasion—that is not to say eternal love, a pledge no one can absolutely keep or break, but truth,
sincerity, inviolable frankness. You will not swear to be ever submissive, but rather never to commit an act of treachery and at least
to declare war before shaking off the yoke. This done, you shall
have the accolade and be acknowledged as sole vassal and loyal
knight.

Adieu, my good friend. The thought of this evening's supper
inspires me with gaiety. Ah! How sweet it will be to see you sharing
my joy.

✤ LETTER XXXVI ✤

From Julie

KISS THIS LETTER and leap for joy at the news I am going to tell you.
But be assured that though I do not leap and have nothing to kiss,
I feel the joy no less keenly. My father, obliged to go to Berne on
account of his lawsuit and from there to Soleure for his pension,
has proposed to take my mother with him, and she has agreed,
hoping for some salutary effect upon her health in the change of
air. They wished to do me the honor of taking me along also, and
I did not consider it appropriate to tell them what I was thinking.
But the difficulty of carriage arrangements made them abandon that
project, and now they are endeavoring to console me for not being in the party. I have to pretend to be sad, and the false role
which I am constrained to play gives me such true sorrow that remorse has almost made the pretense useless.

During my parents' absence, I shall not remain as mistress of the
house but am to be lodged at my uncle's, so that I shall be during
this time wholly inseparable from my cousin. Moreover, my mother
has preferred to take along a maid and leave me Babi as a govern-

ess, a hardly dangerous sort of Argus whose faith may not be corrupted nor her confidence assured but whom one may easily dismiss if need be by offering her the slightest allurement of pleasure or gain.

You understand what opportunities we shall have to meet during these two weeks, but it is in this that discretion must restrain us, and we must voluntarily impose upon ourselves the same reserve which is forced on us at other times. When I am at my cousin's, you must not come there more often than before, for fear of compromising her. I hope that it will not even be necessary to speak to you of the consideration her sex requires, or of the sacred rights of hospitality, and that an honorable man will not need to be instructed in the respect due the friendship which gives his love asylum. I know your ardent disposition, but I know the inviolable limits to it. If you had never renounced virtue, you would not have to make a sacrifice today.

Why that discontented air and that sad eye? Why complain of the restraints which duty imposes upon you? Leave it to your Julie to sweeten them. Did you ever repent having been submissive to her voice? Near the flowery banks of the source of the Vevaise, there is a remote village which sometimes is used as a shelter for hunters but should only serve as a refuge for lovers. Scattered around the main building, which belongs to Monsieur d'Orbe, are some sufficiently remote chalets,* which with their thatch roofs may be able to shelter love and pleasure, the friends of rustic simplicity. The young and discreet milkmaids know enough to keep for others the secret which they need kept for themselves. The streams which run through the meadows are bordered by flowering shrubs and delightful groves. Farther on, some thick woods offer more secluded and shaded refuges.

> Al bel seggio riposto, ombroso e fosco,
> Ne mai pastori appressan, ne bifolci.
> PETRARCH

> In the fair, secluded place, shady and dim,
> Neither shepherds nor plowmen ever come near you.

There, neither art nor the hand of man displays its restless toil. One sees everywhere only the tender care of nature, our common

---

* A sort of wooden house in which cheese and various kinds of milk products are made in the mountains. [*Rousseau*]

mother. It is there, my friend, that one is solely under her protection and may listen only to her laws. At the invitation of Monsieur d'Orbe, Claire has already persuaded her papa to go with some friends to hunt for two or three days in that area and to take along the inseparable cousins. These inseparables have others, as you know only too well. The one, being the master of the house, will naturally do the honors of it; the other with less ceremony will do those of a humble chalet for his Julie, and this chalet, sanctified by love, will be for them the temple of Cnidus.* To carry out this charming project happily and surely, we must only make some arrangements which will easily be settled between us, and which will themselves constitute a part of the pleasure which they are intended to produce. Adieu, my friend, I leave off abruptly for fear of being surprised. Besides, I think that your Julie's heart is flying to the chalet a little too soon.

P.S. All things well considered, I think that we shall be able to meet without indiscretion almost every day—that is to say, at my cousin's every other day and the other while walking in the fields.

✣ LETTER XXXVII ✣

From Julie

THEY LEFT this morning, my tender father and my incomparable mother, overwhelming with the most tender caresses their cherished daughter, too unworthy of their goodness. On my part, I embraced them with a little reluctance in my heart, while deep inside this ungrateful and unnatural heart bubbled with an odious joy. Alas! What has become of that happy time in which I continually led an innocent and wise life under their observation, in which I was not content except near them and could not take a single step from them without displeasure? Now guilty and fearful, I tremble to think of them, I blush to think of myself, all my virtuous sentiments have been corrupted, and I torture myself with

* A shrine housing Praxiteles' statue of Aphrodite and especially dedicated to the worship of that goddess. [*Translator's note*]

vain and barren regrets that do not even arouse a true repentance.
These bitter reflections have brought on all the sorrow which their
farewells had not first effected. A secret grief stifled my soul after
the departure of these dear parents. While Babi was setting
things to rights after them, I mechanically entered my mother's
room, and seeing some of her things still scattered about, I kissed
them all one by one and burst into tears. This state of tenderness
comforted me a little, and I found some sort of consolation in feeling that nature's sweet emotions are not completely extinguished
in my heart. Ah tyrant! In vain do you wish to conquer this tender
and too feeble heart absolutely. In spite of you, in spite of your
fond illusions, it still respects and cherishes some rights more sacred
than yours.

Oh my sweet friend, forgive these involuntary emotions, and do
not fear that I will extend these reflections as far as I should. The
moment in our lives in which our love is perhaps most untroubled
is not one of regret, I know. I wish neither to hide my sorrow from you nor to overwhelm you with it; you must know it,
not to bear but to mitigate it. Into whose bosom should I pour out
my grief, if not yours? Are you not my tender consoler? Do you not
sustain my shaken courage? Do you not foster in my soul the love
for virtue, even after I have lost it? Without you, and without that adorable cousin whose compassionate hand has so often
dried my tears, how many times might I not already have succumbed to the most fatal despondency? But your tender attentions sustain me. I do not dare abase myself as long as you still
esteem me, and I flatter myself that neither of you could love me as
much if I deserved only contempt. I shall fly into the arms of
my dear cousin, or rather, my tender sister, to leave my troublesome sorrow in the bottom of her heart. Come to me this evening
to restore to mine the joy and the serenity which it has lost.

❧ LETTER XXXVIII ❧

To Julie

NO, JULIE, it is not possible for me to see you each day only as I
saw you yesterday. My love must augment and increase forever

with the discovery of your charms, and you are an inexhaustible source of new sentiments which I had not even imagined. What a wonderful evening! What unknown delights my heart experienced because of you! Oh enchanting melancholy! Oh the languor of a tender soul! How these surpass turbulent pleasures, wanton gaiety, extravagant joy, and all the ecstasies that a boundless passion offers to the unbridled desires of lovers! Never, never will the impressive memory of that peaceable and pure bliss which has nothing to equal it in the voluptuousness of the senses be erased from my heart. Gods! What a ravishing sight, or rather, what ecstasy to see two such touching beauties tenderly embracing, your head reclining on Claire's bosom, your sweet tears mingling with hers and bathing that charming bosom just as the dew from Heaven moistens a freshly opened lily! I was jealous of so tender a friendship. I found in it something indefinably more interesting than in love itself, and I wished to be somehow punished for not being able to offer you such tender consolations without disturbing them by the violence of my passion. No, nothing, nothing on earth is capable of exciting so voluptuous a tenderness as your mutual caresses, and in my eyes, the sight of two lovers might have offered a less delightful sensation.

Ah, in that moment I might have been in love with that adorable cousin, if Julie had not existed. But no, it was Julie herself who spread her irresistible charm over everything which surrounded her. Your dress, your finery, your gloves, your fan, your work—everything I saw around you enchanted my heart, and you yourself were responsible for the whole enchantment. Stop, oh my sweet friend! By increasing my intoxication, you would deprive me of the pleasure of feeling it. What you make me experience approaches a true delirium, and I am fearful of finally losing my reason in it. Let me at least know a frenzy which constitutes my happiness; let me enjoy this new rapture, more sublime, more penetrating than all my former ideas of love. What, you can believe yourself abased! What, does passion take away your reason also? I find you too perfect for a mere mortal. I should believe you to be a purer species, if this devouring fire which pierces my being did not unite me to yours and did not make me feel that they are one and the same. No, no one in the world knows you. You do not know yourself. My heart alone knows you, feels you, knows what place you are to occupy in it. My Julie! Ah, if you were only adored, what homage would be robbed from you! Ah! If you were only an angel, how much of your value would you lose!

Tell me how it can be that a passion such as mine can increase? I do not know how, but I feel it. However much you are with me at all times, there are some days above all that your image, more beautiful than ever, pursues me and torments me with an assiduousness from which neither space nor time protects me, and I think you left that image with me in the chalet which you mentioned in the conclusion of your last letter. Since there has been talk of this rustic rendezvous, I have left town three times. Each time my feet have carried me to the same slopes, and each time the prospect of so desirable a visit there has seemed to me more pleasant.

> Non vide il mondo si leggiadri rami,
> Ne mosse 'l vento mai si verdi frondi.
> PETRARCH

> Never did the world see branches so beautiful,
> Nor ever did the wind stir such green leaves.

I find the country more gay, the green more fresh and vivid, the air more pure, the sky more serene. The song of the birds seems to be more tender and voluptuous; the murmur of the brooks evokes a more amorous languor; from afar the blooming vine exudes the sweetest perfumes; a secret charm either embellishes everything or fascinates my senses. One would say that the earth adorns itself to make for your happy lover a nuptial bed worthy of the beauty he adores and of the passion which consumes him. Oh Julie! Oh dear and precious half of my soul, let us hurry to add the presence of two faithful lovers to these ornaments of spring. Let us carry the sentiment of pleasure into the places which afford only an empty idea of it. Let us animate all nature; it is dead without the warmth of love. What! Three days of waiting? Still three days? Drunk with love, greedy for ecstasies, I wait for this delayed moment with a painful impatience. Ah! How fortunate we would be if Heaven removed from life all the tedious intervals which separate such moments!

cf. p 72

✤ LETTER XXXIX ✤

From Julie

YOU DO NOT have one sentiment, my good friend, which my heart does not share, but speak no more to me of pleasure while people who deserve more than we do are suffering, sorrowing, and while I must reproach myself with their misery. Read the enclosed letter and then be tranquil if you can. As for me, knowing the amiable and virtuous girl who has written it, I have not been able to read it without tears of remorse and pity. Regret for my sinful negligence has pierced my soul, and I see with bitter confusion to what point the forgetfulness of my principal duties has brought that of all the others. I had promised to take care of this poor child. I recommended her to my mother, I kept her in some way under my protection, but being unable to protect myself, I abandoned her without thinking and exposed her to worse dangers than those to which I have succumbed. I shudder to think that in two days time, perhaps, it might have been my fault that poverty and seduction ruined a modest and wise girl, who could one day be an excellent mother of a family. Oh my friend, how many men are there in the world base enough to extort from misery the prize which the heart alone should award and to take from a hungry mouth the tender kisses of love!

Tell me, could you not be touched by the filial devotion of my Fanchon, by her honest sentiments, by her innocent simplicity? Are you not touched too by the uncommon tenderness of her lover who will sell himself to assist his mistress? Will you not be only too happy to contribute to the union of such a well-matched couple? Ah, if we were without compassion for the united hearts which people try to separate, from whom could we ever expect any ourselves? For my part, I have resolved to make amends to them for my neglect at no matter what cost and to arrange it so that these two young people may be joined in marriage. I hope that Heaven will bless this undertaking and that it will be a good omen for us. I suggest to you, and I implore you in the name of our friendship, to leave today if

you can for Neuchâtel, or at the very latest tomorrow morning. Go
to negotiate with Monsieur de Merveilleux to obtain the discharge
of that honest boy. Spare neither entreaties nor money. Take with
you my Fanchon's letter; there is no sensitive heart which it cannot
soften. In short, whatever it may cost us both in pleasure and in
money, return only with the absolute release of Claude Anet, or
else be assured that our love will not give me a moment of pure joy
for the rest of my life.

cf. Valmont

I am aware of many objections your heart must raise. Do you
doubt that mine may not have raised them before you? But I am
persistent, for virtue must be only an empty word if it does not demand sacrifices. My friend, my worthy friend, we can meet a thousand times to make up for this disappointed rendezvous; a few
pleasant hours vanish like a lightning flash and are no more. But if
the happiness of an honest couple is in your hands, think of the future you are shaping for them. Believe me, the opportunity to make
people happy is rarer than one thinks; the punishment for having
missed it is to find it again no more, and the use we shall make of
this one will leave us either an eternal contentment or remorse. Forgive my zeal for this superfluous speech; I have said too much to an
honorable man and a hundred times too much to my friend. I know
how much you hate that cruel self-indulgence which hardens us to
the miseries of others. You yourself have said a thousand times that
he is a wretch who does not know how to sacrifice one day of pleasure
to the duties of humanity.

❖ LETTER XL ❖

From Fanchon Regard to Julie

MADEMOISELLE,

Forgive a poor girl in despair who, no longer knowing which
way to turn, dares to have recourse again to your kindness. For
you never grow tired of consoling the afflicted, and I am so unfortunate that I have annoyed everyone but you and our good Lord with
my complaints. I was very sorry to leave the apprenticeship you put

me into, but having had the misfortune of losing my mother that winter, I had to return home to my poor father, whose paralysis keeps him ever in his bed.

I have not forgotten the advice you gave my mother to try to marry me to an honest man who might take care of the family. Claude Anet, who returned from your father's service, is a brave, steady lad who knows a good trade and who has taken a liking to me. Having been already so indebted to your charity, I no longer dared to trouble you, so it was Claude who supported us during the whole winter. He was to marry me this spring; he had set his heart on this marriage. But I had been tormented so much to find money to pay three years rent due at Easter that, not knowing where to get so much, the poor young man enlisted again, without telling me, in the company of Monsieur de Merveilleux, and brought me his enlistment payment. Monsieur de Merveilleux is at Neuchâtel only for seven or eight days more, and Claude Anet must set out in three or four with the rest of the recruits. Thus we do not have the time nor the means to get married, and he is leaving me without any resource. If through your influence or that of your father, the Baron, you could obtain at least a five or six week extension for him, we would try during that time to make some arrangements to get married or else to reimburse that poor lad. But I know him well; he will never want to take back the money he has given me.

This moment there came a very rich gentleman to offer me a great deal more, but thank God, I refused him. He said that he would return tomorrow morning to know my final decision. I told him not to take the trouble to return, for he knew it already. Were God to lead him, he would be received tomorrow as he was today. I could indeed resort to the fund for the poor, but one is so despised after that that it is better to suffer; and then Claude Anet has too much pride to want a girl receiving public assistance.

Forgive the liberty I am taking, my good lady. I dare confess my troubles only to you, and my heart is so oppressed that I can write no more. I am, your very humble and affectionate servant to command,

                                                    Fanchon Regard.

❧ LETTER XLI ❧

Response

I HAVE been deficient in memory and you in confidence, my dear child. We have both been greatly at fault, but mine is impardonable. I shall try at least to make amends for it. Babi, who brings you this letter, is ordered to provide what you most urgently need. She will return tomorrow morning to help you dismiss that gentleman, if he comes back. After dinner, my cousin and I will come to see you, for I know that you cannot leave your poor father, and I want to become acquainted myself with the condition of your little household.

As for Claude Anet, be uneasy no more. My father is away, but in waiting for his return we shall do what we can, and you may be confident that I shall not forget either you or this brave lad. Adieu, my child, may the good Lord console you. You are right not to have recourse to public charity; it is never necessary to do that as long as there is something left in the purse of benevolent people.

❧ LETTER XLII ❧

To Julie

I HAVE received your letter and am setting out immediately. This will be all the answer I shall make. Ah cruel one! How distant is my heart from this hateful virtue which you suppose in me and which I detest! But you command; I must obey. Were I to die a hundred times, I must have Julie's esteem.

❧ LETTER XLIII ❧

To Julie

I ARRIVED yesterday morning at Neuchâtel, and I learned that Monsieur de Merveilleux was in the country. I hurried to see him there, but he was out hunting, so I waited for him until evening. When I had explained the purpose of my trip and after I had begged him to set a price for the discharge of Claude Anet, he raised a great many objections. I thought I could remove them by offering a rather considerable sum and increasing it in proportion to his resistance. But being able to obtain nothing and assuring myself that I would find him in again this morning, I was obliged to take leave of him, quite resolved not to leave him again until I had obtained what I had come to ask him, either with money or importunities or whatever it might require. Having got up very early for that purpose, I was ready to mount my horse, when a messenger brought me the young man's discharge in due form, with this note from Monsieur de Merveilleux:

> Here, Monsieur, is the discharge which you have come to request. I refused it to your offers. I give it to your charitable intentions, and I beg you to believe that I never set a price upon a good deed.

Judge by your own what joy I felt in learning of this happy success. But why must it not be as perfect as it ought? I cannot avoid going to thank and to reimburse Monsieur de Merveilleux, and if this visit delays my departure a day, as I fear it will, have I not the right to say that he has shown himself generous at my expense? No matter, I have done what pleases you; I can bear anything at that price. How happy one is to do good in serving her whom he loves and thus unite the charms of love and of virtue in the same action! Oh Julie! I confess that I left with my heart full of impatience and chagrin. I reproached you for being so sensible of the troubles of others and for considering mine as nothing, as if I were the only person in the world who deserved nothing from you. I thought you cruel, after having enticed me with so sweet a hope, to deprive me needlessly of a blessing that you yourself had deluded me into expecting. All these regrets have vanished; I feel instead an unknown contentment in the bottom of my heart. Already I am experiencing the compensation you promised me, you who have been so well taught the enjoyment of doing good through your habitual benevolence. What a strange control is the one you exercise over me, which can make disappointment as sweet as pleasure and give obeying you the same charm one would find in self-gratification! Ah, I have said a hundred times that you are an angel from heaven, my Julie! With so much authority over my soul, yours is no doubt more divine than human. How can I not be eternally yours, since your reign is celestial, and what use would it be for me to cease loving you since I must always adore you?

P.S. According to my calculations, we still have at least five or six days before the return of your mother. Would it be impossible during that interval to make a pilgrimage to the chalet?

♣ LETTER XLIV ♣

From Julie

DO NOT COMPLAIN so much, my friend, over this unexpected return. It is more advantageous to us than it seems, and if we should have tried to do through skill what we have done through charity, we should not have had more success. Look at what would have happened if we had followed only our inclinations. I would have gone to the country the very day before my mother's return to town, I would have received a message before having met you, I would have had to leave immediately, perhaps without being able to give you notice, and thus leave you in mortal anxiety, and we would have parted just at the moment when it would have been most painful. Moreover, people would have known that we were both in the country. In spite of our precautions, perhaps they might have known that we were there together. At least they would have suspected that we were, and that is enough. Our indiscreet eagerness for the present would have ruined all our expedients for the future, and remorse for having disregarded a good deed would have tormented us all our lives.

Now compare that to our actual situation. First, your absence has produced an excellent result. My Argus will not fail to tell my mother that you were seldom seen at my cousin's. She knows of your trip and its purpose; that is one more reason for esteeming you. And how can they think that two people who have an affection for each other would voluntarily separate during their only moment of freedom? What ruse have we used to avert a distrust which is only too well founded? The only one, in my opinion, consistent with honor is to be discreet to an unbelievable degree so that an attempt to be virtuous may be mistaken for an act of indifference. My friend, how sweet must a love thus concealed be to the hearts which enjoy it! Add to this the pleasure of reuniting two lovers in despair and of making two such deserving young people happy. You have seen my Fanchon; tell me, is she not charming, and does she not truly deserve all you have done for her? Is she not too pretty and too indigent to remain unmarried without disaster? Might Claude Anet, whose natural goodness has miraculously withstood three years of the service, have been able to bear three more without becoming good-for-nothing like all the others? Instead, they are in love and will be united; they are poor and will be assisted; they are honest people and will be able to continue so, for my father has promised to provide for them. What blessings you have procured for them and for us by your kindness, not to mention the esteem I must have for you because of it! Such, my friend, is the assured consequence of the sacrifices one makes to virtue. If they are often painful to make, it is always sweet to have made them, and never has anyone been seen repenting a good deed.

I suspect that at the example of my inseparable cousin, you will also call me "the preacher," and indeed, I do not practice what I preach any better than those who are preachers by profession. But even if my sermons are not as good as theirs, at least I am pleased to see that they are not like water thrown into the wind. I do not deny, my amiable friend, that to your character I should like to add as many virtues as a mad passion has made me lose; and being no longer able to respect myself, I like to respect myself still in you. For your part, you need only to love perfectly, and all will come of itself. With what pleasure must you see that you are continually increasing the debts that love is obliged to pay!

My cousin has learned of the conversations which you have had with her father on the subject of Monsieur d'Orbe, and she is as grateful to you because of them as much as if we had never been indebted to her friendship. Good heavens, my friend, what a fortunate girl I am! How dearly am I loved, and how delighted I am to be so! Father, mother, friend, lover—I cannot cherish all who surround me enough, for I find myself either prevented or outdone. It seems that all the sweetest sentiments in the world continually seek out my soul, and I regret having only one to enjoy all my good fortune.

I forgot to tell you of a visitor you are to receive tomorrow morning. It is Lord Bomston, who has come from Geneva where he spent seven or eight months. He says that he saw you at Sion on his return from Italy. He found you quite melancholy, and moreover, he speaks of you as I do. Yesterday he praised you so well and so opportunely before my father that he completely predisposed me in his favor. Indeed, I found sense, wit, and brilliancy in his conversation. His voice rises and his eye sparkles in telling of great deeds, as it happens with men capable of performing them. He also speaks interestingly of matters of taste, especially of Italian music, which he extols to the heavens, and I thought I was again listening to my poor brother. But he puts more energy than grace into his discourse, and I even find his wit a little unpolished. Adieu, my friend.

❖ LETTER XLV ❖

To Julie

I WAS still only reading your letter for the second time when Edward, Lord Bomston entered. When I had so many other things to tell you, how was I to think, my Julie, to tell you about him? When two people are enough for each other, is one minded to think of a third? But, I will tell you what I know of him, now that you seem to desire it.

Having crossed over the Simplon Pass, he reached Sion before the carriage which runs between Brig and Geneva, and since want of occupation makes men rather sociable, he sought me out. We made as intimate an acquaintance as an Englishman, naturally rather reserved, can make with a very preoccupied man who is seeking solitude. However, we felt that we suited each other. There was a certain harmony of souls which we discerned from the first instant, and we were intimate friends at the end of eight days, but for all our lives, as two Frenchmen would have been at the end of eight hours for merely the time that they had left together. He talked to me of his travels, and knowing him to be English, I thought that he would speak to me of buildings and of paintings. But soon I was pleased to see that pictures and monuments had not made him neglect the study of manners and men. However, he spoke to me of the fine arts with much discernment, but in moderation and without pretention. I judged that his opinions were based more on feeling than knowledge, and determined according to results more than rules, which confirmed for me that he had a sensitive soul. As for Italian music, he seemed as enthusiastic over it as you are; he even had me listen to some, for he has a virtuoso with him. His valet-de-chambre plays the violin very well, and he himself the cello tolerably. He chose for me several of what he claimed to be some very moving pieces, but whether the style was so new for me and required a more practiced ear, or whether the charm of the music, so soothing in its melancholy, was lost in my profound sadness, these pieces gave me little pleasure, and I found their melody in truth pleasant, but bizarre and expressionless.

There was also a discussion of my affairs, and Lord Bomston learned of my situation with interest. I told him as much of it as he ought to know. He offered to take me with him to England with prospects of wealth—impossible since they were in a country where Julie did not live. He told me that he was going to spend the winter in Geneva, the following summer at Lausanne, and that he would come to Vevey before returning to Italy. He has kept his word, and we have seen each other again with renewed pleasure.

As for his character, I believe him fiery and hasty, but virtuous and steady. He prides himself on his philosophy and on those principles of which we have spoken formerly. But I believe him basically to be by temperament what he thinks he is by method, and the stoic polish which he puts on his actions only glosses his heart's inclinations with fine reasoning. However, I have learned with some little pain that he had some affairs in Italy and that he duelled there several times.

I do not know what lack of polish you find in his manners; truly they are not engaging, but I feel there is nothing repelling in them. Although his manner of addressing one may not be as open as his heart, and although he disregards the little proprieties, his behavior nevertheless is agreeable, it seems to me. If he does not have that reserved and circumspect politeness which confines itself only to outward appearances and which our young officers are bringing us from France, he has that humanitarian politeness which prides itself less on distinguishing position and rank at first glance and respects all men in general. Shall I tell you the frank truth? Lack of elegance is a fault which women do not pardon, even in the case of merit, and I am afraid that Julie may have been a woman for once in her life.

Since I am in the mood for sincerity, I shall tell you again, my pretty preacher, that it is useless to wish to put off my rightful deserts and that a starving love is not nourished by sermons. Think, think of the compensations promised and due. All the morality you have offered is very good, but whatever you may say, the chalet is still better.

❧ LETTER XLVI ❧

From Julie

WELL THEN, my friend, always the chalet? Your heart lays excessive stress upon the idea of the chalet, and I clearly see that sometime I must make it up to you. But are you so attached to the places where you never were that one may not compensate you elsewhere, and could not love, which created the palace of Armida in the middle of a desert,* be able to create a chalet for us in town? Hear me— my Fanchon is going to be married. My father, who has no objection to festivals and celebrations, is willing to give her a wedding which we shall all attend. This wedding will not fail to be exciting. Sometimes mystery has been known to spread its veil over the tumultuous joy and din of festivals. You understand me, my friend. Would it not be sweet to recapture the pleasures our benevolence cost us in its result?

It seems to me that you are rather superfluously zealous to vin-

* In Tasso's *Jerusalem Delivered*. [*Translator's note*]

dicate Lord Bomston, for I was far from thinking ill of him. Besides, how could I pass judgment on a man whom I saw only for an afternoon, and how could you yourself judge him on the basis of a few days acquaintance? I speak of him only from conjecture, and you can hardly know him better, for the proposals which he made to you are those vague offers which strangers often make lavishly, because they give them an air of power and because they are easily evaded. But I recognize your usual vivacity and tendency to predispose yourself for or against people, almost at first sight. However, we shall examine his proposals at our leisure. If love favors my project, perhaps something better is promised for us. Oh my good friend, patience is bitter but its fruit is sweet!

To return to your Englishman, I told you that he seemed to me to have a great and strong soul and more intelligence than embellishment in his mind. You say almost the same thing, and then, with that air of masculine superiority, abandoned not even by our humble admirers, you reproach me for having been a woman for once in my life, as if a woman ever should cease being so! Do you remember that, while reading your Plato's *Republic*, we once disputed the point of the moral difference between the sexes? I persist in the opinion which I held then and cannot imagine one common model of perfections for two such different beings. The attack and the defense, the audacity of men, the modesty of women—these are by no means conventions, as your philosophers think, but natural institutions which are easily accounted for and from which all the other moral distinctions are readily inferred. Besides, the purposes of nature not being the same in each sex, its inclinations, perceptions, and sentiments must be directed according to its own views; opposite tastes and constitutions are required for tilling the soil and for nursing children. A taller stature, a stronger voice, and features more strongly marked seem to have no necessary bearing on one's sex, but these exterior modifications indicate the intentions of the creator in the modifications of the spirit. The souls of a perfect woman and a perfect man must not resemble each other more than their appearances. Our vain imitations of your sex are the height of folly; they make the wise man laugh at us and they discourage love. In short, I find that unless we are to be five and a half feet tall, have a bass voice and a beard on our chins, we have no business pretending to be men.

See how unskillful lovers are in insults! You reproach me for a mistake that I have not committed or that you commit as well as I, and you attribute it to a defect in which I pride myself. Do you want me, paying your plain speaking with my own, to tell you frankly what I think of your sincerity? I find it only a refinement of flattery, for the purpose of justifying to yourself by this apparent frankness the enthusiastic praises you heap upon me at every turn. My imaginary perfections blind you so that you do not have the wit to find substantial reproaches to make to me to deny those you secretly make to yourself for your predisposition.

Believe me, do not undertake to tell me my faults; you would do it too poorly. Do the eyes of love, all-penetrating as they are, know how to perceive faults? These attentions belong to honest friendship, and in that your pupil Claire is a hundred times more learned than you. Yes, my friend, praise me, admire me, find me beautiful, charming, perfect. Your praises please me without deluding me because I see that they are the language of error and not of deceit and that you deceive yourself but that you do not wish to deceive me. Oh how delightful are the illusions of love! Its flattery is, in a sense, truth: the judgment keeps silent, but the heart speaks. The lover who praises in us the perfections which we do not possess sees them in fact such as he describes them. He does not lie by telling these falsehoods; he flatters us without debasing himself, and we may esteem him at least even though we do not believe him.

Not without some beating of the heart, I heard a proposal to invite two philosophers tomorrow for supper. One is Lord Bomston; the other is a learned man whose gravity is sometimes a little discomposed at the feet of a young pupil. Do you know him? Exhort him, I beg you, to try to preserve the philosophical decorum a little better tomorrow than usual. I shall take care to warn the young pupil as well to lower her eyes, and to appear in his as unattractive as possible.

❖ LETTER XLVII ❖

To Julie

AH EVIL ONE! Was that the circumspection you promised me? Is it thus that you spare my heart and veil your charms? What infractions of your pledges! First, your finery, for you wore none at all, and you

well know that you are never so bewitching as then. Second, your
demeanor, so sweet, so modest, so calculated to display all your
charms gradually. Your conversation, more refined, more studied,
more witty even than usual, which made us all more attentive and
made our ears and hearts anticipate each word. That air you sang,
in a low pitch which made your voice still sweeter, and which, although French, pleased even Lord Bomston. Your timid glance and
the unexpected flashes of light from your downcast eyes which
threw me into an inevitable disturbance. Finally, that undefinable,
inexpressible enchantment you seemed to have cast over your whole
person to turn everyone's head, without even appearing to dream
of doing so. As for me, I do not know how you do it, but if such is
your way of being as unattractive as possible, I warn you that you
must be much more so for men to act wisely around you.

I strongly fear that the poor English philosopher felt the same
influence a little. After having escorted your cousin home, since we
were all still wide awake, he proposed that we go to his house for
some music and some punch. While his servants were assembling,
he never ceased speaking of you with a warmth which displeased
me, and I did not hear your praises in his mouth with as much pleasure as you had heard mine. On the whole, I confess, I do not like
for anyone except your cousin to speak to me of you; it seems that
each word deprives me of part of my secret or of my pleasures, and
whatever anyone says of you is so suspicious or so short of what I
feel that on that subject I do not like to listen to anyone but myself.

It is not that I am, like you, inclined to be jealous. I know your
soul better than that; I have guaranties which do not even permit
me to imagine your inconstancy to be possible. After your pledges, I
say nothing more to you about other suitors. But this one, Julie!
. . . suitable conditions . . . the prejudices of your father . . .
You well know that it is a matter of my life. Deign then to speak
to me of this matter. One word from Julie, and I am forever tranquil.

I spent the night listening to and playing Italian music, for some
duets were found and I had to venture to do my part in them. I do
not yet dare tell you of the effect which it produced in me. I am
afraid, I am afraid that the impression of last night's supper might
have influenced what I was hearing and that I have mistaken the
effect of your enchantment for the charm of the music. Why should
the same cause which made it disagreeable to me at Sion not make
it pleasing here in a contrary situation? Are you not the prime
source of all the affections of my soul, and am I not at the mercy of

the power of your magic? If the music really had produced that enchantment, it would have affected all those who heard it. But while
those songs kept me in ecstasy, Monsieur d'Orbe slept tranquilly in
an armchair, and in the midst of my raptures, all the praise he be-
stowed was to ask if your cousin knew Italian.

All this will be better clarified tomorrow, for we are to have another musical gathering this evening. His Lordship wishes to make
it complete, and he has sent to Lausanne for a second violin, who
he said is tolerable. I shall bring on my part some operatic music,
some French cantatas, and we shall see!

Upon arriving home, I was in an extreme dejection which has
of late brought upon me the habit of sitting up and which is going
away as I write you. Yet I must try to sleep a few hours. Come with
me, my sweet friend; do not leave me during my sleep. But whether
your image troubles or assists it, whether it brings me the dream
of Fanchon's wedding or not, a delicious moment which cannot escape me and which it prepares for me is the feeling of my happiness
upon awakening.

✤ LETTER XLVIII ✤

To Julie

AH! MY JULIE, what I have heard! What moving sounds! What
music! What a delightful source of sentiments and pleasures! Do
not lose a moment; carefully gather together your operas, your cantatas, and your French music; make a large, very hot fire; throw in
it all that wretched stuff; and fan the flame carefully, so that so
much ice may burn there and give warmth at least once. Make this
propitiatory sacrifice to the god of taste, in order to expiate our
crime in having profaned your voice with this doleful psalmody and
in having so long mistaken a noise which only stuns the ear for the
language of the heart. Oh how right was your worthy brother! In
what an unaccountable error have I lived until now concerning the
productions of this charming art![6] I implore you to hear an experiment of this music soon, whether at home or at your inseparable
cousin's. Whenever you wish, his Lordship will bring over all his

people, and I am sure that with a voice as sensitive as yours and
more knowledge than I had of Italian declamation, a single session
will suffice to bring you to the point where I am and make you share
my enthusiasm. I propose to you and even beg you to profit from
the visit of the virtuoso by taking lessons from him, as I have begun
to do since this morning. His manner of teaching is simple, clear,
and consists in practice more than precept. He does not say what is
to be done, he does it, and in music, as in many other things, example is worth more than rule. I see already that it is only a matter
of marking the tempo, of feeling it well, of phrasing and punctu-
ating with care, of holding the tones equally and not swelling
them, finally of refining the voice from outbursts and all the French
bellowing in order to make it just, expressive, and flexible. Yours,
naturally so soft and so sweet, will easily get into this new habit;
your sensitivity will soon teach you the energy and the vivacity of
the expression which enlivens Italian music.

E'l cantar che nell' anima si sente.
PETRARCH

And the singing that is felt in the soul.

Therefore, abandon forever this wearisome and lamentable
French singing which resembles cries of stomach-ache more than
raptures of passion. Learn to form those divine sounds which sentiment inspires, which alone are worthy of your voice, and which always convey the charm and the fire of sensitive natures.

❧ LETTER XLIX ❧

From Julie

YOU WELL KNOW, my friend, that I can write you only by stealth and
always at the risk of being surprised. Thus, since it is impossible to
write long letters, I limit myself to answering what is most essential
in yours or to supplying what I have not been able to say to you in
our conversations, which are no less furtive than our letters. That

is what I shall do, especially today since your mentioning Lord Bomston makes me forget the rest of your letter.

My friend, you are fearful of losing me and you speak to me of songs! That would be a beautiful issue for a quarrel between lovers who understand one another less than we. Truly you are not jealous, it is evident, but for once I shall not be jealous myself, for I have penetrated into your soul and sense only your confidence where others would have thought to feel your indifference. Oh what a sweet and charming security is that which comes from the feeling of a perfect union! Through it, I know, you derive from your own heart your good opinion of mine; through it also, mine justifies you, and I would think you much less in love if I saw you more alarmed.

I do not know, nor wish to know, if Lord Bomston has any regard for me other than those which all men have for girls of my age. However, it is not a matter of his feelings but of my father's and mine; these are both the same as they were with regard to the pretended suitors, of whom you claim you will say nothing. If his exclusion and theirs will be enough for your repose, be tranquil. Whatever honor we might receive in the courtship of a man of his rank, never with her own or her father's consent will Julie d'Étange become Lady Bomston. That you may count on.

Do not believe, therefore, that his Lordship has even been considered as a suitor. I am sure that of us four you are the only one who even supposed him to have a liking for me. Be that as it may, I know the will of my father in this matter without it being necessary for him to tell me or anyone else, and I should not be better informed if he would positively declare his wishes. That is enough to calm your fears, that is to say, as much as you are to know. The rest is a matter of pure curiosity, and you know that I have resolved not to satisfy it. You reproach me vainly for this reserve and claim it far from our common interest. If I had always been so reserved, it would be less important to me today. Had it not been for the indiscreet account I gave you of some of my father's words, you would not have been disconsolate at Meillerie, you might not have written the letter which ruined me, and I should still be innocent and aspire to happiness. By what a single indiscretion has cost me, judge the fear that I must have of committing others! You have too many fits of passion to be prudent; you could sooner conquer your passions than disguise them. The slightest alarm would put you into a furor; at the slightest glimmer of hope you would be overconfident! All our secrets would be read in your soul, and your zeal would ruin all the success my pains have achieved. Therefore, leave to me the cares of

love, and keep for yourself only the pleasures of them. Is this division so painful, and do you not see that you can do nothing toward
our happiness except not to set up an obstacle to it?

Alas, what use will these late precautions be to me from now on?
Is it time to step cautiously when I am at the bottom of a precipice
and to prevent the evils by which I am crushed? Ah, miserable girl,
it is well for you to speak of happiness! Can there ever be any happiness where shame and remorse reign? God! What a cruel state, to
be able neither to bear my crime nor to repent it, to be beset by a
thousand fears, deceived by a thousand vain hopes, and not even to
enjoy the horrible tranquillity of despair! I am henceforth only at
the mercy of fate. The question is no longer of strength or of virtue,
but of fortune and of prudence, no longer of extinguishing a love
which is to last as long as my life, but of making it innocent or dying
guilty. Consider this situation, my friend, and see if you can trust
in my zeal.

❖ LETTER L ❖

From Julie

AS I LEFT YOU yesterday, I refused to explain the cause of the sadness
for which you reproached me because you were in no state to listen
to me. But I owe you this explanation, in spite of my aversions to
them, for I have made a promise and will hold to it.

I do not know if you remember the strange conversation you held
with me yesterday evening and the manners with which you accompanied it. As for me, I shall not forget them soon enough for
your honor and for my repose, and unfortunately I am too shocked
to be able to forget them easily. Similar expressions have sometimes struck my ear as I passed near the harbor, but I did not think
that they might ever issue from the mouth of an honorable man. I
am quite sure at least that they never entered the vocabulary of
lovers, and I was quite far from thinking that they might pass between us. Good Heavens! What kind of love is yours, thus to season
its pleasures! It is true, you had just come from a prolonged dinner,
and I am aware that in this country one must pardon the excesses

people may be guilty of at such affairs. It is also for this reason that I speak to you. Be assured that if you had treated me that way when you were sober, the interview would have been the last one of our lives.

But what alarms me with regard to you is that often the conduct of a man inflamed with wine is only the effect of what takes place in his inmost heart at other times. Shall I believe that in a condition where nothing is disguised you showed yourself such as you are? What would become of me if you soberly believed what you said last evening? Rather than bear such contempt, I should prefer to extinguish such a gross passion and lose a lover who, knowing how to respect his mistress so poorly, deserves so little esteem. Tell me, you who cherish honest sentiments, have you succumbed to that cruel, mistaken idea that a lover once made happy need no longer be discreet in regard to modesty and that he owes no more respect to the woman whose severity is no longer to be feared? Ah! If you had always thought so, you would have been less to be feared and I should not be so unfortunate! Do not deceive yourself, my friend; nothing is so dangerous to true lovers as the prejudices of the world. So many people speak of love, and so few know how to love, that for its pure and gentle laws most mistake the vile maxims of an abject commerce which, soon satiated, has recourse to the monsters of the imagination and becomes depraved in order to support itself.

I am possibly mistaken, but it seems to me that true love is the most chaste of all bonds. It is true love, it is its divine fire which can purify our natural inclinations by concentrating them in a single object. It is true love which shelters us from temptations and which makes the opposite sex no longer important, except for the beloved one. For an ordinary woman, every man is always the same, but for her whose heart is in love, there is no man but her lover. What do I say? Is a lover no more than a man? Ah, let him be a much more sublime being! There is no man at all for her who is in love: her lover is more, all the others are less, and she and he are the only of their kind. They have no desires; they are in love. The heart does not follow but guides the senses. It throws a delightful veil over their frenzies. No, in true love, there is nothing of the obscene as in debauchery and its coarse language. True love, always modest, does not wrest its favors audaciously; it steals them timidly. Secrecy, silence, and fearful bashfulness sharpen and conceal its sweet ecstasies; its flame honors and purifies all its caresses; decency and chastity accompany it even into the midst of voluptuousness; and it alone knows how to gratify all the desires without trespassing against modesty. Ah! Tell me, you who once knew true pleasures, how could cynical effrontery be joined to them? How could it not fail to banish their delirium and all their charm? How could it not fail to soil that image of perfection in which one likes to contemplate his beloved? Believe me, my friend, debauchery and love could not live together and cannot even be set against each other. The heart creates true happiness when two people are in love, and nothing can take the place of it when they are no longer so.

But if you were unfortunate enough to take pleasure in this immodest language, how could you have prevailed on yourself to use it so indiscreetly and, toward her who is dear to you, to take on a tone and manners which a man of honor must not even know? Since when has it been pleasant to mortify a loved one, and what is this barbarous voluptuousness which delights in enjoying the torment of others? I have not forgotten that I have lost the right to be respected, but if ever I do forget, is it for you to remind me? Is it for the author of my fault to aggravate its punishment? Rather, he should console me. Everyone except you has the right to scorn me. You owe me the price of the humiliation to which you have reduced me, and so many tears poured out over my weakness ought to make you try to alleviate my sorrow. I am neither prudish nor precious in this. Alas, how far I am from it, I who have not even known how to be discreet! You know too well, ingrate, whether this tender heart can refuse anything to love. But at least what it yields, it wishes to yield only to love, and you have taught me its language too well to be able to substitute such a different one in its place. Insults, blows would offend me less than such caresses. Either renounce Julie, or merit her esteem. I have already told you that I do not acknowledge a love without modesty, and whatever it may cost me to lose yours, it would cost me still more to conserve it at that price.

I have many more things left to say on this subject, but I must finish this letter, and I defer them to another time. Meanwhile, you may notice one result of your false precepts on the immoderate use of wine.* Your heart is not guilty, I am sure. However, you have wounded mine, and without knowing what you were doing, as if designedly you afflicted this heart, too quick to take fright and indifferent to nothing which comes from you.

---

* In a deleted description of the peasants of the Valais, the hero speaks of slight intoxication as a positive good, inducing the free flowing of the heart's affections. [*Translator's note*]

❧ LETTER LI ❧

Response

THERE IS NOT one line in your letter which does not freeze my blood, and I have difficulty in believing, after having read it twenty times, that it is addressed to me. Who, I, I? Could I have offended Julie? Could I have profaned her charms? Might she, to whom each instant of my life I offer adoration, have been exposed to my insults? No, I should have pierced my heart a thousand times before so barbarous a design might have come near it. Ah, how poorly you know this heart which idolizes you! This heart which flies to prostrate itself under each of your steps! This heart anxious to invent new praise for you unknown to mortals! How poorly you know it, oh Julie, if you accuse it of lacking that ordinary and common respect that even a common lover would have for his mistress! I cannot believe I am either imprudent or brutal; I hate immodest language and never in my life entered places where one learns it. But let me repeat what you say; let me improve upon your just indignation: had I been the vilest of mortals, had I spent my early years in debauchery, had the liking for shameful pleasures found a place in a heart in which you reign, oh, tell me Julie, angel of heaven, tell me how could I have shown you the effrontery which one can have only before those who like it? Ah no, it is not possible! A single look from you would have kept my mouth in check and purified my heart. Love would have concealed my passionate desires beneath the charm of your modesty, it would have been victorious without insult, and in the sweet union of our souls, their delirium only would have led the senses astray. I appeal to your own testimony. Tell me, if in all the extravagance of a measureless passion I ever ceased to have respect for its charming object? If I received the reward that my ardor had deserved, tell me if I took advantage of my good fortune to insult you in your sweet bashfulness? If an ardent and fearful love sometimes made an attempt upon your charms with a timid hand, tell me if ever a brutal rashness dared to profane them? If an indiscreet transport drew aside for an instant the veil which covers them, did not charming modesty immediately substitute its own? Would this holy vestment abandon you for one moment, if you had none other? Incorruptible as your chaste soul is, have all the fires of mine ever altered it? Is not the union of our souls, so touching and so tender, sufficient for our felicity? Does it not alone constitute the happiness of our lives? Do we know any pleasures in the world outside of those which love gives? Can you conceive how I could in an instant have forgotten chastity, our love, my honor, and the invincible respect I should always have for you, even had I not adored you? No, do not think so; it is not I who could offend you. I have no recollection of it, and if I had been guilty for an instant, could I ever lose my remorse? No, Julie, a demon jealous of a lot too fortunate for a mortal has taken my form to distress it and has left me my heart to make me more miserable.

I abjure, I detest the grave crime which I must have committed, since you accuse me of it, but in which my will had no part at all. How I will abhor this fatal intemperance which once seemed to me favorable to the effusions of the heart and which has so cruelly deceived mine! Irrevocably I swear it to you: from today for life I renounce wine as the most deadly poison. Never shall that fatal liquor disturb my senses, never shall it soil my lips, and no longer shall its mad delirium make me guilty without my knowledge. If I break this solemn vow, my love, heap upon me the chastisement which I shall deserve. At that instant may the image of my Julie forsake my heart forever and abandon it to indifference and to despair.

Do not think that I wish to expiate my crime by so slight a penalty. This is a precaution and not a punishment. I expect from you what I deserve. I beg for it to alleviate my remorse. Let offended love avenge itself and be appeased. Punish me without hating me; I shall suffer without a murmur. Be fair and severe; it is necessary, and I agree to it. But if you want to leave me my life, deprive me of everything but your heart.

❖ LETTER LII ❖

From Julie

WHAT, MY FRIEND, renounce wine for one's mistress? That is what is called a sacrifice! Oh, I defy anyone to find in the four cantons a man more in love than you! Not that there may not be some little Frenchified gentlemen among our young people who drink water through affectation, but you will be the first Swiss whom love ever caused to drink it; that is an example to cite in Switzerland's annals of gallantry. I have even been informed of your conduct, and I have been extremely edified to learn that, supping yesterday with Monsieur de Vueillerans, you let six bottles go the rounds after dinner without touching them and did not spare your glasses of water any more than the other guests did their wine from the coast. However, this penitence has lasted for three days since my letter was written, and three days make at least six dinners. Now, to six dinners observed through faithfulness, we can add six others observed through fear, and six through shame, and six through habit, and six through obstinacy. How many motives can prolong these painful privations for which love alone would have all the credit? Could love condescend to credit itself with what it cannot claim?

These pleasantries are more unpleasant than the wicked words you spoke to me; it is time to put a stop to them. You are by nature serious. I have noticed that lengthy raillery overheats you, as a long walk overheats a stout man; but I am almost revenged upon you as Henri IV was revenged upon the Duc de Mayenne, and your sovereign wishes to imitate the clemency of the best of kings. Also I am afraid that by virtue of remorse and excuses you might in the end make a merit of a fault so fully atoned, and I want to forget it immediately, for fear that if I waited too long it might no longer be generosity but ingratitude.

With regard to your resolution to renounce wine forever, it does not have as much luster in my eyes as you might think; vigorous passions think little of these trifling sacrifices, and love does not take nourishment from gallantry. Besides, sometimes there is more shrewdness than courage in making a present advantage of an uncertain future and in paying oneself in advance for an eternal abstinence which may be renounced when one wishes. Ah my good friend! In everything which pleases the senses, is the abuse therefore inseparable from the enjoyment? Is drunkenness necessarily attached to a taste for wine? And would philosophy be vain or cruel enough not to offer another way to prevent immoderate use of things which give pleasure besides that of depriving oneself of them completely?

If you keep your pledge, you deprive yourself of an innocent pleasure and risk your health by changing your manner of living. If you break it, love will be doubly offended, and even your honor will suffer. Therefore, I make use of my privilege on this occasion, and not only do I release you from a vow worthless for being made without my permission, but I even forbid you to observe it beyond the term which I am going to prescribe. Tuesday we shall have Lord Bomston's concert here. At the refreshment time, I shall send you a cup half full of a pure and wholesome nectar. I want you to drink it in my presence and for my sake, after having made an expiatory libation to the graces with a few drops. Then my penitent friend will resume at his meals the sober use of wine tempered with the crystal of fountains, and as your good Plutarch says, moderate Bacchus's ardors by communication with the Nymphs.[7]

Until Tuesday then, my dear friend, my teacher, my penitent, my apostle. Alas! That you are not mine at all! Why must it be that with so many rights you lack only one title?

P.S. Do you know that there is talk of a pleasant party on the lake like the one we had two years ago with poor Chaillot? How timid my artful teacher was then! How he trembled in giving me his hand to get out of the boat! Ah, the hypocrite! . . . He has greatly changed.

❖ LETTER LIII ❖

From Julie

THUS EVERYTHING disconcerts our plans, everything disappoints our expectation, everything betrays the passions that heaven should have rewarded! Base playthings of a blind fortune, sad victims of a mocking hope, shall we endlessly draw near fleeing pleasure without ever reaching it? This wedding so fruitlessly desired was to have taken place at Clarens. Bad weather thwarted us, and it was necessary to have it in town. We were to have contrived a meeting there; both beset by troublesome people, we could not elude them at the same time, and the moment when one of the two escaped was that when it was impossible for the other to join him. Finally a favorable instant was presented, the cruelest of mothers arrived to wrench it from us, and this instant was close to being the ruin of two unfortunate people whom it ought to have made happy! But, far from dismaying my courage, so many obstacles have stimulated it. I don't know what new power is animating me, but I feel in myself a fearlessness which I never had before; and if you dare share it, tonight, this very night can discharge my promises and once and for all pay all the debts of love.

Consider well, my friend, and determine to what point life is sweet for you, for the measure I am proposing can lead us both to death. If you fear it, do not finish this letter; but if the point of a sword does not frighten your heart any more today than the abysses of Meillerie frightened it before, mine will run the same risk and not hesitate. Listen.

Babi, who usually sleeps in my room, has been ill for three days, and although I have indeed wished to take care of her, she has been carried elsewhere in spite of me. But since she is better, perhaps she will return as early as tomorrow. The room where we eat is far from the staircase which leads to my mother's apartment and to mine; at the supper hour the whole house is deserted, except for the kitchen and the dining room. Moreover, night in this season has already fallen by that hour; its cover can easily conceal passers-by in the street from spectators, and you are perfectly acquainted with the members of the household.

That is enough to make myself understood. Come this afternoon to my Fanchon's. I shall explain the rest to you and give you the necessary instructions, but if I cannot come, I shall leave them in writing in the old hiding-place for our letters, where, as I have informed you, you will find this one already, for the subject is too important to dare confide to anyone.

Oh how I see your heart beating now! How I read in it your ecstasies, and how I share them! No, my sweet friend, no, we shall not leave this short life without having tasted happiness for an instant. But yet remember that this instant is surrounded by the horrors of death; that to come is to be subject to a thousand hazards, to stay is dangerous, to leave is extremely perilous; that we are ruined if we are discovered, and that to avoid it everything must assist us. Let us not deceive ourselves. I know my father too well to doubt that I might see him stab you to the heart immediately with his own hand, if indeed he did not begin with me; for surely I should not be spared, and do you think that I should expose you to this danger if I were not sure of sharing it?

Still, remember that it is not a matter of depending upon your courage. You must not think of it and I even forbid you quite expressly to carry any weapon for your defense, not even your sword. Besides, it would be perfectly useless to you, for if we are surprised, my plan is to throw myself into your arms, to grasp you strongly in mine, and thus to receive the deadly blow so that we may be parted no more, happier at the moment of my death than I was in my life.

Yet, I hope that a kinder fate is reserved for us. I feel at least that we deserve it, and fortune will grow weary of being unjust to us. Come then, heart of my heart, life of my life, come and be reunited with yourself. Come under the auspices of tender love to receive the reward for your obedience and your sacrifices. Come to swear, even in the midst of pleasures, that from the union of hearts they draw their greatest charm.

❧ LETTER LIV ❧

To Julie

I ARRIVE full of an emotion which increases upon entering this retreat. Julie! Here I am in your rooms; here I am in the sanctuary of all my heart adores. The torch of love has guided my steps, and I have passed through the house without being perceived. Charming room, fortunate room, which formerly saw so many tender looks repressed, so many eager sighs stifled, which saw my first fires born and nourished and for the second time will see them rewarded, witness of my everlasting constancy, be the witness of my happiness, and conceal forever the pleasures of the most faithful and the most fortunate of men.

How is this secret room so charming? Everything in it pleases and nourishes the ardor which devours me. Oh Julie! It is full of you, and the flame of my desires spreads over all traces of you. Yes, all my senses are at once intoxicated by them. An indefinable perfume, almost imperceptible, sweeter than the rose and more delicate than the iris is here exhaled from every part of the room. I imagine that I hear the pleasing sound of your voice. All the parts of your scattered dress present to my ardent imagination those of your body that they conceal. This delicate headdress which sets off the large blond curls which it pretends to cover; this happy bodice shawl against which at least once I shall not have to complain; this elegant

and simple gown which displays so well the taste of the wearer; these
dainty slippers that a supple foot fills so easily; this corset so slender
which touches and embraces . . . what an enchanting form . . .
in front two gentle curves . . . oh voluptuous sight . . . the whale-
bone has yielded to the force of the impression . . . delicious im-
prints, let me kiss you a thousand times! . . . Gods! Gods! What
will it be when . . . Ah, I think I am already feeling that tender
heart beating under my happy hand! Julie! My charming Julie! I see
you, I feel you everywhere, I breathe you in with the air that you
have breathed; you penetrate my entire being. How inflaming and
painful your room is for me! My impatience is terrible. Oh come,
fly, or I am lost.

What good fortune to have found ink and paper! I am expressing
my feelings in order to temper their excess; I moderate my ecstasy by
describing it.

It seems to me I hear a noise. Could it be your cruel father? I do
not consider myself a coward . . . but at this moment, would not
death be horrible to me? My despair would be equal to the ardor
which is consuming me. Heaven! I ask for one more hour to live,
and I give up the rest of my life to your severity. Oh desires! Oh
fear! Oh cruel palpitations! . . . The door is opening! . . . Someone is coming in! . . . It is she! . . . It is she! I catch a glimpse of
her, I have seen her, I hear the door being closed. My heart, my
feeble heart succumbs to so many agitations. Ah, let it seek strength
to bear the happiness which overwhelms it!

❧ LETTER LV ❧

To Julie

OH LET US DIE, my sweet friend! Let us die, beloved of my heart!
What shall we do henceforward with an insipid youth, now that we
have exhausted all its delights? Explain to me, if you can, what I
felt during that inconceivable night; give me hope for a life spent
in that way, or let me leave this one which has no more experiences
like that which I have just had with you. I had tasted pleasure and
thought I understood happiness. Ah, I had known only an empty
dream and imagined only the happiness of a child! My senses de-

ceived my unrefined soul; only in them did I search for the ultimate good, and I found that their exhausted pleasures were only
the beginning of mine. Oh unique masterpiece of nature! Divine
Julie! Delicious possession with whom all the transports of the most
ardent love are hardly sufficient! No, it is not those transports
which I now miss most; ah, no, if it is necessary, withdraw those in-
toxicating favors for which I would give a thousand lives, but give
me back all that does not depend upon them and surpasses them a
thousand times. Give me back that intimate union of souls, which
you had told me of and which you have made me enjoy so well.
Give me back that languor so sweet, filled with the overflowings of
our hearts; give me back that enchanting sleep found in your bosom; give me back that still more delightful instant of awakening,
and those broken sighs, and those sweet tears, and those kisses that
a voluptuous languor made us savor slowly, and those murmurs so
tender, during which you pressed together those hearts which were
made to be united.

Tell me, Julie, you who through your own sensibility know how
to judge that of others so well, do you think that what I felt before
was really love? My sentiments, do not doubt it, have undergone a
natural change since yesterday; they have taken on an indefinable
quality, less impetuous but sweeter, more tender and more charming. Do you remember that whole hour we spent in peacefully
speaking of our love and of that obscure and fearful future by which
the present was made still more tender for us—that hour, too short,
alas, during which a slight touch of sadness made the conversation
so moving? I was tranquil, and yet I was near you; I adored you and
desired nothing. I did not even imagine another felicity than that
of feeling your face next to mine, your breath on my cheek, and
your arms around my neck. What calm in all my senses! What pure,
continuous, complete voluptuousness! The charm of possession was
in the soul, no longer momentary but eternal. What a difference
between the frenzies of love and a situation so peaceful! That was
the first time in my life that I experienced it near you, and yet consider the strange change which I experienced. It is of all the hours of
my life the one which is most dear to me, and the only one which I
should have wished to prolong eternally.* Julie, tell me, then, if before I did not love you at all or if now I no longer love you?

* Too compliant woman, do you wish to know if you are loved? Examine your
lover as he leaves your arms. Oh love! If I miss the age at which you are
enjoyed, it is not for the hour of possession; it is for the hour which follows it.
[Rousseau]

If I no longer love you? What a fear! Have I then ceased to exist, and is my life not more in your heart than in mine? I feel, I feel that you are a thousand times more dear to me than ever, and I have found in the abatement of my desire new strength to cherish you still more tenderly. The sentiments I have conceived for you are more peaceable, it is true, but more affectionate and more varied; without becoming weakened they have multiplied. The sweetness of friendship tempers the frenzies of love, and I can scarcely imagine any sort of attachment which may not unite me with you. Oh my charming mistress, oh my wife, my sister, my sweet friend! How little I shall have expressed for what I feel, even after having exhausted all the names dearest to the heart of man!

I must confess to you a suspicion I have conceived, to my shame and humiliation. It is that you are more capable of love than I. Yes, my Julie, it is indeed you who constitute my life and my being. I adore you with all the powers of my soul, but yours is more loving; love has penetrated it more profoundly. One sees, one feels that love inspires your charms, reigns in your speech, gives that penetrating sweetness to your eyes, those accents so touching to your voice. It is love which through your presence alone communicates imperceptibly to other hearts the tender emotion of your own. How far I am from that charming state which is enough in itself! I wish to enjoy and you wish to love; I have ecstasies and you have passion. All my frenzies are not equal to your delightful languor, and the sentiment with which your heart is nourished is the only supreme felicity. It is only since yesterday that I have enjoyed that voluptuousness so pure. You have left me something of that inconceivable charm which is in you, and I think that with your sweet breath you breathed a new soul into me. Hurry, I implore you, to finish your work. Take from my soul all which remains of me and put yours completely in its place. No, angelic beauty, celestial soul, it is only sentiments like yours which can do honor to your charms. You alone are worthy of inspiring a perfect love; you alone are capable of feeling it. Ah, give me your heart, my Julie, so that I may love you as you deserve!

✤ LETTER LVI ✤

From Claire to Julie

MY DEAR COUSIN, I have to give you some news which concerns you. Last night your friend had a quarrel with Lord Bomston which could become serious. Here is what was told to me about it by Monsieur d'Orbe, who was present and who, uneasy over the results of this affair, came this morning to give me an account of it.

They had both supped at his Lordship's, and after an hour or two of music they began to chat and drink punch. Your friend drank only a single glass diluted with water; the other two were not so sober, and although Monsieur d'Orbe may not admit being intoxicated, I intend to tell him my opinion of that matter at another time. The conversation naturally lit upon you, for you are not unaware that Lord Bomston likes to speak of no one else. Your friend, whom these confidences always displease, received them with such little grace that his Lordship, heated with punch and nettled by this curtness, finally dared say in complaining of your coldness that it was not so general as one might think and that whoever said nothing about it was not so poorly treated as he. At that instant your friend, whose impetuosity you know, contradicted these words with an insulting outburst that occasioned a charge of "liar," and they leaped for their swords. Lord Bomston, half-intoxicated, sprained his ankle in running, which compelled him to sit down. His leg swelled immediately, and that calmed the quarrel better than all the trouble Monsieur d'Orbe had taken to do so. But as he was attentive to all that was going on, he observed your friend, upon leaving, approach Lord Bomston, and he heard him whisper in his ear, "As soon as you are in condition to walk, send me notice, or I shall take care to inform myself."

"Do not bother," said his Lordship with a mocking smile. "You will know it soon enough."

"We shall see," replied your friend coldly, and left.

In delivering this letter, Monsieur d'Orbe will explain the whole thing to you in more detail. Your discretion must suggest to you the means of suppressing this unfortunate affair or tell me what I must

do on my part to help. In the meantime, the bearer of this letter is
at your service; he will do all that you command him, and you may
rely upon his secrecy.

You are going to be ruined, my dear; my friendship forces me to
tell you so. Your attachment cannot remain hidden for a long time
in a small town like this, and considering that it is more than two
years since it began, it is a miracle of good fortune that you have
not yet been a subject of public talk. But you will be if you do not
take care; you would be already if you were less beloved by the
townspeople. But there is such a general reluctance to speak ill
of you that doing so is a poor way of crediting oneself and a very
sure one of becoming despised. However, everything comes to an
end; I fear that the end of your love's secrecy may have come, and
there is great likelihood that Lord Bomston's suspicions have come
to him through some unpleasant remarks he may have heard.
Think it over well, my dear child. Some time ago the night-police-
man said that he saw your friend leave your house at five in the
morning. Fortunately the latter found out about this talk at the
outset; he hurried to the man and discovered the secret of silencing
him. But what is such a silence if not the way of confirming the secretly widespread rumors? Also, your mother's mistrust grows from
day to day; you know how many times she has made you aware of
it. She has spoken to me of it afterwards in a rather serious way,
and if she did not fear your father's violence, no doubt she might
have already spoken to him about it; but she dares even less to do
so because he will blame her the most if the news comes from her.

I cannot repeat it too much: think of yourself while there is still
time. Send your friend away before people talk; prevent the growing suspicions that his absence will surely dispel. For what, finally,
can people believe that he is doing here? Perhaps in six weeks or in
a month it will be too late. If the slightest word reaches your father's ears, be fearful of the result of the indignation of an old sol-
dier obstinate about the honor of his house, and of the impatient
irritation of a passionate young man who cannot brook anything.
But you must first terminate the affair with Lord Bomston in one
way or another, for you would only anger your friend and obtain a
just refusal if you spoke to him of separation before that is finished.

❧ LETTER LVII ❧

From Julie

I HAVE BEEN carefully informed, my friend, of what took place between you and Lord Bomston. With a perfect understanding of the facts, I wish to discuss with you how you ought to conduct yourself on this occasion according to the sentiments which you profess and of which I suppose you do not merely make a vain and false parade.

I have not inquired if you are well versed in the art of fencing, or if you think yourself in condition to cope with a man who in Europe has a superior reputation for handling his weapon and who, having duelled five or six times in his life, has always killed, wounded, or disarmed his man. I understand that in such a case as yours, people do not consult their skill but their courage, and that the proper way of revenging yourself upon a man who insults you is to let him kill you. Let us pass over such a judicious maxim! You will tell me that your honor and mine are more dear to you than life. This, then, is the principle from which we must reason.

Let us begin by what concerns you. Could you ever tell me in what respect you were personally insulted by a conversation which was about me alone? Whether you ought to have espoused my cause on this occasion is what we shall presently see; meanwhile you cannot deny that the quarrel is perfectly irrelevant to your private honor, unless you take the suspicion that I am in love with you as an affront. You have been insulted, I admit, but after having begun the quarrel yourself with an odious insult; and I, whose family is full of soldiers and who have heard these horrible questions debated so much, am not unaware that one outrage in response to another does not annul it and that the man first insulted remains the only one offended. It is the same as in the case of an unexpected fight, in which the aggressor is the only criminal and in which the one who kills or wounds the other in self-defense is not considered guilty of murder.

Turning now to me, let us grant that I was insulted by Lord Bomston's words, although he was only doing me justice. Do you know what you are doing in defending me with so much warmth and indiscretion? You are aggravating his insult; you are proving that he was right; you are sacrificing my honor to a false point-of-honor; you are defaming your mistress in order at most to win the reputation of a good swordsman. Show me, please, what connection there is between your way of vindicating me and my real vindication? Do you think that to espouse my cause with so much ardor is great proof that there is no intimacy at all between us, and that it is sufficient to reveal that you are brave to show that you are not my lover? Be assured that all Lord Bomston's remarks do me less wrong than your conduct; it is you alone who by this scandal are responsible for publishing and confirming them. As for his Lordship, he can easily evade your sword in the duel, but never will my reputation, or my life perhaps, evade the deadly blow you are dealing it.[8] *argument against dueling*

You know that my father had the misfortune in his youth to kill a man in a duel. This man was his friend; they fought reluctantly, compelled by an absurd point of honor. The fatal blow which deprived one of his life robbed the other of his peace of mind forever. Since that time, painful remorse has never left his heart. Often we hear him cry and lament in private; he thinks he still can feel the blade thrust by his cruel hand piercing his friend's heart. In his nightmares he sees the pale and bloody body. Trembling, he gazes upon the mortal wound; he would like to staunch the flowing blood; terror seizes him; he cries out; the frightful corpse does not cease pursuing him. Since five years ago when he lost the dear support of his name and the hope of his family, he has reproached himself with the death as if it were a just punishment from Heaven, who upon his only son avenged the unfortunate father whose son he had killed.

I confess that all this, added to my natural aversion to cruelty, inspires in me such a horror of duels that I regard them as the last degree of brutality to which men can descend. He who goes to fight out of sheer wantonness is in my eyes only a ferocious beast who endeavors to tear another to pieces; and if the slightest natural sentiment remains in their souls, I find the one who perishes less to be pitied than the victor. Look at these men accustomed to blood: they defy remorse only by stifling the voice of nature; they gradually become cruel, insensible; they sport with the lives of others; and the penalty for having been deficient in humanity is finally to lose it completely. What do they do in that state? Answer me, do you wish to become like them? No, you are not made for that odious brutality; be fearful of the first step which can lead you into it. Your soul is still innocent and wholesome; at the hazard of your life do not begin to deprave it by an action without virtue, a crime without approbation, a point of honor without reason.

I have said nothing to you of your Julie; she will win her point no doubt, by permitting your own heart to speak. One word, a single word, and I leave you to it. You have sometimes honored me with the tender name of wife; perhaps at this moment I am to bear that of mother. Will you leave me a widow before a sacred bond unites us?

P.S. I use in this letter an authority which wise men have never resisted. If you refuse to submit yourself to it, I have nothing further to say to you, but first consider it well. Take a week for reflection, to meditate upon this important subject. I ask you for this delay not for the sake of reason but for my own. Remember that I am using on this occasion the prerogative which you yourself gave me and that it extends at least to this point.

❖ LETTER LVIII ❖

From Julie to Lord Bomston

IT IS NOT to complain of you, my Lord, that I am writing. Since you speak against me, I must necessarily have wronged you without knowing it. How could I believe that an honest gentleman might wish to dishonor an estimable family without cause? Satisfy your vengeance then, if you believe it just. This letter will provide you with an easy method of ruining an unfortunate girl who can never forgive herself for having offended you and who is putting at your discretion the honor you wish to deprive her of. Yes, my Lord, your charges were correct; I have a lover. He is the master of my heart and of my person; death only can break so sweet a bond. This lover is he whom you honored with your friendship; he is worthy of it for he is attached to you and he is virtuous. Nevertheless, he will die by your hand. I know that blood is needed to appease an outraged honor; I know that his own courage will destroy him; I know that in a duel, little for you to fear, his intrepid heart will bravely seek the deadly blow. I have tried to curb his inconsidered zeal; I have spoken in the name of reason. Alas! Even while writing my letter, I was aware of its uselessness, and whatever respect I have for his virtues, I do not expect from him those sublime enough to detach him from a false point of honor. You may enjoy beforehand the pleasure you will have in stabbing your friend, but be assured, cruel man, that at least you will not have that of enjoying my tears and of gazing upon my despair. No, I swear by the love which grieves my heart—you may be the witness to an oath which is not taken in vain—I shall not survive him for whom I breathe one day; and you will have the glory of putting into the tomb with a single blow two unfortunate lovers who did not offend you intentionally and who took pleasure in honoring you.

People say, my Lord, that you have a beautiful soul and a sensitive heart. If these allow you to enjoy tranquilly a vengeance which I cannot understand and to delight in causing unhappiness, can they inspire in you when I shall be dead a little compassion for an inconsolable father and mother who will yield to eternal grief over the loss of the only child left to them?

❧ LETTER LIX ❧

From Monsieur D'Orbe to Julie

IN OBEDIENCE to your orders, Mademoiselle, I hasten to give you an account of the errand with which you entrusted me. I have just come from the lodging of Lord Bomston, whom I found still suffering from his sprain and unable to walk in his room except with the help of a cane. I gave him your letter, which he opened eagerly; he seemed moved in reading it. He mused for some time; then he read it again with more perceptible agitation.

After finishing it, he said to me, "You know, Monsieur, that affairs of honor have their rules from which one cannot depart. You have seen what happened in this affair; it must be settled according to the rules. Choose two friends, and give yourself the trouble to return here with them tomorrow morning; then you will know my decision."

I again urged him that it would be better if the affair, having taken place among us, might be terminated the same way. "I know what is proper," he said brusquely, "and I shall do what is necessary. Bring your two friends, or I have nothing further to say to you."

I left, uselessly racking my brain to fathom his bizarre plan. Whatever it may be, I shall have the honor of seeing you this evening, and tomorrow I shall carry out what you command. If you find it proper for me to wait on his Lordship with my men, I shall choose them from those whom I may depend upon at all events.

✤ LETTER LX ✤

To Julie

CALM YOUR FEARS, tender and dear Julie, and from the following account of what has just happened, know and share the sentiments which I am experiencing.

I was so full of indignation when I received your letter that I could scarcely read it with the attention it deserved. I should have made fine work in refuting it; blind anger had the upper hand. You may be right, I said to myself, but never speak to me of allowing you to be disparaged. Were I to lose you and die a criminal, I shall not allow anyone to be wanting in the respect which is due you, and as long as I have a breath of life left, you will be honored by all who approach you just as you are in my heart. However, I did not hesitate for a week only because you asked me to; Lord Bomston's accident and my vow of obedience concurred in making that delay necessary. Resolved, according to your command, to use that interval in meditating upon the subject of your letter, I busied myself ceaselessly in rereading it and reflecting upon it, not with a view, however, to change my opinion but to justify it.

This morning, I had returned to that letter, too wise and judicious to my thinking, and I was rereading it uneasily when there was a knock at the door of my room. A moment later, Lord Bomston entered, without his sword, leaning upon a cane; three persons followed him, among whom I recognized Monsieur d'Orbe. Surprised by this unexpected visit, I was silently awaiting what was to come of it when his Lordship begged me to hear him for a moment and to permit him to proceed and speak without interference.

"I ask your word not to interrupt," he said. "The presence of these gentlemen, who are your friends, ought to satisfy you that you are not pledging it indiscreetly."

I promised without hesitating; scarcely had I finished when, with an astonishment you can well imagine, I saw Lord Bomston fall on his knees before me. Surprised by such a strange attitude, I wished to raise him up immediately; but after reminding me of my promise, he spoke to me in these words.

"I have come, Monsieur, to retract openly the injurious things which intoxication caused me to say in your presence. The injustice of them makes them even more offensive to myself than to you, and I owe myself a public retraction of them. I submit to whatever punishment you wish to impose upon me, and I shall not believe my honor restored until my fault shall have been atoned. Whatever the price may be, grant me the pardon I ask of you, and give me back your friendship."

"My Lord," I said immediately, "I recognize now your great and generous soul. And I can readily distinguish the words your heart dictates from those you speak when you are not yourself; may those be forever forgotten." At that instant I helped him raise himself and we embraced.

After that Lord Bomston, turning toward the witnesses, said to them, "Gentlemen, thank you for your obligingness. Men of honor like you," he added with a proud air and an animated tone, "know that whoever makes amends for his injurious actions in this way will not be submissive and take insults from anyone. You may make public what you have seen." Then he invited all four of us to supper for this evening, and the gentlemen left.

Scarcely were we alone when he returned to embrace me in a more tender and friendly manner; then he took me by the hand and sat beside me. "Fortunate mortal," he exclaimed, "enjoy the happiness you deserve. Julie's heart is yours; could you both . . ."

"What are you saying, my Lord?" I interrupted. "Have you lost your mind?"

"No," he said, smiling, "but I was very near losing it, and it had perhaps been all over with me if she who took away my reason had not restored it to me." Then he gave me a letter which I was surprised to see written by a hand which never wrote to any man but

myself.* What emotions I felt in reading it! I saw an incomparable
lover willing to ruin herself in order to save me, and I recognized
my Julie. But when I came to that place wherein she protests that
she will not survive the most fortunate of men, I shuddered at the
risks I had run, I complained that I was loved too well, and my terror convinced me that you are only mortal. Ah, restore to me the
courage you have taken from me; I had enough to face the death
which threatened only my person, but I have none for dying completely.

While my heart was indulging in these bitter reflections, his
Lordship was saying things to which I paid little attention at first.
However, he called it forth by speaking of you, and what he said to
me pleased my heart and no longer excited my jealousy. He seemed
pierced with regret for having disturbed our passion and your tranquillity; he respects you more than anyone in the world, and not
daring to bring to you the excuses he made me, he begged me to
receive them in your name and to prevail upon you to accept them.

"I look upon you," he said, "as her representative, and I cannot
humble myself too much before the one she loves, since I am unable to speak to her in person or even to name her without compromising her." He confessed that he had entertained feelings for
you which no one can resist upon seeing you very closely, but they
were of a tender admiration rather than love. These feelings have
never prompted him to pretentions or to hope; he sacrificed them
all to our sentiments at the instant he became acquainted with
them, and the injurious remark which escaped him was the result
of punch and not of jealousy. He discusses love like a philosopher
who believes his soul to be above passions. But I am deceived if he
has not already experienced some passion which now prevents others
from taking deep root. He mistakes the weakening of his affection
for the effect of reason, but I am certain that to love Julie and to
renounce her is not humanly possible.

He desired to know in detail the story of our love and the obstacles which stand in the way of my good fortune. I thought that
after your letter a superficial confidence was dangerous and imper-
tinent; I made a complete breast of it, and he listened to me with an
attention that attested to his sincerity. More than once I saw his eyes
moist and his heart affected; I especially noticed the powerful impression that all the triumphs of virtue made on his soul, and I

---

* One must, I think, except her father. [Rousseau]

think I have obtained a new protector for Claude Anet who will be no less zealous than your father.

"There are neither intrigues nor adventures in what you have told me," he said, "and yet the catastrophes of a novel would interest me much less, so much do your sentiments take the place of its situations and your honest behavior that of its striking action. Your two souls are so extraordinary that they cannot be judged by common rules. For you, happiness neither is to be attained by the same manner nor is it of the same kind as that of other men; they seek only power and the attention of others, but you need only tenderness and peace. Joined to your love is an emulation of virtue which elevates you, and you would both be less worthy if you were not in love."

He dared to add that love will pass. (Let us forgive him for this blasphemy uttered in the ignorance of his heart.) "Love will pass," he said, "but virtue will endure." Ah, may it endure as long as love, my Julie! Heaven will require no more.

At last I see that philosophical and national austerity does not affect the natural humanity of this honest Englishman and that he is truly interested in our difficulties. If influence and riches could be useful to us, I believe we should have cause to rely upon him. But alas! What use is power and money in making our hearts happy?

This conversation, during which we did not count the hours, brought us to dinnertime. I had a chicken brought up, and after dining we continued to talk. He spoke of his course of action this morning, and I could not keep from evidencing some surprise at a proceeding so notable and so uncommon. But, repeating the reason he had already given me, he added that to give a partial satisfaction was unworthy of a courageous man, that a full one was necessary or nothing, lest he debase himself without making amends for anything, and lest a step taken half-heartedly and grudgingly be attributed to fear.

"Besides," he added, "my reputation is established; I can be just without being suspected of cowardice. But you who are young and just beginning in the world, you must emerge so clean from the first affair of honor that no one is tempted to involve you in a second. The world is full of those clever scoundrels who seek, as they say, to feel out their man, that is, to discover someone who may be even more of a cowardly scoundrel than they and at whose expense they can push themselves forward. I wish to spare a man of honor like you the unglorious necessity of punishing one of this sort, and if they need a lesson I prefer them to receive it from me rather than from you; for one more duel takes nothing from a man who has already had several. But to have had only one is always a kind of disgrace, and Julie's lover must be exempt from that."

This is the résumé of my long conversation with Lord Bomston. I thought it necessary to give you an account of it so that you may prescribe the manner in which I ought to behave to him.

Now that your fears must be allayed, I implore you to dispel those distressing ideas which have taken possession of you for the past few days. Remember the precautions made necessary by the uncertainty of your present condition. Oh, if soon you could triple my life! If soon an adored pledge . . . will an expectation already disappointed once come to deceive me again? . . . oh desires! oh fear! oh difficulties! Charming friend of my heart, let us live in order to love, and let Heaven dispose of us as it may.

P.S. I forgot to tell you that his Lordship gave me back your letter and that I raised no objections about taking it, considering that such a treasure should not remain in the hands of a third party. I shall give it back to you at our first meeting, because, as for me, I no longer need it. It is written too well in my heart for me ever to need to read it again.

⚜ LETTER LXI ⚜

From Julie

TOMORROW, bring Lord Bomston here so that I may throw myself at his feet as he did at yours. What greatness! What generosity! Oh, how small we are compared to him! Preserve this precious friend as you would the pupil of your eye. Perhaps he would be less deserving if he were more even-tempered. Was there ever a man without faults who had great virtues?

A thousand anxieties of all kinds had thrown me into dejection, but your letter has rekindled my extinguished courage. By dissipating my fears, it has made my troubles more supportable. Now I feel strong enough to bear them. You live, you love me, neither your blood nor that of your friend has been shed, and your honor is saved. Therefore I am not completely miserable.

Do not fail our meeting tomorrow. Never have I had such great need of you, nor so little hope of seeing you for very long. Adieu, my dear and only friend. You have not spoken well, it seems to me, in saying that we should live in order to love. Ah! You should have said, let us love in order to live.

❧ LETTER LXII ❧

From Claire to Julie

MUST I ALWAYS, dear cousin, perform for you only the most disagreeable offices of friendship? Must I always, in the bitterness of my heart, afflict yours with cruel information? Alas! All our sentiments are the same, as you well know, and I can give you no new griefs unless I have already experienced them. Would that I could hide your misfortune from you without augmenting it! Or that our tender friendship had as many recompenses as your love! Ah! Would that I could promptly efface all the misery I give you!

After the concert yesterday, your mother having accepted the arm of your friend to return home and you that of Monsieur d'Orbe, our two fathers remained here with his Lordship to talk about politics, a subject I am so tired of that boredom drove me to my room. A half-hour later, I heard the name of your friend being mentioned several times with some vehemence. I knew that the subject of the conversation had been changed and I listened to it. I guessed by the talk which followed that his Lordship had ventured to propose your marriage to your friend, whom he was openly calling his own and on whom as such he was offering to make a suitable settlement. Your father scornfully rejected this proposal, and upon that the conversation began to grow heated.

"Understand," his Lordship said, "that in spite of your prejudices he is of all men most worthy of her and perhaps most suited to make her happy. He has received from nature all the gifts which are independent of men, and to them he has added all the talents which depended upon himself. He is young, tall, well-made, robust, and skillful. He has education, sense, manners, and courage. He has a fine wit, a sound mind. What, then, does he lack in order to deserve your consent? A fortune? He shall have one. A third of my estate will suffice to make him the richest individual in the Vaud region. If necessary I shall give him as much as half of it. Nobility? An empty prerogative in a country where it is more injurious than useful.* But he has nobility even so, do not doubt it, not written in ink on old parchment but engraved on his heart in indelible characters. In short, if you prefer reason to prejudice, and if you love your daughter better than your titles, you will give her to him."

Thereupon your father flew into a lively passion. He called the proposal absurd and ridiculous. "What! My Lord," he said, "can an honorable man like yourself even think that the last surviving branch of an illustrious family might lose or degrade its name by taking that of a nobody, without a home and reduced to living on charity?"

"Stop," interrupted his Lordship. "You are speaking of my friend. Consider that I take as if done myself all the injuries done him in my presence, and that names which are injurious to an honorable man are even more so to the one who utters them. Such nobodies are more respectable than all the country squires in Europe, and I challenge you to find any means of coming by a fortune more honorable than accepting acknowledgments of esteem and gifts of friendship. If the son-in-law whom I propose to you does not have, like you, a long succession of forefathers, always doubtful, he will be the foundation and the honor of his own house, just as your first ancestor was of yours. Could you, then, consider yourself dishonored by the marriage of the founder of your family, without this disdain falling back upon yourself? How many great families would sink back into oblivion if only those which began with a respectable man were considered? Let us pass judgment on the past by looking at the present: for the two or three citizens who become illustrious by virtuous means, every day a thousand rogues raise their families to the rank of nobility, and what does this nobility, of which their descendants will be so proud, prove if not the thievery and the infamy of their ancestor. I confess that one sees a great many dishonest men

* Daniel Mornet provides the following explanation for this remark: Berne had conquered the Vaud region, after which all the Vaud nobility had been excluded from public office; since there was little commerce or industry in which they cared to engage, they were reduced to a life of idleness or expatriation. [*Translator's note*]

among the common people, but the odds are always twenty to one
against a gentleman that he is descended from a scoundrel." [9]

if attack on nobility

Imagine, my dear, what I was suffering in seeing this honest gentleman through an ill-timed bitterness thus injure the interests of
the friend he wished to help. In fact, your father, irritated by so
many stinging invectives, however general, began to counter them
with personal remarks. He said to his Lordship outright that never
had a man of his position spoken in such words as he had just used.

"Do not uselessly plead the cause of someone else," he added in a
brusque tone. "Great Lord that you are, I doubt if you could uphold
your own very well on the subject under consideration. You are asking for my daughter for your so-called friend without knowing if you
yourself could be suitable for her, and I am well enough acquainted
with English nobility to have, from your discourse, a mediocre opinion of yours."

"By Jove!" said his Lordship. "Whatever you think of me, I should
be very sorry to have no other proof of my merit than the name of a
man dead for five hundred years. If you are acquainted with the
English nobility, you know that it is the most enlightened, the best
educated, the wisest and bravest of Europe. With all that, I have no
need to ask whether it is the most ancient, for when we speak of what
it is, we never mind what it has been. We are not, it is true, slaves
of the Prince but his friends, nor are we oppressors of the people
but their leaders. Guardians of liberty, pillars of the country and
supports of the throne, we maintain an invincible equilibrium between the people and the king. Our first duty is to the nation, the
second to the one who governs it. It is not his will but his prerogative
which we consult. Supreme judges of the laws in the House of Peers,
sometimes even legislators, we render equal justice to the people and
to the king, and we allow no one to say 'God and my sword' but
only 'God and my right.'

"Such, Monsieur," he continued, "is this respectable nobility, as
ancient as any other but more proud of its merit than its ancestors,
of which you speak without knowledge. I am not the lowest in rank
in this illustrious order, and I think myself equal to you in every
respect, in spite of your pretentions. I have an unmarried sister. She
is of the nobility, young, amiable, and rich. She is inferior to Julie
only in those attributes which you consider as nothing. If it were
possible for him who has perceived your daughter's charms to turn
his eyes and his heart elsewhere, what honor it would be for me to
accept for my brother-in-law, though without a fortune, the man
whom I propose for your son-in-law with half my wealth!"

I knew by your father's reply that this conversation would only grow more bitter, and, although I was moved with admiration for Lord Bomston's generosity, I felt that such an inflexible man was likely only to ruin forever the business he had undertaken. I hurried, therefore, to return before things might go any further. My entrance broke off this conversation, and a moment later, they parted rather coldly. As for my father, I found that he behaved very well in this quarrel. At first he seconded the proposal with concern; but seeing that your father would not hear of it at all and that the argument was beginning to become animated, he took, as was fitting, his brother-in-law's side again, and interrupting each of them pertinently with moderate words, he kept both within the bounds they would probably have broken had they remained alone. After their departure, he told me in private what had just taken place, and as I foresaw what would come of it, I hastened to tell him that, things being in this state, it was no longer proper for the person in question to see you here so often, and that it would not be proper for him even to come at all, if that had not constituted a kind of affront to Monsieur d'Orbe, who is his friend, but that I should beg him to invite him, and Lord Bomston as well, less frequently. That, my dear, is the best I could do so as not to close our door completely to them.

This is not all. The crisis I see you in forces me to return to my former counsel. The affair between Lord Bomston and your friend has created all the talk in the town that one might expect. Although Monsieur d'Orbe has kept secret the cause for the quarrel, too many clues betray it for it to remain hidden. People suspect, they make conjectures, and you are named; the report of the night policeman is not so well suppressed that they do not remember it, and you are not unaware that in the eyes of the public the suspicion of truth is quite close to evidence. All that I can tell you for your consolation is that in general your choice is approved, and that everyone would look upon the union of such a charming couple with pleasure, which confirms my idea that your friend has behaved well in this country and is loved hardly less than you. But what is the public voice to your inflexible father? All this talk has reached him or will reach him, and I tremble at the effect it can produce, if you do not hasten to prevent his anger. You must expect from him an interpretation terrible for yourself, and perhaps worse yet for your friend; not that I think that at his age he may want to test his strength against a young man whom he does not think worthy of his sword, but the influence he has in the town could furnish him, if he wished, a thousand means of getting rid of him, and it is to be feared that his fury may excite his wish to do so.

I implore you on my knees, my sweet friend, to think of the dangers which surround you, the risk of which increases every moment. An extraordinary good fortune has preserved you so far in the midst of all these perils; while there is still time, put the seal of prudence on the secrecy of your love affair, and do not strain your luck to its breaking point, lest it may entangle in your misfortunes the man who has been the cause of them. Believe me, my angel, the future is uncertain; a thousand accidents, with time, may offer unexpected expedients. But as for the present, I have told you and now repeat it more forcefully: send your friend away, or you are undone.

❧ LETTER LXIII ❧

From Julie to Claire

ALL THAT you had foreseen, my dear, has happened. Yesterday, an hour after our return, my father entered my mother's room, his eyes flashing, his countenance inflamed with anger—in short, in a state in which I had never before seen him. Immediately I understood that he had just had a quarrel or that he was going to begin one, and my guilty conscience made me tremble in advance.

He began by exclaiming sharply but in general terms against mothers who indiscreetly invite into their homes young men without fortune or family, whose acquaintance brings only shame and scandal to those who pay attention to them. Then, seeing that that was not enough to draw any response from an intimidated woman, with no discretion he brought up as an example what has happened in our house since she had introduced a so-called fine wit, an empty babbler, more fit to corrupt a chaste girl than to give her any good education. My mother, who saw that she would gain little by keeping silent, stopped him at the word corruption and asked him what he found in the conduct or in the reputation of the honorable man he was speaking of which might authorize such suspicions.

"I did not think," she added, "that intelligence and merit might constitute reasons for exclusion from society. To whom, then, must we open your house, if talent and manners may not obtain admittance?"

"To suitable people, Madame," he replied angrily, "who can repair a girl's honor when they have offended it."

"No," she said, "rather to honest people who will not offend it."

"Learn," he said, "that it is an insult to the honor of a house to dare solicit an alliance without a title for obtaining it."

"Far from seeing an insult in that," said my mother, "I see on the contrary only a mark of esteem. Besides, I am not aware that the man against whom you are declaiming may have done anything like that with regard to your house."

"He has, Madame, and will do worse yet if I do not see to him. But do not doubt that I shall attend to the charges which you execute so ill."

Then began a dangerous quarrel which let me know that my parents were unaware of the rumors you say are about the town, but during which your undeserving cousin could have wished herself buried a hundred feet in the earth. Imagine the best and the most deceived of mothers speaking in praise of her guilty daughter and lauding her, alas, for all the virtues which she has lost, in the most honorable, or I should say, the most mortifying terms. Picture to yourself an angry father, profuse of injurious expressions, who yet in all his rage did not utter one which indicated the slightest doubt as to the chastity of her who in his presence is rent by remorse and crushed with shame. Oh, what unbelievable torment from my guilty conscience I had in reproaching myself with crimes that anger and indignation could not even suspect! What an oppressive and insupportable weight is that of unmerited praise and esteem which the heart secretly rejects! I felt so oppressed that in order to rid myself of such a cruel burden I was ready to confess everything, if my father would have given me the chance, but in the impetuosity of his fury he kept saying the same things over a hundred times and yet changed the subject every moment. He noticed my downcast looks, distraught and humbled, an indication of my remorse. If he did not deduce from them the result of my weakness, he did deduce my love, and in order to make me feel more ashamed of it he insulted its object in terms so odious and so scornful that in spite of all my efforts I could not let him go on without interrupting him.

I do not know, my dear, where I found so much courage or what frantic moment made me so forget my duty and modesty; however, if for one instant I dared break a respectful silence, I paid the penalty rather severely, as you will see.

"In the name of Heaven," I said to him, "calm yourself. A man who deserved so many insults could never be a danger to me."

At that moment, my father, who thought he felt a reproach in these words and whose fury awaited only a pretext, flew upon your poor friend. For the first time in my life I received a blow; nor was that all, but giving himself up to his fit of passion with a violence equal to the effort he was making, he beat me mercilessly, although my mother had thrown herself between us, covered me with her body, and received some of the blows which were intended for me. In shrinking back to avoid them, I stumbled, I fell, and my head struck the leg of a table, which caused me to bleed.

At this point, the triumph of anger was ended and that of nature began. My fall, my bleeding, my tears and my mother's moved him. He raised me up with an anxious and earnest expression, and having placed me in a chair, they both sought attentively if I was hurt. I had only a slight bruise on my forehead and was bleeding only from my nose. However, I saw by the change in my father's manner and voice that he was unhappy about what he had just done. He was not reconciled to me with caresses; his paternal dignity would not suffer so abrupt a change. But he apologized to my mother with tender excuses, and I saw quite well by the looks that he cast furtively on me that half of them were indirectly addressed to me. No, my dear, there is no embarrassment as touching as that of a tender father who thinks himself to blame for his injustice. A father's heart feels that it is made to pardon and not to have need of being pardoned.

It was supper time. They delayed eating so as to give me time to compose myself, and my father, not wishing the servants to see anything of my disorder, went himself to fetch me a glass of water while my mother bathed my face. Alas, that poor mother! Already languishing and ill, she could well have done without such a scene and almost had more need of assistance than myself.

At the table, my father did not speak to me, but this silence was from shame and not from disdain. He pretended to find everything good in order to tell my mother to serve me some, and what touched me most sensibly was to notice that he sought opportunities to call me his daughter and not Julie, as he usually does.

After supper, the air was so chilly that my mother had a fire lit in her room. She sat on one side and my father on the other. I was go-

ing to get a chair in order to put myself between them, when, laying
hold of my dress and drawing me to him without saying anything,
he placed me on his knees. All this was done so suddenly and by a
kind of quite involuntary impulse that he was almost regretful the
moment afterwards. However, I was on his knees, he could no
longer push me away, and what was more discomposing, he had to
hold me clasped in his arms in this embarrassing position. All this
was done in silence, but now and then I felt his arms press against
my sides and heard a rather poorly stifled sigh. I do not know what
false shame prevented these paternal arms from giving themselves
up to these sweet embraces. A certain gravity which he dared not
abandon, a certain confusion which he dared not overcome put between the father and his daughter this charming embarrassment
that modesty and passion cause in lovers; meanwhile, a tender
mother, beside herself for joy, was secretly devouring this very sweet
sight. I saw, I felt all this, my angel, and could no longer hold back
the tenderness which was overcoming me. I pretended to slip; to
prevent myself, I threw an arm around my father's neck. I laid my
face close to his venerable cheek, and in an instant it was covered
with my kisses and bathed with my tears. I knew by those which
rolled from his eyes that he himself was relieved of a great sorrow.
My mother shared our rapture. Only sweet and peaceful innocence
was wanting in my heart to make this natural scene the most delightful moment of my life.

This morning, weariness and the pain from my fall having kept
me in bed a little later than usual, my father came into my room
before I was up. He sat at the side of my bed, inquiring tenderly
after my health; he took my hand in his and bent to kiss it several
times, calling me his dear daughter and proving to me his remorse
for his anger. For myself, as I told him, I should think myself only
too happy to be beaten every day for this reward, and there was no
treatment so harsh that a single caress from him could not efface
from my heart.

Then assuming a more serious manner, he reminded me of yesterday's subject and signified his will to me in polite but precise
terms.

"You know," he said to me, "the husband I have decided upon
for you. I made that known to you as soon as I returned and
I shall never change my mind in this matter. As for the man of
whom Lord Bomston spoke, although I do not dispute the
merit which everyone allows him, I do not know if he himself has
conceived the ridiculous hope of an alliance with my family or if

someone has inspired it in him, but even if I had no one in view and if he owned all the guineas in England, be assured that I would never accept such a man for a son-in-law. I forbid you as long as you live either to see him or to speak to him, and that is as much for the sake of his honor as for yours. Although I always felt but little regard for him, now I hate him above all for the outrages he caused me to commit, and I shall never forgive him for my violence."

With these words, he left without waiting for my answer and almost with the same air of severity as that which he had just reproached himself for assuming before. Ah, my cousin, what infernal monsters are these prejudices, which deprave the best hearts and silence the voice of nature at every moment?

There, my Claire, is how the explanation you had foreseen took place, the cause of which I could not understand until your letter informed me. I cannot tell you very well what a revolution has taken place within me, but since that moment I have changed. It seems to me that I look with more regret upon the happy time when I lived tranquil and content in the bosom of my family, and that I feel the weight of my fault increase along with that of the blessings it has caused me to lose. Tell me, cruel one! Tell me if you dare, is the time of love gone, no longer to return? Ah, do you really see all that is somber and horrible in that distressing thought? Yet my father's command is precise; my lover's danger is certain! Do you know what has happened within me because of so many contradicting emotions which destroy each other? A sort of stupidity which renders me almost insensible and permits me to use neither my passions nor my reason. The moment, as you have told me, is critical, and I am aware of it. Yet I was never less capable of acting. Twenty times I have tried to write my lover; at each line I was ready to faint and could not write two more. Only you are left for me, my sweet friend; please think, speak, act for me. I deliver up my fate into your hands; whatever course you take, I confirm in advance all that you do. To your friendship I entrust this fatal power over my lover which I have bought so dear. Part me forever from myself, kill me if I must die, but do not force me to pierce my heart with my own hand.

Oh my angel! My protectress! What a horrible task I am leaving to you! Will you have the courage to perform it? Will you find means to soften its severity? Alas! It is not my heart only that you must rend. Claire, you know, you know how much he loves me! I do not even have the consolation of being the most to be pitied. For mercy's sake! Let my heart speak through your lips, let yours be affected with the tender compassion of love, and console an unfortunate man. Tell him a hundred times . . . Ah, tell him . . . Do you not think, dear friend, that in spite of all prejudices, all obstacles, all misfortunes, Heaven has made us for each other? Yes, yes, I am sure of it; we are destined to be united. It is impossible for me to lose sight of this prospect; it is impossible for me to give up the hope which accompanies it. Tell him to guard himself against discouragement and despair. Do not trouble yourself exacting in my name love and faithfulness from him; still less promise him as much from me. Is not such assurance firmly rooted in our hearts? Do we not feel that they are inseparable and that we no longer have but one between us? Therefore, only tell him to hope, and, if fortune persecutes us, to put his trust at least in love; for I know, my cousin, in one way or another love will compensate for the evils it has caused us, and however Heaven may dispose of us, we shall not live separated for a long time.

P.S. After I had written my letter, I went into my mother's room and there became so ill that I was compelled to return to my bed. I even perceived . . . I fear . . . ah, my dear! I quite fear that my fall yesterday may have some consequence more disastrous than I had thought. Thus all is finished for me; all my hopes abandon me at once.

MISCARRIES—
see p 153

⚜ LETTER LXIV ⚜

From Claire to Monsieur D'Orbe

THIS MORNING, my father gave me an account of the conversation he had with you yesterday. I see with pleasure that everything is proceeding toward what you are pleased to call your good fortune. I hope, you know, that it will prove to be mine as well. You have won my esteem and friendship, and all the more tender sentiments which my heart can harbor are yours also. But do not deceive yourself in this; as a woman I am a kind of monster, and, I know not by what caprice of nature, my friendship outweighs my love. When

contrast
Julie

I tell you that my Julie is dearer to me than you, you only laugh, and yet nothing is more true. Julie knows it so well that she is more jealous in your place than you are, and while you seem content, she is always finding that I do not love you enough. What is more, I have such an affection for everyone who is dear to her that both her lover and you hold almost the same place in my heart, although in different ways. For him I have only friendship, but it is more intense; for you I think I feel a little love, but it is more calm. Although all this might seem ambiguous enough to disturb the tranquillity of a jealous man, I do not think that you will be very upset by it.

How far those poor children are from this sweet tranquillity which we presume to enjoy, and how ill does this contentment become us while our friends are in despair! It is all over; they must part. This is perhaps the moment of their eternal separation, and the reason for the sadness for which we reproached them on the day of the concert was perhaps a presentiment that they were seeing each other for the last time. However, your friend knows nothing of his ill fortune. In the security of his heart he still enjoys the happiness he has lost; at the very instant of despair he mentally savors the shadow of felicity, and like one who is carried off by an unexpected death, the wretch thinks of life and does not see the fate which is about to seize him. Alas! It is from my hand that he must receive this terrible blow! Oh divine friendship! The only idol of my soul! Come to inspire me with your pious cruelty. Give me the courage to be barbarous and to serve you worthily in such a sorrowful duty.

I am depending on you in this case, and I would depend upon you even if you loved me less, for I know your heart. I know that you have no need of love's zeal when humanity pleads. You must first persuade our friend to come to my house tomorrow morning. Take care, however, not to warn him of anything. Today I am free and I shall spend the afternoon with Julie; try to find Lord Bomston and come alone with him to see me at eight o'clock so that we may together determine on means to persuade the unfortunate man to leave and to prevent his despair.

I am expecting much from his courage and from our precautions. I am expecting even more from his love. Julie's will, the risks her life and her honor are running are reasons he will not resist. Whatever may happen, I declare to you that there will be no talk of our marriage until Julie has peace of mind and that my friend's tears will never water the knot which is to unite us. Thus, Monsieur, if it is true that you love me, your interest in this case will second your generosity, and this affair is not so much another's as it is also your own.

❧ LETTER LXV ❧

From Claire to Julie

ALL HAS BEEN DONE, and in spite of her imprudence my Julie is safe. The secrets of your heart are buried in the shadow of mystery; you are again in the midst of your family and your people, cherished, honored, enjoying a spotless reputation and a universal esteem. Consider and tremble for the risks you have run through shame or love, by doing too much or too little. Learn to desire no more to reconcile incompatible sentiments, and praise Heaven, you too foolish lover or too fearful girl, for good fortune which it reserved only for you.

I wanted to spare your sorrowing heart the details of this departure, so cruel and so necessary. But you desired to know them, I promised you should, and I shall keep my word with the same sincerity that is common to us and which never weighs advantage with good faith. Therefore, read this, dear and wretched friend; read since you must, but take courage and maintain your resolution.

All the measures which I had formulated and of which I told you yesterday have been carried out exactly. Returning home, I found Monsieur d'Orbe and Lord Bomston. I began by declaring to the latter that we knew of his heroic generosity, and I showed him how much both of us were affected by it. Next I revealed to them the powerful reasons we had for your friend's immediate departure and the difficulties I foresaw in bringing it about. His Lordship was perfectly sensible that it was necessary and showed much grief over the result which his unconsidered zeal had produced. They agreed that it was important to hasten the departure of your friend, and to seize the moment of consent in order to forestall any new irresolution and remove him from the continual danger of delay. I wanted to charge Monsieur d'Orbe with the task of making the suitable preparations without your friend's knowledge, but his Lordship, regarding this affair as his own, desired to take care of them. He promised me that his carriage would be ready this morning at eleven o'clock, adding that he would accompany it as far as necessary, and he proposed first to get him away on some other pretext, in order to tell him the real reason more leisurely. This expedient did not seem to me sufficiently sincere for us and for our friend, nor did I want to expose him at a distance from us to the first effects of a despair which might more easily escape his Lordship's eyes than mine. For the same reason I did not accept the proposal he made to speak alone to him to obtain his consent. I foresaw that this business would be delicate, and I desired to entrust no one but myself with it, for I am more certainly acquainted with the sensitive places of his heart, and among men I know that a harshness always prevails which a woman can better soften. However, I conceived that the attentions of his Lordship would not be useless to us in the preparations. I saw the entire effect that could be produced in a virtuous heart by the discourse of a sensitive man who thinks himself only a philosopher, and I knew what warmth the voice of a friend could give to the arguments of wisdom.

I therefore persuaded Lord Bomston to spend the evening with him and, without saying anything which might have direct bearing on his situation, imperceptibly to dispose his mind to stoic courage. "You who know your Epictetus so well," I told him, "here or never is the opportunity to employ it usefully. Distinguish carefully between apparent advantages and real advantages, between those which depend on us and those outside our control. At this moment when he is about to be threatened from without, prove to him that he alone can give himself pain and that the man who keeps his wisdom with him at all times also has his happiness everywhere in his own power."

I knew by his answer that this touch of irony, which could not make him angry, was enough to excite his zeal and that he very much expected to send me your friend well prepared the next day. This was all that I had intended, for although basically I do not value all this verbose philosophy any more than you do, I am persuaded that an honest man always has some shame at changing his opinions overnight and at denying in his heart as early as the next day all that his reason dictated to him the night before.

Monsieur d'Orbe wished also to be in the plan and spend the evening with them, but I begged him to do nothing of the sort; that would only have disturbed or restrained the conversation. The interest I have in him does not keep me from seeing that he is not a match for the other two. The masculine turn of thought in strong minds, which gives them such a peculiar idiom, is a language the grammar of which he does not know. Leaving them, I thought of the punch, and fearing anticipated disclosures, I slipped in a word about it laughingly to his Lordship.

"Be reassured," he said to me. "I indulge in the habit when I see no danger in it, but I never make myself slave to it. This concerns Julie's honor and perhaps the destiny of a man's life, of my friend's life. I shall drink punch according to my custom, lest I give the conversation some air of preparation, but this punch will be lemonade, and since he abstains from drinking it he shall not notice it at all."

Do you not, my dear, find it quite a mortification to have contracted habits which compel such precautions?

I spent the night in much agitation which was not all on your account. The innocent pleasures of our first youth, the sweetness of an old familiarity, the still closer intimacy between us begun a year ago because of the difficulty he had in seeing you—all that burdened my heart with the bitterness of this separation. I felt that along with half of yourself, I was about to lose a part of my own existence. I counted the hours uneasily, and at dawn it was not without dread that I saw the break of the day which was to determine your fate. I spent the morning thinking over my words and reflecting upon the impression they could make. Finally, the time came and I saw your friend enter. He had an uneasy manner and hurriedly asked me for news of you, for since the day after your scene with your father he had known you were ill, and Lord Bomston had confirmed to him yesterday that you had not left your bed. In order to avoid entering into details on this subject, I immediately told him that I had left you much improved last evening, and I added that he would learn more in a moment by the return of Hanz whom I had just sent to you. My precaution was useless; he asked me a hundred questions about your condition, and as they were leading me far from my purpose, I made short answers and began in turn to question him.

I began by sounding the condition of his spirit. I found him serious, methodical, and ready to put sentiment into the balance with reason. Thank Heaven, I said to myself, here was my philosopher quite prepared. Nothing now remained but to put him to the test. Though the ordinary custom of announcing sad news is by degrees, my knowledge of his ardent imagination which at a word carries him to extremes decided me to follow a contrary course, and I pre-

ferred to overwhelm him at once in order to administer consolations
later rather than needlessly to multiply his griefs, giving him a thousand instead of one. Assuming therefore a more serious tone and
looking at him fixedly, I said to him, "My friend, do you know the
limits of courage and virtue in a strong mind, and do you believe
that to renounce the person one loves requires an effort beyond the
powers of humanity?"

At that instant he started up like a madman; then clasping his
hands together and striking them against his forehead, he cried, "I
understand, Julie is dead. Julie is dead!" he repeated in a tone that
made me shudder. "I know it by your misleading precautions,
by your vain circumspection which only makes my death slower and
more cruel."

Although alarmed by such an unexpected emotion, I soon guessed
the cause of it, and for the first time I saw how the news of your illness, Lord Bomston's moral reflections, this morning's meeting, his
evaded questions, those I had just put to him—all had managed to
give him a false alarm. I also saw clearly what advantage I could
draw from his mistake by leaving him in it for a few moments, but
I could not bring myself to that cruelty. The thought of a loved
one's death is so frightful that anything else is a kind substitute,
and I hastened to profit from this advantage.

"Perhaps you will see her no more," I told him, "but she lives and
she loves you. Ah! If Julie were dead, could Claire have anything to
say to you? Thank Heaven which, unfortunate as you are, spares
you from the evils which might have crushed you."

He was so astonished, so stricken, so distracted, that after having
made him sit down again, I had time to tell him the details in sequence of all that it was necessary that he know, and as best as I
could I asserted the worthiness of Lord Bomston's conduct, in order
to give his noble heart some diversion from its sorrow by means of
the appeal of gratitude.

"That, my dear," I continued, "is the actual state of things. Julie
is at the edge of the abyss, ready to be overwhelmed by public disgrace, by her family's indignation, by the violence of an enraged father, and by her own despair. The danger increases every moment.
Whether in her father's hand or in her own, at every moment of her
life the dagger is within an inch of her heart. Only one way is left
to prevent all these misfortunes, and this way depends upon you
alone. The fate of your lover is in your hands. See if you have the
courage to save her by leaving her, since she is no longer permitted
to see you, or if you prefer to be the author and the witness of her

ruin and her disgrace. After having done everything for you, she will see what your heart can do for her. Is it surprising that her health has succumbed to her sorrows? You are uneasy about her life; know that it depends on you."

He listened without interrupting me, but as soon as he comprehended what was involved, I saw disappear that animated gesture, that furious look, that frightened but nervous and impetuous manner which he had before. A somber veil of sadness and consternation covered his face; his dull eye and his gloomy countenance betrayed the dejection of his heart. He hardly had the strength to open his lips to answer me.

"I must leave," he said to me in a tone that someone else would have thought tranquil. "Well, I shall leave. Have I not lived long enough?"

"No, not so," I instantly replied, "you must live for her who loves you. Have you forgotten that her life depends on yours?"

"Then we should not be separated," he added immediately. "She could and still can elope with me."

I pretended not to hear these last words and was trying to cheer him up with a few hopes to which his heart remained closed when Hanz came back and brought me good news of your health. In the moment of joy he felt over this, he cried, "Ah, may she live! May she be happy . . . if it is possible. I wish only to say my last farewell to her . . . and I shall leave."

"Do you not know," I said, "that she is not permitted to see you? Alas! Your farewells are said, and you are already separated! Your lot will be less cruel when you are farther from her. At least you will have the consolation of having made her secure. Fly today, this instant. Be fearful that even such a great sacrifice may be too late. Tremble lest even yet you cause the ruin of her to whose security you have devoted yourself."

"What!" he said to me with a kind of furor, "should I leave without seeing her again? What! Should I see her no more? No, no, we shall both perish if we must. I know she will not think it painful to die with me. But I shall see her, whatever happens. I shall leave my heart and my life at her feet, before I am thus torn from myself."

It was not difficult for me to show him the madness and the cruelty of such a project. But this "What, shall I see her no more!" which he repeated ceaselessly in a more sorrowful voice seemed to require at least some consolations for the future. "Why," I said to him, "do you imagine your misfortunes worse than they are? Why do you renounce hopes that Julie herself has not lost? Do you think that she could thus part from you if she thought it might be forever? No, my friend, you ought to know her heart better. You ought to know how much she prefers her love to her life. I fear, I fear too much (I added these words, I confess) that she will soon prefer it to everything. Believe, then, that she has hopes, since she consents to live. Believe that the precautions which her prudence dictates have you in view more than it may seem, and that she is more careful of herself on your account than her own."

Then I took out your last letter, and showing him the tender hopes of that deluded girl who believes her lover gone, I cheered his with this sweet warmth. Those few lines seemed to distill a salutary balm into his irritated wound. I watched his looks soften and his eyes moisten; I saw tenderness gradually succeed despair. But your last words, so moving, when your heart makes you say "We shall not live separated for a long time," made him burst into tears.

"No Julie, no my Julie," he said raising his voice and kissing the letter, "we shall not live separated for a long time. Heaven will unite either our destinies on earth or our hearts in the eternal resting place."

This was the state of mind I had hoped for. His dry and sullen grief disturbed me. I should not have allowed him to leave in that disposition of mind, but as soon as I saw him weep and heard your cherished name come tenderly from his lips, I had no more fear for his life, for nothing is less tender than despair. At that instant he drew from the emotion of his heart an objection which I had not foreseen. He spoke to me of the condition you suspected yourself *pregnant?* in, swearing that he would rather die a thousand times than abandon you to all the dangers that were about to threaten you. I took care not to tell him of your accident; I simply told him that your expectation had again been mistaken and that there was no longer any hope.

"Thus," he said to me, sighing, "there will remain no living memorial of my good fortune. It has disappeared like a dream that was never real."

It remained for me to execute the last part of your commission, and I did not think that, after the intimacy in which you have lived, neither preparation nor mystery was necessary for that. I should not even have shunned a little argument over this slight point in order to avoid the one which could have risen again over that of our whole conversation. I reproached him for his negligence in the care of his affairs. I told him that you feared that for a long time he has not been attentive to them and that until he is in a better position you ordered him to take care of himself for your sake, to attend to his needs better, and for this purpose to take the small present which I had to give to him from you. He neither seemed humiliated by this proposal nor pretended to make an affair of it. He said to me simply that you well knew that nothing came to him from you which he might not receive with joy, but that your precaution was superfluous and that a little house in Grandson which he had just sold,* the remainder of his small inheritance, had furnished him with more money than he had ever had in his life.

"Besides," he added, "I have a few talents from which I can draw my subsistence anywhere. I shall be only too happy to find in their exercise some diversion from my misfortunes, and since I have more closely seen the use to which Julie puts her superfluous money, I regard it as the sacred treasure of widows and orphans, from whom humanity does not permit me to take anything."

I reminded him of his journey to the Valais, your letter, and the preciseness of your orders. "The same reasons hold good now," I said.

"The same!" he interrupted in a tone of indignation. "The penalty then for my refusal was never to see her again. Let her therefore permit me to stay and I will accept. If I obey, why will she punish me? If I refuse, what worse will she do to me? . . . The same!" he repeated with impatience. "Then our intimacy was just beginning. Now it is at an end. Perhaps I shall be parted from her forever. There is no longer any connection between us. We shall be strangers to one another."

He pronounced these last words with such a shrinking of the heart that I trembled to see him fall back into the state of mind from which I had had so much trouble extricating him.

"You are a child," I affected an air of gaiety to say to him. "You still need a tutor, and I shall be yours. I am going to take charge of this, and in order to dispose of it properly in the business we shall engage in together, I desire to be informed of all your affairs."

I tried thus to turn aside his distressing ideas by that of a familiar correspondence to be kept up between us, and his simple soul, which seeks only to cling, so to speak, to whatever is near you, easily

* I have a little trouble in understanding how this lover, without a family name, who it will be hereafter said is not yet twenty-four, could sell a house, not having reached his majority. These letters are so full of like absurdities that I shall speak no more of them; it is enough to have given notice of them. [Rousseau]

At that time in Switzerland, the legal age of manhood was twenty-five. [Translator's note] accepted the diversion. We then settled upon addresses for our let-ters, and as these plans could only be agreeable to him, I prolonged their details until the arrival of Monsieur d'Orbe, who signaled to me that everything was ready.

Your friend readily understood what was meant; immediately he desired to write you, but I took care not to permit him. I foresaw that an excess of tenderness would overcome his heart too much and that he would hardly get to the middle of his letter when we would have no more means of making him leave.

"All delays are dangerous," I said to him. "Hasten to arrive at the first stop where you can write her at your leisure."

While saying this, I motioned to Monsieur d'Orbe; I went for-ward to your friend, and, my heart heavy with sobs, I pressed my face to his. I no longer knew what was happening; tears clouded my sight, my head began to spin, and it was time for my part to be finished.

A moment after, I heard them hurriedly descend. I went out onto the landing to look after them. My distress needed only this last blow. I saw the madman throw himself onto his knees in the middle of the stairs, kissing the steps a thousand times, and Monsieur d'Orbe could hardly wrest him from that cold stone to which he clung with his whole body, heaving long sighs. I felt mine ready to burst forth in spite of myself, and I went back in quickly, for fear of making a scene in front of the whole house.

Some moments later, Monsieur d'Orbe returned, holding his handkerchief to his eyes. He told me that it was done, that they were on their way. Upon arriving home, your friend found the car-riage at his door. Lord Bomston was waiting there also; he ran up to him and clasped him to his breast.

"Come, unfortunate man," he said to him in an emotional tone, "come pour out your sorrows into this heart which loves you. Come, you will perhaps feel that all on earth is not lost when you have found a friend such as I."

Immediately after, he helped him into the carriage with a vigor-ous gesture, and they left clasping each other tightly by the arm.

PART II

❧ LETTER I ❧

To Julie*

A HUNDRED TIMES I have picked up and flung down my pen. I hesitate at the first word. I do not know what tone I ought to assume, I do not know where to begin, and yet it is to Julie that I would write! Ah, wretch that I am! What has happened to me? The time, then, is no more when a thousand delicious sentiments flowed from my pen like an inexhaustible torrent! Those sweet moments of confidence and effusion of hearts are gone. We live no longer for each other, we are no longer the same persons, and I no longer know to whom I write. Will you condescend to receive my letters? Will you condescend to read them? Will you find them sufficiently reserved, sufficiently circumspect? Dare I preserve in them our former familiarity? Dare I speak of an extinguished or disdained passion, and am I not to be more distant than on the first day I wrote you? What a difference—oh Heaven—between those days, so charming and so sweet, and my frightful present misery! Alas! I was beginning to live and I sunk into nothing. The hope of life was warming my heart; now I have nothing before me but the prospect of death, and three years have circumscribed the happiness of my life. Ah, would that I had ended them before I outlived myself! Would that I had followed my first feelings just after those rapid moments of delight, when I no longer saw anything in life worthy of prolonging it! Without a doubt, either I should have terminated it after those three years or those moments should have been removed from that period. It is preferable never to have tasted happiness than to taste

---

* I think I hardly need to mention that in this second part and the one which follows it, the two separated lovers do nothing but speak irrationally and deliriously; the poor creatures no longer have any presence of mind. [*Rousseau*]

it and lose it. If I had been exempted from that fatal interval, if I had evaded that first look which made another being of me, I should still be in possession of my reason, I should still discharge a man's duties, and I should perhaps sow some virtues during my insipid career. A moment's mistake has changed everything. My eye dared to look upon what it was not supposed to see. That spectacle has finally produced its inevitable result. After having been gradually led to ruin, I am now only a fool whose mind is deranged, a cowardly slave without strength and without courage who ignominiously drags his chain and his despair.

Idle delusions of a distracted mind! False and misleading desires, immediately disclaimed by the heart which has formulated them! What good is it for real ills to invent imaginary remedies which we should reject when they are offered us? Ah! Who will ever know love, see you, and be able to believe that there may be any possible felicity which I would purchase at the expense of my first passion? No, no, let Heaven keep its blessings and leave me, along with my misery, the remembrance of my past good fortune. I prefer the pleasures which are in my memory and the regrets which rend my soul than happiness forever without my Julie. Come adored image, make complete a heart which beats only for you. Follow me in my exile, console me in my misery, cheer and sustain my extinguished hope. This unfortunate heart will forever be your inviolable sanctuary, from which neither fate nor society can ever remove you. If I am lost to happiness, I am not to the love which makes me worthy of it. This love is invincible, like the charms which gave rise to it. It is based on the firm foundation of merit and virtue; it cannot perish in an immortal soul. It no longer needs hope as a support, and the memory of the past will sustain it for eternity.

But you, Julie, oh you who once knew what it is to love! How can your tender heart have forgotten life? How can this holy flame have been extinguished in your pure soul? How can you have lost the taste for those heavenly pleasures which you alone were capable of feeling and inspiring? You drive me away pitilessly, you banish me with shame, you give me up to my despair, and you do not see, in the error which misleads you, that by making me miserable you are depriving yourself of your life's happiness. Ah Julie, believe me, you will look vainly for another heart akin to yours! A thousand will adore you, no doubt; mine alone knew how to love you.

Answer me, now, my deceived or deceiving lover, what has become of those projects formed with such secrecy? Where are those vain expectations with which you so often ensnared my credulous simplicity? Where is that holy and desired union, the sweet object of so many ardent sighs, with which your pen and your lips used to flatter my hopes? Alas! On the faith of your promises, I dared aspire to that holy name of husband, and thought myself already the happiest of men. Tell me, cruel one! Did you deceive me only to make my sorrow finally more intense and my humiliation more profound? Have I occasioned my misfortune through my own fault? Have I failed in obedience, in docility, in discretion? Did you see me so weak in my desires to deserve to be dismissed, or else preferring my passionate desires to your supreme will? I have done everything to please you and you renounce me! You were entrusted with my happiness and you destroyed me! Ungrateful one, give me an account of the treasure I confided to you. Give me an account of myself, after having seduced my heart in that supreme felicity that you showed me and now take from me. Heavenly angels, I might have scorned your lot! I might have been the happiest of beings . . . Alas! I am no longer anything. One instant has deprived me of everything. Instantaneously, I have passed from the summit of pleasure to eternal remorse. I am still reaching after the happiness which escapes me . . . I still reach after it and lose it forever! . . . Ah, if I could believe that! If the vestiges of a vain hope did not sustain . . . Oh crags of Meillerie, which my wandering eye measured so many times, why did you not assist my despair! I should have less regretted leaving life before I had experienced its value.

✤ LETTER II ✤

From Lord Bomston to Claire

WE HAVE ARRIVED in Besançon, and my first concern is to give you news of our journey. It passed, if not peacefully, at least without accident, and your friend is as healthy as possible for a man so sick at heart. He would even like to affect a kind of outward tranquillity. He is ashamed of his condition and is much restrained in my presence, but everything betrays his secret distress; and if I pretend to be deceived, it is to let him grapple with it himself and thus occupy one part of his soul's faculties in repressing the effect of the other.

The first day he was extremely dejected. Seeing that the speed of our journey was increasing his sorrow, I cut it short. He did not speak to me at all, nor I to him; ill-timed condolence only embitters violent afflictions. Indifference and coldness easily find words, but sadness and silence are in those cases the true language of friendship. I began yesterday to perceive the first sparks of the anger which infallibly succeeds this lethargy; at dinner, we had been stopped scarcely a quarter of an hour when he approached me with an air of impatience.

"Why do we delay our departure?" he said to me with a bitter smile. "Why are we staying for one moment so near to her?"

In the evening, he affected to speak a great deal, without saying a word about Julie. He began again to ask questions I had already answered ten times. He wanted to know if we were already on French soil, and then he asked if we would soon reach Vevey. The first thing he did at each stop was to begin some letter which a moment later he tore up or crumpled. I have saved two or three of these fragments from the fire, by which you will be able to get an imperfect notion of the state of his mind. However, I think he has succeeded in writing a complete letter.

The outburst of passion which these first symptoms threaten is easily foreseen, but I could not say what its result or duration will be, for that depends upon a combination of the man's character, the nature of his passion, the circumstances which can arise—a thousand things which no human knowledge can determine. As for me, I can answer for his rage but not for his despair, for do as we will, every man is always the master of his life.

I flatter myself, however, that he will have respect for his person and my attentions, but for that I rely less upon the zeal of friendship, which will not be spared, than upon the character of his passion and that of his mistress. A soul can hardly occupy itself very much and for a long time with one object without contracting the dispositions related to that object. Julie's extreme sweetness must temper the intensity of the passion she inspires, and I do not doubt either that love, from a man of such lively passions as he, makes her a little more ardent than she would naturally be without him.

I dare also to depend upon his heart; it is made for struggling and conquering. Such a love as his is not so much a weakness as a strength badly exerted. An ardent and unhappy passion is for a time, for always perhaps, capable of smothering some of his faculties, but it is itself a proof of their excellence and of the use he could *contrast 2 couples*

make of them in cultivating wisdom; for the highest reason is only attained through the same power of the soul which gives rise to great passions, and we serve philosophy worthily only with the same ardor that we feel for a mistress.

Be sure, charming Claire, that I am no less interested than you in the fate of this unfortunate couple, not out of a sentiment of pity, which can only be a weakness, but out of a concern for justice and order which desires everyone to be disposed of in the manner most advantageous to himself and to society. These two beautiful souls left nature's hand made for each other. It is in a sweet union, it is in the midst of happiness, free to display their talents and exercise their virtues, that they might enlighten the world with their example. Why must an absurd prejudice reverse eternal directions and overturn the concord of thinking beings? Why does the vanity of a cruel father thus hide their light under a bushel and cause tender and gracious beings to grieve tearfully, those who were born to dry the tears of others? Is not the conjugal tie the freest as well as the holiest of engagements? Yes, all the laws which obstruct it are unjust; all fathers who presume to form or break it are tyrants. That chaste, natural knot is subject neither to a sovereign's power nor to paternal authority, but only to the authority of our common Father, who has command over hearts and who, decreeing their union, can make them love each other.[10]

i.e. or fathers

You are more fortunate, charming Claire; you have a father who does not pretend to know wherein your happiness consists better than you. Perhaps it is neither through great insight into wisdom nor through an excessive tenderness that he thus leaves you mistress of your destiny, but what does the cause matter if the effect is the same and if, in the freedom he allows you, indolence supplies the place of reason? Far from an abuse of this liberty, the choice you have made at twenty would have the approval of the wisest father. Your heart, absorbed by an unparalleled friendship, has had little room for the fires of love. For them you substitute all which can make up for that deficiency in marrriage. Though less a lover than a friend, if you are not the most tender wife, you will be the most virtuous, and this union which wisdom has created is to increase with age and last as long as wisdom itself. The heart's impulse is blinder, but it is more irresistible; the way to ruin is to put oneself under the necessity of resisting it. Happy are those whom love unites as reason would have done and who have no obstacle to surmount or prejudices to combat! Such would our two lovers be without the unjust resistance of a stubborn father. Such might they still be in spite of him, if one of the two were well advised.

The example of you and Julie equally shows that it is only for the parties themselves to judge if they suit each other. If love is not predominant, reason alone will make the choice; that is your case. If love prevails, nature has already chosen; that is Julie's case. Such is nature's sacred law which man is not permitted to transgress, which he never transgresses with impunity, and which consideration for positions and ranks can repeal only at the cost of unhappiness and crime.

Although winter is coming on and I have to get to Rome, I shall not leave the friend I have under my protection until I see his soul in a stable condition on which I may rely. He is a treasure dear to me because of his worthiness and because you have entrusted him to my care. If I cannot make him happy, I shall try at least to make him prudent and bear the evils of humanity like a man. I have determined to spend two weeks here with him, during which I hope that we shall receive news from Julie and you and that you will both help me to put some balm on the wounds of this broken heart which cannot yet listen to reason unless it speaks the language of sentiment.

I am enclosing a letter for your friend. Do not confide it, I beg you, to any messenger, but give it to her yourself.

Fragments Attached to the Preceding Letter

(1)

Why could I not see you before departing? Did you fear that I might die while taking leave of you? Pitiful heart! Be reassured. I am well . . . I do not suffer . . . I am still alive . . . I am thinking of you . . . I am thinking of the time I was dear to you . . . my heart is a little oppressed . . . the carriage makes me giddy . . . I am depressed . . . I shall not be able to write you long today. Tomorrow, perhaps, I shall have more strength . . . or I shall no longer need any. . . .

(2)

Where are these horses dragging me with such speed? Where is this man who calls himself my friend leading me with such zeal? Is it far from you, Julie? Is it by your command? Is it to places where you will not be? . . . Ah foolish girl! . . . I examine the road which I am traveling so rapidly. Where have I come from? Where am I going? And why so much speed? Are you afraid, cruel ones, that I will not run fast enough to my ruin? Oh friendship! Oh love! Is this your contrivance? Are these your kindnesses? . . .

(3)

Have you well consulted your heart in driving me away so abruptly? Could you, tell me Julie, could you renounce forever . . . no, no, that tender heart loves me, I am sure of it. In spite of fortune, in spite of itself, it will love me until death . . . I see it, you gave way to persuasions* . . . what eternal remorse you are preparing for yourself! . . . alas! it will be too late . . . what, could you forget . . . what, I could have misunderstood you! . . . Ah, think of yourself, think of me, think of . . . listen, there is still time . . . you drove me away cruelly. I am fleeing faster than the wind . . . Say a word, one word, and I shall return quicker than lightning. Say one word and we shall be united forever. We must be . . . we shall be . . . Ah! I complain to the winds! . . . and yet I am fleeing; I am going to live and die far from her . . . live far from her! . . .

✤ LETTER III ✤

From Lord Bomston to Julie

YOUR COUSIN will give you news of your friend. Besides, I think he has written you by this post. First satisfy your impatience with that letter, so that you can next read this one calmly, for I warn you that its subject will demand your whole attention.

I know men, I have lived a great deal in a few years, I have acquired much experience at my own expense, and it is the path of passions that has led me to philosophy. But of all I have observed

---

* The sequel shows that these suspicions fell upon Lord Bomston and that Claire applied them to herself. [*Rousseau*]

until now, I have never seen anything so extraordinary as you and
your lover. It is not that either of you have any peculiar character-
istic which at first glance can be distinguished, and it could be quite
possible that this difficulty in differentiating you might cause a superficial observer to mistake you for ordinary souls. But that it is
impossible to differentiate you is actually what distinguishes you,
and the features of the common model, some of which are always
lacking in every individual, are all equally clear in you. In like
manner, each print of an engraving has its particular defects which
furnish it with character, but if one happens to be perfect, though it
may be found beautiful at first glance, it must be considered for a
long time for its perfection to be recognized. The first time I saw
your lover, I was struck by a new sentiment, which only increased
from day to day in proportion as reason justified it. In respect to
you, it was completely otherwise, and the sentiment you inspired
was so intense that I was mistaken about its nature. This impression
resulted not so much from the difference between the sexes as from a
character still more stamped by perfection than a heart, even one
independent of love, can know. I well see what you would be without your friend; I do not see in the same way what he would be
without you. Many men may resemble him, but there is only one
Julie in the world. After an injury to you for which I shall never
pardon myself, your letter arrived to enlighten me about my real
sentiments. I realized that I was not jealous nor, consequently, in
love; I realized that you were too good for me. You require the first
fruits of the heart, and mine would not be worthy of you.

Since that moment I have taken a tender interest in your mutual happiness which shall not be extinguished. Thinking to remove all obstacles, I took an indiscreet step with regard to your
father, the ill success of which is only one more reason that my zeal
should be inspired. Condescend to hear me, and I can still make
amends for all the pain I have caused you.

Examine your heart carefully, oh Julie, and see if it is possible
for you to extinguish the flame with which it is devoured. There
was a time, perhaps, when you could stop its progress, but if a pure
and chaste Julie nevertheless fell from innocence, how will she be
redeemed after her fall? How will she resist triumphant love, armed
with the dangerous memory of all past pleasures? Young lover, deceive yourself no longer about it, and renounce the self-reliance
which seduced you. You are lost, if you must still battle with love;
you will be disgraced and conquered, and the sense of your shame
will gradually stifle all your virtues. Love has insinuated too deeply

into the substance of your soul for you ever to be able to drive it out; like a corrosive acid, it intensifies and penetrates all your features. You shall never efface love's strong impression without at the same time effacing all the exquisite sentiments which you received from nature, and when you will no longer be in love, you will have nothing left deserving regard. Therefore, what must you do now, being able no more to alter the condition of your heart? Only one thing, Julie. You must make it legitimate. For that I am going to propose the only method which is left for you. Profit from it, while there is still time; restore to innocence and to virtue the exercise of that sublime reason with which Heaven endowed you, or be fearful of forever debasing the most precious of its gifts.

In Yorkshire I have a rather considerable estate, which was for a long time the seat of my ancestors. The mansion house is old, but good and comfortable; the countryside is solitary, but pleasant and variegated. The river Ouse, which runs through the end of the park, presents both a charming prospect to the view and a means of transportation convenient for provisions. The income from the land is enough for the honest upkeep of the master and could double under his supervision. Hateful prejudices have no access into this happy country. The peaceable inhabitant there still preserves the simple manners of earlier times, and one finds there a likeness of the people of the Valais as described by your friend's pen with such affecting touches. This estate is yours, Julie, if you deign to live on it with him, and it is there together that you could fulfill all the tender hopes with which the letter I speak of concludes.

Come, unique pattern for true lovers. Come, charming and faithful couple, and take possession of a place made to serve as the refuge of love and of innocence. Come and there, in the presence of God and man, tie the sweet knot which unites you. Come and with the example of your virtues do honor to a country in which they will be worshipped and simple people will be prone to imitate them. In this tranquil place, may you be able to enjoy forever, with the sentiments which unite you, the happiness of pure souls. May Heaven there bless your chaste passions with children who resemble you. May your days be prolonged there in respectable old age and be terminated at last peacefully in the arms of your children. May posterity, perusing with secret delight that monument to conjugal felicity, one day say in the tenderness of its heart, "Here was the refuge of innocence; here was the home of two lovers."

Your destiny is in your hands, Julie. Carefully weigh the proposal I am making to you and examine only the main point, for as to the rest, I charge myself beforehand with irrevocably engaging your friend in the pledge I am making. I charge myself also with the security of your departure and with attending, along with him, to that of your person until your arrival. Once there, you can immediately be married publicly without difficulty, for among us a girl of marriageable age has no need of another's consent to dispose of herself. Our wise laws do not abrogate those of nature, and if from this pleasant harmony some problems result, they are much fewer than those which it prevents. I have left my valet at Vevey, a man to be trusted, brave, prudent, and faithful in every event. You will easily be able to consult with him by word of mouth or in writing with the help of Regianino, without the latter knowing anything of the affair. When it is time, we shall set out to join you, and you will not leave your father's house except under the protection of your husband.

I leave you to your reflections, but, I repeat, be fearful of the error of prejudice and the seduction of scruples which often lead to vice along the road of honor. I foresee what will happen to you if you reject my offers. The tyranny of an obstinate father will plunge you into the abyss, which you will recognize only after your fall. Your extreme gentleness sometimes degenerates into timidity; you will be sacrificed to the chimerical distinction of rank.* You will be forced to contract an alliance disavowed by your own heart. Public approval will incessantly be contradicted by the cry of your conscience. You will be respected but contemptible. It is preferable to be forgotten but virtuous.

P.S. In doubt about your decision, I am writing you without your friend's knowledge, for fear that a refusal on your part might succeed in at once destroying all the effects of my care.

* The chimerical distinction of rank! This is an English lord who is speaking in this way! Must not all this be fictitious? Reader, what do you say about it? [*Rousseau*]

✤ LETTER IV ✤

From Julie to Claire

OH, MY DEAR! What distress you left me in last night, and what a night I have spent pondering that fatal letter! No, never did a more dangerous temptation worry my heart, never did I experience such disturbance, and never was I more at a loss to quiet it. Formerly some light of wisdom and reason directed my will; in every perplexing occasion, I would first discern the most honest course and follow it immediately. Now, debased and continually overcome, I can only fluctuate between contending passions. My frail heart has now no other choice but between its foibles, and such is my deplorable blindness that if by chance I succeed in following the best course, my choice will not be directed by virtue and I shall feel no less remorse than if I followed the worse. You know the husband my father has determined for me; you know what bonds love has imposed on me. Would I be virtuous? Obedience and faithfulness impose opposite duties upon me. Would I follow the inclination of my heart? Whom shall I favor, my lover or my father? Alas, listening to love or to nature, I cannot avoid driving either one or the other to despair. Sacrificing myself to duty, I cannot avoid committing a crime, and whatever course I take, I am forced to die both unhappy and guilty.

Ah! Dear and tender friend, you who were ever my only resource and who have so many times saved me from death and despair, think of the present horrible state of my mind and see if your helpful consideration was ever more necessary! You know how I listen to your opinions; you know how I follow your advice; you have just seen how, at the expense of my life's happiness, I can defer to the counsel of friendship. Pity, then, the dejection to which you have reduced me; put an end to it, since you have begun; do duty for my crestfallen spirits; think for her who no longer thinks but through you. Lastly, read this heart which loves you; you know it better than I. Teach me, then, what I desire and decide for me, since I no longer have the strength with which to desire nor the reason with which to decide.

Read over the letter from that generous Englishman; read it a thousand times, my Angel. Ah! Be affected by the charming picture of happiness which love, peace, and virtue can still promise me! Sweet and enchanting union of souls! Inexpressible delights, even in the midst of remorse! Heavens! What could they be to my heart in the midst of conjugal fidelity? What! Could happiness and innocence be still within my power? Oh, I could expire for love and joy between an adored husband and the dear pledges of his tenderness! . . . But I hesitate for one moment, and I do not fly to atone for my fault in the arms of him who caused me to commit it. And I delay becoming a virtuous wife and chaste mother. . . . Oh that my parents might see me raised from my debasement! That they might witness the way I should perform in my turn the sacred duties that they have performed for me! . . . But mine toward them? Ungrateful and unnatural daughter, who will perform those duties for them while you forget them? Is it by plunging a dagger into the heart of a mother that you prepare to become one yourself? Will she who dishonors her family teach her children to honor her? Unworthy object of the blind fondness of a doting father and mother, abandon them to regret for having given you birth, heap their old age with sorrow and shame . . . and enjoy, if you can, a happiness purchased at this price.

My God! What horrors surround me! To leave my country furtively, dishonor my family, abandon at once father, mother, friends, relatives, and you! You, my sweet friend! You, the darling of my heart! You from whom since my childhood I can scarcely remain parted for a single day. To flee from you, to leave you, to lose you, to see you no more! . . . Ah no! May never . . . what torments rend your unfortunate friend! At once she senses all the evil which she must choose, without the consolation of any of the good which will remain. Alas, I am bewildered. So many struggles surpass my strength and disturb my reason. I am losing both my courage and my wits. I have no further hope except in you alone. Either decide for me or allow me to die.

❧ LETTER V ❧

Response

YOUR PERPLEXITY is only too well founded, my dear Julie. I foresaw it but could not prevent it. I feel it and cannot relieve it, and what is worse in your situation is that no one can extricate you except yourself. When it is a matter of prudence, friendship may come to the aid of a disturbed soul; when a choice must be made between good and evil, mistaken passion may be overruled by disinterested advice. But in this case, whatever course you take, nature both authorizes and condemns it, reason both blames and approves it, duty either is silent or contradicts itself. The consequences from both courses are equally to be feared; you can neither remain undecided nor decide wisely. You have only evils to choose between, and your heart alone is the judge of them. As for me, the importance of your deliberation frightens me and its result saddens me. Whatever destiny you choose, it will still be unworthy of you, and being able neither to point out to you an agreeable course of action nor to conduct you to true happiness, I do not have the courage to decide your destiny. This is the first refusal you ever received from your friend, and I know indeed by what it is costing me that it will be the last; but I should betray you by consenting to direct you in a case in which reason itself imposes silence and in which the only rule to follow is to listen to your own inclination.

Do not be unjust toward me, my sweet friend, and do not condemn me too soon. I know that there are some circumspect friends who, fearing to compromise themselves, refuse advice in difficult cases, and whose reserve increases with the peril of their friends. Ah! You will know if this heart which loves you is capable of those timid precautions! Allow me, instead of advising you in your affairs, to speak for a moment of mine.

Have you never noticed, my Angel, to what degree all who are near you become attached to you? That a father and a mother may cherish an only daughter is not, I know, much to wonder at; that an ardent young man is inflamed by a charming girl is no more extraordinary. But that at a mature age a man as cold as Monsieur de

Wolmar may by seeing you become tender for the first time in his life; that a whole family may dote unanimously on you; that you may be dear to my father, a man with so little sensibility, as much as and more, perhaps, than his own children are; that friends, acquaintances, servants, neighbors, and the entire village may adore you unanimously and take the most tender interest in you—all that, my dear, is a less likely coincidence which would not have occurred if there were not in your person some particular reason. Do you know what this reason is? It is neither your beauty, nor your wit, nor your grace, nor anything of all that known as the talent of pleasing. It is, rather, that tender heart and that sweetness of affection which is matchless; it is the talent of loving, my child, which makes you loved. One can resist everything except benevolence, and there is no surer means of acquiring the affection of others than by giving them your own. A thousand women are more beautiful than you; several have as many graces. Only you have, along with these graces, an indefinably more seductive quality which not only pleases but affects and ravishes every heart. One feels that your heart asks only to give itself, and the delightful sentiment which it is looking for comes in turn to look for it.

You see with surprise, for example, the incredible affection of Lord Bomston for your friend. You see his zeal for your happiness. With wonder, you receive his generous offers; you attribute them to his virtue alone, and my Julie is affected! An error, a mistake, charming cousin! God forbid that I should diminish his Lordship's beneficence or that I should disparage his great heart. But believe me, this zeal, wholly disinterested as it is, would be less ardent if under the same circumstances he had to do with other people. It is your and your friend's invincible influence which, without his perceiving it even, determines him with such force and makes him do through affection what he thinks he is only doing through generosity.

That is what must happen to all souls of a certain temper. They transform others into their own likeness, so to speak. They have a sphere of influence in which nothing resists them. It is impossible to know them without wishing to imitate them, and from their sublime height they attract all who are about them. It is for that reason, my dear, that neither you nor your friend will perhaps ever know mankind, for you will see them much more as you fashion them than as they would be in themselves. You will lead the way for all who live with you. They will flee from you or become like you, and perhaps you will meet with no one in the world similar to all those whom you have seen.

Let us turn now to me, cousin; though I have an opposite temperament, the same blood, the same age, and above all a perfect conformity of tastes and moods have united us since childhood.

> Congiunti eran gl' alberghi,
> Ma più congiunti i cori:
> Conforme era l'etate,
> Ma 'l pensier più conforme.
> TASSO

> Our homes were close by,
> But closer were our hearts:
> Our ages were matched,
> But our thoughts matched more perfectly.

What do you think it is that has produced in her who has spent her life with you this charming influence which is felt by everyone who comes near you? Do you think it can be only an ordinary connection between us? Do not my eyes convey to you the sweet joy I receive each day when they meet yours? Do you not perceive in my tender heart my pleasure in sharing your sorrows and in weeping with you? Can I forget that in the first ecstasies of a budding love, my friendship was not troublesome to you and that the complaints of your lover were not able to prevail upon you to send me from you or to conceal from me the spectacle of your frailty? That was a critical moment, my Julie; I know what a sacrifice your modest heart made in confessing a shame which I escaped. Never should I have been your confidante if I had been but half a friend to you, and our souls feel themselves too intimately united now for anything to be able to part them henceforward.

What is it that makes friendships between women so lukewarm and so short-lived, I mean between women who are capable of love? It is the selfishness of love, it is the influence of beauty, it is jealousy over conquests. Now, if anything of that kind could have separated us, this separation would already have taken place; but were my heart more sensible of love, were I even unaware that your passions are so much a part of your nature as to be extinguished only with your life, your lover is my friend—that is to say, my brother—and who has ever seen a true friendship like that one end in love? As for Monsieur d'Orbe, he will assuredly have to be well pleased with your feelings for him for a long time before I dream of complaining of them, and I am not more tempted to hold him by force than you are to tear him from me. Ah, my child! Would to Heaven that at the cost of his affection I might cure you of yours. I keep him with pleasure; I would resign him with joy. [11]

You grow impatient to know what I am driving at. Here it is. I cannot give you the advice you ask of me. I have told you the reason for it, but the course you will follow for yourself will be at the same time that which you follow for your friend, for whatever your fortune may be I am determined to share it. If you leave, I shall follow you; if you stay, I shall stay. I have formed an unshakable resolution; it is my duty and nothing can turn me from it. My fatal indulgence caused your undoing; your destiny must be mine, and because we have been inseparable since childhood, my Julie, we must be so until death.

I foresee that you will find much rashness in this project, but at base it is more reasonable than it seems, and I do not have the same reasons for indecision as you. First, as to my family, if I leave an easy father, I am leaving a rather indifferent one, who allows his children to do all they please more through negligence than through indulgence, for you know that European affairs interest him much more than his own and that his daughter is considerably less dear to him than the Pragmatic Sanction.* Besides, unlike you I am not his only child, and among those that remain he will hardly be aware if one is missing.

Am I leaving a marriage agreement ready to be concluded? *Manco male,* my dear. It is for Monsieur d'Orbe, if he loves me, to console himself. As for me, although I esteem his character, although I am not without an affection for his person, and although I would regret losing a very honest gentleman, next to my Julie he is nothing to me. Tell me, my child, does the soul have a sex? In truth, I hardly feel one in mine. I may have fancies but very little love. A husband may be useful to me, but he would ever be for me only a husband, and of those, still free and as tolerable as I am, I can find one anywhere in the world.

Take care, cousin, for although I do not hesitate, I do not say

---

* The Pragmatic Sanction is the name given to the decree of 1713 by which, in the absence of a male heir, the Emperor Charles VI declared his eldest daughter, Maria-Theresa, successor to all his Hapsburg dominions. At his death in 1740, however, support of this alteration of the law of succession was weakened, and Maria-Theresa was refused recognition by Elector Charles Albert of Bavaria, later Charles VII. The ensuing quarrel precipitated the War of the Austrian Succession, 1740–48. [*Translator's note*]

that you ought not to hesitate; nor would I suggest to you to take the course that I shall take if you leave. The difference between us is great and your duties are much more rigorous than mine. You still know that an unparalleled affection almost fills my heart and so well absorbs all the other sentiments that they are as if stifled. An invincible and sweet habit has attached me to you since my childhood. I love no one else perfectly, and if I have a few ties to break by following you, I shall be encouraged by your example. I shall say to myself, "I am imitating Julie," and I shall think myself justified.

Note from Julie to Claire

I understand you, incomparable friend, and I thank you. For once at least, I shall do my duty and shall not be completely unworthy of you.

❖ LETTER VI ❖

From Julie to Lord Bomston

YOUR LETTER, my Lord, fills me with tenderness and admiration. The friend whom you deign to protect will not be less moved when he knows all you have wanted to do for us. Alas! It is only the unfortunate who know the value of benevolent hearts. Already we know in only too many ways all the worth of yours, and your heroic virtues will affect us always, but they will no longer surprise us.

How sweet it would be for me to be happy under the auspices of so generous a friend and to have from his kindness the good fortune that fate has denied me! But, my Lord, I see with despair that fate frustrates your good designs. My cruel destiny triumphs over your zeal, and the delightful prospect of the blessings you offer me serves only to make their loss more poignant for me. You would offer two persecuted lovers a pleasant and secure refuge; there you would make their passion legitimate, their union sacred; and I know that under your protection I should easily elude the pursuits of my angered family. That is a great deal for love; is it enough for happiness? No, if you wish me to be peaceful and content, give me some refuge still more secure, in which I can elude shame and remorse. You anticipate our needs, and with an unprecedented generosity for our maintenance you deprive yourself of a part of your wealth destined for your own. Richer, more honored by your charity than by my own patrimony, with you I may recover everything, and you will deign to take the place of a father for me. Ah my Lord! Shall I deserve to find one, after having abandoned the one nature has given me?

This is the source of the reproaches my frightened conscience gives me and of the secret pangs which rend my heart. I do not concern myself with whether I have the right to dispose of myself contrary to the will of my parents but whether I can do so without mortally afflicting them, whether I can abandon them without driving them to despair. Alas! This is equal to debating whether I have the right to kill them. When before has virtue thus had to balance the rights of blood and of nature? When before has a sensitive heart had to distinguish so carefully the bounds of gratitude? Is it not already to be a criminal to consent to proceed to the point at which we begin to become one, and do we question so minutely the extent of our duty unless we are tempted to go beyond it? Who, I? Should I pitilessly abandon those by whom I breathe, those who maintain for me the life they have given me and make dear for me, those who have no other hope, no other pleasure except in me alone? A father almost sixty! A mother ever languishing! I, their only child, should I leave them helpless in the solitude and the weariness of old age, when it is the time to return to them the tender solicitude they have lavished on me? Should I give their last days up to shame, to remorse, to tears? Terror, the cry of my disturbed conscience, would ceaselessly represent to me my father and mother dying without consolation and cursing the ungrateful daughter who has forsaken and dishonored them. No, my Lord, the virtue I abandoned in turn abandons me and no longer speaks to my heart, but this horrible idea speaks to me in virtue's place; it would follow me as my torment every instant of my life and would make me miserable in the midst of happiness. In a word, if my destiny is such that the rest of my life must be given up to regrets, this one regret is too frightful to bear; I prefer to run the risk of all the others.

I cannot make a suitable answer to your arguments, I confess; I am only too inclined to find them just. But, my Lord, you are not married. Do you not feel that one must be a father to have the right to advise the children of others? As for me, my resolution is taken. My parents will make me unhappy, I am convinced, but it will be less cruel for me to grieve for my own misery than to have caused theirs, and so I shall never desert my father's house. Go, then, delightful fancy of a sensitive soul, happiness so charming and so desired, go vanish like a dream; for me you shall have no more substance than that. And you, too generous friend, forget your pleasant projects, and let no trace of them remain except in the bottom of a heart too grateful to forget them. If the excess of our grief does not discourage your great soul, if your generous kindness is not exhausted, there is still a way for you to put it to use with renown, and he whom you honor with the title of friend may under your care deserve to become one. Do not judge him by the condition in which you now see him; his distraction springs not from cowardice but from an ardent and proud spirit which stiffens in the face of adversity. There is often more insensitivity than courage in an apparent moderation; common people do not know violent sorrows, and great passions hardly develop in feeble men. Alas! Into his passion he has put that vigor of feeling which characterizes noble souls, and it is that which is the cause of my present shame and despair. My Lord, deign to believe me; if he was only an ordinary man, Julie had never been undone.

No, no, this secret affection which predisposes you to a manifest esteem for him has not betrayed you. He is worthy of all you have done for him before knowing him well; you will do even more, if that is possible, after you know him better. Yes, be his comforter, his protector, his friend, his father, I implore you both for your sake and for his. He will justify your confidence, he will esteem your kindnesses, he will put your precepts into practice, he will imitate your virtues, and he will learn your wisdom. Ah, my Lord! If in your hands he becomes all that he is capable of being, how proud you will be one day of your work!

❧ LETTER VII ❧

From Julie

YOU TOO, my sweet friend! You, my only hope, you have just wounded my heart again while it is dying of sorrow! I was prepared for fortune's blows; long have my presentiments announced them to me. I should have borne them patiently. But you for whom I suffer them! Ah, only those which come to me through you are unbearable, and it is frightful for me to see my distress aggravated by the one who ought to alleviate it. What sweet consolations which I had promised myself vanish with your courage! How many times I flattered myself that your strength would urge me from my languor, that your merit would efface my error, that your virtues would raise my debased soul. How many times have I dried my bitter tears in saying to myself, I am suffering for him, but he is worthy of it; I am sinful, but he is virtuous; a thousand troubles beset me, but his constancy sustains me; and in his heart I find recompense for all my losses. Vain hope which the first trial has destroyed! Now where is that sublime love which could elevate all your sentiments and display your virtues? Where are your fine principles? What has become of your imitation of great men? Where is that philosopher whom misfortune could not shake but who succumbs to the first accident which parts him from his mistress? What pretext will henceforth excuse my shame in my own eyes, when I see in him who seduced me nothing but a man without courage who is enervated by pleasures, a cowardly heart crushed by the first reverse of fortune, a madman who renounces his reason as soon as he needs it? Oh God! In this utter humiliation am I to see myself reduced to shame for my choice as well as for my frailty?

Consider how far you are forgetting yourself. Is your distracted and cringing soul stooping to cruelty? Do you dare reproach me? Do you dare complain of me? . . . of your Julie? . . . Barbarous one! . . . Why did your remorse not hold back your hand? Why did not the sweetest proofs of the most tender love ever deprive you of the courage to insult me? Ah, if you could doubt my heart, how despicable yours would be! . . . But no, you do not doubt it, you cannot doubt it. I defy your anger; and at this very moment while I am hating your injustice, you see only too well the source of the first emotion of anger that I ever experienced.

Can you lay the blame on me, if I was led astray through blind confidence and if my plans have not succeeded? How you would be ashamed of your harsh words if you knew what hope had seduced me, what projects I dared form for our mutual happiness, and how they have vanished with all my hopes! Some day, I dare hope still, you will know better, and then your remorse will avenge me for your reproaches. You know my father's prohibition; you are not unaware of public talk. I foresaw the consequences of these things, I had my cousin make them clear to you, you were as sensible of them as we, and for our mutual preservation we had to submit to the fate which separated us.

I have driven you away, then, as you dare to say. But for whom have I done so, you indelicate lover? Ungrateful man! It was for the sake of a heart much kinder than he believes it to be, who would rather die a thousand times than see me disgraced. Tell me, what shall become of you when I am given up to opprobrium? Are you hoping to be able to bear the sight of my dishonor? Come back, cruel one, if you think you can; come back to receive the sacrifice of my reputation with as much courage as I can offer it up to you. Come, do not be afraid of being disclaimed by her to whom you were dear. I am ready to declare in the face of Heaven and earth all that we have felt for each other; I am ready to name you openly as my lover, to die in your arms of love and of shame. I would rather the entire world knew of my tenderness than see you doubt it for one moment, for your reproaches are more bitter than ignominy to me.

Let us forever end these mutual complaints, I implore you. They are intolerable to me. Oh God! How can we quarrel when we are in love, and by torturing each other lose the moments in which we have such great need of consolation? No, no my friend, what use is it to pretend a disagreement which does not exist? Let us complain about fate but not about love. Never has love formed so perfect a union; never has it formed one more lasting. Our hearts, too intimately blended, are no longer capable of separation, and we can no longer live parted from each other but as two parts of one being. How then can you feel only your own griefs? How is it you do not feel your friend's too? Why are you not aware of her heart-felt

sighs in your breast? How much more grief-stricken they are than
your passionate outbursts! If you shared my sufferings, how much
more cruel they would be to you than even your own!

You find your situation deplorable! Consider your Julie's, and
cry only for her. Consider the different position of my sex and of
yours in our common misfortunes, and decide which of us is most
to be pitied. To pretend to be insensitive while in the grip of passion, to appear joyful and content while prey to a thousand griefs,
to have a calm appearance and a distressed mind, to speak always
otherwise than we think, to disguise all we feel, to be deceitful
through obligation and to speak untruths through modesty—that
is the usual position of all girls of my age. Thus we spend the prime
of our youth under the tyranny of propriety, which at length is
augmented by that of our parents who force us into an unsuitable
marriage. But in vain are our inclinations restrained; the heart
gives laws only to itself. It escapes enslavement; it bestows itself
of its own accord. Under an iron yoke, not imposed by Heaven, only
the body but not the soul is subdued; person and faith remain
separately engaged, and an unfortunate victim is forced into crime
by being forced in one respect or the other to fail in the sacred duty
of fidelity. Are there girls more prudent than I? Ah, I know there
are! Are there those who have not been in love at all? How fortunate they are! Have they resisted passion? I have attempted to resist. Are they more virtuous? Do they love virtue better than I? Had
it not been for you, for you alone, I should have always loved
it. Is it then true that I no longer love virtue? . . . You have
ruined me, and it is I who console you! . . . But what is going to
become of me? . . . How weak is friendship's consolation where
that of love is lacking! Who will console me, then, in my misery?
What a frightful fate I face, I who for having lived in sin see nothing but a fresh sin in the marriage bonds, abhorred and perhaps
inevitable! Where shall I find tears sufficient to weep for my fault
and my lover if I yield? Where shall I find strength enough
to resist in my present dejection? I think I already can see the fury
of an angered father! I think I already can feel my inmost self
moved by the cry of nature, or my heart rent by the pangs of love!
Deprived of you, I remain without resource, without support, without hope. The past degrades me, the present afflicts me, the future affrights me. I thought I was doing everything for our happiness by sending you away; I have only made us more miserable by
preparing the way for a more cruel separation. Our fleeting pleas-

ures are no more, remorse remains behind, and the shame which humiliates me is without alleviation.

It is for me, it is for me to be weak and miserable. Let me weep and suffer; my tears are as inexhaustible as my fault is irreparable, and even all-healing time only offers me fresh reasons for tears. But you who have no violation to fear, whom shame does not degrade, whom nothing forces basely to disguise your real sentiments, you who feel only the blow of misfortune and at least enjoy your former virtues, how dare you lower yourself to the point of sighing and sobbing like a woman and of flying into a passion like a madman? Have I not deserved enough scorn on your account without your augmenting it by making yourself scornful, and without your crushing me with both my own shame as well as yours? Recall, then, your resolution, learn how to bear misfortune, and be a man. Be again, if I dare say so, the lover Julie has chosen. Ah, if I am no longer worthy of inspiring your courage, remember at least what I once was, deserve what for your sake I have ceased to be, and do not dishonor me twice.

No, my respectable friend, it is not you at all whom I recognize in that effeminate letter which I wish to forget forever and which I consider already disclaimed by you. I hope, wholly debased, wholly confused as I am, I dare to hope that my memory does not inspire feelings so base, that my image still reigns with more honor in a heart which once I could inflame, and that I shall not have to reproach myself, along with my frailty, for the cowardice of the one who caused it.

Happy in your misfortune, you have found the most precious compensation which is known to sensitive souls. Heaven, in your grief, gives you a friend and allows you to wonder if that which it gives you is not worth more than that which it takes away. Admire and cherish that too generous man who at the expense of his ease deigns to take care of your life and your reason. How affected you would be if you knew all that he has wished to do for you! But what use is it to inspire your gratitude by aggravating your grief? You do not need to know how much he loves you to be aware of all his worth, and you cannot respect him as he deserves to be without loving him as you must.

❧ LETTER VIII ❧

From Claire

YOU ARE more passionate than delicate, and you know better how to make sacrifices than to turn them to account. What do you mean by writing to Julie with a reproachful tone in her present condition, and because you are suffering must you lay the blame on her who is suffering even more? I have told you a thousand times that in my life I have never seen a lover so grumbling as you. You are always ready to argue over everything, and love for you is only a state of war; or if sometimes you are tractable, it is for the purpose of then complaining that you have been so. Oh, how such lovers are to be feared and how fortunate I consider myself to have never desired any but those whom I can dismiss when I like without it costing anyone a tear!

Believe me, change your language with Julie if you want her to survive; it is too much for her to bear both her own misery and your displeasure. Learn for once to treat her overly sensitive heart with caution; you owe her the most tender consolations. Be fearful of increasing your own misfortunes by complaining of them, or at least complain of them only to me who am solely responsible for your separation. Yes, my friend, you have guessed correctly. I suggested to her the course which the danger to her honor necessitated, or rather, I forced her to take it by exaggerating the hazard. I prevailed also on you to depart, and we all have done our duty. I did more, however; I prevented her from accepting his Lordship's offers. I have kept you from being happy, but Julie's happiness is dearer to me than yours. I knew that she could not be happy after having left her parents in shame and despair, and I have difficulty, with my knowledge of you, in understanding what happiness you could enjoy at the expense of hers.

Be that as it may, such was my conduct and my offense, and since you take pleasure in scolding those who love you, you may blame me alone for that. If in this you do not cease being ungrateful, you at least cease being unjust. As for me, in whatever manner you behave to me, I shall always be the same towards you. You will be dear to me as long as Julie loves you, and I could not possibly say more. I am sorry neither for assisting nor for opposing your love. The disinterested zealousness of friendship which has always guided me justifies me equally in what I have done for and against you, and if at any time I took an interest in your passion, more perhaps than would seem to become me, the testimony of my heart is enough for my tranquillity. I shall never blush for the services I have been able to render my friend, and reproach myself only for their uselessness.

I have not forgotten what you once taught me of the fortitude of the wise man under misfortunes, and I should be able, it seems to me, to remind you of some precepts to that purpose. But Julie's example teaches me that a girl of my age is to a philosopher of yours as bad as a preceptor as she is dangerous as a pupil, and it would not become me to give lessons to my teacher.

⚜ LETTER IX ⚜

From Lord Bomston to Julie

WE HAVE TRIUMPHED, charming Julie. Our friend's mistake has brought back his reason. The shame of having found himself for a moment in the wrong has dissipated all his fury and has made him so tractable that henceforth we shall manage him all we please. With pleasure I see that the fault with which he reproaches himself leaves him more remorse than resentment, and I know he esteems me, for he is humble and confused before me, but not embarrassed or constrained. He senses his injustice too well for me to remember it, and wrongs thus acknowledged do more honor to the one who atones for them than to the one who pardons them.

I have profited from this change and from the effect it has produced to enter into some necessary arrangements with him before we separate, for I cannot defer my departure much longer. As I expect to return next summer, we have agreed that he should go wait for me in Paris and that afterwards we should go to England together. London is the only stage worthy of great talents, where their career is most extensive.* His are superior in many respects, and I do not despair of seeing him, in a short time with the help of some friends, make a career for himself worthy of his merit. I shall explain my view to you in more detail when I pass through your neighborhood. Meanwhile, you know that through success one can remove many difficulties, and that there are modes of distinction which can compensate for an inferior birth, even in your father's mind. That, it seems to me, is the only expedient left to be tried to bring about your mutual happiness, since fortune and prejudice have deprived you of all others.

I have written to Regianino to come join me post haste, so that I may profit from him during the eight or ten days I will still spend with our friend. His sadness is too profound to leave room for much conversation. Music will fill the empty silences, allow him to dream, and gradually change his sorrow into melancholy. I am waiting for that state in order to leave him to himself. I should not dare trust him alone before. As for Regianino, I shall return him to you when I pass through and shall not take him back until I return from Italy, a time when, judging by the musical progress that you both have already made, you will no longer need him. As for the present, surely he is useless to you, and I am depriving you of nothing by taking him from you for a few days.

✤ LETTER X ✤

To Claire

WHY MUST I finally have my eyes opened? Would that I had shut them forever, rather than look on the degradation into which I have

---

* This is to entertain a curious prejudice in favor of his country, for I hear talk that there is no place in the world where, generally speaking, foreigners are less well received and find more obstacles to their advancement than in England. Because of the taste of the nation, they are encouraged in nothing there. But let us also agree that the Englishman hardly asks others for the hospitality that he refuses them in his country. In what court outside that of London does one see these proud islanders cringing servilely? To what country outside their own do they go to seek to make their fortunes? They are hard-hearted, it is true; this hardness does not displease me when it is consistent with justice. I think it well that they should be nothing but Englishmen, since they have no occasion to be men. [*Rousseau*]

fallen, rather than find myself the least of men, after having been the most fortunate! Charming and generous friend, you who were so often my protectress, again I dare to pour out my shame and my grief to your compassionate heart; again I dare to beg for your consolations against the feeling of my own unworthiness. Abandoned by myself, I dare to resort to you. Heavens, how could so despicable a man ever be loved by her, or how could so divine a passion fail to refine my soul? How she must now be ashamed of her choice, she whom I am no longer worthy to name! How she must sigh to see her image profaned in a heart so cringing and so base! How she must disdain and hate the man who could love her and yet be nothing but a coward! You shall know all my mistakes, charming cousin;* you shall know my crime and my repentance. Be my judge and let me die, or be my intercessor and let the person who creates my destiny condescend again to be its arbiter.

I shall not speak to you of the effect which this unforeseen separation had on me. I shall say nothing to you of my stunned grief and my insane despair. You will judge me only too much by the incredible distraction into which they both led me. The more aware I was of the horror of my situation, the less I believed it possible for me to renounce Julie voluntarily; and the bitterness of these sentiments, joined with the astonishing generosity of Lord Bomston, made me conceive suspicions which I shall never remember without horror and which I cannot forget without ingratitude to the friend who has pardoned me for them.

In my delirium, putting together all the circumstances attending my departure, I imagined I recognized a premeditated plan in it, and I dared to attribute it to the most virtuous of men. Scarcely had this frightful suspicion entered my mind than everything seemed to me to confirm it. His Lordship's conversation with Baron d'Étange; the tone, a little insinuating, which I reproached him for having affected during it; the quarrel which ensued; the prohibition against Julie's seeing me; the resolution to make me leave; the diligence and the secrecy of the preparations; the conversation which he had with me the night before; finally the rapidity with which I was forced rather than led away—everything seemed to prove a plan on his Lordship's part to separate me from Julie, and his return near her which I knew he intended ended by revealing, to my way of thinking, the purpose of his attentions. I resolved, however, to get still better information before bringing it out in the open, and with

* In imitation of Julie, he calls her "my cousin"; also in imitation of Julie, Claire calls him "my friend." [*Rousseau*]

this intention I contented myself in examining things with greater care. But everything increased my ridiculous suspicions, and his zealous humanitarianism inspired no kindness toward me from which my blind jealousy did not extract some indication of his perfidy. In Besançon, I knew that he had written to Julie, without communicating to me the contents of his letter, without even speaking to me of it. Therefore, I considered myself sufficiently convinced and I waited only for her reply, over which I indeed expected to find him displeased, to come to the explanation with him which I was contemplating.

Last night we got in rather late, and I knew that there had been mail from Switzerland, which I did not mention as we parted. I allowed him time to open it; in my room I heard him murmuring some words as he read. I listened attentively.

"Ah Julie!" he was saying in broken sentences, "I wanted to make you happy . . . I respect your virtue . . . but I pity your mistake. . . ."

At these words and others like them which I distinguished perfectly, I was no longer in control of myself. I put my sword under my arm; I opened, or rather, I burst in the door; I went in like a madman. No, I shall not defile this paper nor your eyes with the insults that rage dictated to me in order to urge him to duel with me immediately.

Oh my cousin! It was then above all that I was able to recognize the influence of true wisdom, even over the most sensitive men, when they will listen to its voice. At first he could understand nothing of my words, and he mistook them for a real delirium. But the perfidy of which I was accusing him, the secret plans for which I was reproaching him, that letter from Julie which he was still holding and which I was mentioning to him incessantly finally made him recognize the reason for my furor.

He smiled, then said coolly to me, "You have lost your reason, and I do not duel with madmen. Open your eyes, blind as you are," he added in a more gentle tone. "Is it really I whom you accuse of betraying you?"

I sensed in the tone of these words an inexpressible quality which was not that of a perfidious man. The sound of his voice struck my heart; I had no sooner met his looks before all my suspicions vanished, and I began with dismay to see my folly. He instantly perceived this change; he held out his hand to me.

"Come," he said to me, "if you had not recollected yourself before my justification, I should never have seen you again. Now that you are rational, read this letter and for once recognize your friends."

I wanted to refuse to read it, but the ascendancy which so many advantages gave him over me made him insist in an authoritative tone, so that, in spite of my dissipated suspicions, my secret desire to read it was only too well assisted.

Imagine what state I found myself in after reading that letter which informed me of the extraordinary beneficence of the man whom I was presuming to berate with so much indignity. I threw myself at his feet, and with a heart charged with admiration, with remorse, and with shame, I clasped his knees with all my strength, unable to utter a single word. He received my penitence as he had received my insults, and required from me as the price of the pardon he condescended to grant me only that I should never put myself in opposition to the good he would try to do for me. Ah, let him henceforth do what he pleases! His sublime soul is above that of mankind, and we are no more permitted to resist his beneficence than we are to withstand that of the Deity.

Next he gave me the two letters which were addressed to me, which he had not wanted to give me before he had read his own and was informed of your cousin's decision. Reading them, I saw what kind of lover and friend Heaven has given me; I saw how it has gathered sentiments and virtues about me in order to make my remorse more bitter and my meanness more despicable. Tell me, who then is this unique mortal whose least influence is in her beauty, and who, like the eternal powers, makes herself equally adored both through the good and through the evil she does? Alas! She has robbed me of everything, the cruel woman, and I love her more for it. The more miserable she makes me, the more I find her perfect. It seems that all the torment she causes me is a new instance of her merit for me. The sacrifice she has just made to the sentiments of nature makes me desolate and enchants me; in my eyes it augments the value of that which she has made to love. No, her heart can make no refusal that is not of equal value to what it grants.

And you, worthy and charming cousin, you unique and perfect model of friendship that alone shall be cited among all women and whom hearts which do not resemble yours will dare to consider imaginary—ah, speak to me no more of philosophy! I scorn that deceiving parade which consists only of idle words, that phantom which is only a delusion, which stirs us to defy passions at a distance and leaves us like a blustering bully at their approach. Deign not to abandon me to my distraction; deign to restore your former kindnesses to this unfortunate man who no longer deserves them, but who desires them more ardently and needs them more than ever; deign to call me back to myself and let your sweet voice take the place of reason's in this sick heart.

No, I dare hope, I have not sunk into perpetual degradation. I feel rekindled in me that pure and holy fire with which I once burned. The example of so many virtues will not be lost on the one who occasioned them, who loves them, admires them, and wishes to imitate them ceaselessly. Oh my dear lover, whose decision I must respect! Oh my friends whose esteem I wish to regain! My soul is revived and recovers its strength and its life from yours. Chaste love and sublime friendship will restore the courage that a cowardly despair was ready to take from me. The pure sentiments of my heart will supply the place of wisdom for me. Through you I shall be all that I ought to be, and I shall compel you to forget my fall if for one moment I can raise myself again. I do not know nor wish to know what destiny Heaven is reserving for me; whatever it may be, I want to make myself worthy of that which I have already enjoyed. That deathless image which I carry within me will serve me as a shield and will make my soul invulnerable to the blows of fortune. Have I not lived enough already for the sake of happiness? Now it is for her glory that I must live. Ah, may I be able to astonish the world with my virtues so that people may one day say in admiring them, "Could he have done less? He was loved by Julie!"

P.S. Marriage bonds abhorred and *perhaps inevitable!* What do these words signify? They are in her letter. Claire, I expect anything; I am resigned, ready to bear my destiny. But these words . . . whatever happens, I shall never leave this place until I have had an explanation of those words.

❖ LETTER XI ❖

From Julie

IS IT TRUE, therefore, that my soul is not closed to pleasure and that a sentiment of joy can still penetrate it? Alas, since your departure I thought myself sensible only to sorrow, away from you I thought myself capable only of suffering, and in your absence I did not even imagine any consolations. Your extremely pleasing letter to my cousin has come to undeceive me; I read it and kissed it with tears of tenderness. It sprinkled a fresh, gentle dew upon my heart, dried by troubles and withered by sadness, and I felt by the serenity which it left within me that far away you have no less influence than close by over your Julie's affections.

My friend! What delight for me to see you recover that vigor of sentiment which becomes a courageous man! I shall esteem you more for it, and I shall despise myself less for not having completely debased the dignity of a chaste love nor corrupted two hearts at once. I shall tell you more, now that we can speak freely of our affairs; what was aggravating my despair was to see that yours was depriving us of the only resource which we had left, the use of your talents. Now you know the worthy friend that Heaven has given you. Your whole life would not be too long to deserve his good deeds; it will never be long enough to atone for the injury which you have just done him, and I hope that you will no longer need another lesson in order to restrain your impetuous imagination. It is under the protection of that respectable man that you will enter the world; it is with the help of his influence, it is guided by his experience that you will try to revenge yourself for neglected merit, for the severity of fortune. Do for him what you would not do for yourself; try at least to respect his kindness by not making it useless. Look what a joyous prospect is still offered you; look what success you are to expect in a career in which everything conspires to favor your zeal. Heaven has lavished its gifts on you; your auspicious nature, cultivated by your taste, has endowed you with every talent. At less than twenty-four, you combine the graces of your age with the maturity that compensates later for the passage of the years.

Frutto senile in su 'l giovenil fiore.
PETRARCH

Aged fruit surpasses the youthful.

Study has not blunted your vivacity nor made your person less active; insipid gallantry has not contracted your spirit nor besotted your reason. Ardent love, by inspiring in you all the sublime sentiments which are its offspring, has given you that elevation of thought and that justness of mind from which it is inseparable.* In

---

* Justness of mind inseparable from love? Simple Julie, it does not show here in yours. [Rousseau]

its gentle warmth, I have seen your soul unfold its splendid qualities, like a flower opening in the sun's rays. You have both all that
which leads to fortune and all that which sets you above it. To obtain the world's respects, you needed only to condescend to lay claim
to them, and now I hope that an object more dear to your heart
will give you the ardor for them which they do not in themselves
deserve.

Oh my sweet friend, are you going far away from me? . . . Oh my
beloved, are you going to fly from your Julie? . . . It must be so;
we must separate if one day we wish to see each other happy again,
and the result of the pains you are going to take is our last hope.
May so dear an idea inspire you, console you during this bitter
and long separation! May it inspire you with that ardor which sur-
mounts obstacles and masters fortune! Alas, the world and its affairs
will be continual distractions for you and will be a helpful diversion
from the pangs of absence! But I am to remain left to myself alone
or subject to persecutions, and everything will compel me to miss
you ceaselessly. I shall be fortunate at least if groundless alarms do
not aggravate my real torments and if besides my own evils I do
not feel within me all those to which you are going to be exposed!

I shudder to think of the risks of a thousand kinds that your life
and your morals are going to run. In you I place all the confidence that a man can inspire; but since fate separates us, ah my
friend, why are you only a man? What advice you will need in that
unknown world in which you are about to entangle yourself! It is
not fitting for me—young, inexperienced, less qualified by study
and reflection than you—to give you advice on this head; that is a
duty I leave to Lord Bomston. I limit myself to charging you with
two things, for they pertain more to sentiment than to experience,
and though I know the world very little, I think I know your heart
very well: never forsake virtue, and never forget your Julie.

I shall not remind you of all those subtle philosophical arguments
which you yourself have taught me to despise, which fill so many
books and have never made one man virtuous. Ah! Those sorry
reasoners! What sweet delights their hearts have never felt nor
given! Leave these idle moralists, my friend, and consult your inmost heart; it is there that you will always rediscover the source of
that sacred fire which inflamed us so many times with love for the
sublime virtues. It is there that you will see that eternal image of
true beauty, the contemplation of which inspires us with a holy enthusiasm, an image which our passions defile ceaselessly but can

never efface.* [12] You have received from Heaven that happy
inclination for all that is good and virtuous. Listen only to your own
desires; follow only your natural inclinations; think above all of our
first affections. As long as those innocent and delightful moments
shall come back in your memory, it is not possible that you should
cease to love that which made them so sweet, that the charm of
the morally beautiful should be effaced from your soul, nor that you
should ever desire to obtain your Julie by methods unworthy of
you. How can one enjoy a pleasure for which he has lost the taste?
No, to be able to possess what one loves, it is necessary that the heart
that loved it should be kept the same.[13]

Therefore, never forget this Julie who was yours and whose heart
will never be another's. I can say nothing more to you, in the dependent state in which Heaven has placed me. But after having
charged you with fidelity, it is only fair to leave you with the sole
pledge of mine that is in my power. I have consulted not my duties
—my distracted mind no longer knows them—but my heart, the last
guide of those who can follow no other, and here is the result of its
inspirations: I shall never marry you without the consent of my
father, but I shall never marry anyone else without your consent.
On that I give you my word, which will be sacred whatever happens,
for there is no human power which can make me be unfaithful.
Therefore, be not disquieted over what may befall me in your absence. Go, my amiable friend, and seek under the auspices of tender
love a fortune worthy of rewarding it. My destiny is in your hands,
as much as it is in my power to commit it to you, and it will never
be altered except with your consent.

* The true philosophy of lovers is that of Plato; while the passion lasts, they
never have any other. A sensitive man cannot forsake this philosopher; a cold
reader cannot endure him. [Rousseau]

✤ LETTER XII ✤

To Julie

O Qual fiamma di gloria, d'onore,
Scorrer sento per tutte le vene,
Alma grande parlando con te!
                        METASTASIO

O what flame of glory, of honor
I feel coursing through my veins,
Great soul, in speaking with you!

JULIE, let me catch my breath. You make my blood course, you thrill
me, you make me palpitate. Like your heart, your letter burns with
the holy love of virtue, and you have brought its celestial flame to the
inmost recesses of mine. But why so many exhortations when only
commands were required? Be sure that if I ever forget myself to the
point of needing reasons in order to do good, at least it is not your
fault; your will alone is enough for me. Are you not aware that I
shall always do what pleases you and that I would even do evil before being able to disobey you? Yes, I should have burned down
the Capitol if you had commanded me to, because I love you more
than everything. But do you really know why I love you so? Ah! Incomparable girl! It is because you can never desire anything but
good, and because my love for your virtue makes my love for your
charms more invincible.

I am leaving, encouraged by the pledge you have just given me,
but you could have spared yourself the trouble, for to promise to be
no other's without my consent is to promise only to be mine, is it
not? As for me, I speak more freely, and right now as a man of honor
I give you my word, never to be broken: in the career in which I am
going to try my hand to please you, I do not know to what destiny
fortune is calling me, but never will the bonds of love or of marriage unite me to another than Julie d'Étange. I live, I exist only
for her, and I shall die either unmarried or as her husband. Adieu,
time is short and I am leaving immediately.

❖ LETTER XIII ❖

To Julie

LAST NIGHT I arrived in <u>Paris</u>, and he who could not live separated from you by two streets is now more than a hundred leagues from you. Oh Julie! Pity me, pity your unhappy friend. If slow streams of my blood had marked that extremely long road, it would have seemed shorter to me, and I would not have felt my spirits fail with more languor. Ah, if at least I knew the time which was to rejoin us as well as the space which separates us, I could compensate for the distance between places by the progress of time, and every day taken from my life I could count the steps which would bring me closer to you! But this career of sorrows is covered by the gloom of the future. The time which is to bring it to an end is concealed from my feeble sight. Oh doubt! Oh torment! My restless heart seeks you and finds nothing. The sun rises and no longer gives me hope of seeing you. It sets and I have not seen you. Void of pleasure and joy, my days slip away in one long night. In vain I have tried to rekindle my extinguished hope; it offers me only uncertain assistance and suspicious consolation. Dear and tender friend of my heart—alas!— what miseries must await me if they are to equal my past happiness?

Let this sadness not alarm you, I beg you; it is the passing effect of solitude and reflections of my journey. Do not be afraid of the return of my former weaknesses. My heart is in your hands, my Julie, and since you sustain it, it will no longer permit itself to be depressed. One of the consoling ideas which are the fruit of your last letter is that at present I find myself supported by a double strength, and though love should have prostrated mine, nevertheless I should still gain, for the courage which comes to me from you sustains me much better than I could sustain myself. I am convinced that it is not good for a man to be alone. Human souls need to be joined together in pairs in order to be worth their full value, and the united strength of two friends, like that of the bars of an artificial magnet, is incomparably greater than the sum of their individual forces. Divine friendship, this is your triumph! But what is even friendship next to that perfect union which connects the whole energy of friendship with bonds a hundred times more sacred? Where are those gross men who represent the transports of love as only a fever of the senses, as a desire of a debased instinct? Let them come, let them observe, let them feel what is taking place in my inmost heart. Let them see an unhappy lover, separated from her he loves, uncertain of ever seeing her again, hopeless of recovering his lost felicity, but yet inspired by those immortal fires which he received from your eyes and which your sublime sentiments have fed, ready to defy fortune, to undergo its reverses, to see himself even deprived of you, and to practice the virtues that you have instilled in him as the worthy tribute to that adorable image which will never be effaced from his soul. Julie, ah, what would I have been without you? Dispassionate reason would have enlightened me, perhaps; as a cool admirer of virtue, at least I should have respected it in others. Now I shall do more; I shall be capable of practicing it zealously, and penetrated by your wise lessons, I shall one day cause those who have known us to say, "Oh, what men we should all be if the world were full of Julies and of hearts who were capable of loving them!"

Meditating on your last letter while traveling, I decided to gather together all those you have written me, now that I can no longer receive your counsel from your own lips. Although there is not one of them which I do not know by heart—and know well by heart, you can believe me—I still like to reread them ceaselessly, were it only to see again the characters of that dear hand which alone can constitute my happiness. But the paper wears away imperceptibly, and before they are in pieces I intend to copy them all in a blank book which I have just chosen expressly for that purpose. It is rather thick, but I am thinking of the future, and I hope I do not die young enough to be limited only to this volume. I am setting apart my evenings to this charming occupation, and I shall proceed slowly in order to prolong it. This precious collection will never leave me during my life. It will be my manual in the world I am about to enter; it will be the antidote for me against the maxims that are inhaled there; it will console me in my misery; it will prevent or correct my mistakes; it will instruct me during my youth; it will edify me always—and to my knowledge these will be the first love letters ever put to this use.

As for the last one, which I have now before me, excellent as it seems to me, I nevertheless find in it one thing to omit. This is a view already quite strange, but what must be even more so is that this thing is precisely one which concerns you, and that I reproach you for even having thought of writing it. Why do you speak to me of fidelity, of constancy? Once you knew my love and your power better. Ah Julie! Do you inspire perishable sentiments, and though I had promised you nothing, could I ever cease being yours? No, no it was at the first glance from your eyes, at the first word from your lips, at the first ecstasy of my heart that in it was lit this eternal flame which nothing can extinguish any more. Had I seen you only that first moment, it had already been done; it was too late ever to be able to forget you. And should I forget you now? Now that, intoxicated with my past happiness, the very remembrance of it is sufficient to make me happy still? Now that, subdued by the force of your charms, I live only in them? Now that my former heart has disappeared and that I live by the one you have inspired in me? Now, oh Julie, that I am out of temper with myself for expressing so poorly to you all that I feel? Ah! Let all the beauties of the universe try to seduce me! Is there another beside yours in my eyes? Let everything conspire to wrench you from my heart. Let them pierce it, let them rend it, let them break this faithful mirror of Julie; her pure image will not cease to be reflected even in the smallest fragment. Nothing is capable of destroying it. No, the supreme power itself could not go that far; it can annihilate my soul, but not permit it to exist and then make it cease to adore you.

When he passes through, his Lordship has taken it upon himself to give you an account of what concerns me and of his projects in my favor, but I am afraid that he will not strictly fulfill this promise in regard to his present arrangements. Learn that he dares to abuse the right that his benevolence gives him over me by extending it even beyond propriety. I see myself, through a pension which he has been careful to make irrevocable, in a condition to make an appearance much above my birth, and that is perhaps what I shall be forced to do in London in order to submit to his designs. As for here, where no affairs engage me, I shall continue to live in my own manner, and shall not be tempted to use the surplus of my maintenance in frivolous expenditures. You have taught me, my Julie, that the principal needs, or at least the most sensible ones, are those of a beneficent heart, and as long as one individual lacks the necessaries of life, what virtuous man has a surplus?

❧ LETTER XIV ❧

To Julie

WITH A SECRET horror I am entering this vast wasteland of a world. This chaos offers me only a frightful solitude, in which a dismal silence reigns. My oppressed soul seeks to burst forth but finds itself everywhere restrained more closely. I am never less alone than when I am by myself, an ancient writer said; as for me, I am only alone in the crowd, where I can be neither with you or with others. My heart would speak, but it senses that it is not heard. It would answer, but nothing is said which can reach it. I do not understand the language of the country, and no one here understands mine.

It is not that I have not been shown a great welcome, much friendliness, and kind attentions, or that a thousand officious solicitudes do not seem on the wing to oblige me. But that is precisely what I complain of. How can one be the friend so quickly of someone he has never seen before? The honest concern for humanity, the simple and touching outpouring of a sincere heart has a language quite different from the false demonstrations of politeness and the misleading appearances that the custom of society demands. I am greatly afraid that the man who treats me at first sight like a friend of twenty years standing might treat me at the end of twenty years like a stranger, if I had some important service to ask of him; and when I see such profligate men take so tender an interest in so many people, I readily presume that they are really taking one in nobody. [14]

Thus the men to whom one speaks are not at all those with whom one communicates. Their sentiments do not come from their hearts, their insight is not in their character, their speech does not represent their thoughts. Of them only their appearance is perceived, and one is in a company almost as if before a moving picture, where the unmoving spectator is the only being capable of self-motion.

Such is the idea I have formed of society at large based on that which I have seen in Paris. This idea is perhaps more pertinent to my individual situation than to the real state of things and will no doubt be reformed under new illuminations. Besides, I only frequent the groups to which Lord Bomston's friends have introduced me, and I am convinced that one must descend into the other classes to know the true manners of a country, for those of the rich are everywhere almost all the same. I shall try to inform myself better later. Meanwhile, judge if I am right in calling this crowded scene a wasteland, and of being alarmed by a solitude in which I find only an empty appearance of sentiment and of sincerity which changes every instant and falsifies itself, in which I see only spectres and phantoms which strike the eye for a moment and disappear as soon as one tries to touch them? Until now I have seen a great many masks; when shall I see the faces of men?

❧ LETTER XV ❧

From Julie

YES, MY FRIEND, we shall be united in spite of our separation; we shall be happy despite fate. It is the union of hearts which constitutes their true felicity. Their attraction does not understand the law of distances, and ours would be in contact from the two poles of the earth. Like you, I find that lovers have a thousand means of soothing the feeling of absence and of being brought together in a moment. Sometimes we even see each other still more often than when we saw each other every day, for as soon as one of us is alone, immediately both are together. If you enjoy this pleasure every evening, I enjoy it a hundred times a day. I am more alone, I am surrounded by remembrances of you, and I would be incapable of looking upon the objects gathered about me without seeing you ever near me.

> Qui cantò dolcemente, e qui s'assise:
> Qui si rivolse, et qui ritenne il passo;
> Qui co' begli occhi mi trafise il core:
> Qui disse una parola, et qui sorrise.
> PETRARCH

> Here he sang sweetly, and here he sat:
> Here he turned about, and here he paused;
> Here with fair eyes he pierced my heart:
> Here he spoke a word, and here he smiled.

But you, are you capable of placing yourself in these peaceful situations? Are you capable of enjoying a tranquil and tender love which speaks to the heart without stirring the senses, and are your griefs today more prudent than your desires once were? The tone of your first letter causes me to tremble. I fear these deceiving raptures, so much the more dangerous when the imagination which excites them has no limits, and I am afraid that you are insulting your Julie in your very love for her. Ah, you do not feel, no, your too indelicate heart does not feel how much love is offended by vain homage. You consider neither that your life is mine nor that one often hastens to his death in believing he is helping nature. Sensual man, will you never know how to love? Remember, remember that sentiment, so calm and so sweet, which once you experienced and which you described in a manner so touching and so tender.* If such is the most delightful that has ever been savored by happy lovers, it is the only one permitted to separated lovers, and when one has been able to enjoy it, though for a moment, he should no longer regret the loss of any other. I remember some reflections we made, while reading your Plutarch, on a depravity of taste which insults nature. Were such sorry pleasures only not mutual, that would be enough, we said, to make them insipid and despicable. Let us apply the same conclusion to the wanderings of an over-active imagination; it will be no less applicable. Wretch! What do you enjoy when you are the only one to enjoy it? These solitary, sensual pleasures are lifeless pleasures. Oh love! Yours are animated. It is the union of souls which gives life to them, and the pleasure we excite in those we love makes that which it gives us valuable.[15]

The inseparable cousin, in whose room I am writing you this letter, claims that I was at the beginning in that state of playfulness that love inspires or allows, but I don't know what has become of it. In proportion as I proceeded, a certain languor pervaded my heart and hardly leaves me strength to write you the abuses the wicked creature wanted to address to you.[16]

But do you really know what put us both in such good humor? It is her forthcoming marriage. The contract was signed last night, and the day fixed is a week from Monday. If ever a love was gay, it is assuredly hers. We have never in our life seen a girl so jestingly in love. The good Monsieur d'Orbe, whose head also is turned, is enchanted by so gay a reception. Less hard to please than you once were, he takes pleasure in joking and looks upon the art of divert-

* Part One, Letter LV. [*Translator's note*]

ing his mistress as a masterpiece in making love. As for her, we may preach to her as we please, point out the dictates of decorum to her, tell her that, so near her marriage, she ought to assume a demeanor more serious and more grave and do honor a little better to the state she is about to leave. She considers all that as foolish affectations, and she maintains in front of Monsieur d'Orbe that on the day of the ceremony she will be in the best humor in the world and that people could not go too cheerfully to their weddings. But the little dissembler does not tell everything. I found her this morning with red eyes, and I wager that the tears of the night indeed pay for the laughs of the day. She is going to form new ties which will relax the gentle bonds of friendship; she is going to begin a manner of living different from that which was dear to her. She was content and tranquil; she is going to run the risks to which even the best marriage exposes one, and whatever she may say of it, as a pure and calm sea begins to be disturbed at the approach of the storm, her timid and chaste heart does not see the forthcoming change in her condition without some alarm.

Oh my friend, may they be happy! They are in love; they are going to be married; they will enjoy their love without obstacles, without fears, without remorse! Adieu, adieu, I can say no more.

P.S. We saw Lord Bomston only for a moment, so much was he pressed to continue his journey. With a heart full of our obligations to him, I tried to show him my feelings and yours, but I had a kind of shame about them. In truth, it is to insult a man like him to thank him for anything.

❖ LETTER XVI ❖

To Julie

WHAT CHILDREN do impetuous passions make of men! How readily does an extravagant love feed itself on shadows, and how easy it is to mislead violent desires with the most trivial objects! I received your letter with the same rapture that your presence would have caused me, and in the passionate outburst of my joy, a mere piece of paper took your place for me. One of the greatest miseries of absence, and the only one for which reason can do nothing, is the uneasiness over the actual condition of the person one loves. Her health, her life, her repose, her love—nothing escapes the apprehensions of him who has everything to lose. We are no more sure of the present than of the future, and every possible accident is realized ceaselessly in the mind of a lover who is fearful of them. At last, I can breathe, I can live: you are well, you love me, or rather, ten days ago all that was true. But who will assure me for today? Oh absence! Oh torment! Oh bizarre and distressing situation, in which we can enjoy only the past moment and in which the present does not yet exist![17]

In spite of my slow pace, in spite of my inevitable distractions, my collection of your letters was finished when your last fortunately arrived to prolong it, and I am astonished, seeing it is so short, at how many things your heart was capable of saying to me in so little space. No, I maintain that there is no reading so delightful, even for someone who does not know you, if he has a heart similar to ours. But how can one not know you as he reads your letters? How can one ascribe such an affecting manner and such tender sentiments to a character other than yours? At each sentence does one not see the sweet look in your eyes? At each word does one not hear your charming voice? What woman other than Julie has ever loved, thought, spoken, acted, written as she? Do not be surprised, then, if your letters which describe you so well sometimes have the same effect as your presence on your idolatrous lover. Rereading them, I lose my reason, my head strays in a continual delirium, a devouring flame consumes me, my blood takes fire and boils over, a frenzy causes me to tremble. I imagine I see you, touch you, press you to my breast . . . adored object, enchanting girl, source of delight and voluptuousness, seeing you, how can one not see the angelic companions created for the blessed? . . . ah come! . . . I feel her . . . she vanishes, and I embrace only a shadow . . . It is true, dear friend; you are too beautiful and you were too indulgent for my frail heart. It can forget neither your beauty nor your caresses. Your charms triumph over absence; they follow me everywhere. They make me fear solitude, and my greatest misery is that I dare not always preoccupy myself with thoughts of you.

Our friends, then, will be joined, in spite of obstacles, or rather, they are married at the moment I am writing. Amiable and worthy pair! May Heaven bestow upon them the happiness that they deserve through their prudent and peaceful love, the innocence of their conduct, the goodness of their hearts! May it give them this precious happiness of which it is so sparing toward hearts created to enjoy it! Fortunate will they be, if it grants them, alas, all that it takes from us! But nevertheless, do you not feel some sort of consolation in our grief? Do you not feel that our excessive misery is not without compensation, and that if they have pleasures which we are deprived of, we have some also which they cannot know? Yes, my sweet friend, in spite of absence, privations, alarms, in spite of despair itself, the powerful exertion of two hearts toward each other is always attended by a secret pleasure unknown to tranquil souls. It is one of the miracles of love to make us find pleasure in suffering, and we should regard as the worst of misfortunes a state of indifference and oblivion which would take all the feeling of our misery from us. Let us lament our fate, oh Julie! But let us not envy anyone. On the whole, there is perhaps no existence preferable to ours, and like the goddess who derives all her happiness from herself, hearts which glow with a celestial fire find in their own sentiments a kind of pure and delightful pleasure, independent of fortune and of the rest of the universe.

❧ LETTER XVII ❧

To Julie

AT LAST, here I am completely in the torrent. My collection of letters finished, I have begun to frequent the public diversions and take supper in the city. I spend my entire day in society, I lend my ears and my eyes to everything which impresses them, but perceiving nothing which resembles you, I wrap myself up in meditation and secretly commune with you in the midst of the noise. It is not that this busy and tumultuous life does not have some kind of attraction, or that the vast diversity of objects does not offer certain pleasures to one just come to town, but to experience them, the heart must be empty and the mind idle. Love and reason seem to unite in giving me an aversion to them. As everything is only vain appearance and all changes every instant, I have neither the time to be affected by nor the time to examine anything.

Thus I am beginning to see the difficulties in a study of the world, and I do not even know what position one must take in order to understand it well. The philosopher is too far from it; the man of the world is too close to it. The one sees too much to be able to reflect on any part; the other sees too little to pass judgment on the total picture.[18]

What course shall I take, then, I, a foreigner who can have no business in this country and whom the difference of religion alone would prevent from aspiring to anything? * I am reduced to being humble in order to instruct myself, and unable ever to be useful, to trying to make myself entertaining. I exert myself as much as possible to become polite without falseness, obliging without servility, and to taking so well what good there is in society without adopting its vices that I may be admitted to it. Every idle man who wishes to see the world must assume its manners at least up to a certain point, for by what right could one demand to be admitted among people to whom he is good for nothing and for whom he would not know the art of being agreeable? But also, when he has discovered that art, no more is asked of him, especially if he is a foreigner. He can exempt himself from taking part in cabals, in intrigues, in quarrels. If he behaves kindly toward everyone, if he neither excludes nor prefers certain women, if he keeps the secret of each group into which he is received, if he does not expose the foolishness of one house to another, if he avoids confidences, if he withstands bickering, if he retains a certain dignity everywhere, he will be able to observe the world peaceably, preserve his morals, his integrity, even his sincerity, provided that it comes from a free and not a partisan spirit. That is what I have tried to do on the advice of some informed people whom I have chosen as guides from among the acquaintances Lord Bomston has provided me. I have therefore begun to be admitted into some less numerous and more select groups. Until now I had found myself only at those regular dinner parties where one sees no other woman but the mistress of the house, where all the idlers of Paris are received however little they are known, where each pays for his dinner as he can with wittiness or flattery, and where the noisy and confused conversation does not differ much from that of tables at public taverns.

Now I am initiated into more secret mysteries. I attend private suppers, where the door is closed to all chance guests and where one

* Protestants, from Switzerland or elsewhere, were generally refused employment in France at this time. [*Translator's note*]

is sure to find only people who are all agreeable, if not to each other at least to those who receive them. There the women are less on their guard, and one can begin to study them. There more refined and more satirical conversation prevails with more decorum. It is there that, instead of public news, plays, promotions, deaths, and marriages—which were the topics of the morning—the anecdotes of Paris are discreetly reviewed; that all the secret articles of the scandalous chronicle are divulged; that the good and the bad alike are turned to pleasantry and ridicule; and that describing the characters of others, skillfully and according to his particular interest, each speaker undesignedly describes his own still much better. It is there that a little surviving circumspection in front of the lackeys has invented a certain ambiguous language, under which, pretending to make their satire more oblique, people only make it more biting. It is there, in short, that people carefully sharpen the dagger, under the pretext of making it less hurtful, but in fact in order to sink it more deeply.[19]

Thus, whatever way one looks at things, everything here is merely babble, jargon, inconsequential talk. On the stage as in society, attentive as one may be to what is said, he learns nothing of what is done, but what need is there to learn it? As soon as a man has spoken, is one not informed of his conduct? Has he not done everything? Is he not judged? Here the good man is not he who does good deeds but he who says good things, and a single unconsidered word, let fall without reflection, can do to him who speaks it an irreparable wrong which forty years of integrity would not erase. In short, although the conduct of men hardly resembles their speech, I see that they are depicted only by their words without regard for their actions. I see also that in a large city society appears more genteel, more agreeable, even more safe than among less learned people, but are the men here in fact more humane, more temperate, more just? I know nothing of it. I still see only appearances, and under these exteriors, so open and so pleasant, their hearts are perhaps more hidden, more buried within than ours. Foreign, isolated, without business, without connections, without pleasures, and desiring only to have recourse to myself, how can I pass judgment upon them?

However, I am beginning to feel the intoxication into which this busy and tumultuous life plunges those who lead it, and I am becoming giddy like a man before whose eyes a multitude of objects is made to pass rapidly. None of those which impress me engage my heart, but all together disturb and suspend its affections to the point that sometimes I forget what I am and whose I am. Each day in leaving my room, I lock up my sentiments, in order to take on others which are connected with the frivolous objects that await me. Insensibly I make judgments and reason as I hear everyone making judgments and reasoning. If sometimes I try to shake off prejudices and see things as they are, immediately I am overwhelmed with a kind of torrent of words which greatly resembles reasoning. People prove to me with illustrations that it is only a half-witted philosopher who looks at the reality of things, that the truly wise man considers them only by appearances, that he must take prejudices for principles, decorum for law, and that the highest wisdom consists in living like fools.

Compelled in this way to pervert the order of my moral affections, compelled to give a value to shadows and to impose silence on nature and on reason, I thus see disfigured that divine model I bear within me, which served both as the object of my desires and as the guide of my conduct. I float from caprice to caprice, and my tastes being incessantly enslaved by opinion, I cannot be sure for a single day of what I shall approve the next.

Confused, humiliated, struck with consternation over feeling human nature in me being degraded, and seeing myself fallen so low from that innate greatness to which our impassioned hearts had reciprocally raised us, I return in the evenings pierced by a secret sorrow, overwhelmed by a mortal disgust, my heart empty and puffed up like a balloon full of air. Oh love! Oh the pure sentiments which I possess because of it! . . . With what delight I recollect myself! With what ecstasy do I find still within me my former affections and my former dignity! How I rejoice to see there the image of virtue shining in all its brilliance, to contemplate your image there, oh Julie, seated on a throne of glory and with a breath dissipating all those delusions! I feel my oppressed soul revive, I seem to have recovered my existence and my life, and along with my love I regain all the sublime sentiments which make it worthy of its object.

❖ LETTER XVIII ❖

From Julie

I HAVE just enjoyed, my good friend, one of the sweetest sights which could ever delight my eyes. The most prudent and the most amiable of girls has at last become the most deserving and the best of wives. Full of esteem and love for her, the honest man whose hopes she has fulfilled lives only to cherish her, adore her, make her happy, and I am enjoying the inexpressible delight of being witness to the happiness of my friend, that is to say, of sharing it. You will not share it less, I am quite sure, you whom she always loved so tenderly, you who were dear to her almost since her childhood and who were the recipient of so much of her benevolence, which must have made her even more dear to you. Yes, all the sentiments she is experiencing are felt in our hearts as in hers. If they are pleasures for her, they are consolations for us, and such is the value of the friendship which unites us that the felicity of one of the three is enough to mitigate the misery of the other two.

Let us not pretend, however, that this incomparable friend is not going to forsake us in some measure. Now she is in a new order of things; now she is subject to new engagements, to new duties, and her heart which once was only ours is now owed to other affections to which friendship must give first place. What is more, my friend, we must become more scrupulous on our part in the services we impose on her zeal. We must not only consult her attachment for us and our need for her, but also what is fitting in her new situation and what can please or displease her husband. We have no need to ask what virtue would demand in such a case; the laws of friendship alone are enough. Would anyone who in his own self-interest could compromise a friend deserve to have one? When she was unmarried, she was free, she had to answer only to herself for her conduct, and the uprightness of her intentions was enough to justify her in her own eyes. She considered us as man and wife destined for each other, and her sensitive and pure heart reconciling the most chaste modesty in regard to herself with the most tender compassion for her guilty friend, she concealed my fault without sharing it. But now all is changed. She must account for her conduct to another. She has not only pledged her faith; she has resigned her liberty. Now that she is entrusted with the honor of two people at the same time, it is not enough for her to be respectable; she must be respected as well. It is not enough for her to do nothing but good; she must moreover do nothing which is not approved. A virtuous woman must not only deserve her husband's esteem but also obtain it. If he blames her, she is to blame, and even were she innocent, she is in the wrong as soon as she is suspected, for even keeping up appearances is part of her duty.

I do not clearly see if all these reasons are good ones; you will be the judge of that. But a certain inner feeling warns me that it is not good for my cousin to continue to be my confidante, nor to be the first to tell me so. I have often found myself in error over my arguments, but never over the secret feelings on which they are founded, and that makes me have more confidence in my instinct than in my reason.

From this consideration, I have already found a pretext for taking back your letters that fear of surprise made me give to her. She returned them to me with an oppression of the heart which my own made me perceive and which convinced me that I had done what was necessary. We did not have an explanation, but our expressions took the place of one. Weeping, she embraced me. Saying nothing to each other, we felt what little need the tender language of friendship has of the assistance of words.

In regard to an address to substitute for hers, I first had thought of Fanchon Anet, and she is indeed the safest intermediary we could choose. But if that young woman is in a class lower than my cousin's, is that a reason for having less respect for her in what concerns virtue? Is it not, on the contrary, to be feared that her less elevated sentiments may not make my example more dangerous for her, that what was for one only the effort of a sublime friendship may be for the other the first step to corruption, and that in abusing her gratitude I may be compelling virtue itself to serve as the instrument of vice? Ah, is it not enough for me to be guilty without procuring accomplices and without augmenting my faults with the weight of another's? Let us not consider it, my friend. I have thought of another expedient, much less safe, in truth, but also less reprehensible in that it compromises no one and involves us with no confidant. It is to write me under a fictitious name—for example, Monsieur du Bosquet—and to send the letter in an envelope addressed to Regianino, which I shall take care to intercept. Thus Regianino himself will know nothing; at the most he will have only suspicions which he would not dare confirm, for Lord Bomston, on whom his fortune depends, has answered to me for his fidelity. While our correspondence is continuing by this method, I shall see if we can return to the person whom we used during your trip to the Valais, or someone else who may be permanent and safe.

Even if I did not know the state of your heart, I should perceive by the prevailing humor of your correspondence that the life you are leading is not to your liking. The letters of Monsieur Muralt, which are complained of in France, were less severe than yours.* Like a child who is out of temper with his tutors, you revenge yourself for being obliged to study the world on the first people who teach you about it. What surprises me most is that the thing which began by disgusting you is that which predisposes all foreigners in favor of the French, namely, their reception of strangers and the general manners of their society, although by your own admission you personally should be well pleased with them. I have not forgotten your distinction between Paris in particular and large cities in general, but I see that, being unaware of what is applicable to either one or the other, you criticize without consideration, before knowing if it is slander or observation. Whatever it may be, I like the French nation, and you do not oblige me by speaking ill of it. I am indebted for the greater part of the education that we acquired together to the fine books which come from France. If our country is barbarous no longer, to whom but France are we obligated? [20] My friend, if each people has its good and its bad qualities, you should pay attention at least to the commendable facts as well as the reproachable facts.

I shall tell you more: why do you waste in idle visits the time you have left to spend where you are? Is Paris less of a theatre for talents than London, and do foreigners make their way less easily there? Believe me, all the English are not Lord Bomstons, and all the French do not resemble these fine talkers who displease you so much. Attempt something, try, make some experiments, were it only to examine their manners thoroughly, and judge these people who speak so well by their deeds. My cousin's father says that you know the constitution of the Empire and the interests of the princes. His Lordship also finds that you have studied political principles and the various systems of government rather well. I have got it in my

* Muralt was a Swiss traveler who in 1725 published his *Lettres sur les Anglais et les Français et sur les voyages,* which was generally unfavorable to the French. [*Translator's note*]

head that the country in the world where merit is most respected is that which is best for you and that you only need to be known to be employed. As for religion, why should yours be more injurious to you than another? Is not good sense security against intolerance and fanaticism? Are people more bigoted in France than in Germany? And who would prevent you from being able to follow the same career that Monsieur de Saint-Saphorin did in Vienna? * If you consider the end, must not the earliest attempts speed success? If you compare the means, is it not even more honest to advance yourself by your talents than by your friends? If you think . . . ah that sea! . . . an even longer journey . . . I would like England better if it was on this side of Paris.

With respect to this large city, should I dare mention an affectation that I notice in your letters? You who spoke to me of the women of the Valais with so much pleasure, why do you say nothing to me of Parisian women? Are these elegant and celebrated women less worth the trouble to describe than a few simple and coarse mountain women? Are you perhaps afraid of giving me some uneasiness by a picture of the most seductive creatures in the universe? Undeceive yourself, my friend. The worst you can do for my peace of mind is not to speak of them at all, and whatever you may say of them, your silence in that respect is much more suspicious to me than your praises. [21]

I don't know if it is worth the trouble to tell you that two suitors came again to see me a few days ago as if by appointment at the occasion of the wedding. One from Yverdon, lodging and hunting from chateau to chateau; the other from Germany by the Berne coach. The former is a kind of a dandy, who speaks rather boldly in order to have his repartee found witty by those who listen only to the manner of it. The other is a great timid simpleton, not with that amiable timidity which arises from the fear of displeasing but that which comes from the distress of a fool who knows not what to say and from the awkwardness of a libertine who does not feel in place near a virtuous girl. Knowing very positively my father's intentions in regard to these two gentlemen, with pleasure I took the liberty he gave me to treat them according to my whim, but I do not think that this whim may allow her who inspired them to come here to tolerate them a long time. I hate them for presuming to attack a heart in which you reign, without weapons to dispute it with you;

* Saint-Saphorin was a Swiss general who entered the service of England and became English minister to Vienna. [*Translator's note*]

if they had some I should hate them still more, but where should they acquire them, they or any other men in the whole world? No, no, be tranquil, my amiable friend. Even if I should find a merit equal to yours, if another like you should present himself, the first would still be the only one heard. Do not be uneasy, then, about these two types whom I hardly condescend to mention to you. What pleasure I should have in measuring out to them two such perfectly equal portions of aversion, so that they might resolve to leave together as they came and I might inform you of the departure of both at once.[22]

Adieu, my too dear friend. I would not end so soon but I am awaited, I am called away. I leave you regretfully, for I am cheerful and I like to share my pleasures with you. What inspires and increases them is that my mother has been better for a few days. She felt strong enough to attend the wedding and to act as a mother for her niece, or rather, her second daughter. Poor Claire wept for joy to see her. Think how I felt, I who deserve to keep her so little and am always fearful of losing her. In truth, she did the honors of the celebration with as much grace as if she were in her most perfect health; it even seems that some remaining languor makes her natural manners still more affecting. No, never was this incomparable mother so good, so charming, so worthy of being adored! . . . Do you know that several times she has asked Monsieur d'Orbe for news of you? Although she does not speak to me about you, I am not unaware that she likes you, and that if ever she were heard, our mutual happiness would be her first concern. Ah! If your heart can be sensible of this, what need it has to be so, and what debts it has to pay!

❖ LETTER XIX ❖

To Julie

WELL, MY JULIE, chide me, quarrel with me, whip me, and I shall bear everything, but nonetheless I shall continue to tell you what I think. With whom will I entrust all my sentiments if not with you who enlighten them, and with whom would my heart be permitted to speak if you refused to hear it? When I give you an account of

my observations and my judgments, it is so that you may correct
them, not so that you may approve them, and the more liable I am
to commit errors, the sooner must I inform you of them. If I censure
the evil customs which impress me in this large city, I do not excuse
myself because I write to you in confidence, for I never say anything
of a third party that I am not ready to say to his face, and in all that
which I have written to you about the Parisians, I merely repeated
what they say every day to themselves. They do not resent me for it;
they agree on a great many things. They complained of our Muralt,
I know. One sees, one feels how much he hates them, even in the
praises he gives them, and I am much mistaken if even in my adverse criticism the contrary is not to be perceived. The esteem and
the gratitude which their kindnesses inspire in me only increases my
frankness; it cannot be useless to some people, and by the way in
which everyone endures the truth from my lips, I dare believe that
they deserve to listen to it and I to speak it. In this case, my Julie,
true censure is more honorable than true praise, for praise serves
only to corrupt those who enjoy it, and the most worthless are always the most greedy after it. But censure is useful and only the deserving are capable of enduring it. I tell you sincerely that I respect
the French as the only people who truly love mankind and who are
beneficent by nature. But for that very reason, I am less disposed
to grant them that general admiration to which they lay claim, even
for the faults that they acknowledge. If the French had no virtues
at all, I should say nothing about them; if they had no vices at all,
they would not be human. They have too many praiseworthy qualities for indiscriminate praise.

As for the experiments which you mention, they are impractical,
because to carry them out I should be obliged to employ means
which do not suit me and which you yourself have forbidden. Republican austerity is not in fashion in this country; here more
flexible virtues are needed which can bow better than mine to the
interests of friends or patrons. Merit is respected, I agree; but here
the talents which lead to fame are not those which lead to fortune,
and if I should have the misfortune to possess the latter, would Julie
consent to become the wife of a parvenu? In England, it is another
thing altogether, and though manners there are perhaps still less
praiseworthy than in France, that does not prevent one from being
able to rise to fortune by more honest methods, because, the people
having more share in the government, public esteem is there a
greater means of distinguishing oneself. You are not unaware that
his Lordship's project is to use this means to my advantage and

mine to justify his zeal. The place on earth where I am farthest from you is that where I can do nothing which may bring me back to you. Oh Julie! If it is difficult to obtain your hand, it is even more so to deserve it, and that is the noble task which love imposes on me.

You relieve me of a great anxiety by giving me better news of your mother. Before my departure, I saw you already so uneasy about her that I did not dare tell you what I thought, but I found her thin, changed, and I feared some dangerous sickness. Save her, because she is dear to me, because my heart respects her, because her kindness is my only hope, and above all because she is my Julie's mother.

As for the two suitors, I shall own that I do not like that word, even in jest. Yet the manner with which you speak to me of them keeps me from fearing them, and I no longer hate those unfortunate men since you believe you hate them. But I wonder at your simplicity in thinking you are capable of hatred. Do you not see that it is insulted love which you mistake for hate? The white dove murmurs in this way when someone pursues its mate. No, Julie, no, incomparable girl, when you are able to hate something, I shall be able to cease loving you.

P.S. How I pity you for being beset by these two importunate men! For your own sake, hasten to send them away.

✤ LETTER XX ✤

From Julie

MY FRIEND, I have given Monsieur d'Orbe a package which he is charged to send to you at the address of Monsieur Silvestre, from whom you will be able to receive it, but I warn you to wait until you are alone and in your room to open it. You will find in the package a little trinket for your use.

It is a kind of amulet that lovers willingly wear. The manner of using it is curious. You must contemplate it every morning for a quarter of an hour until you feel yourself penetrated with a certain tenderness. Then you press it to your eyes, your lips, and your heart; that serves, it is said, as a preservative during the day against the

noxious air of a country infected by gallantry. To these kinds of
talismans, people even attribute a very singular electric quality, but
one which acts only between faithful lovers. It is supposed to communicate to one the impression of the other's kisses from a distance
of more than a hundred leagues. I do not guarantee the success of
the experiment; I simply know that it is your fault only if you do
not try it.

Calm yourself with regard to the two gallants, or suitors, call
them what you will, for from now on the title is unimportant to
the thing. They have left. Peace go with them. Since they are out of
my sight, I no longer hate them.

❧ LETTER XXI ❧

To Julie

YOU HAVE desired it, Julie; I must, then, describe them for you,
these charming women of Paris. Vain girl! Your charms were lacking
this tribute. Notwithstanding all your pretended jealousy, your modesty, and your love, I see more vanity than fear hidden under this
curiosity. Be that as it may, I shall be truthful; I can be so, and I
should be so with better will, even if I had more to praise. Would
they were a hundred times more charming! Would they had sufficient
allurements to render new honor to yours by the comparison!

You complained of my silence? Ah, good heavens, what should
I have told you? In reading this letter you will feel why I liked to
speak of your neighbors, the women of the Valais, and why I did
not speak at all of the women of this country. It is because the first
reminded me incessantly of you, and because the others . . . read
this, and then you will pass judgment on me. Besides, few people
think as I do about French ladies, if indeed in respect to them I am
not completely alone in my opinion. Fairness obliges me to warn you
of this, so that you may realize that I am representing them to you
not perhaps as they are but as I see them. Nevertheless, if I am unjust toward them, you will not fail to censure me again, and you will
be more unjust than I, because the fault is entirely yours alone.

Let us begin with their appearance. That is what satisfies the greater part of the observers. If I imitate them in this, the women of this country should have great cause to complain. They have an exterior character as well as an exterior face, and as neither is much more to their advantage than the other, one does them injury by judging them only by that. At the most, they have a tolerable appearance and are generally rather ill-favored than good-looking; I leave aside the exceptions. Slender rather than well-proportioned, they do not have a good figure; thus they readily prefer fashions which disguise it, and I find women of other countries rather simple for trying hard to imitate these fashions made to hide defects which they do not have.[23]

Their features are not very regular, but if they are not beautiful, they have something in their countenance which makes up for beauty and sometimes eclipses it. Their eyes are quick and brilliant but nevertheless neither penetrating nor soft. Although they pretend to animate them with the help of rouge, the expression they acquire by this means has more of the fire of anger than that of love. By nature they have sprightliness only, or if they sometimes seem to ask for a tender sentiment, they never promise it.*[24]

I warned you that I am by no means of the ordinary opinion in respect to the women of this country. People unanimously find that they give the most enchanting welcome, that their graces are most seductive, their coquetry most refined, their elegance sublime, and their art of pleasing superlative. For my part, I find their welcome shocking, their coquetry disgusting, their manners immodest. I should imagine that one's heart would be closed to all their advances, and I shall never be persuaded that they can speak of love for a moment without showing themselves incapable equally of inspiring or feeling any.

On the other hand, report teaches one to be mistrustful of their character; it represents them as frivolous, guileful, false, heedless, flighty, as talking well but not thinking at all, feeling still less, and thus wasting all their merit in idle chatter. All that seems to me to be part of their outward appearance, like their hoop-petticoats and their rouge. In Paris, one must acquire the fashionable vices, which conceal their basic sense, reason, humanity, and good nature. They are less indiscreet, less given to fidgeting than women among us, less perhaps than women of any other country. They are more

* Speak for yourself, my dear philosopher. Why should others not be more fortunate? It is only a coquette who promises everyone what she ought to reserve for one man only. [Rousseau]

soundly educated and their education is of better service to their judgment. In short, if they displease me by disfiguring all that characterizes their sex, I esteem them for their resemblances to ours which do us credit, and I find that they should be worthy men a hundred times sooner than amiable women.

Conclusion: even if Julie had not existed, if my heart had been able to allow some attachment other than that for which it was created, I should never have taken my wife in Paris, still less my mistress, but I should have readily chosen a friend there, and this treasure might have consoled me, perhaps, for not finding the other two.*

❖ LETTER XXII ❖

To Julie

SINCE I received your letter, I have gone every day to Monsieur Silvestre's to ask for the small package. It was always not yet come, and devoured by a mortal impatience, seven times I made the trip uselessly. At last, the eighth time I received the package. Scarcely did I have it in my hands than, without paying the postage, without inquiring what it was, without saying a word to anyone, I left in a daze, and having only the thought to return home, I ran so precipitously through streets I did not know that at the end of a half-hour, looking for the rue de Tournon where I lodge, I found myself in the marsh at the other end of Paris. I was obliged to take a hackney coach to get back more promptly. That was the first time this happened to me in the morning. I only use them in the afternoons for some visits, and then even with regret, for I have two very good legs and I should be quite angry if a little more affluence in my fortune made me neglect their use.

I was very nervous in my hackney coach with my package. I did not want to open it except in my room; that was your command. Besides, a sort of voluptuousness, which permits me to forget comfort

---

* I shall restrain myself from commenting upon this letter, but I doubt that a judgment which allows to the women he observes qualities which they scorn, and which denies them the only ones they value, will be very likely to please them. [Rousseau]

in ordinary things, makes me seek it carefully in true pleasures. In those I cannot bear any sort of distraction, and thus I wish to have time and ease to savor all that comes to me from you. I held that package, therefore, with an impatient curiosity which I could not overcome. I endeavored to feel what it could contain through the wrappings, and you would have said it was burning my hands to see the continual transfer it was undergoing from one to the other. It was not that by its size, its weight, the manner of your letter, I did not have some suspicion of the truth, but how could I conceive you to have found the artist and the opportunity? That is what I still cannot guess. It is a miracle of love. The more it surpasses my reason, the more it enchants my heart, and one of the pleasures it gives me is that of understanding nothing of it.

At last I arrived at my lodgings, I flew up, I locked myself in my room, I sat down out of breath, and I put a trembling hand on the seal. Oh, the first effect of the talisman! I felt my heart palpitating at each paper I removed, and I soon found myself so overcome that I was forced to get my breath for a moment at the last wrapping . . . Julie! . . . Oh my Julie! . . . the veil is torn away . . . I see you . . . I see your divine features! My lips and my heart pay them first homage; my knees bend . . . adored charms, once more you enchant my eyes. How immediate, how powerful is the magic effect of these cherished features! No, it does not require a quarter of an hour, as you claim, to feel this effect. One minute, one instant was enough to tear a thousand ardent sighs from my breast and bring back along with your image remembrance of my past happiness. Why must it be that the joy of possessing so precious a treasure is mingled with such cruel bitterness? With what anguish the portrait reminded me of the times which are no more! Seeing it, I imagined I was seeing you again; I imagined I found those delightful moments again, the memory of which now creates my life's unhappiness, the moments which Heaven gave me and took from me in its anger. Alas, the next instant undeceives me. All the grief of absence is rekindled and sharpened as the delusion which suspended it vanishes, and I am like those wretches whose torments are interrupted only to make them more sensitive to them. Gods! What torrents of passion my avid eyes absorb from this unexpected object! Oh how it revives in my inmost heart all the impetuous emotions that your presence used to call into being! Oh Julie, if it were true that it might transmit to your senses the delirium and the illusion of mine. . . . But why should it not be so? Why should not the impressions which my soul sends forth with such rapidity not reach as far as you? Ah dear friend! Wherever you may be, whatever you may be doing at the moment I am writing this letter, at the moment when your portrait is receiving all the homage your idolatrous lover addresses to your person, do you not feel your charming face bathed with tears of love and sadness? Do you not feel your eyes, your cheeks, your lips, your bosom caressed, pressed, overwhelmed by my ardent kisses? Do you not feel yourself surrounded completely by the fire from my burning lips! . . . Heavens, what do I hear? Someone is coming . . . Ah let us lock up, let us conceal my treasure . . . the importunate one! . . . Cursed be the cruel person who comes to interrupt such sweet ecstasies! . . . May he never be in love . . . or else may he live far from the one he loves![25]

11-p. letter on opera

❧ LETTER XXIV ❧

From Julie

YES, YES, I see it well. Fortunate Julie is ever dear to you. The same fire which once sparkled in your eyes glows in your last letter. In it I found again all the passion which gives me courage, and mine is excited again. Yes, my friend, fate separates us in vain. Let us press our hearts together, let us by this communication preserve their natural warmth against the chill of absence and of despair, and let all that which should loosen our attachment serve only to bind it incessantly closer.

But admire my simplicity. Since I received that letter, I have experienced something of the enchanting effects which you mention, and that jest about the talisman, although my own invention, has nevertheless taken me in and appears to me now to be true. A hundred times a day when I am alone, a trembling seizes me as if I felt you near me. I imagine that you are holding my portrait, and I am so foolish that I think I can feel the pressure of the caresses you are giving it and the kisses you are bestowing on it. My lips imagine they are receiving them; my tender heart imagines it is enjoying them. Oh sweet illusions! Oh imagination, last resource of the unhappy! Ah, if possible, be to us a reality! You are yet something to those for whom happiness no longer exists.

As for the way I devised to have this portrait done, it is indeed a contrivance of love, but believe me, if it were true that mine might work miracles, it would not have chosen this one. Here is the explanation for your bewilderment. Some time ago, we had here a miniaturist who came from Italy. He had some letters from Lord Bomston, who in giving them to him perhaps had in view what has happened. Monsieur d'Orbe wanted to profit from this opportunity to have a portrait of my cousin. I wished to have one also. She and my mother wanted to have mine, and at my request the painter secretly made a second copy. Then without troubling myself about the copy or the original, I cunningly chose the best likeness of the three to send to you. This was a deception over which I did not hesitate much, for a little more or less resemblance hardly matters to my mother and my cousin; but the homage you would pay to a face other than mine would be a sort of infidelity, by so much the more dangerous as my portrait would be better than I, and I do not want you in any manner whatsoever to acquire a liking for charms I do not possess. Moreover, if it had rested with me, I should have been a little less negligently dressed, but I was not heard, and my father himself wanted the portrait to remain such as it is. I beg you at least to believe that except for the head-dress, that apparel was not drawn from mine, that the painter did all as he pleased, and that he adorned my person with works of his imagination.[26]

❧ LETTER XXVI ❧

To Julie

JULIE! Oh Julie! Oh you whom once I dared call mine, whose name I now profane! The pen falls from my trembling hand; my tears flood the paper. I have difficulty in tracing the first words of a letter which ought never to be written. I can neither keep silent nor speak! Come, respectable and dear image, come to purify and fortify a heart debased by shame and broken by remorse. Sustain my failing courage; give to my contrition the power to confess the involuntary crime which your absence allowed me to commit.

What scorn you will have for me in my guilt, but much less than I have for myself! However low I shall be in your eyes, I am a hundred times more so in my own, for in seeing myself such as I am, what humiliates me most yet is to see you, to feel you in my inmost heart, in a place henceforth so little worthy of you, and to think that the memory of the truest pleasures of love was not able to protect my senses against a snare that had no lure and a crime that had no appeal.

Such is the excess of my confusion that in appealing to your clemency, I am even afraid to defile your eyes with these lines in which I confess my heinous offense. Pure and chaste soul, forgive an account which I should spare your modesty if it were not a means of atoning for my ill-conduct. I am unworthy of your kindness, I know; I am vile, base, contemptible, but at least I shall be neither hypocritical nor deceitful, and I prefer that you deprive me of your heart and my life rather than deceive you for a single moment. For fear of being tempted to seek excuses, which would only make me more criminal, I shall confine myself to giving you an exact account of what happened to me. It will be as sincere as my remorse; that is all I shall permit myself to say in my defense.

I had made the acquaintance of some officers of the guards and other young fellows among our countrymen in whom I found a worthy character which I was sorry to see spoiled by the imitation of I know not what false airs that were not suitable for them. In turn, they scoffed to see me preserve in Paris the simplicity of the old Swiss morals. They construed my precepts and my manners into indirect censure of theirs, at which they were offended, and they resolved at whatever cost to make me change my attitude. After several attempts which did not succeed at all, they contrived a better one which succeeded only too well. Yesterday morning, they came to me to propose supper at the home of the wife of a certain Colonel they mentioned, who from the report of my good sense desired, they said, to make my acquaintance. Foolish enough to be taken in by this idle story, I represented to them the propriety of first paying her a call, but they scoffed at my scruple, telling me that Swiss frankness did not agree with so much formality and that those ceremonious manners would only serve to give her an ill opinion of me. At nine o'clock, therefore, we betook ourselves to the lady's home. She came out to receive us on the staircase, something which I had not yet observed anywhere else. Entering, I saw old candles over the chimney which had just been lit and throughout a certain air of preparation which did not please me at all. The mistress of the house appeared pretty, although a little past her prime; other women almost of the same

age and with a similar figure were with her. Their rather brilliant
dress was more gaudy than tasteful, but I had already observed that
in this country this is a sign by which one can in no way judge the
position of a woman.

The first civilities took place almost as usual; the custom of
society teaches one to cut them short or to turn them into pleasantry
before they become tiresome. It was not wholly as usual as soon as
the conversation became general and serious. I thought these ladies
seemed to have a repressed and constrained manner, as if this
serious tone were not familiar to them, and for the first time since
I had been in Paris, I saw women at a loss to support a rational conversation. In order to find an easy topic, they brought up their family affairs, and as I was not acquainted with any of them, each one
spoke as she pleased. Never did I hear so much talk of the Colonel,
which astonished me in a country where the custom is to call people
by their name rather than by their rank, and where those who have
one of the latter ordinarily use other titles.

This affected dignity soon gave place to more natural behavior.
They began to chat in low voices, and unthinkingly assuming a
scarcely decent tone of familiarity, they whispered, they smiled as
they were looking at me, while the lady of the house was question-
ing me on the state of my heart in a certain bold manner hardly
suited to entice it. Supper was served, and the freedom of the table,
which seems to make no distinctions between persons but which imperceptibly puts everyone in his place, finally taught me what sort of
a place I was in. It was too late for me to back out. Therefore, putting my confidence in my aversion, I decided to devote that evening to my function as an observer and resolved to use in studying
this type of women the only opportunity I might ever have for it. I
drew little profit from my observations; they were so insensible
of their present situation, so scarcely apprehensive for the future,
and except for the tricks of their profession, they were so stupid in
all respects that contempt soon effaced the pity I first entertained
for them. In speaking even of pleasure itself, they were, I saw, incapable of feeling any. They seemed to me excessively avid after all
that could tempt their avarice. Except in that respect, I heard from
their lips no word which came from the heart. I wondered how these
honest men could endure such disgusting company. A cruel punishment to impose upon them, in my opinion, would be to condemn
them to keep such company as they themselves chose.

However, the supper was prolonged and became noisy. For want
of love, wine inflamed the guests. The talk was not tender but im-

modest, and the women tried by disordering their dress to excite the desires which should have caused that disorder. At first, all this only had a contrary effect on me, and all their efforts to seduce me served but to repel me. Sweet modesty, I said to myself, is the supreme voluptuousness of love! How a woman loses her charm at the moment she renounces it! If they knew its power, what pains they would take to preserve it, if not through virtue at least through coquetry! But one does not counterfeit modesty. There is no ruse more ridiculous than that of the woman who tries to affect it. What a difference, I was thinking still, between the coarse impudence of these creatures with their licentious ambiguities and those timid and impassioned looks, those conversations full of modesty, grace, and sentiment which . . . I dared not finish; I was ashamed of these unworthy comparisons . . . I reproached myself as if it were a crime for the delightful memories which were pursuing me in spite of myself . . . In what place was I daring to think of her . . . Alas! Being unable to dispel your dear, dear image from my heart, I endeavored to veil it.

The noise, the talk I heard, the objects which presented themselves to my view, insensibly inflamed me. My two supper partners did not cease giving me enticements which finally were pushed too far to leave me any composure. I knew that my head was whirling. I had been drinking my wine always strongly diluted. I put still more water in it, and at last I determined to drink pure water. Only then did I perceive that this pretended water was white wine, and that I had been deceived during the whole meal. I made no complaints, which would only have subjected me to raillery; I stopped drinking. It was too late; the evil was done. Drunkenness did not delay in depriving me of what little consciousness I had left. I was surprised, in coming to my senses, to find myself in a secluded bedroom, in the arms of one of these creatures, and at the same moment I knew the despair of feeling myself as guilty as I could be . . .

I have finished this frightful story. Let it no longer defile your eyes nor my memory. Oh you from whom I await my judgment, I beg for your severity, I deserve it. Whatever my punishment may be, it will be less cruel to me than the memory of my crime.

✤ LETTER XXVII ✤

Response

SET YOUR MIND at rest over the fear of having made me angry. Your letter has caused me more sorrow than anger. It is not me, it is yourself whom you have offended by licentiousness in which your heart had no part at all. But I am more afflicted by this. I should prefer to see you insult me rather than debase yourself, and the injury you do to yourself is the only kind which I cannot forgive.

Looking only at the fault for which you are ashamed, you find yourself much more guilty than you are, and I hardly see anything but imprudence in this case for which to reproach you. But what I blame you for proceeds from further back and has a deeper root than you perceive, and my friendship for you is obliged to uncover it.

Your first error was to have taken a wrong path in entering the world. The more you advance, the more you go astray, and I tremble to observe that you are lost unless you retrace your steps. You have allowed yourself to be imperceptibly led into the snare I had feared. The gross enticements of vice could not first seduce you, but evil company began by deceiving your reason in order to corrupt your virtue and has already made the first trial of its maxims on your morals.[27]

In spite of all your passion, you are the most easy-tempered of men, and in spite of the maturity of your judgment, you allow yourself to be so led by those with whom you associate that you cannot keep company with people of your age without regressing and becoming a child again in their hands. Thus you degrade yourself in thinking they are suitable for you, and you lower yourself by not choosing friends more prudent than you.

I do not reproach you for having been inadvertently led into a dishonest house, but I do reproach you for having been led there by young officers whom you should not have known, or whom at least you should not have permitted to direct your amusement. As for your project of making them converts to your principles, I find in it more zeal than prudence. If you are too serious to be their comrade, you are too young to be their tutor, and you ought to meddle with reforming others only when you have nothing left to reform in yourself.

A second fault, still more serious and much less pardonable, is to have voluntarily spent the evening in a place so little worthy of you and not to have fled the first instant you knew what sort of house you were in. Your excuses on that score are pitiable. *It was too late to back out!* As if there was some kind of decorum in such places, or that decorum ought ever to outweigh virtue, or that it was ever too late to stop oneself from doing evil! As for the confidence which you placed in your aversion, I shall say nothing of it; the event has shown you how well founded it was. Speak more sincerely to her who can read your heart; it was shame that held you back. You feared that they might make fun of you as you left. A moment of jeering made you afraid, and you preferred to expose yourself to remorse rather than raillery. Do you know what maxim you followed in that case? That which first introduces vice into an innocent soul, stifles the voice of conscience by public clamor, and represses the resolution to do good by the fear of censure. By such a maxim, one would overcome temptations yet yields to bad examples; he is ashamed of being virtuous and becomes brazen through shame, and this evil shame corrupts more chaste hearts than evil inclinations do. That is chiefly what you have to guard yourself against, for whatever you do, the fear of the ridicule that you pretend to scorn dominates you even in spite of yourself. You would sooner face a hundred dangers than one jeer, and never has so much timidity been seen united with so intrepid a heart.[28]

I do not know if your accommodating philosophy has already adopted the maxims that are said to be established in large cities for the toleration of such places, but I hope at least that you are not among those who have sufficient contempt for themselves to permit them to frequent them, under the pretext of I know not what imaginary need, felt only by men of debauched lives, as if the two sexes were in this respect of different natures and as if in absence or celibacy the honest man had need of some resources which the honest woman did not require. But if this error does not lead you to prostitutes, I am indeed afraid that it will continue to deceive your thoughts. Ah! If you are determined to be contemptible, be so at least without pretext, and do not add lying to debauchery. All these pretended needs do not have their source in nature, but in the voluntary depravity of the senses. The fond illusions of love are purified in a chaste heart and corrupt only a heart already corrupted. On the contrary, chastity is sustained by itself; desires constantly repressed become accustomed to remaining at rest, and temptations are multiplied only by the habit of succumbing to them. Friendship has twice made me overcome my reluctance to treat such a subject; this will be the last time, for in what name should I hope to obtain that influence over you which you have refused to virtue, *3/p advice* to love, and to reason?[29]

I ought to use with you all the frankness of friendship in the critical situation you seem to me to be in, for fear that a second step toward licentiousness might finally plunge you into it past all hope before you might have the time to recollect yourself. But now I cannot conceal from you, my friend, how much your prompt and sincere confession has affected me, for I know how much the shame of that avowal has cost you and consequently how much that of your fault weighs upon your heart. An involuntary error is pardoned and forgotten easily. But for the future, hold well to this maxim from which I shall never swerve: he who can be deceived twice on these occasions was not actually deceived the first time.

Adieu, my friend. Look after your health carefully, I beg you, and bear in mind that there must remain no trace of a crime which I have pardoned.[30]   *1p on politics*

✤ LETTER XXVIII ✤

From Julie

ALL IS RUINED! All is discovered! I no longer find your letters in the   *up 1st.* place where I had hidden them. They were still there yesterday evening. They could have been taken away only today. My mother alone can have found them. If my father sees them, it means my life! Oh, what good would it be if he did not see them, if I must renounce . . . Oh God! My mother sends for me. Where shall I fly?   *present* How shall I bear her looks? Why can I not conceal myself in the center of the earth! . . . My whole body trembles, and I am unable to take a step . . . shame, humiliation, piercing reproaches . . . I have deserved everything, I shall endure everything. But the grief, the tears of a distressed mother . . . Oh my heart, how they pierce it! . . . She is waiting for me; I can delay no longer . . . she will want to know . . . it will be necessary to tell her all . . . Regianino will be dismissed. Write me no more until you hear further . . . who knows if ever . . . I might . . . what, lie? . . . lie to my mother . . . Ah, if we must be saved by lying, adieu, we are destroyed!

PART III

❖ LETTER I ❖

From Madame d'Orbe

WHAT MISERY you cause those who love you! What tears have already been shed on your account in an unfortunate family whose tranquillity you alone disturb! Be fearful of adding the anguish of mourning to our tears. Be fearful lest the death of an afflicted mother may be the last effect of the poison you have poured into the heart of her daughter, and lest an extravagant love may at length become the source of your eternal remorse. Friendship made me endure your folly as long as a shadow of hope could nourish it, but how can I tolerate a vain constancy which honor and reason condemn and which, causing only unhappiness and grief, deserves but the name of obstinacy?

You know in what manner the secret of your passions, concealed so long from my aunt's suspicions, was discovered to her by your letters. How sensibly this tender and virtuous mother felt such a blow. Less angry with you than with herself, she lays the blame only on her blind negligence; she deplores her fatal delusion. Her most cruel affliction arises from having had too high esteem for her daughter, and her sorrow is for Julie a punishment a hundred times worse than her reproaches.

The extreme dejection of my poor cousin cannot be imagined. You must see her to realize it. Her heart seems stifled by grief, and the violence of the sentiments which oppress her gives her a stunned manner, more frightful than piercing cries. She remains day and night on her knees at her mother's bedside, with a mournful look and her eyes fixed on the ground, keeping a profound silence. She serves her with more attention and vivacity than ever, then immediately relapses into a state of dejection which would cause one to mistake her for another person. It is very evident that it is the sickness of the mother which sustains the strength of the daughter, and if the ardent desire to serve did not kindle her zeal, her dim eyes, her paleness, her extreme despondency would make me apprehensive that she herself had great need of all the attentions which she gives her mother. My aunt perceives it too, and I see by the uneasiness with which she privately recommends her daughter's health to my care how much her heart struggles against the constraint they both impose upon themselves, and how much you should be hated for disturbing so charming a union.

This constraint is augmented even more by the care of hiding it from the eyes of the passionate father, from whom the mother, trembling for the life of her daughter, wishes to hide this dangerous secret. They make it a rule to keep their old familiarity in his presence, but if maternal tenderness takes advantage of this pretext with pleasure, a confused daughter dares not yield her heart to caresses which she believes feigned and which are as cruel to her as they would be sweet if she dared have confidence in them. In receiving those of her father, she looks toward her mother with an air so tender and so humble that her heart seems to say to her through her eyes, "Ah, would that I were still worthy of receiving as much from you!"

Madame d'Étange has conversed with me privately several times, and I have easily recognized by the mildness of her reprimands and by the tone in which she spoke to me of you that Julie has made great efforts to calm her too just indignation toward us, and that she has spared no pains to justify us both at her own expense. Even your letters convey, in the depiction of an excessive love, a sort of excuse which has not escaped her; she reproaches you less for abusing her confidence than she reproaches herself for her simplicity in granting it to you. She esteems you enough to believe that no other man in your place would have resisted better than you; she blames virtue itself for your faults. She understands now, she says, that it is not an overly praised integrity which prevents an honest man in love from corrupting a chaste girl if he can, and from unscrupulously dishonoring a whole family to satisfy a moment of ardor. But what use is it to go back over the past? It is now a matter of concealing this odious mystery under an everlasting veil, of effacing the slightest trace of it if possible, and of assisting the goodness of Heaven which has left no visible evidence. The secret is confined to six safe people. The tranquillity of all whom you have

loved, the life of a mother in despair, the honor of a respectable
house, your own virtue, all these still depend on you. All prescribe
your duty to you. You can make amends for the evil you have
caused; you can make yourself worthy of Julie and justify her fault
by renouncing her, and if your heart has not deceived me, nothing
but the grandeur of such a sacrifice can be equal to the love which
requires it. Relying on the esteem I always had for your sentiments
and on the strength which must be added to it by the tenderest
union that ever was, I have promised in your name all that
you must do. Dare to undeceive me if I have presumed too much of
you, or be now what you ought to be. You must sacrifice either your
mistress or your love for each other, and show yourself either the
most cowardly or the most virtuous of men.

renounce

This unfortunate mother resolved to write you; she had even
begun a letter. Oh God, what stabs her bitter complaints would
have given you! How her affecting reproaches would have torn your
heart! How her humble prayers would have pierced you with shame.
I tore to pieces this distressful letter that you could never have endured. I could not bear this last degree of horror, to see a mother
humbled before her daughter's seducer. You are at least worthy
enough that with you one does not use such means, designed
to soften monsters and kill a sensitive man.

If this were the first effort that love had demanded of you, I might
doubt its success and hesitate over the esteem you deserve, but the
sacrifice you have made to Julie's honor by leaving this country is a
guarantee to me of that which you will make to her peace of mind
by breaking off this useless affair. The first efforts of virtue are always the most painful, and you will waste the advantage of an effort which has cost you so much by insisting on maintaining a futile
correspondence, the risks of which are terrible for your lover, without the least compensation for either, a correspondence which
only fruitlessly prolongs the torments of both. Doubt it no longer:
this Julie who was so dear to you must be nothing to him she loved
so much. In vain do you dissemble your misfortunes; you lost her
the moment you parted from her. Or rather, Heaven took her from
you, even before she gave herself to you, for her father had promised her to another before his return, and you know only too well
that the word of this inflexible man is irrevocable. Whatever you
do, insurmountable fate opposes your desires, and you will never
possess her. The only choice left for you to make is either to hurl
her into an abyss of misery and shame, or to respect in her what

you have adored and to restore to her, in place of lost happiness, at least the prudence, peace, and security of which your fatal affair deprives her.

How afflicted you would be, how consumed with regret you would be, if you could gaze on the real state of our unhappy friend and the self-abasement to which remorse and shame reduce her! How dulled is her brightness! How languid are her graces! All her sentiments, so charming and so sweet, are sadly dissolving into the single one which absorbs them. Even friendship is cooled by it; scarcely does she still share the pleasure I enjoy when we meet, and her sick heart no longer can feel anything but love and sorrow. Alas, what has become of that fond and sensitive character, that pure taste for virtuous things, that tender interest in the pains and pleasures of others? I confess, she is still sweet, generous, compassionate; the amiable habit of doing good cannot be effaced in her, but it is now only a blind habit, an inclination without reflection. She does all the same things, but she no longer does them with the same zeal. Those sublime sentiments have grown weak, that divine flame has cooled, and that angel is now no more than an ordinary woman. Ah, what a soul you have seduced from virtue!

❖ LETTER II ❖

To Madame d'Étange

PENETRATED with a sorrow which is to last as long as my life, I throw myself at your feet, Madame, not to show you a repentance which does not rest with my heart, but to atone for an involuntary crime by renouncing all that could make my life a pleasure. Just as never did human feelings approach those which your adorable daughter inspired in me, never was there any sacrifice equal to that which I shall make to the most respectable of mothers; but Julie has taught me too well how one must sacrifice happiness to duty. She has too courageously set an example for me at least once not to be capable of imitating her. If my blood would suffice to remove your distress, I should shed it in silence and complain only of giving you such a feeble proof of my zeal. But to break the sweetest, the purest, the holiest tie that has ever united two hearts, ah, that is an effort which the whole universe might not have obliged me to make, and which you alone have the right to obtain!

Yes, I promise to live far from her as long as you require it; I shall abstain from seeing her and from writing her. I swear it by your precious life, so necessary to the preservation of hers. I submit, not without fear but without a murmur, to all you deign to command of her and of me. I shall say much more still: her happiness can console me for my misery, and I shall die content if you give her a husband worthy of her. Ah, let him be found! And let him dare say to me, "I shall be more capable of loving her than you!" Madame, in vain will he have all I lack; if he does not have my heart he has nothing for Julie. But I have only this honest and tender heart. Alas! I have nothing more. Love, which unites everyone, does not elevate the person; it elevates only the sentiments. Ah! If I had dared to listen only to mine for you, how many times in speaking to you might my lips have pronounced the sweet name of mother?

Deign to rely upon oaths which will not be empty and a man who is not false. If once I could deceive your esteem, I deceived myself first. My inexperienced heart recognized the danger only when there was no longer time to escape, and I had not yet learned from your daughter that cruel art of conquering love with its own weapons that she has since so well taught me. Banish your fears, I implore you. Is there a person in the world to whom her peace of mind, her happiness, her honor are more dear than to me? No, my word and my heart are securities to you of the pledge I am taking in the name of my renowned friend as well as in my own. No indiscretion will be committed, be sure of it, and I shall breathe my last sigh without divulging to anyone what sorrow caused the end of my life. Therefore, calm that distress which consumes you and with which mine is increased. Dry the tears which wring my heart, recover your health, restore to the most tender daughter who ever lived the happiness she renounced for you, be yourself happy through her, and live, finally, so that she may value life. Ah, in spite of our love's mistakes, to be Julie's mother is still sufficient cause for happiness in life.

❧ LETTER III ❧

To Madame d'Orbe

(With the preceding letter enclosed.)

WELL, CRUEL ONE, here is my response. Burst into tears as you read it, if you know my heart and if yours is still sensitive. But above all, overwhelm me no more with that unpitying esteem which I so dearly purchase and with which you create the torment of my life.

Your barbarous hand, then, has dared to break these sweet bonds, formed under your eyes almost since childhood, which your friendship seemed to share with so much pleasure? I am, therefore, as wretched as you would have me and as I can be. Ah! Do you understand all the evil you are doing? Are you well aware that you are wringing my heart, that what you take from me is without compensation, and that it is a hundred times better to die than no longer to live for each other? Why do you speak to me of Julie's happiness? Can there be any without the heart's consent? Why do you speak to me of her mother's danger? Ah, what is a mother's life, what is my own, yours, even hers, what is the existence of the whole world next to the delightful sentiment which united us? Senseless and fierce virtue! I obey its undeserving voice; I abhor it while I do everything for it. What use are its vain consolations against the distressful agonies of the soul? No, the sullen idol of wretches, it only increases their misery by depriving them of the resources which fortune offers them. Yet, I shall obey. I shall become, if possible, insensible and ferocious like yourself. I shall forget everything in the world that was dear to me. I will no longer hear or pronounce Julie's name or yours. I will no longer be reminded unbearably of them. A resentment, an inflexible rage embitters me against so many misfortunes. A harsh obstinacy will take the place of my courage. It has cost me too much to be sensitive; it is preferable to renounce humanity.

❧ LETTER IV ❧

From Madame d'Orbe

YOU HAVE written me a distressing letter, but there is so much love and virtue in your conduct that it effaces the bitterness of your complaints. You are too generous for anyone to have the spirit to quarrel with you. Whatever anger one permits to burst forth, when he is capable of sacrificing himself in this way to the one he loves, he deserves more praise than reproach, and in spite of your insults, you were never so dear to me as you are now since I am so fully aware of all you are worth.

Give thanks to that virtue which you think you hate, and which does more for you than even your love. There is not one of us, not even my aunt, whom you have not won over by this sacrifice, the whole cost of which she knows. She could not read your letter without becoming tender; she even had the weakness to allow her daughter to see it, and the effort that poor Julie made to restrain her sighs and her tears as she read it caused her to fall in a faint.

This tender mother, whom your letters had already powerfully affected, is beginning to perceive from all she sees how much your two hearts are above ordinary rules, and how much your love contains a natural sympathy which neither time nor human efforts could efface. She who has such great need of consolation would readily console her daughter, if propriety did not hold her back, and I see her too ready to become Julie's confidante to fear she will not pardon me for having been one. Propriety forsook her yesterday to the point of saying in Julie's presence, a little indiscreetly, perhaps, "Ah, if it rested only with me. . . ." * Although she restrained herself and did not finish, I saw by the ardent kiss that Julie impressed on her hand that she had understood only too well. I am even certain that she has been minded several times to speak to her inflexible husband, but, whether it was the danger of exposing her daughter to the fury of an angered father, or whether it was fear for herself, her timidity has always held her back, and her illness, her

* Claire, in telling him this, are you less indiscreet? Is this the last time you will be so? [*Rousseau*]

pain increases so visibly that I am afraid she will be unable to execute her resolution before she has well formed it.

Be that as it may, in spite of the faults you have caused, that integrity of heart which is felt in your mutual love has given her such an opinion of you that she confides in the promise you have both made to discontinue your correspondence, and she has taken no precaution to watch more closely over her daughter; indeed, if Julie did not measure up to her confidence, she would no longer be worthy of her solicitude, and it would be necessary to treat you both severely if you were again capable of deceiving the best of mothers and of taking advantage of the esteem she has for you.

I do not seek to rekindle in your heart a hope which I myself do not entertain, but I would indicate to you, since it is true, how the most virtuous course is also the most prudent, and how if your love has any resource left, it is in the sacrifice that honor and reason impose on you. Mother, relatives, friends—all are now for you, except the father who by this method will be won over or nothing will be able to do it. Whatever imprecation that a moment of despair may have been able to dictate to you, you have a hundred times proved to us that there is no road to happiness more sure than that of virtue. If one succeeds, the happiness is purer, sounder, and sweeter because of virtue; if one fails, virtue alone can be the compensation. Therefore, resume your courage, be a man, and be yourself again. If I know your heart well, the most cruel way for you to lose Julie would be to make yourself unworthy of obtaining her.

❖ LETTER V ❖

From Julie

SHE LIVES NO MORE. My eyes have seen hers close forever; my lips have received her last sigh; my name was the last word she uttered, her last look was fixed on me. No, it was not life that she seemed to leave; too little had I known how to make it dear to her. It was from me alone that she was torn. She saw me without guidance and without hope, overwhelmed by my misfortune and my faults; to die was nothing to her, and her heart grieved only to abandon her daughter in this condition. She was only too right. What on earth did she have to regret? Here below, what could be worth in her eyes the immortal reward for her patience and her virtues which was awaiting her in Heaven? What was left for her to do in the world except to weep for my shame? Pure and chaste heart, worthy life, and incomparable mother, you live now in a place of glory and felicity. You live, and I, given up to repentance and despair, deprived forever of your solicitude, of your advice, of your sweet caresses, I am dead to happiness, to peace, to innocence. I feel only your loss; I see only my shame. My life is nothing but grief and sorrow. My mother, my tender mother, alas, I am much more dead than you!

My God! What delirium bewilders an unfortunate girl and makes her forget her resolutions? To whom have I just shed my tears and vented my sighs? It is the cruel man who has caused them with whom I entrust them! It is with him who has made my life miserable that I dare to lament it! Yes, yes, barbarous one, share the torments you make me suffer. You for whom I plunged a dagger into a mother's breast, grieve over the misfortunes which come to me from you, and feel with me the horror of a matricide which was your doing. In whose eyes dare I appear as contemptible as I am? Before whom shall I debase myself at the bidding of my remorse? Who else besides the accomplice of my crime can understand it sufficiently? It is my most insupportable burden to be accused only by my own heart, and to see attributed to the goodness of my disposition the impure tears that bitter repentance wrings from me. I saw, shuddering I saw sorrow poison and hasten the last of my sad mother's days. In vain did her pity for me prevent her from admitting it; in vain did she pretend to attribute the progress of her illness to the cause which had originally brought it on; in vain was my cousin prevailed upon to hold to the same story. Nothing could deceive my heart, torn with regret, and as my everlasting torment I shall carry to the tomb the frightful idea of having shortened the life of her to whom I owe mine.

Oh you whom Heaven in its anger created to make me miserable and guilty, for the last time receive in your breast the tears you have occasioned. I no longer come, as before, to share with you the griefs which ought to be mutual. These are the sighs of a last adieu which escape me in spite of myself. It is all over. The empire of love is extinguished in a heart given up to despair alone. I am devoting the rest of my life to mourning the best of mothers; I shall sacrifice to her the passion which cost her her life. I should be only too happy if it might cost me as much to conquer it, in order to atone for all that it has made her suffer. Ah, if her immortal soul penetrates to my inmost heart, she knows well that the victim I am sacrificing to her is not completely unworthy of her! Share an effort which you have made necessary for me. If you have any respect left for the memory of a bond so dear and so disastrous, by that I implore you to fly from me forever, to write me no more, to sharpen my remorse no longer, to allow me to forget, if possible, what we were to each other. May my eyes look upon you no more; may I never more hear your name; may remembrance of you come no longer to disturb my heart. I dare still speak in the name of a love which must no longer be. To so many causes of grief, do not add that of seeing her last wish defied. Adieu, then, for the last time, dear and only . . . ah foolish girl . . . adieu forever.

❖ LETTER VI ❖

To Madame d'Orbe

AT LAST the veil is torn away. The long illusion is vanished. That sweet hope has been extinguished. I have nothing left to feed an eternal flame but a bitter yet delightful memory which sustains my life and nourishes my torments with a vain consciousness of a happiness which is no more.

Is it true, then, that I have tasted the supreme felicity? Am I indeed the same being who once was happy? Whoever can feel what I am suffering, was he not born for eternal suffering? Whoever could enjoy the blessings I have lost, can he lose them and still live, and can such opposite sentiments spring from the same heart? Days of pleasure and glory, no, they were not those of a mortal! They were too beautiful to have perished. A gentle ecstasy filled their whole duration, and converged them like eternity into a point. There was neither past nor future for me, and I tasted the delights of a thousand centuries at once. Alas! They have disappeared like a flash of lightning! That eternity of happiness was but an instant of my life. Time has resumed its slow pace in my days of despair, and weariness measures out the unhappy remainder of my life in long years.

In order to make them completely unbearable for me, the more afflictions overwhelm me, the more I seem to lose all that was dear to me. Madame, it is possible that you love me still, but other cares call you, other duties occupy you. My complaints, which you used to hear with interest, are now indiscreet. Julie! Julie herself is disheartened and forsakes me. Sad remorse has driven love away. All is changed for me; only my heart is ever the same, and thus my fate is more frightful.

But what does it matter what I am and what I am to be. Julie is suffering; is it the time to think of myself? Ah, it is her grief which makes mine more bitter. Yes, I had rather she might cease loving me and be happy. . . . Cease loving me! . . . does she hope for that? . . . Never, never. In vain she forbids me to see her and write her. It is not the torment which she removes; alas, it is the comforter! Is the loss of a tender mother to deprive her of an even more tender friend? Does she think she is alleviating her griefs by multiplying them? Oh love! Can nature be revenged at your expense?

No, no. In vain she pretends to forget me. Will her tender heart be able to separate itself from mine? Do I not retain it in spite of her? Can we forget sentiments such as we have experienced, and can we remember them without experiencing them still? Conquering love was the bane of her life; conquered love will only make it more pitiable. She will spend her days in sorrow, tormented at once by vain regrets and vain desires, unable ever to satisfy either love or virtue.

Yet, do not think that by complaining of her delusions I am exempting myself from respecting them. After so many sacrifices, it is too late to learn to disobey. Since she commands, it is enough; she will hear of me no more. Judge: is my fate not frightful? My greatest despair is not in renouncing her. Ah! It is in her heart that my most keen sorrows are, and I am more unhappy over her ill fortune than over my own. You whom she loves more than everything and who alone, next to me, are able to love her worthily, Claire, amiable Claire, you are the only blessing she has left. It is precious enough to make the loss of all the others bearable for her. Compensate her for the consolations of which she is deprived and for those she refuses. Let a holy friendship make up at once for the tenderness of a mother, for that of a lover, for the charms of all the sentiments which ought to have made her happy. May she be so, if it is possible, whatever the cost. May she recover the peace and the tranquillity of which I have deprived her; I shall then be less sensible of the torments she has given me. Since now I am nothing in my own eyes, since it is my fate to spend my life in dying for her, let her consider me as already dead; I consent to it if this idea makes her more tranquil. May she be able with you to recover her former virtues, her former happiness! May she be able through your solicitude to be again all that she might have been without me!

Alas! She was but a girl, and no longer has a mother! This is the loss which is not repaired and for which she can never be consoled as long as she reproaches herself with it. Her disturbed conscience calls for that tender and cherished mother, and in such cruel sorrow, a horrible remorse is joined to her affliction. Oh Julie, ought you to feel that frightful sentiment? Claire, you who were witness to the illness and the last moments of that unfortunate mother, I beg you, I implore you, tell me what I must believe. Tear out my heart if I am guilty. If grief over our faults sent her to the tomb, we are both monsters unworthy of existence. It were a crime even to dream of such a fatal union; it were a crime to live. No, I dare believe that a fire so pure cannot have produced such dark results. Love inspired in us sentiments too noble for us to commit the heinous crimes of unnatural hearts. Heaven, could Heaven be unjust, and could she who was able to sacrifice her happiness to her parents deserve to cost them their life?

❦ LETTER VII ❦

Response

HOW COULD I love you less when each day I esteem you more? How could I lose my former feeling for you when each day you earn it anew? No, my dear and worthy friend, for the rest of our lives we shall be all that we were to each other since our early youth, and if our mutual attachment is no longer strengthened, it is because it can be strengthened no more. The whole difference is that I used to love you as my brother, and now I love you as my child, for although we are both younger than you and even were your pupils, I consider you in some measure as ours. While teaching us to think, you have learned from us to feel, and whatever your English philosopher may say, this education is truly as good as the other. If it is reason which constitutes the man, it is sentiment which guides him.[31]

If the reproaches that my afflicted cousin makes herself over her mother's death were well-founded, this cruel memory would, I confess, poison that of your love, and such a distressing idea should forever extinguish it, but do not believe in her grief. It deceives her, or rather, the imaginary cause with which she likes to increase it is only a pretence to justify its excess. Her tender heart is always fearful of not being sufficiently afflicted, and it is a kind of pleasure for her to add to her anguish all that which can sharpen it. She deludes herself, you may be sure; she is not sincere with herself. Ah! If she sincerely thought she had shortened her mother's life, could her heart bear the frightful remorse? No, no, my friend, she would not mourn her; she would have followed her. Madame d'Étange's illness was well understood; it was a pleurisy from which she could not recover, and we despaired of her life even before she had discovered your correspondence.[32]

Quite far from adopting Julie's black thoughts, you may be sure that everything which one could expect on her part from human assistance and heartfelt consolation contributed to retarding the progress of her mother's illness, and that certainly Julie's tenderness and her solicitude saved her mother for us longer than we would have been able to otherwise. A hundred times my aunt herself told me that her last days were the sweetest moments of her life and that her daughter's happiness was the only thing missing in her own.

If it is necessary to attribute her death to grief, this grief comes from further back, and it is her husband alone who is to blame. Unsteady and inconstant for a long time, he wasted the fire of his youth on a thousand objects less worthy of inspiring affection than his virtuous companion, and when age had brought him back to her, he treated her with that inflexible severity with which unfaithful husbands are accustomed to aggravate their faults. My poor cousin has felt the effects of it. A vain obstinacy about his nobility and that rigidity of disposition which nothing softens have produced your misfortunes and hers. Her mother, who always had some inclination for you and who fathomed her love when it was too late to extinguish it, had for a long time secretly endured the sorrow of not being able to overcome either the inclinations of her daughter or the obstinacy of her husband, and of being the original cause of an evil which she could no longer remedy. When your intercepted letters taught her to what point you had misused her confidence, she was afraid of losing all by trying to save all, and of endangering her daughter's life in order to restore her honor. Several times she sounded her husband unsuccessfully. Several times she resolved to hazard an entire confidence and show him the full extent of his duty; her terror and timidity always held her back. She hesitated while she was able to talk; when she would have told him, it was too late. Her strength failed her; she died with the fatal secret, and I, who know the temper of that severe man without knowing to what point natural sentiments might be able to moderate it, breathe easily to see Julie's life, at least, in safety.

She knows all this, but shall I tell you what I think about her apparent remorse? Love is more ingenious than she. Pierced with grief for her mother, she would willingly forget you, but in spite of herself, love troubles her conscience by forcing her to think of you. Love wants her tears to be connected with the one she loves. She no longer dares employ her thoughts directly with you; love forces her to do so still, at least through her repentance. Love deceives her with so much art that she prefers to suffer more so that you might enter the reason for her grief. Your heart does not perhaps understand these subterfuges of hers, but they are nonetheless natural, for the love of each of you although equal in force is not similar in effects. Yours is fiery and violent; hers is gentle and tender. Your sentiments are breathed forth vehemently; hers turn back on herself and, penetrating the substance of her soul, insensibly alter and change it. Love animates and supports your heart; it overwhelms and humbles hers. All her energies are relaxed, her strength is gone, her courage is extinguished, and her virtue no longer counts for anything. All her heroic faculties are not annihilated but suspended; a momentary crisis can restore them to full vigor or efface them past all hope. If she takes one more step toward discouragement, she is lost; but if her excellent soul is raised for one instant, she will be greater, stronger, more virtuous than ever, and there will be no further question of a relapse. Believe me, my amiable friend, you must learn in this perilous situation to respect what you loved. Any letter that comes to her from you, even were it against your interest, can only be fatal to her. If you are persistent with her, you will be able to triumph easily, but vainly you will think you possess the same Julie. You will never more find her again.

❖ LETTER VIII ❖

From Lord Bomston

I HAD acquired some rights over your heart, you were necessary to me, and I was ready to come join you. What do my rights, my needs, my eagerness matter to you? You have forgotten me; you no longer deign to write me. I hear of your solitary and sullen life. I fathom your secret designs: you are weary of living.

Die, then, young fool. Die, both fierce and cowardly man. But know that in dying you leave in the heart of an honest man, to whom you were dear, the grief of having served merely an ingrate.

❖ LETTER IX ❖

Response

COME, MY LORD. I thought I could no longer enjoy earthly pleasures, but we shall see each other again. You cannot truly call me an ingrate; your heart is not formed to meet with any, nor mine to be one.

Note from Julie

It is time to renounce the errors of our youth and to abandon an illusive hope. I shall never be yours. Restore to me, then, the freedom which I have pledged to you and of which my father will dispose, or complete my misery by a refusal which will ruin us both without being of any advantage to you.

Julie d'Étange.

❧ LETTER X ❧

From Baron d'Étange

(In which the preceding note was enclosed.)

IF SOME SENTIMENT of honor and of humanity can remain in the heart of a deceiver, answer this note from a wretched girl whose heart you have corrupted and who would live no more if I dared to suspect that she had forgotten herself any further. I shall be little surprised if the same philosophy which taught her to throw herself at the first man she saw may teach her even to disobey her father. Consider this, however. On every occasion, I like to use gentle and kind methods, when I hope that they will suffice, but if I am willing to use them with you, do not think that I do not know how a gentleman's honor is avenged when he is insulted by a man who is not a gentleman.

❧ LETTER XI ❧

Response

SPARE YOURSELF vain threats, Monsieur, which do not frighten me at all, and unjust reproaches which cannot humble me. Know that between two persons of the same age, there is no deceiver other than love, and that it will never be your right to disparage a man whom your daughter honored with her esteem.

What sacrifice do you dare impose on me and by what authority do you demand it? Is it to the author of all my misfortunes that I must sacrifice my last hope? I will respect Julie's father, but let him condescend to be mine if I must learn to obey him. No, no, Monsieur, whatever opinion you may have of your rights, they do not oblige me for your sake to renounce pretensions so dear and so well deserved by my heart. Since you cause the unhappiness of my life, I owe you nothing but hatred, and your claims are without foundation. But Julie has spoken; here is my consent. Ah! May she be always obeyed! Someone else will possess her, but I shall be more worthy of her.

If your daughter had deigned to consult me about the limits of your authority, do not doubt that I might not have taught her to offer opposition to your unjust pretensions. Whatever the influence which you abuse, my rights are more sacred than yours; the tie which unites us marks the extent of paternal power, even before human tribunals, and if you dare object to nature, it is you alone who are defying its laws.

Nor do not urge that honor, so capricious and so delicate, which you speak of avenging; no one offends it but yourself. Respect Julie's choice and your honor is secure, for my heart respects you despite your insults—and despite your medieval ideas, an alliance with an honorable man will never dishonor another. If my presumption offends you, attack my life; I shall never defend it against you. Moreover, I am very little anxious to know in what consists a gentleman's honor, but as for that of a virtuous man, it concerns me, I am able to defend it, and I shall keep it pure and spotless until my last breath.

Go, barbarous father, scarcely worthy of so sweet a name, meditate the frightful destruction of your child, while a tender and submissive daughter sacrifices her happiness to your prejudices. Your remorse will one day avenge me for the injury you do me, and too late you will know that your blind and unnatural hatred was no less disastrous to you than to me. I shall be unhappy, without doubt, but if ever the voice of nature rises up in your inmost heart, how much more unhappy yet will you be for having sacrificed your only child to vain notions, a child unique in the world in beauty, in merit, in virtue, to whom Heaven, lavish with its gifts, neglected only to give a better father!

Note

(Enclosed in the preceding letter.)

I RESTORE to Julie d'Étange the right to dispose of herself, and to give her hand without consulting her heart.

S.G.*

---

* The name Saint-Preux, by which the hero of this novel is always known, is actually only a pseudonym, as Part Three, Letter XIV explains. [*Translator's note*]

❧ LETTER XII ❧

From Julie

I WANTED to describe to you the scene which has just taken place and which has produced the note that you have had to receive, but my father timed it so exactly that it was finished only a moment before the postman's departure. His letter has no doubt arrived at the post in time; it cannot be so for this one. Your resolution will be taken and your answer sent even before this reaches you. Thus all detailed explanations would be useless now. I have done my duty; you will do yours. But fate overwhelms us; honor betrays us. We shall be parted forever, and to complete the horror, I am going to be forced into the arms of . . . Alas! I could have lived in yours! Oh duty, what use is it? Oh Providence! . . . I must grieve and keep silent.

The pen falls from my hand. I have been unwell for a few days; this morning's interview has greatly disturbed me . . . my head and my heart give me pain . . . I feel myself growing faint . . . Will Heaven take no pity on my suffering? . . . I cannot support myself . . . I am forced to go to bed and console myself with the hope of never rising from it. Adieu, my only love. Adieu, for the last time, dear and tender friend. Ah! If I am to live for you no longer, have I not already ceased to live?

❧ LETTER XIII ❧

From Julie to Madame d'Orbe

IS IT TRUE, then, dear and cruel friend, that you have called me back to life and sorrow? I had a glimpse of the happy moment when I would rejoin the tenderest of mothers; your inhuman solicitude has detained me only so that I may grieve for her longer. But while the desire to follow her tears me from this earth, regret over leaving you holds me back. If I am consoled for having lived, it is by the hope of not having escaped death entirely. They exist no longer, these beauties of my face that my heart has bought so dearly. The illness from which I am recovering has freed me from them. This fortunate loss will abate the gross ardor of a man sufficiently deprived of delicacy to dare marry me without my consent. No longer finding in me what pleased him, he will care little about the rest. Without breaking my promise to my father, without offending the friend to whom he owes his life, I shall be able to repulse that intruder; my lips will keep silent, but my face will speak for me. His disgust will protect me from his tyranny, and he will find me too ugly to deign to make me unhappy.

Ah, dear cousin! You knew a heart more constant and more tender, which would not be so repulsed. His inclination did not confine itself to my features and my person; it was me he loved and not my face. We were united to each other in every part of our being, and so long as Julie had lived, her beauty could have fled but love might have always remained. Yet he could consent . . . the ingrate! . . . but he had to, since I could demand it. Who would retain by their word those who wish to withdraw their heart? Have I, then, wished to withdraw mine? . . . Have I done it? . . . Oh God! Must everything incessantly remind me of a time which is no more and of a passion which must no longer be? In vain I tried to tear that cherished image from my heart; I feel it too strongly attached there. I tear at it without dislodging it, and my efforts to efface so sweet a memory only engrave it more deeply.

Shall I dare tell you about a delirium of my fever which, far from diminishing with it, torments me even more since my recovery? Yes, you must know and pity the disordered mind of your unfortunate friend, and give thanks to Heaven for having preserved your heart from the horrible passion which brings on this disorder. In one of the moments when I was most ill, during the violence of a paroxysm, I thought I saw that unfortunate man by the side of my bed, not such as he formerly delighted my eyes during the short period of my life's happiness, but pale, thin, wild, despair in his eyes. He was on his knees; he took one of my hands, and without being repelled by its condition, without fearing infection from so terrible a disease, he covered it with kisses and tears. At the sight of him, I felt that keen and delightful emotion which his unexpected appearance used to give me before. I wanted to rush to him; I was held back. You tore him from me, and what affected me most severely were his groans that I thought I heard increase as he withdrew.

I cannot describe to you the astonishing effect which this dream produced in me. My fever was long and violent, I lost consciousness for several days, and I often dreamed of him in my delirium. But none of these dreams left such a profound impression on my imagination as this last one. It is such that it is impossible for me to efface it from my memory and from my mind. Every minute, every instant it seems I see him in the same attitude; his manner, his dress, his gestures, his sad look are again before my eyes. I believe I feel his lips pressed on my hand, I feel it moistened by his tears, the sound of his plaintive voice makes me tremble, I see him taken away from me, I make an effort still to hold him back—this whole imaginary scene recurs in my mind with more intensity than events which really happened to me.

For a long time, I have hesitated to tell you this secret. Shame keeps me from telling it to you by word of mouth, but far from becoming calm, my disturbance is only increased from day to day, and I can no longer resist the need to confess my madness to you. Ah! Let it get complete possession of me. Would that I could completely lose my reason in this way, since the little I have left only serves now to torment me!

I return to my dream. My cousin, laugh at me, if you will, for my simplicity, but there is in this vision something indefinably mysterious which distinguishes it from ordinary delirium. Is it a presentiment of the death of the best of men? Is it a sign that he already lives no more? Does Heaven deign to guide me once at least, and does it invite me to follow the one whom it made me love? Alas! The command to die will be for me the first of its blessings.

In vain I am reminded of all those vain words with which philosophy amuses people who feel nothing. They no longer awe me, and I feel that I despise them. Spirits are invisible, I believe, but would not two souls so intimately united be able to have an immediate communication between them, independent of the body and of the senses? Cannot one's direct impression from the other be transmitted to the brain, and cannot the other receive in turn the sensations it has been sent? . . . Poor Julie, what folly! How credulous passion makes us, and how painfully a heart severely affected relinquishes even errors that it perceives.

❖ LETTER XIV ❖

Response

AH, UNHAPPY and sensitive girl, were you born, then, only to suffer? In vain I would spare you from sorrow; you seem to seek it ceaselessly, and the influences which determine your destiny are stronger than all my solicitude. But to so many real causes for grief at least do not add imaginary ones, and since my caution is more injurious than useful to you, free yourself from an error which torments you. Perhaps the melancholy truth will be even less cruel for you. Learn, then, that your dream was not a dream, that it was not the phantom of your friend which you saw but his person, and that that affecting scene incessantly present to your imagination actually took place in your room three days after you were most ill.

The night before, I had left you rather late, and Monsieur d'Orbe, who was going to relieve me with you that night, was ready to leave, when suddenly we saw that poor wretch enter abruptly and throw himself at our feet in a pitiable condition. He had taken the post-stage as soon as he received your last letter. Travelling day and night, he made the trip in three days, and stopped only at the last station to wait for night in order to enter the town. I confess to you, to my shame, that I was less eager than Monsieur d'Orbe to embrace him; without yet knowing the reason for his journey, I foresaw the consequence. So many bitter memories, your danger, his own, the discomposure in which I saw him—all marred so agreeable a surprise, and I was too startled to make much over him. Nevertheless, I embraced him with a heart-felt emotion that he shared and which reciprocally displayed itself in this silent embrace, more eloquent than cries and tears.

His first words were, "How is she? Ah, how is she? Am I to live or die?" I understood then that he was informed of your illness, and supposing he knew the nature of it as well, I spoke without precaution other than to extenuate the danger. As soon as he knew that it was smallpox, he cried out and became ill. Fatigue and want of sleep, joined to the uneasiness of his mind, had thrown him into such prostration that we were a long time in bringing him to himself. He could scarcely speak; we put him to bed.

Overcome by nature, he slept twelve hours successively, but with so much agitation that such a sleep must have exhausted more than restored his strength. The next day, a new difficulty: he absolutely insisted on seeing you. I urged to him the danger of occasioning a relapse in your illness; he offered to wait until there was no more risk. But his presence alone was a terrible one; I tried to make him feel it. He interrupted me sharply.

"Cease your cruel eloquence," he said in a tone of indignation. "You go too far in using it for my ruin. Do not hope to drive me away again as you did when I went into my exile. I should come from the ends of the earth a hundred times to see her for a single instant. But I swear by my creator," he added impetuously, "that I shall not leave here without having seen her. Let us try for once whether I shall move you with compassion or if you will make me guilty of perjury."

His resolution was taken. Monsieur d'Orbe was of the opinion that we should seek the means of satisfying him, in order to be able to send him back before his return was discovered, for he was not known in the house except by Hanz alone, of whom I was sure, and we had called him in front of our servants by a name other than his own.* I promised him that he would see you the following night, on condition that he would stay only an instant, that he would not speak to you, and that he would leave again the next day before daybreak. I demanded his word on it; then I was calm, I left my husband with him, and I came back to you.

I found you perceptibly better; the eruption was complete. The doctor restored my courage and hope. I laid my plan beforehand with Babi, and since the paroxysm, although slight, had still left you light-headed, I took this opportunity to dismiss everyone and send word to my husband to bring his visitor, judging that before your attack was over you would be less likely to recognize him. We had all the difficulty in the world to send away your disconsolate father, who stubbornly determined to sit up with you each night. Finally, I told him angrily that he would not spare anyone the trouble, that I was likewise determined to sit up, and that he was assured, though he was your father, that his tenderness was no more vigilant than mine. He left reluctantly; we remained alone. Monsieur d'Orbe arrived at eleven o'clock and told me that he had left

* In Part Four it will be seen that this substituted name was *Saint-Preux*. [*Rousseau*]

your friend in the street. I went to fetch him. I took him by the hand; he trembled like a leaf. Passing through the outer room, his strength failed him; he breathed with difficulty and was forced to sit down.

Then discerning a few objects by the faint gleam of a distant light, he said, with a profound sigh, "Yes, I recognize these rooms. Once in my life I passed through them . . . at the same hour . . . with the same secrecy . . . I was trembling then as now . . . my heart beat the same way . . . Oh rash creature! I was only mortal, and I dared enjoy . . . What am I going to see now in this same refuge where everything breathes forth the voluptuousness with which my heart was intoxicated? What shall I see in the same person who constituted and shared my ecstasy? The image of death, the display of sorrow, afflicted virtue, and dying beauty!"

Dear cousin, I shall spare your poor heart the details of that moving scene. He saw you and kept silent; he had promised it. But was this silence? He fell on his knees; sobbing, he kissed the curtains of your bed. He lifted up his hands and his eyes, he uttered muffled groans, and he could scarcely contain his sorrow and his cries. Without seeing him, you mechanically put out one of your hands; he seized it with a sort of furor. The fiery kisses which he pressed on that sick hand awakened you sooner than all the noise and voices around you. I saw that you had recognized him, and despite his resistance and his complaints, I forced him from the room immediately, hoping to elude the idea of so fleeting an apparition under the pretext of delirium. But then, seeing that you said nothing to me of it, I thought you had forgotten it; I forbade Babi to mention it to you, and I know she has kept her word. A needless caution which love has disconcerted, and which has only allowed a memory to ferment which it is too late to efface!

He left as he had promised, and I made him swear that he would not stop in the neighborhood. But, my dear, that is not all. I must, moreover, finish telling you what you could not long fail to know. Lord Bomston came through two days afterwards; he hurried to catch up with your friend. He joined him at Dijon and found him ill. The wretch had caught smallpox. He had kept it secret from me that he had not had it before, and I had led him to you without taking precautions. Being unable to cure your sickness, he determined to share it. Remembering the way he kissed your hand, I cannot doubt that he inoculated himself voluntarily. He could not have been worse prepared to receive it, but it was the inoculation of love; it was successful. The Father of life has preserved it for the tenderest lover who ever was; he is recovered, and according to his Lordship's last letter, they are by this time set out again for Paris.

There, too amiable cousin, is something with which to banish the melancholy terrors which alarmed you without cause. A long time ago you renounced the person of your friend, and his life is safe. Think only, then, of preserving your own and of performing with good grace the sacrifice your heart has promised to paternal love. Cease at last to be the plaything of a vain hope and to feed yourself with shadows. You are in too much hurry to be proud of your ugliness; be more humble, believe me. You have yet only too much cause to be so. You have undergone a cruel attack, but your face has been spared. What you mistake for scars are only inflammations which will soon disappear. I was more ill-treated by the disease than that, and yet you see that I am not too ugly still. My angel, you will remain beautiful in spite of yourself. And will the indifferent Wolmar, whom three year's absence could not cure of a love conceived in a week, be cured of it when he sees you every hour? Oh, if your only resource is in being disagreeable, how desperate is your condition!

❖ LETTER XV ❖

From Julie

IT IS TOO MUCH, it is too much. Friend, you have conquered. I am not proof against so much love; my resistance is exhausted. I have exerted all my strength; my conscience gives me consoling evidence of it. Let Heaven not call me to account for more than it has given me. This sorrowful heart which you purchased so many times and which cost yours so dear belongs to you without reservation; it was yours from the first moment my eyes saw you. It will remain yours until my last breath. You have deserved it too well to lose it, and I am tired of serving an imaginary virtue at the expense of justice.

Yes, tender and generous lover, your Julie will be yours forever; she will love you always. I must, I will, I ought. I resign to you the empire which love has given you; it will be taken from you no more. In vain a deceitful voice murmurs in my inmost soul; it will no longer delude me. What are the vain duties which it urges upon me against those of forever loving the one whom Heaven has made me love? Is not my most sacred duty of all toward you? Have I not promised everything to you alone? Was not the first vow of my heart never to forget you, and is not your inviolable constancy a new bond for mine? Ah! In the ecstasy of love with which I am restored to you, my only regret is for having struggled against such dear and legitimate sentiments. Nature, oh sweet nature, resume all your rights! I abjure the cruel virtues which destroy them. Will the inclinations that nature has given me be more deceiving than reason which so many times misleads me?

Respect these tender inclinations, my amiable friend. You are too much indebted to them to hate them, but allow the dear and sweet division of them; let not the rights of blood and friendship be extinguished by those of love. Do not think that to follow you I shall ever abandon my father's house. Do not expect me to reject the bonds that a sacred authority imposes on me. The cruel loss of one of my parents has taught me too well to be afraid of afflicting the other. No, she whom he expects to be his whole comfort henceforth will not grieve his heart, overwhelmed with sadness; I shall not destroy both those who gave me life. No, no, I understand my crime but cannot hate it. Duty, honor, virtue, all these considerations no longer influence me, but yet I am not a monster. I am weak but not unnatural. My resolution is taken; I will not grieve any of those I love. Let a father enslaved by his promise and jealous of a vain title dispose of my hand as he has pledged; let love alone dispose of my heart; let my tears incessantly flow into the bosom of my tender cousin. Let me be vile and unhappy, but let all who are dear to me be happy and content if it is possible. May all three of you constitute my only existence, and may your happiness make me forget my misery and my despair.

❧ LETTER XVI ❧

Response

WE ARE REBORN, my Julie. All the true sentiments of our hearts resume their courses. Nature has preserved our existence, and love restores us to life. Could you doubt it? Did you dare think you could take your heart away from me? No, I know it better than you do, that heart which Heaven created for mine. I feel them joined in a common existence which they can lose only in death. Does it rest with us to separate them, or even to desire to do so? Are they held to each other by bonds which men have formed and which they can break? No, no, Julie, if cruel fate denies us the sweet name of husband and wife, nothing can take from us that of faithful lovers. It will be the consolation of our melancholy lives, and we shall carry it to the tomb.[33]

What have you told me? . . . What do you dare make me understand? . . . You, to be forced into the arms of another? . . . Another to possess you? . . . No longer to be mine? . . . Or rather, to complete my horror, not to be mine alone! I? Should I suffer that frightful torment? . . . Should I see you survive yourself? . . . No. I prefer to lose you rather than share you . . . Would that Heaven had given me a courage equal to the passion which shakes me! . . . Before you might be debased in that fatal union, abhorred by love and condemned by honor, with my own hand I should plunge a dagger into your breast. I should drain your chaste heart of blood which infidelity might not taint. With this pure blood I would mix that which burns in my veins with a fire that nothing can extinguish. I would fall into your arms, I would yield my last breath on your lips . . . I would receive yours . . . Julie dying! . . . Those eyes, so charming, dulled by the horrors of death! . . . That breast, the throne of love, torn open by my hand, gushing forth copious streams of blood and life . . . No, live and suffer; endure the punishment for my cowardice. No, I wish you lived no longer, but I do not love you enough to stab you.

Oh, if you knew the state of this heart oppressed with anguish! Never did it burn with so holy a fire. Never were your innocence and your virtue so dear to it. I am a lover, I know how to love, I feel it, but I am only a man, and it is beyond human strength to renounce supreme felicity. One night, one single night has changed my soul forever. Take from me that dangerous memory and I am virtuous. But that fatal night reigns in my inmost heart and will overshadow the rest of my life. Ah Julie! Adored object! If we must be miserable forever, let us have one more hour of happiness and then eternal regret!

Listen to the one who loves you. Why should we alone try to be more prudent than all the rest of mankind, and with a childish simplicity pursue the imaginary virtues which everyone talks about and which no one practices? What! Shall we be better moralists than those crowds of philosophers with which London and Paris are peopled, who all laugh at conjugal fidelity and consider adultery as a game? Instances of it are not scandalous; it is not even permitted to find fault with it, and all reasonable people would laugh here at the man who through respect for marriage would resist the inclination of his heart. In fact, they say, is not an injury which consists only in opinion no injury at all when it remains secret? What harm does a husband receive from an infidelity of which he is unaware? With what obligingness cannot a woman make up for her faults? * What endearments does she not use to prevent or remove his suspicions? Deprived of an imaginary good, he actually lives more happily, and this supposed crime about which so much stir is made is only one more thing which holds society together.

God forbid, oh dear friend of my heart, that I might wish to reassure yours by these shameful maxims. I abhor them without being able to confute them, and my conscience answers them better than my reason. Not that I am confident of a courage which I detest, nor that I seek a virtue bought so dear, but I believe I am less guilty to reproach myself for my faults than to strain to justify them, and I consider as the height of crime the desire to stifle remorse.[34]

I have long ago forgotten those vain prospects of fortune which have so grossly deluded me. Now I shall occupy myself exclusively with the duties I owe Lord Bomston. He wishes to take me off to England; he pretends that I can be of service to him there. Well, I shall follow him. But I shall steal away every year; I shall secretly come back near you. If I cannot speak to you, at least I shall see you. I shall at least kiss your footsteps; one look from your eyes will give me life for ten months. Forced to return, to console myself as I go from her I love, I shall count the steps which will bring me back to her. These frequent journeys will delude your unhappy lover. As he sets out to see you, he will believe he is already enjoying the sight of you. The memory of his ecstasies will enchant him as he returns. In spite of cruel fate, his melancholy years will not be completely wasted; there will be none which is not marked by pleasures, and the short moments that he spends near you will be repeated during his whole life.

* And where had the simple Swiss seen this? A long time ago women of spirit assumed more imperious airs. They begin by boldly establishing their lovers in the house, and if they deign to permit the husband there too, it is only as long as he behaves toward them with the respect he owes them. A woman who would conceal an illicit affair would cause it to be thought that she is ashamed of it and she would be dishonored; not one reasonable woman would take notice of her. [Rousseau]

❧ LETTER XVII ❧

From Madame d'Orbe

YOUR MISTRESS is no more, but I have recovered my friend, and you have acquired one whose heart can give you a great deal more than you have lost. Julie is married and worthy of making happy the honest man who has just joined his lot to hers. After so many indiscretions, give thanks to Heaven which has saved you both, her from shame and you from the remorse of having dishonored her. Respect her new condition; do not write her, she begs you. Wait until she writes you; she will do so shortly. Now is the time when I shall find out if you deserve the esteem I have entertained for you and if your heart can feel a pure and disinterested friendship.

❧ LETTER XVIII ❧

From Julie

YOU HAVE for so long been the confidant of all the secrets of my heart that it could no longer forsake such a sweet habit. In the most important occasion of my life, it desires to open itself to you. Open yours to it, my amiable friend.

Bound by an indissoluble tie to the fate of a husband, or rather to the will of a father, I am entering a new way of life which is to end only with my death.[35] All is changed between us. Your heart must necessarily change as well. Julie de Wolmar is no longer your former Julie; the change of your sentiments for her is inevitable, and the only choice left you is to give the credit for this change to vice or to virtue. I have in mind a passage from a writer whom you will not deny. "Love," he said, "is deprived of its greatest charm when honesty abandons it. To feel its whole value, the heart must delight in it, and it must ennoble us by ennobling the one we love.

Take away the idea of perfection, and you take away enthusiasm; take away esteem, and love is nothing. How could a woman honor a man who dishonors himself? How could he adore a woman who has no fear of abandoning herself to a vile seducer? This way, mutual contempt soon results, love is nothing for them but a shameful relationship, and they lose honor without finding happiness." * This is our lesson my friend; it is you who have prescribed it. Were our hearts ever more delightfully in love, and was honor ever as dear to them as in the happy time when that letter was written? Consider then to what we now would be led by guilty passions nourished at the expense of the sweetest ecstasies which enchant the soul. The horror of vice which is so natural to us both would soon extend to the partner of our guilt; we should hate each other for having loved too much, and love would be extinguished in remorse. Is it not better to purify so dear a sentiment to make it lasting? Is it not better to save of it at least that part which can concur with innocence? Is that not to save all of it that was most charming? Yes, my good and worthy friend, in order to be forever in love, we must renounce each other. Let us forget all the rest, and be the lover of my soul. This idea is so sweet that it is the consolation for everything.

I shall love you always, do not doubt it. The sentiment which attaches me to you is still so tender and so lively that another woman would perhaps be alarmed by it; as for me, I knew one too different to be wary of this one. I feel that its nature has changed, and at least in this respect my past faults lay the foundation for my present security. I know that exacting decorum and the external show of virtue would demand still more and would not be content until you were completely forgotten. I think I have a more certain rule and I abide by it. I listen secretly to my conscience; it reproaches me for nothing, and it never deceives a heart which sincerely consults it. If that is not enough to justify me before the world, that is enough for my own tranquillity. How has this happy change come about? I do not know. What I do know is that I have ardently desired it. God alone has done the rest. I should think that a soul once corrupted is so forever, and no longer returns to good by itself, unless some unexpected revolution, some abrupt change of fortune and situation suddenly alters its connections and, with a violent shock, helps it to recover a desire for good. All its habits being broken and all its passions modified in this general revolution, it sometimes recovers its

* See Part One, Letter XXIV. [Rousseau]

primitive character and becomes like a new creature recently formed by nature's hands. Then the memory of its former baseness can serve as a deterrent against a relapse. Yesterday we were abject and weak; today we are strong and high-minded. By thus closely contemplating ourselves in two such different conditions, we become more sensible of the value of that to which we have risen, and we become more attentive to sustain ourselves there. My marriage has made me experience something like what I am trying to explain to you. This bond, so feared, delivers me from a servitude much more fearful, and my husband becomes dearer to me for having restored me to myself.

We were too united, you and I, for our union to be destroyed by a change of this kind. If you are losing a tender mistress, you are gaining a faithful friend, and whatever we said of it in our delusion, I doubt that this change may be disadvantageous to you. Draw from it the same resolution as I have, I implore you, to become better and wiser and to refine the lessons of philosophy by Christian morals. I shall never be happy unless you too are happy, and more than ever I feel that there is no happiness without virtue. If you love me truly, give me the sweet consolation of seeing that our hearts are in accord in their return to virtue no less than they were in their error.

Before I close, I have one favor left to ask of you. A cruel burden weighs on my heart. Monsieur de Wolmar is ignorant of my past conduct, but an unreserved frankness constitutes a part of the faithfulness I owe him. I should have already confessed everything a hundred times; you alone have kept me back. Although I know Monsieur de Wolmar's discretion and moderation, to name you is yet to compromise you, and I have not wanted to do it without your consent. Would asking it of you displease you, or should I have presumed too much of you or of myself in expecting to obtain it? Consider, I beg you, how this reserve is inconsistent with innocence, how each day it is more cruel for me, and how until I receive your answer I shall not have an instant of tranquillity.

❧ LETTER XIX ❧

Response

AND WILL you no longer be my Julie? Ah! Do not say that, worthy and respectable woman. You are more mine than ever. You are she who deserves the homages of the whole universe. You are she whom I adored as I began to be sensible of true beauty; you are she whom I shall not cease to adore, even after my death, if there still remains in my soul some remembrance of the truly celestial charms which enchanted it during my life. This courageous effort by which you recover all your virtue only makes you more equal to yourself. No, no, whatever torment I experience in feeling and saying it, never were you more my Julie than at the moment you renounced me. Alas! It is by losing you that I have found you again. But I, whose heart shudders at the mere prospect of imitating you, I who am tormented by a criminal passion which I can neither support nor suppress, am I the man I thought I was? Was I worthy of inspiring your affection? What right had I to trouble you with my complaints and my despair? It was a great deal for me to presume to live for you! Ah! What was I that I should love you?

Fool! As if I did not experience enough humiliation without seeking more! Why should I think about the distinctions between us that love made disappear? Love elevated me, it made me equal to you, its flame sustained me, our hearts were blended, all their sentiments were mutual, and mine shared the grandeur of yours. Here I am, then, fallen back into all my baseness! Sweet hope which fed my soul and deceived me for so long, are you extinguished, then, never to return? Will she not be mine? Have I lost her forever? Is she making another happy? . . . Oh rage! Oh hell's torment! . . . Faithless one! Ah! Ought you ever . . . Pardon, pardon, Madame, take pity on my madness. Oh God! You said it only too well, she is no more . . . she is no more, that tender Julie to whom I could disclose all the emotions of my heart. What, would I complain when I was unhappy? . . . Would she listen to me? But was I unhappy? . . . What am I now, then? . . . No, I shall no longer make you ashamed either of yourself or of me. It is over. We must renounce each other; we must part. Virtue itself has dictated the order; your hand could write it. Let us forget each other . . . forget me, at least. I am resolved, I swear it; I shall speak no more to you of myself.

May I dare speak still of you and preserve the only interest in the world left for me—that of your happiness? In describing for me the state of your mind, you said nothing to me of your present situation. Ah! As the reward for a sacrifice which you must feel, deign to deliver me from this unbearable doubt. Julie, are you happy? If you are, give me the only consolation to which I am susceptible in my despair; if you are not, through pity deign to tell me. I shall be unhappy, then, for a shorter time.

The more I reflect on the confession which you contemplate, the less I can agree to it, and the same reason which always deprived me of the courage to refuse you must make me inflexible in this case. The subject is of the utmost importance, and I exhort you to weigh my reasons well. First it seems to me that your extreme delicacy leads you into error in this matter, and I do not see on what grounds the most rigid virtue could demand such a confession. No engagement in the world can have a retroactive effect. You cannot put yourself under obligation for the past, nor promise what you no longer have the power to perform. Why should you owe an account to the one to whom you pledge yourself of the previous use you made of your liberty and of a fidelity you did not promise to him? Do not deceive yourself, Julie; it is not to your husband, it is to your friend that you have broken your word. Before your father's tyranny, Heaven and nature had united us. By forming other ties, you have committed a crime that neither love nor honor perhaps may pardon, and it is for me alone to reclaim the prize that Monsieur de Wolmar has stolen from me.

If there are cases when duty can demand such a confession, it is when the danger of a relapse obliges a prudent woman to take precautions for her security. But your letter has given me more insight into your real sentiments than you think. In reading it, I felt in my own heart how much yours would have abhorred, even in the midst of love, the first hand experience of a criminal liaison, the horror of which was removed by its distance.[36]

Believe me, virtuous Julie, beware a fruitless and unnecessary zealousness. Keep a dangerous secret which nothing obliges you to reveal, the discovery of which can destroy you and is of no use to your husband. If he is worthy of this confession, his heart will be saddened by it, and you will have afflicted him without reason. If he is not worthy, why will you give him a pretext for using you ill? How do you know whether your virtue, which has sustained you against the assaults of your heart, would likewise sustain you against ever reappearing domestic griefs? Do not voluntarily make your misfortunes worse, lest they become stronger than your courage and lest through scruples you fall back into a condition worse than that from which you have had difficulty in rising. Prudence is the basis of all virtue; consult it, I implore you, in this most important occasion of your life, and if this fatal secret weighs on you so cruelly, at least wait to unburden yourself until time and the years give you a more perfect knowledge of your husband and add to the effect of your beauty in his heart the still more certain effect of the charms of your character and the delightful habit of perceiving them. Finally, if these reasons, good as they are, do not persuade you, do not close your ears to the voice which exposes them to you. Oh Julie, listen to a man capable of some virtue, who deserves from you at least some sacrifice in return for the one which he made to you today.

I must finish this letter. I know I cannot keep myself from resuming a tone which you ought to hear no more. Julie, I must leave you! So young still, must I already renounce happiness? Oh the time which is to return no more! The time forever past, source of eternal sorrow! Pleasures, transports, sweet ecstasies, delicious moments, celestial raptures! My love, my only love, honor and delight of my life! Adieu, forever.

✤ LETTER XX ✤

From Julie

YOU ASK ME if I am happy. This question affects me, and in asking it you help me to answer it, for far indeed from trying to forget you as you say I should, I own that if you should cease loving me I could not be happy; but I am so in every respect, and my happiness lacks nothing except yours. If in my previous letter I avoided speaking of Monsieur de Wolmar, I did it through regard for you. I know your sensitivity too well not to fear to sharpen your anguish, but your uneasiness over my situation obliging me to speak to you about the man on whom it depends, I can speak to you of him only in a manner worthy of him, as it befits his wife and a friend to the truth.

Monsieur de Wolmar is almost fifty. His simple, regulated life and the serenity of his passions have preserved in him a constitution so healthy and a manner so sprightly that he hardly appears to be forty, and he has no traits of an advanced age except experience and wisdom. His features are noble and kind, his manner of address simple and open; his manners are more prudent than officious, and he speaks little and with much good sense but without affecting either preciseness or sententiousness. He is the same toward everyone, he neither seeks out nor shuns anyone, and he never has other than rational preferences.

In spite of his natural coolness, his heart, seconding my father's intentions, thought it felt that I was suited to him, and for the first time in his life he formed an attachment. This moderate but lasting affection is so well guided by decorum and is maintained with such equilibrium that he had no need to change his behavior in changing his condition, and since his marriage he has kept the same manners with me as he had before, without violating conjugal solemnity. I have never seen him either gay or sad, but always content; he never speaks to me of himself, rarely of me. He does not seek me out, but he is not angry when I seek his company, and he leaves me rather unwillingly. He does not laugh; he is serious without disposing others to be so. On the contrary, his serene manner of address seems to invite me to sprightliness, and as the pleasures I enjoy are the only ones to which he appears sensible, one of the duties I owe him is to try to amuse myself. In short, he wants me to be happy; he does not tell me so, but I see it, and is not to desire the happiness of one's wife to have obtained it?

With all the trouble that I have taken to observe him, I have not been able to find passion of any kind in him except that which he has for me. Yet this passion is so even and so temperate that one would say that he loves only as much as he wishes to and that he wishes to only as much as reason permits. He is actually what Lord Bomston believes himself to be. In this respect, I find him much superior to all our men of feeling whom we ourselves admire so much, for our hearts deceive us in a thousand ways and act only according to an always secret principle; but the reason has no other end except that which is good, its rules are sure, clear, practicable in the conduct of life, and never is it misled except in idle speculations which are not intended for it.

Monsieur de Wolmar's greatest delight is observation. He likes to pass judgment on men's characters and the actions he sees. He judges them with a profound wisdom and the most perfect impartiality. If an enemy did him injury, he would examine the motives and the means of it with as much composure as if it was a matter of indifference. I do not know how he has heard of you, but he has several times spoken of you to me with much esteem, and I know him incapable of dissimulation. I thought I sometimes noticed that he was observing me during these conversations, but there is great likelihood that this supposed notice is only the secret reproach of an alarmed conscience. Whatever it may be, I have done my duty in this respect; neither fear nor shame has inspired an unjust reserve in me, and I have done you justice with him, as I do him justice with you.[37]

There, my good friend, is a short but faithful account of Monsieur de Wolmar's character, as well as I can know it since I have been living with him. Such as he appeared to me the first day, so he appears to me now without any alteration, which makes me hope that I have observed him well and that I have nothing left to discover about him, for I do not imagine that he could show himself otherwise except to his disadvantage.

On the basis of this description, you can anticipate your answer yourself, and you must despise me a great deal not to believe me happy with so much reason to be so.* What has long misled me and what perhaps still misleads you is the thought that love is necessary to form a happy marriage. My friend, that is an error; honor, virtue, a certain conformity, not so much of stations and ages as of characters and temperaments, are enough between two partners, which does not prevent this union from resulting in a very tender attachment which, though not precisely love, is no less sweet and is only more lasting. Love is accompanied by a continual uneasiness over jealousy or privation, little suited to marriage, which is a state of enjoyment and peace. People do not marry in order to think exclusively of each other, but in order to fulfill the duties of civil society jointly, to govern the house prudently, to rear their children well. Lovers never see anyone but themselves, they incessantly at-

* Apparently she had not yet discovered the fatal secret which torments her so greatly in the sequel, or else she did not then wish to confide it to her friend. [*Rousseau*]

tend only to themselves, and the only thing they are able to do is love each other.[38]

As for Monsieur de Wolmar, no illusion predisposes us toward each other; we see each other such as we are. The sentiment which joins us is not the blind ecstasy of impassioned hearts but the immutable and constant attachment of two respectable and reasonable people who, being destined to spend the rest of their days together, are content with their lot and try to make it pleasant for each other. It seems that if we had been created expressly to be united, it could not have been more successful. If he had a heart as tender as mine, it would be impossible for so much sensitivity on both sides not to come sometimes into collision and for quarrels not to result. If I were as calm as he, too much coldness would reign between us and would make our union less agreeable and less sweet. If he did not love me at all, we should live together uneasily; if he loved me too much, he would be troublesome to me. Each of us is precisely what the other needs; he instructs me and I enliven him. We are of greater value together, and it seems that we are destined to have only a single mind between us, of which he is the understanding and I the will. There is nothing, even to his somewhat advanced age, which does not turn to mutual advantage, for with the passion with which I was tormented, it is certain that if he had been younger, I should have married him with more difficulty yet, and that extreme repugnance had perhaps impeded the fortunate revolution which has occurred within me.

My friend, Heaven guides the good intentions of fathers and recompenses the docility of children. God forbid that I should want to insult you in your affliction. Nothing but my desire to reassure you fully about my situation makes me add what I am going to say. If with the feelings I had before for you and the knowledge I have now, I were free again and mistress of my own choice of a husband—I call upon God, who deigns to enlighten me and who reads my inmost heart, to witness my sincerity—it is not you whom I should choose, it is Monsieur de Wolmar.

It is perhaps important to your complete recovery that I tell you all that remains in my heart. Monsieur de Wolmar is older than I. If in order to punish me for my faults Heaven would deprive me of the worthy husband whom I so little deserve, my firm resolution is never to take another. If he has not had the good fortune to find a chaste girl, he at least will leave behind a chaste widow. You know me too well to believe that after having made this declaration to you I may ever retract it.[39]

This is the last letter you will receive from me. I beg you also to write me no more. However, since I shall never cease taking the most tender interest in you and since this sentiment is as pure as the light which shines on me, I shall be very glad to have news of you now and then and to see you attain the good fortune you deserve. From time to time you can write to Madame d'Orbe on the occasions when you have some interesting event to inform us of. I hope that the integrity of your soul will be always expressed in your letters. Besides, my cousin is virtuous and prudent, and she will communicate to me only what is fitting for me to see, suppressing this correspondence if you were capable of misusing it.[40]

Adieu, my amiable friend. Adieu forever. So inflexible duty commands. But you may believe that Julie's heart is incapable of forgetting him who was dear to it . . . My God! What am I doing? . . . You will see only too well by the condition of this paper. Ah! Is it not permissible to dissolve in tenderness as one says the last adieu to a friend?

❖ LETTER XXI ❖

To Lord Bomston

YES, MY LORD, it is true. My soul is oppressed by the weight of life. For a long time it has been a burden to me; I have lost all that could make it dear and nothing is left but weariness. But I am told that it is not permissible for me to dispose of my life without the order from Him who gave it to me. I also know that it belongs to you for more reasons than one. Your solicitude has twice saved my life, and your kindness ceaselessly maintains it. I shall never dispose of it until I am sure I may without committing a crime or as long as the slightest hope remains of being able to use it in your service.

You said that I was necessary to you; why do you deceive me? Since we have been in London, so far from thinking of employing me in your concerns, you make me your only concern. What superfluous pains you are taking! My Lord, you know that I abhor crime even more than life. I adore the Eternal Being, I owe you everything, I am fond of you, and on this earth I am attached to you alone. Friendship and duty can detain an unfortunate being here; pretexts and sophistry will not chain him here at all. Enlighten my understanding; speak to my heart. I am prepared to hear you, but remember that my despair is not to be deluded.[41]

For a long time I have meditated this serious subject. You must know this, for you are acquainted with my situation, and yet I am alive. The more I reflect, the more I find that the question may be reduced to this fundamental proposition: to seek happiness and avoid misery in that which does not affect another is a natural right. When our life is misery for us and is not a pleasure for anyone, it is therefore permissible to free ourselves from it. If there is a self-evident and absolute maxim in the world, I think it is this one, and if anyone succeeded in subverting it, there is no human action which might not be made a crime.[42]

You have deigned to open your heart to me. I am acquainted with your troubles; you do not suffer less than I. Your misery is without remedy in the same way as mine, and so much the more without remedy as the laws of honor are more immutable than those of fortune. You bear it, I confess, with fortitude. Virtue sustains you; furthermore, it redeems you. You entreat me to suffer; my Lord, I dare entreat you to end our sufferings, and I leave you to judge which of us is most dear to the other.

Why do we delay in taking a step that we must eventually take? Shall we wait until age and years attach us basely to life after having deprived us of its delights, and until with effort, ignominy, and sorrow we drag along an infirm and broken body? We are at the age when the soul's vigor easily frees itself from its shackles and when a man still knows how to die; later he lets himself be wrested from life reluctantly. Let us profit from a time when the weariness of life makes death desirable for us; let us be afraid that it may come with its horrors at a moment when we shall no longer desire it. I remember the time when I asked Heaven for only an hour and when I should have died despondent if I had not obtained it. Ah, what difficulty one has in breaking the ties which bind our hearts to the world, and how wise it is to leave it as soon as they are broken! I feel, my Lord, that we are both worthy of a purer habitation; virtue points it out to us and fate invites us to seek it. May the friendship which joins us unite us even at our last hour. Oh what pleasure for two true friends voluntarily to end their days arm in arm, to mingle their last breath, to give up their mutual soul at once! What sorrow, what regret can poison their last moments? What are they leaving behind in going from the world? They are going together; they are leaving nothing behind.

❧ LETTER XXII ❧

Response

YOUNG MAN, a blind passion distracts you. Be more discreet; do not give counsel while you are asking for it. I have been acquainted with misfortunes other than yours. I have a firm soul; I am English. I know how to die, for I know how to live, to suffer like a man. I have seen death near at hand, and I regard it with too much indifference to go in search of it. Let us speak of you.

It is true, you were necessary to me; my soul needed yours. Your attentions could be useful to me; your reason could enlighten me in the most important affair of my life.* If I do not make use of it, whom do you blame? What are you good for in your present state? What services can I expect from you? A senseless sorrow makes you stupid and unconcerned. You are not a man, you are nothing, and if I did not consider what you could be, such as you are now I see nothing in the world more abject.[43]

[handwritten marginalia: 78 Against suicide]

Listen to me, young madman. You are dear to me; I pity your errors. If there remains the slightest sentiment of virtue in the bottom of your heart, come, let me teach you to be reconciled to life. Each time you are tempted to quit it, say to yourself, "Let me do one more good deed before I die." Then go seek some poor person to aid, some unfortunate person to console, some oppressed person to defend. Bring to me the wretches whom my manner of address intimidates; fear to abuse neither my purse nor my credit. Take, consume my wealth; make me rich. If this consideration restrains you from suicide today, it will restrain you tomorrow; after tomorrow, for all your life. If it does not restrain you, die; you are merely worthless.

* A reference to Lord Bomston's proposed marriage, which subsequent parts of the novel will disclose. [*Translator's note*]

❖ LETTER XXIII ❖

From Lord Bomston

I SHALL NOT be able, my dear friend, to greet you today as I had hoped to, for I am detained for two more days at Kensington. The way of the court is that one works very much there without doing anything, and that all the affairs run in succession without being terminated. The business which has kept me here for a week did not require two hours, but since the most important concern of the Ministers is always to have a busy air, they waste more time in putting me off than they would have spent in dispatching my case. My impatience, a little too evident, does not shorten these delays. You know that the court hardly suits me; it has been still more intolerable for me since we have been together, and I had rather share your melancholy a hundred times than be annoyed by the knaves who populate this country.

However, in talking with these officious idlers, an idea has come to me which concerns you, and I wait only for your consent to dispose of you. I see that in combatting your grief you are suffering both from misery and from resisting it. If you wish to live and be cured, it is less to satisfy the demands of honor and reason than to please your friends. My dear man, that is not enough. You must resume the relish for life in order to fulfill its obligations adequately, and with so much indifference about everything, you will never succeed in anything. We may both of us talk as we will, but reason alone will not restore your reason. A multitude of new and striking objects must withdraw you from that attention that your heart gives only to the one object which occupies it. To recover yourself, you must get outside yourself, and it is only in the excitement of an active life that you can find serenity again.

For this purpose an opportunity is presented which is not to be disregarded. It is a matter of a great, noble enterprise, such that many ages will not see the like. It rests with you to be a spectator to it and to contribute to it. You will see the greatest sight which man's eyes ever beheld; your penchant for observation will be satisfied. Your duties will be honorable; they will require, along with the talents that you possess, only courage and health. You will encounter in your duties more danger than confinement; they will only suit you the better. Finally, your obligation will not be for very long. I cannot tell you any more today because this project, on the point of breaking into the open, is nevertheless still a secret which I am not at liberty to disclose. I shall add only that if you neglect this fortunate and rare opportunity, you will probably never find it again and will regret it, perhaps, your whole life.

I have ordered my servant, who brings you this letter, to find you wherever you may be and not to return without your response, for the affair is urgent and I must give my answer before leaving here.

❧ LETTER XXIV ❧

Response

IT IS DONE, my Lord. Dispose of me. I shall agree to anything. Until I am worthy to serve you, at least I shall obey you.

❧ LETTER XXV ❧

From Lord Bomston

SINCE YOU APPROVE of the idea which has come to me, I will not delay a moment in informing you that everything has just been concluded and in explaining to you what it concerns, according to the authority you gave me to speak for you.

You know that a squadron of five warships has just been fitted out at Plymouth, and that it is ready to set sail. The man who is to command it is Mr. George Anson, a skillful and valiant officer, my old friend. It is destined for southern waters where it is to go through the Straits of Le Maire and to return by the East Indies. Thus, you see, it is a matter of no less than a world tour, an ex-

pedition which we estimate ought to last about three years. I could
have had you enlisted as a volunteer, but to give you more importance in the crew, I have had a title added, and you are on the list
in the capacity of engineer of landing forces, which suits you all the
better because, engineering being your first ambition, I know that
you have studied it since your childhood.

I expect to return to London tomorrow and present you to Mr.
Anson within two days. Meanwhile, think about your equipment
and about providing your instruments and books, for the embarka-
tion is at hand and they only await the order to depart. My dear
friend, I hope that God will bring you back from this long voyage
whole in body and heart and that at your return we shall rejoin
each other, never to part again.

❧ LETTER XXVI ❧

To Madame d'Orbe

I AM LEAVING, dear and charming cousin, to make a tour of the
world. I am going to another hemisphere to seek the peace which I
could not enjoy in this one. Fool that I am! I am going to wander
in the universe without finding a place to rest my heart; I am going
to seek a refuge in the world where I may be far from you! But I
must respect the will of a friend, of a benefactor, of a father. Without hoping to be cured, I must at least try to be, since Julie and
virtue command it. In three hours I am going to be at the mercy of
the waves; in three days I shall no longer look on Europe; in three
months I shall be in unknown waters where everlasting storms
prevail; in three years perhaps . . . how frightful it would be to
see you no more! Alas! The greatest peril is in the bottom of my
heart, for whatever my fate may be, I have resolved, I swear that
you will see me worthy of appearing before your eyes or you will
never see me again.

Lord Bomston, who is returning to Rome, will deliver this letter
to you as he passes through and will give you a detailed account of
what concerns me. You know his heart, and you will easily guess
what he will not tell you. You knew mine; form a judgment also on

what I myself do not tell you. Ah, my Lord! Your eyes will see her
again!

Your friend, then, as well as yourself, has had the good fortune
to become a mother. She must now be so? . . . Inexorable Heaven!
. . . Oh my mother, why in its anger did it give you a son? . . .

I must end, I know. Adieu, charming cousins. Adieu, incomparable beauties. Adieu, pure and celestial souls. Adieu, tender
and inseparable friends, women unique on the earth. Each of you
is the only object worthy of the other's heart. May you constitute
each other's happiness. Deign sometimes to call to mind an unfortunate man who existed only to share with you all the sentiments of
his soul and who ceased to live at the moment he parted from you.
If ever . . . I hear the signal and the sailors' shouts; I see the
wind blowing and unfolding the sails. I must climb on board; I
must leave. Vast sea, immense sea, which perhaps is to engulf me in
its midst, would that I might find again on its waves the calm which
forsakes my troubled heart!

PART IV

✿ LETTER I ✿

From Madame de Wolmar
to Madame d'Orbe

HOW LONG you delay in returning! All this going and coming does not please me at all. How many hours you lose in traveling to the place where you ought always to stay, and what is worse, in going from it! The thought of seeing each other for such a short time spoils all the pleasure of being together. Do you not feel that thus to be alternately at your house and at mine is not really to be anywhere, and can you not contrive some means by which you may be at both at the same time?

What are we doing, dear cousin? What precious moments we are losing when we have none left to waste! The years multiply, youth begins to vanish, life slips away, the fleeting happiness which it offers is in our possession, and we neglect to enjoy it! Do you remember the time when we were still girls, those early days so charming and so sweet that no other time of life affords and that the heart forgets with such difficulty? How many times, obliged to part for a few days or even for a few hours, we used to say as we sadly embraced, "Ah! If ever we are our own mistresses, no one will see us separated again." We are now our own mistresses, and we spend half of the year far from each other. What! Do we love each other any less? Dear and tender friend, we are both aware how time, habit, and your kindness have made our attachment stronger and more indissoluble, and I can no longer live for an instant without you. [44]

½ page on aging

Ah! My dear, my poor heart has loved so much! It was exhausted so early that it grew old before its time, and so many diverse affections have so absorbed it that it has no room left for new attach-

ments. You have seen me successively a girl, a friend, a mistress, a
wife, and a mother. You know how all these titles have been dear
to me! Some of these bonds are destroyed; others are relaxed. My
mother, my tender mother lives no more; I have only tears left to
give to her memory, and I do but half enjoy the sweetest sentiment
of nature. Love is extinguished forever, and that is one more place
that will not be filled. We have lost your worthy and good husband
whom I loved as the dear half of yourself, and who so well deserved
your tenderness and my friendship. If my sons were bigger, maternal
love would fill all these voids, but that love, like all others, needs to
be returned, and what return can a mother expect from a child of
four or five? Our children are dear to us long before they are aware
of it and love us in turn, and yet we have such great need of telling
someone who understands us how much we love them! My husband
understands me, but he does not respond enough to my liking. His
head is not turned by love as mine is; his tenderness for them is
too reasonable. I desire one more animated and more like my own.
I need a friend, a mother who is as foolish as I about my children
and her own. In short, motherhood makes friendship even more
necessary to me, for the pleasure of speaking incessantly about my
children without being wearisome. I feel that I doubly enjoy my
little Marcellin's caresses when I see you sharing them. When I embrace your daughter, I imagine I am pressing you to my bosom.
We have said a hundred times, as we see our little babies playing
together, that our united hearts mix them, and we no longer know
to which one of us each of the three belongs.

That is not all; I have strong reasons for desiring you constantly
near me, and your absence is cruel for me in more than one respect.
Think of my aversion to all dissimulation and of this continual
reserve in which I have lived for almost six years with the man who
is most dear to me in the world. My odious secret oppresses me
more and more, and yet silence seems each day to become more in-
dispensable. The more honesty prompts me to reveal it, the more
prudence obliges me to keep it. Can you conceive what a frightful
state it is for a wife to carry mistrust, lying, and fear even into a husband's arms, not to dare open her heart to the one who possesses
her, and to conceal half her life from him in order to ensure the
tranquillity of the other? From whom, great God, must I conceal
my most secret thoughts and hide the recesses of a soul with which
he should have cause to be so content? From Monsieur de Wolmar,
from my husband, from the most worthy spouse with whom Heaven
could have rewarded the virtue of a chaste girl. For having de-

ceived him once, I must deceive him every day and feel myself constantly unworthy of all his kindness to me. My heart dares not accept any display of his esteem; his most tender caresses make me
blush, and all the marks of respect and consideration which he
gives me are interpreted by my conscience as opprobrium and
signs of contempt. It is very cruel to have to say to myself incessantly, "It is another than myself whom he is honoring. Ah, if he
knew me, he would not treat me in this way!" No, I cannot bear
this frightful state; I am never alone with that respectable man than
I am ready to fall on my knees before him, confess my fault to him,
and die of sorrow and shame at his feet.

Nevertheless, the reasons which have restrained me from the
beginning each day acquire new force, and I do not have a motive
for speaking which is not a reason for keeping silent. In considering
the peaceable and pleasant state of my family, I cannot reflect without fright that a single word can cause an irreparable disturbance
to it. After six years spent in so perfect a union, shall I disturb the
tranquillity of a husband so wise and so good, who has no other
will but that of his fortunate wife nor pleasure but that of seeing
order and peace reign in his house? Shall I with domestic troubles
sadden the old age of a father whom I see so content, so delighted
with the happiness of his daughter and his friend? Shall I render
these dear children, these charming children who give promise of
so much, liable to have merely a neglected or scandalous education,
to become the melancholy victims of their parents' discord, between
a father inflamed with a just indignation, disturbed by jealousy,
and a mother wretched and guilty, always bathed in tears? I am acquainted with a Monsieur de Wolmar who esteems his wife; how
do I know what he will be if he esteems her no longer? Perhaps he
is so temperate only because the passion which would dominate in
his character has not yet had room to develop. Perhaps he will be
as violent in the outburst of anger as he is gentle and calm as long
as he has no cause for irritation.

If I owe so much consideration to all those about me, do I not
also owe some to myself? Do six years of an honest and regular life
efface nothing of youth's errors, and must I be still exposed
to punishment for a fault which I have lamented for so long? I
swear to you, my cousin, that I do not look upon the past without
aversion; it humiliates me to the point of despondency, and I am
too sensitive to the shame to endure the thought of it without falling back into a kind of despair. The time which has passed since
my marriage is what I must consider to reassure myself. My present

state inspires me with self-confidence of which importunate memories try to deprive me. I love to nourish in my heart the sentiments of honor that I believe I find within myself again. The rank of wife and mother elevates my soul and sustains me against remorse for my former condition. When I see my children and their father about me, it seems to me that everything breathes forth virtue; they drive from my mind the very thought of my former faults. Their innocence is the security for mine; they become more dear to me by making me better, and I have so much horror for all that violates honor that I can scarcely believe myself the same being who formerly could forget it. I feel myself so far from what I was, so sure of what I am, that I nearly consider what I have to declare as a confession which does not concern me and which I am no longer obliged to make.

That is the state of uncertainty and anxiety in which I constantly waver during your absence. Do you know what will happen because of it some day? My father is soon going to leave for Berne, resolved not to return until after he has seen the end of that long law-suit, the burden of which he does not wish to leave to us, nor does he rely too much, I think, on our zeal to proceed with it. In the interval between his departure and his return, I shall remain alone with my husband, and I feel that it will be almost impossible for my fatal secret not to escape me. When we have visitors, you know that Monsieur de Wolmar often leaves the company and willingly takes solitary strolls in the neighborhood. He chats with the peasants, he inquires into their situation, he examines the condition of their land, and he helps them in case of need, both with his purse and with his advice. But when we are alone, he strolls only with me; he seldom leaves his wife and his children, and he lends himself to their little games with such charming simplicity that then I feel for him something even more than usual tenderness. These tender moments are so much the more dangerous to my reserve, as he himself furnishes me the opportunities to disregard it, and he has a hundred times held conversations with me which seemed to inspire me to confidence. Sooner or later, I shall have to open my heart to him, I know, but since you want harmony to prevail between us and the confession made with all the precautions that prudence sanctions, return and be away for shorter times, or I can no longer answer for anything.

My sweet friend, I must conclude, but what remains to be said is sufficiently important to be most painful for me. You are not only necessary to me when I am with my children or with my husband, but above all when I am alone with your poor Julie; solitude is dangerous precisely because it is pleasant for me and because I often seek it without intending to. It is not, you know, that my heart still feels the effects of its old wounds; no, it is cured, I feel. I am very sure of it; I dare believe myself virtuous. It is not the present that I fear; it is the past which torments me. There are memories as fearful as the original sensation. I grow tender in reminiscing, I am ashamed to feel myself crying, and I only cry the more because of it. These are tears of pity, of regret, of repentance; love has no more share in them. Love is nothing to me now, but I lament the misfortunes it has caused. I weep for the fate of a worthy man whom indiscreetly nourished passions have deprived of tranquillity and perhaps life. Alas! Without a doubt he has perished in that long and perilous voyage which despair caused him to undertake. If he lived, he would have sent us news of himself from the ends of the earth. Almost four years have elapsed since his departure. 4 yrs It is said that the squadron he was with has suffered a thousand disasters, that it has lost three-quarters of its crew, that several vessels have sunk, that no one knows what has become of the rest. He lives no more, he lives no more. A secret presentiment tells me so. The unfortunate man has not been spared any more than so many others. The sea, illness, melancholy, which is much more cruel, have shortened his life. Thus all that glitters for a moment on the earth is extinguished. My tormented conscience wanted only to reproach me for the death of an honest man. Ah my dear! What a soul was his! . . . How he could love! . . . He deserved to live . . . He will present before the Supreme Judge a feeble soul, but one which is sound and loves virtue . . . I endeavor in vain to drive away these sad thoughts; every moment they return in spite of me. To banish them, or to control them, your friend needs your help, and since I cannot forget that unfortunate man, I prefer to talk with you about him than to think of him by myself.

You see how many reasons increase my continual need to have you with me! If you, who have been more prudent and more fortunate, do not have the same reasons, does your heart feel the same need any less? If it is indeed true that you do not wish to remarry, having such little satisfaction with your family, what house can suit you better than this one? As for me, I suffer to see you in your own, for despite your dissimulation, I know your manner of living there and am not fooled by the playful air which you have just displayed for us at Clarens. You have reproached me many times for the faults in my life, but I have a very great one for which to reproach you in turn. It is that your grief is always confined and solitary. You hide in order to grieve, as if you were ashamed to weep in front of your friend. Claire, I do not like this. I am not unjust like you; I do not disapprove of your grief. I do not want you to cease honoring the memory of such a tender husband at the end of two years, or of six, or of your whole life. But I blame you, after having spent your best days in weeping with your Julie, for stealing from her the pleasure of weeping in turn with you and of washing away with more honorable tears the shame of those which she poured out into your bosom. If you are vexed about your grief, ah, you do not know true affliction! If you take a sort of pleasure in it, why do you not want me to share it? Do you not know that the communion of hearts imparts to sadness something indefinably sweet and affecting which contentment does not have? And has not friendship been given especially to the wretched as the solace of their misery and the consolation for their pains?

There, my dear, are the things you ought to take into consideration, to which I must add that in proposing that you come live with me, I am speaking in my husband's name no less than in my own. Several times he has appeared surprised, almost scandalized, that two friends such as we do not live together; he assures me he has told you so, and he is not a man to speak inadvertently. I do not know what course you will take on the basis of my remonstrances; I have reason to hope that it will be such as I desire. Be that as it may, mine is resolved upon and I shall not change it. I have not forgotten the time when you were willing to follow me to England. Incomparable friend, it is now my turn. You know my aversion for the city, my preference for the country, for rustic occupations, and the attachment that a three year stay has given me for my house at Clarens. You are also aware of what trouble it is to move with a whole family and how it would be to abuse my father's good nature to move him so often. Well, if you will not leave your household and come govern mine, I am determined to take a house in Lausanne where we shall all go to live with you. Everything requires it. My heart, my duty, my happiness, the preservation of my honor, the recovery of my reason, my condition, my husband, my children, myself—I owe you everything. All the blessings I have come to me from you; I see nothing which does not remind me of it, and without you I am nothing. Come then, my beloved, my guardian angel. Come preserve your work; come enjoy your beneficence. We have but one family, just as we have but one heart with which to cherish it. You will supervise the education of my sons; I shall supervise

that of your daughter. We shall share the duties of a mother, and
we shall double the pleasures. We shall lift our hearts together to the
One who purified mine through your solicitude, and having nothing further to desire in this world, in the midst of innocence and
friendship we shall peacefully await the next.

❖ LETTER II ❖

Response

GOOD HEAVENS, cousin, what pleasure your letter has given me! [45]
I had no sooner lost my husband than you filled the void he had left
in my heart. While he lived, he shared its affections with you;
when he was gone, I was yours alone, and as you observe with respect
to the agreement of maternal tenderness and friendship, my daughter herself was only one more bond between us. Since then, not only
have I resolved to spend the rest of my life with you, but I formed a
more extensive plan. So that our two families may constitute only
one, I intend one day, supposing all the circumstances suitable, to
marry my daughter to your eldest son, and the name of husband he
first took in jest seemed to me a happy omen of his taking it one day
in earnest.[46]

It remains for me to vindicate myself from the reproach of hiding my misery and preferring to grieve far from you. I do not deny
it; that is the way I pass the better part of the time I spend here. I
never enter my house without finding in it traces of the one who
made it dear for me. I do not take a step, I do not stare at an object
without perceiving some sign of his tenderness and of the goodness of his heart. Would you wish mine to be unaffected? When I
am here, I feel only the loss I have sustained. When I am with you,
I see only what I have left. Can you consider your power over my
humor as my crime? If I weep in your absence and if I laugh in
your company, why is this difference? Little ingrate, it is because you
console me for everything, and because I can no longer grieve over
anything while I have you.[47]

What displeases me most about the business which detains me
here is the risk to your secret, always ready to escape your lips. Con-

sider, I implore you, that what persuades you to keep it is a strong and substantial reason, and that what persuades you to reveal it is only a blind sentiment. Our very suspicion that it is no longer a secret for the one it concerns is an additional reason for declaring it to him only with the greatest circumspection. Perhaps your husband's reserve is an example and a lesson for us, for in such matters there is often a great difference between what one pretends not to know and what one is forced to know. Wait, therefore, I urge you, until we consider the matter once more. If your presentiments were well-founded and your unfortunate friend lived no more, the best course left to take would be to leave his story and his misfortunes buried with him. If he lives, as I hope he does, the case may be different, but this case still needs to arise. In any event, do you not think you owe any respect to the last wishes of a wretched man, all of whose misfortunes were your doing?

In respect to the dangers of solitude, I understand and I approve of your fears, although I know them very ill-founded. Your past faults make you fearful; I foresee so much the better for the present, for you would be much less fearful if you had more cause to be so. But I cannot approve of your terror over the fate of our poor friend. Now that your affections have changed their nature, believe me, he is not less dear to me than he is to you. Yet I have presentiments completely contrary to yours, and more in accord with reason. Lord Bomston has twice received news from him, and wrote me upon receiving the second letter that he was in the South Seas, having already escaped the dangers you mention. You know this as well as I and you afflict yourself as if you knew nothing of it. But what you do not know and what I must tell you is that the ship he is on was seen two months ago off the Canaries, making sail for Europe. That is what my father heard from Holland and what he did not fail to communicate to me, according to his custom of informing me of public affairs much more precisely than of his own. My heart tells me that we shall not be long before receiving news of our philosopher, and that your tears will be dried, unless after having wept for his death you do not weep that he is alive. But, thank God, you are no longer at that point.

This is my answer. She who loves you proposes and shares the sweet hope of an eternal reunion. You see that you have not formed the plan for it either solely or first, and that the execution of it is further along than you think. Therefore, have patience for this summer, my sweet friend. It is better to be delayed in rejoining each other than to have to part again.

Well, good Madame, have I kept my word, and is not my triumph complete? Come, fall on your knees, kiss this letter respectfully, and humbly acknowledge that at least once in her life Julie de Wolmar has been outdone in friendship.*

✤ LETTER III ✤

To Madame d'Orbe

MY COUSIN, my benefactress, my friend, I have come from the ends of the earth, and I bring back a heart full of you. I have crossed the equator four times. I have passed through the two hemispheres, I have seen the four quarters of the world, I have put the distance of its diameter between us, I have circled the entire globe, and I have not been able to escape you for a moment. We may try as we like to flee from what is dear to us; its image, quicker than the sea and the winds, follows us to the end of the universe, and everywhere we go we carry there what gives us life. I have suffered a great deal; I have seen others suffer more. How many wretches I have seen die! Alas, they set such a high price on life! And I, I have survived them . . . Perhaps, in fact, I was less to be pitied; the miseries of my companions affected me more than my own. I saw them entirely miserable; they must have suffered more than I. I said to myself, "I am wretched here, but there is a corner of the earth where I am happy and peaceful." And I was compensated beside the Lake of Geneva for what I was enduring on the ocean. I have the good fortune upon arriving to see my hopes fulfilled; Lord Bomston informs me that you both are enjoying peace and health and that if you in particular have lost the sweet title of wife, you retain that of friend and mother, which must be enough for your happiness.

I am in too much of a hurry to send you this letter to give you at present a detailed account of my voyage. I dare hope soon to have a more convenient opportunity. I have spent almost four years in the

* How fortunate this good Swiss woman is to be gay as she is gay, without wit, without ingenuity, without artifice! She is unconscious of the affectations which are necessary among us for good humor to succeed. She does not know that we do not have this good humor for ourselves but for others, and that we do not laugh to laugh but to be applauded. [*Rousseau*]

long voyage I have just mentioned to you and have returned in the same ship in which I had left, the only one of the squadron which the commander has brought back.[48]

How shall I tell you of my recovery? It is from you that I must learn to understand it. Do I return more free and more prudent than I departed? I dare think so, and yet I cannot affirm it. The same image reigns always in my heart; you know whether it is possible for it to be effaced. But her dominion is more worthy of her, and if I am not deluding myself, she reigns in this unfortunate heart just as she does in yours. Yes, my cousin, it seems to me that her virtue has subdued me, that I am for her only the best and the most tender friend ever, that I do no more than adore her as you yourself adore her; or rather, it seems to me that my sentiments are not weakened but rectified, and however carefully I examine myself, I find them as pure as the object which inspires them. What more can I say to you until I am put to the test by which I can learn to judge myself? I am sincere and honest, I want to be what I must be, but how can I answer for my heart with so many reasons to distrust it? Am I in control of the past? Can I prevent a thousand passions from formerly having devoured me? How shall my imagination alone distinguish what is from what was? And how shall I picture her as a friend whom I never saw except as a mistress? Whatever you may think, perhaps, of the hidden motive for my eagerness to see her, it is honest and reasonable; it deserves your approval. I answer in advance for my intentions at least. Allow me to see you and examine me yourself, or let me see Julie and I shall know myself.

I am to accompany Lord Bomston to Italy. Shall I travel close by you and not see you? Do you think that can be? Ah! If you had the cruelty to demand it, you would deserve not to be obeyed! But why would you demand it? Are you not that same Claire, as good and compassionate as you are virtuous and prudent, who has deigned to love me since her most tender youth and who must love me much more still, now that I owe her everything?* No, no, dear and charming friend, such a cruel refusal would be just neither from you nor to me; it will not complete my misery. Once more, once more in my life, I shall lay my heart at your feet. I shall see you; you will consent to it. I shall see her; she will consent to it. You both know my respect for her only too well. You know whether I am a man to present myself to her if I felt myself unworthy of appearing before

---

* Why does he owe so much, then, to her who occasioned the misfortunes of his life? Wretched questioner! He owes her the honor, the virtue, the tranquillity of the one he loves; he owes her everything. [Rousseau]

her. She has for so long deplored the work of her charms; ah, let her see for once the work of her virtue!

P.S. His Lordship is detained here for some time by business. If it is permissible for me to see you, why should I not set out before him in order to be with you sooner?

❧ LETTER IV ❧

From Monsieur de Wolmar

ALTHOUGH we are not yet acquainted, I am charged with writing to you. The most prudent and the most cherished wife has just opened her heart to her fortunate husband. He believes you worthy of having been loved by her, and he offers you his house. Innocence and peace prevail in it; there you will find friendship, hospitality, esteem, and confidence. Consult your heart, and if there is nothing in it which alarms you, come without fear. You will not depart without leaving behind a friend.

Wolmar

P.S. Come, my friend, we await you eagerly. I should be pained if you were to refuse us.

Julie

❖ LETTER V ❖

From Madame d'Orbe

(In which the preceding was enclosed.)

WELCOME! A hundred times welcome, dear Saint-Preux, for I am pretending that you have kept this name, at least in our society.* I think this is sufficient to tell you that we do not intend to exclude you from it, unless you exclude yourself. Seeing by the enclosed letter that I have done more than you asked of me, you may learn to have a little more confidence in your friends and no longer blame their hearts for the griefs they share when reason forces them to afflict you with them. Monsieur de Wolmar wants to see you; he offers you his house, his friendship, his counsel. This is more than requisite to calm all my apprehensions about your coming, and I should offend myself if I could distrust you for a moment. Monsieur de Wolmar does more; he intends to cure you, for he says that neither Julie, nor he, nor you, nor I can be perfectly happy without that. Although I expect much from his wisdom and more from your virtue, I do not know if this undertaking will be a success. What I do know is that with the wife he has, the trouble he proposes to take is out of pure generosity for you.

Come then, my amiable friend, in the security of an honorable heart, to satisfy the eagerness we all have to embrace you and see you peaceful and content. Come to your country and among your friends to rest from your voyages and forget all the hardships you have suffered. The last time you saw me I was a serious matron and my friend was dying; but now that she is well and I am single again, here I am completely as gay and almost as pretty as before my marriage. One thing at least which is quite certain is that I have not changed toward you, and that you will tour the world many times before finding in it someone who loves you as I do.

---

* It is the one she had given him before her servants during his preceding visit. See Part Three, Letter XIV. [*Rousseau*]

❧ LETTER VI ❧

To Lord Bomston

I HAVE RISEN in the middle of the night to write you. I could not find a moment's rest. My excited, ecstatic heart cannot be contained within me; it needs to be opened. You who have so often preserved it from despair, be the dear confidant of the first pleasures it has enjoyed for such a long time.

I have seen her, my Lord! My eyes have beheld her! I have heard her voice; her hands have touched mine; she has recognized me; she has shown joy at seeing me; she has called me her friend, her dear friend; she has received me in her house. Happier than I ever was in my life, I am lodging under the same roof with her, and now as I am writing you, I am thirty steps from her.

My thoughts are too quick to be in order. They present themselves all at once; they impede each other. I must pause and catch my breath, to try to put some order into my account.

After so long an absence, I had no sooner surrendered myself to the first ecstasies of my heart in greeting you as my friend, my deliverer, and my father, than you thought of taking a trip to Italy. You made me desire it in the hope of finally relieving myself of the burden of my uselessness to you. Unable to terminate immediately the business which kept you in London, you proposed my leaving first in order to have more time to wait for you here. I asked permission to come here; I obtained it, I left, and although Julie's image offered itself beforehand to my sight, while I was dreaming of meeting her I felt regret at leaving you. My Lord, we are even; this sentiment alone has paid you for everything.

It is not necessary to tell you that during the whole trip I was preoccupied only with the object of my journey, but one thing to observe is that I began to see this same object, which had never left my heart, from another point of view. Up to then, I had always remembered Julie glowing as before with the charms of youth. I had always seen her beautiful eyes enlivened with the fire that she kindled in me. Her cherished features used to offer to my eyes only the surety of my happiness; our love used to be so interwoven with her person that I could not separate them. Now I was going to see Julie married, Julie a mother, Julie indifferent! I was uneasy about the changes that an eight year interval could make in her beauty. She had had smallpox; she was changed by it, but to what degree? My imagination stubbornly resisted marks on that lovely face, for as soon as I saw a smallpox scar on it, it was no longer Julie's. I thought again of the meeting we would have, of the reception she would give me. This first meeting presented itself to my imagination under a thousand different forms, and that moment which was to pass by so rapidly recurred a thousand times a day for me.

When I perceived the peaks of the mountains, my heart beat violently and said to me, "She is there." The same thing had happened to me on the sea at the sight of the European coast. The same thing had happened to me before at Meillerie as I discovered the house of the Baron d'Étange. The world is ever divided for me into only two regions, where she is and where she is not. The first is extended when I am going away and grows smaller in proportion as I approach, like a place which I am never to reach. It is at present confined by the walls of her room. Alas! That place alone is inhabited; all the rest of the universe is empty.

The closer I came to Switzerland, the more excited I felt. The instant when from the heights of the Jura I discovered the Lake of Geneva was an instant of ecstasy and rapture. The sight of my country, of that cherished country where torrents of pleasure had flooded my heart; the Alpine air so wholesome and so pure; the gentle breeze of the country, more fragrant than the perfumes of the orient; that rich and fertile land, that matchless countryside, the most beautiful ever beheld by human eyes; that charming place to which I had found nothing equal in my tour of the world; the aspect of a happy and free people; the mildness of the season, the serenity of the weather; a thousand delightful memories which aroused again all the sentiments I had enjoyed—all threw me into ecstasies which I cannot describe and seemed to infuse me with all the joy of my whole life at once.

In coming down toward the far side of the lake, I felt a new sensation which I did not understand. It was a certain emotion of fright which oppressed my heart and disturbed me in spite of myself. This fright, the cause of which I could not discern, increased as I drew near the town; it abated my eagerness to arrive, and finally made such progress that I was as much disturbed about my speed as I had been until then about my slowness. Entering Vevey, I experienced a sensation which was something less than agreeable.

I was seized with a violent palpitation which prevented me from breathing; I spoke in a changed and trembling voice. I had trouble in making myself understood as I asked after Monsieur de Wolmar, for I never dared to call his wife by name. I was told he lived at Clarens. This news took a five hundred pound weight off my breast, and considering the two leagues which I had left to travel as a respite, I was delighted with what might at another time have made me desolate, but I learned with real sorrow that Madame d'Orbe was at Lausanne. I went into an inn to regain the strength which was failing me. It was impossible for me to swallow a single bite; I choked as I drank and could not empty a glass except with several sips. My terror doubled when I saw the horses hitched to leave again. I think that I should have given the whole world to have seen a wheel broken on the way. Julie was no longer before my eyes; my disturbed imagination presented only confused objects to me. My soul was in a general tumult. I had experienced grief and despair; I should have preferred them to this horrible state. In short, I can say that I have never in my life experienced distress more cruel than that in which I found myself during that short journey, and I am convinced that I could not have endured it for a whole day.

Upon arriving, I had the carriage stop at the gate, and feeling myself in no condition to take a step, I sent the postilion to say that a stranger was asking to speak to Monsieur de Wolmar. He was strolling with his wife. They were informed, and they came round another way, while, my eyes fixed on the main avenue, I waited in mortal terror to see someone appear there.

Julie had no sooner seen me than she recognized me. Immediately, seeing me, crying out, running, and throwing herself into my arms were for her but a single act. At the sound of her voice, I felt myself tremble; I turned around, I saw her, I felt her. Oh my Lord! Oh my friend! . . . I could not speak . . . Farewell dread, farewell terror, fright, fear of what people might say. Her look, her cry, her gesture in a moment restored to me confidence, courage, and strength. I received warmth and life from her arms; I sparkled with joy in clasping her in mine. A sacred ecstasy kept us tightly embraced in a long silence, and it was only after such a delightful shock that our voices began to be confused and our eyes to intermingle their tears. Monsieur de Wolmar was there, I knew; I looked at him, but what was I capable of seeing? No, if the entire universe had been united against me, if instruments of torture had surrounded me, I should not have screened my heart from the least of these caresses, tender beginnings of a pure and holy friendship which we shall bear with us into Heaven!

This first impetuosity abated, Madame de Wolmar took me by the hand and, turning toward her husband, said to him with a certain air of innocence and candor with which I felt myself affected, "Although he is my former friend, I do not present him to you, I receive him from you, and it is only honored by your friendship that he will henceforward have mine."

"If new friends have less ardor than old ones," he said as he embraced me, "they in turn will become old ones, and will not be inferior in affection to the others." I received his embraces, but my heart had just been exhausted and I did nothing but receive them.

After this short scene, I observed in the corner of my eye that my trunk had been taken down and my carriage sent away. Julie took my arm and I went with them toward the house, almost overcome with joy to see that they were determined I should be their guest.

It was then that, contemplating more calmly that adored face which I had thought I would find disfigured, I saw with a bittersweet surprise that she was actually more beautiful and more sparkling than ever. Her charming features are even improved; she has put on a little more flesh, which only adds to her dazzling fairness. The smallpox has left only some slight, almost imperceptible marks on her cheeks. In place of that humble modesty which formerly made her lower her eyes incessantly, one sees the security of virtue in her chaste look, joined to sweetness and to sensitivity. Her countenance, not any less modest, is less timid. A freer air and franker manners have succeeded that restrained behavior mixed with tenderness and shame, and if the sense of her fault made her more affecting then, that of her purity makes her more celestial today.

We were scarcely in the parlor than she disappeared and returned a moment later. She was not alone. Whom do you think she brought with her? My Lord, her children! Her two children, more beautiful than the day and bearing already in their childish features the charm and attraction of their mother. What happened to me at that sight? That can neither be described nor understood; you must feel it. A thousand contrary emotions seized me at once. A thousand cruel and delightful memories divided my heart. Oh what a sight! Oh what regrets! I felt myself torn with sorrow and transported with joy. I saw her who was so dear to me multiplied, so to speak. Alas! I saw at the same instant the too convincing proof that she was no longer anything to me, and my losses seemed to be multiplied with her.

She led them by the hand to me. "Here," she said in a tone which pierced my soul, "these are your friend's children. They will one day be your friends. Be theirs henceforth."

Immediately these two little creatures pressed around me, took my hands, and overwhelming me with their innocent caresses, turned all my emotions into tenderness. I took them both in my arms, and pressing them against my throbbing heart, I said with a sigh, "Dear and charming children, you have a great task to perform. May you be able to resemble those from whom you received your life. May you be able to imitate their virtues and by yours one day console their unfortunate friends."

Enchanted, Madame de Wolmar embraced me a second time and seemed to desire to pay with her caresses for those I was bestowing on her two sons. But what difference between the first embrace and this one! I experienced it with surprise. It was a mother of a family whom I was clasping. I saw her surrounded by her husband and her children; this group was imposing. I found an air of dignity in her countenance which had not impressed me at first. I felt myself forced to pay her a new kind of respect. Her familiarity was almost a burden to me; however beautiful she appeared to me, I should have kissed the hem of her dress with better heart than I kissed her cheek. From that instant, in short, I knew that she and I were no longer the same, and I began in earnest to feel optimistic about myself.

Taking me by the hand, Monsieur de Wolmar led me next into the rooms which were prepared for me. Upon entering, he said to me, "Here is your apartment. It is not that of a stranger. It will no longer be another's, for henceforth it will remain either empty or occupied by you."

You may judge if that compliment was agreeable for me! But I still did not deserve it enough to hear it without confusion. Monsieur de Wolmar saved me the embarrassment of a reply. He invited me to walk around the garden. There he behaved so that I found myself more at ease, and assuming the tone of a man informed of my former errors but full of confidence in my integrity, he spoke to me like a father to his child, and through his esteem for me made it impossible for me to belie him. No, my Lord, he is not mistaken; I shall not forget that I have his esteem and yours to justify. But why must my heart shrink at his beneficence? Why must a man whom I am bound to love be Julie's husband?

This day seemed destined to put me to every kind of trial I could undergo. After we had returned to Madame de Wolmar, her husband was called away to give some order, and I was left alone with her.

I found myself then in new perplexity, the most painful and the least expected of all. What should I say to her? How should I begin? Should I dare remind her of our former connection and of the time so present to my mind? Should I permit her to think that I had forgotten them or that I no longer cared about them? What torment it was to treat as a stranger her whom I carry in my inmost heart! But what baseness to abuse hospitality by speaking words to her which she must hear no more! In this perplexity, I was put out of countenance, color mounted to my face, I dared not speak nor lift my eyes nor make the least movement, and I think I would have remained in that distressed state until her husband's return if she had not extricated me from it. As for her, it appeared that this private interview had in no way embarrassed her. She preserved the same manner and the same behavior that she had before; she continued to speak to me in the same tone, except that I thought I perceived that she was trying to infuse it with still more gaiety and freedom, joined with a look, not timid or tender but sweet and affectionate, as if to encourage me to be reassured and emerge from my constraint which she could not fail to notice.

She spoke to me of my long voyage; she wanted to know its details, especially those of the risks I had run, the suffering I had endured, for she knew, she said, that she was bound in friendship to make me some reparation for them.

"Ah Julie!" I said to her sadly, "I have been with you only for a moment. Do you already want to send me back to the Indies?"

"No," she said, laughing, "but I would go there in my turn."

I told her that I had written you an account of my voyage, a copy of which I brought to her. Then she eagerly asked me for news of you. I spoke of you and could not do so without recounting the suffering I had undergone and that which I had caused you. She was affected; she began in a more serious tone to enter into her own justification and to show me that she had had to do all that she had done. Monsieur de Wolmar returned in the middle of her explanation, and what astounded me was that she continued it in his presence exactly as if he had not been there. He could not keep himself from smiling as he discerned my astonishment.

After she had finished, he said to me, "You have seen an example of the openness which prevails here. If you sincerely wish to be virtuous, learn to imitate it. That is the only request and the only

advice I have to give you. The first step toward vice is to shroud innocent actions in mystery, and whoever likes to conceal something
sooner or later has reason to conceal it. A single moral precept can
take the place of all the others. It is this one: never do or say anything you do not want the whole world to see and hear. As for me, I
have always regarded as the most estimable of men that Roman
who wanted his house to be built in a way that people might see
everything that was done there.

"I have," he continued, "two courses of action to propose to you.
Freely choose the one which will suit you best, but choose one or
the other."

Then, taking his wife's hand and mine, he said as he clasped
them together, "Our friendship now begins. Here is the dear bond.
May it be indissoluble. Embrace your sister and friend. Treat her
constantly as such. The more familiar you will be with her, the better
I shall think of you. But behave when alone as if I were present or
before me as if I were not. That is all I ask of you. If you prefer the
latter course, you can choose it without uneasiness, for since I reserve for myself the right to inform you of all that displeases me, as
long as I shall say nothing to you, you will be certain of not having
displeased me."

Two hours before, this speech would have much embarrassed
me, but Monsieur de Wolmar was beginning to assume such great
authority over me that I was already almost accustomed to it. We
all three began again to chat peacefully, and each time I spoke to
Julie, I did not fail to call her *Madame*.

"Tell me frankly," her husband finally said, interrupting me,
"in your conversation a little while ago, did you call her *Madame*?"

"No," I said, a little disconcerted, "but decorum. . . ."

"Decorum," he resumed, "is only the mask of vice. Where virtue
prevails, it is useless. I do not desire any. Call my wife *Julie* in my
presence, or *Madame* in private. It is indifferent to me."

I began then to understand with what sort of man I had to deal,
and I resolved indeed to keep my heart always in a state to bear
his examination.

Exhausted with fatigue, my body had great need of refreshment
and my spirit of rest. I found both at the table. After so many years
of absence and of sorrow, after such long journeys, I said to myself
in a sort of rapture, "I am with Julie, I am looking at her, I am
speaking with her, I am at the table with her, she is looking at me
without uneasiness, she is welcoming me without fear, and nothing

is disturbing the pleasure we have in being together." Sweet and precious innocence, I had not enjoyed its charms before, and it is only today that I have begun to exist without suffering!

At night as I retired, I passed before the master bedroom of the house. I saw them enter it together. I sadly reached my own, and that moment was not for me the most agreeable of the day.

There, my Lord, are the events of this first meeting, so passionately desired and so cruelly feared. I have tried to collect myself since I have been alone. I have forced myself to examine my heart, but the excitement of the preceding day is still prolonged, and it is impossible for me so soon to determine my true state. All that I know very certainly is that if my sentiments for her have not changed their nature, they have at least changed their form, that I intend always to see a third person with us, and that I fear being alone with her as much as I once desired it.

I expect to go to Lausanne in two or three days. I have yet but half seen Julie since I have not seen her cousin, that amiable and dear friend to whom I owe so much, who will ceaselessly share with you my friendship, my solicitude, my gratitude, and all the sentiments of which my heart has remained the master. At my return, I shall not delay in telling you more. I need your advice, and I will watch myself closely. I know my duty and will do it. However pleasant it is for me to stay in this house, I have resolved, I swear, that if ever I perceive that I am too fond of it, I shall leave immediately.

✤ LETTER VII ✤

From Madame de Wolmar to Madame d'Orbe

IF YOU HAD agreed to stay with us as we asked of you, you would have had the pleasure of embracing your protégé before your departure. He arrived the day before yesterday and wanted to go see you today, but a kind of stiffness, the result of fatigue and his journey, keeps him in his room, and he has been bled this morning.* Besides, I had fully resolved, in order to punish you, not to let him leave so

* Why bled? Is that also the fashion in Switzerland? [*Rousseau*]

soon, and you must come here to see him, or I promise you that you will not see him for a long time. Really it would be unthinkable for him to see the inseparables separately!

In truth, my cousin, I know not what idle terrors had fascinated my mind about his coming, and I am ashamed that I was opposed to it with so much obstinacy. The more afraid I was to see him again, the more sorry I should be today for not having seen him, for his presence has destroyed the fears which still disturbed me and which could have become legitimate by fixing my attention on him. The attachment I feel to him is now so far from frightening me that I believe if he were less dear to me I would distrust myself more, but I love him as tenderly as ever, without loving him in the same way. It is by comparing what I experience now at the sight of him to what I formerly experienced that I derive the security of my present state, and the difference of such opposite sentiments is perceived in proportion to their vivacity.

As for him, although I recognized him the first instant, I have found him greatly changed, and—what formerly I should hardly have imagined possible—he seems to me in many respects changed for the better. The first day he showed some signs of embarrassment, and I myself had much difficulty in hiding mine from him. But it was not long before he assumed the resolute tone and the open manner which is in accord with his character. I had always seen him timid and bashful; the dread of displeasing me, and perhaps the secret shame of acting a part scarcely worthy of a man of honor, gave him an indefinably servile and abased look before me, which you have justifiably ridiculed more than once. In place of a slavish submission, he now shows the respect of a friend who knows how to honor what he esteems. He speaks honestly and with assurance, he has no fear that his virtuous maxims may be contrary to his interests, he fears neither to do himself injury nor to affront me by praising what is praiseworthy, and one senses in everything he says the confidence of an upright and self-confident man, who derives from his own heart the approval which he formerly sought only in my eyes. I find also that the customs of the world and experience have taken away his dogmatic and peremptory tone which men contract in their study, that he is less prompt to pass judgment on men since he has observed them a great deal, that he is less in a hurry to establish general propositions since he has seen so many exceptions, and that in general the love of the truth has cured him of a systematic mind, with the result that he has become less brilliant and more rational, and one learns much more from him now that he is no longer so learned.

His person is also changed but not for the worse. His bearing is more assured, his countenance is more open, and his manner is more proud. He has brought back from his travels a certain martial air, which becomes him all the more because his gestures, lively and quick when he is animated, are otherwise more serious and sober than formerly. He is a sailor whose attitude is calm and cool and whose speech fiery and impetuous. Past thirty, his face is that of a man in his prime and combines the dignity of a mature age with the spirit of youth. His complexion is not recognizable; he is as dark as a Moor and quite scarred by smallpox as well. My dear, I must tell you everything: to look at these scars causes me some uneasiness, and I often catch myself looking at them in spite of myself.

I think I notice that if I examine him, he is no less attentive in examining me. After such a long absence, it is natural for us to contemplate each other with a sort of curiosity, but if this curiosity seems to retain anything of our old eagerness, what a difference there is in its manner as well as in its motive! If our eyes meet less often, we look at each other with more freedom. It seems that we have a tacit agreement for examining each other alternately. Each feels when it is the other's turn, as it were, and in his turn averts his eyes. Although the emotion may no longer be present, can we see again without pleasure the person we loved so tenderly before and love so purely now? Who knows whether vanity is not endeavoring to justify past mistakes? Who knows if, when passion ceases to blind us, we both do not still like to say to ourselves that we did not choose too badly? Be that as it may, I tell you again without shame that I retain very sweet sentiments for him which will last as long as I live. Far from reproaching myself for these sentiments, I congratulate myself for them; I should be ashamed not to have them, as for a defect in my character and the mark of a wicked heart. As for him, I dare believe that next to virtue he loves me best in the world. I feel that he prides himself in my esteem; I pride myself in turn in his, and I shall deserve to keep it. Ah! If you saw with what tenderness he caresses my children, if you knew what pleasure he takes in speaking of you, cousin, you would recognize how dear I still am to him.

That which doubles my confidence in the opinion that we both have of him is that Monsieur de Wolmar shares it and that since he has met him he thinks from his own observations fully as well of our friend as we had told him he should. He has spoken to me of him a great deal these past two evenings, congratulating himself for the course he has taken and for struggling against my opposition.

"No," he said to me yesterday, "we shall not leave so honest a man in doubt about himself. We shall teach him to have more confidence in his virtue, and perhaps one day we shall enjoy with more benefit than you think the fruit of the trouble we are going to take. As for the present, I must tell you that already his character pleases me and that I esteem him above all for a reason which he hardly suspects, that is, to see the reserve he has in front of me. The less friendship he shows me, the more he inspires me to it. I could not tell you how much I feared his embrace. That was the first trial that I prepared for him. A second one is to take place, during which I shall watch him.* After that I shall watch him no more."

"As for this trial," I said to him, "it proves nothing else but the openness of his character. For never before could he resolve himself to assume a submissive and compliant manner with my father, although it was greatly to his interest and I had earnestly begged him to do so. With sorrow I saw that he was depriving himself of that single resource, but I could not resent him for being unable to be hypocritical in any way."

"This case is very different," my husband replied. "Between your father and him there is a natural antipathy based on the opposition of their precepts. As for myself who have neither systems nor prejudices, I am sure that he has no natural aversion to me. No man hates me. A man without passions cannot inspire aversion in anyone. But I have stolen his property from him; he will not immediately forgive me for it. He will love me more tenderly only when he is perfectly convinced that the injury I have done him does not prevent me from looking upon him with a favorable eye. If he embraced me now, he would be a hypocrite; if he never embraced me, he would be a monster."

There, my Claire, is our situation, and I am beginning to think that Heaven will bless the integrity of our hearts and the kind intentions of my husband. But I am indeed kind to go into all this detail; you do not deserve that I should take so much pleasure in talking with you. I have resolved to say nothing further, and if you want to know more, come to learn it.

* The letter which concerns this second trial has been suppressed, but I shall take care to mention it at the proper time. [*Rousseau*]

P.S. Yet I must tell you more of what has taken place. You know with what indulgence Monsieur de Wolmar received the delayed confession that this unexpected return forced me to make. You saw with what gentleness he could dry my tears and dispel my shame. Whether I had told him nothing new, as you have rather reasonably surmised, or whether he was in fact affected by a measure which nothing but repentance could dictate, not only has he continued to live with me as before, but he seems to have doubled his solicitude, confidence, and esteem, and to wish to compensate me with attention for the confusion which that confession cost me. My cousin, you know my heart; judge the impression that such conduct makes on it! [49]

❖ LETTER VIII ❖

Response

WHAT COUSIN! Has our traveler arrived and have I not yet seen him at my feet laden with spoils from America? It is not he, I inform you, whom I accuse of this delay, for I know that he suffers from it as much as I, but I see that he has not forgotten his old role as a slave as well as you say he has, and I complain less of his neglect than of your tyranny. I too find you very kind to wish that a grave and formal prude such as I should make the first advances, and that abandoning all my affairs, I should run to kiss a black and pockmarked face which has spent four years in the sun and seen the land of spices! But you make me laugh above all when you are in a hurry to scold for fear that I may scold first. I would like to know why you attempt this? Quarreling is my talent; I take pleasure in it, I acquit myself marvelously, and it becomes me very well. But you, no one can be more awkward than you in quarreling, and it becomes you not at all. On the other hand, if you knew how graceful you are in being in error, how charming your confused manner and your supplicating eye make you, instead of scolding, you would spend your life asking pardon, if not through duty, at least through coquetry. [50]

I come to the principal subject of your letter. You know that when our friend wrote, I flew to you; the matter was serious. But now if you knew what trouble that short absence from my home has caused me and how much business I have all at once, you would sense the impossibility of my abandoning my house again without causing myself new inconveniences and putting myself under an obligation to spend the winter here again, which is not my intention nor yours. Is it not better to abstain from seeing each other hastily for two or three days and rejoin each other six months sooner? I also think that it will not be useless if I chat privately and somewhat leisurely with our philosopher, either to probe and strengthen his heart, or to give him some useful advice on the way he is to conduct himself with your husband and even with you, for I do not imagine you can speak to him quite freely on that subject, and I see even by your letter that he needs advice. We have gotten so much into the habit of governing him that in our own conscience we are a little responsible for him, and until his reason is completely freed, we must make up for it. As for me, this is a trouble I shall always take with pleasure, for he has paid such costly deference to my advice, which I shall never forget, and there is no man in the world since my husband is no more whom I esteem and whom I love as much as him. I also am reserving for his benefit the pleasure of doing me some services here. I have a great many papers in disorder which he will help me to clear up and some intricate business in which I shall in turn need his understanding and his solicitude. Nevertheless, I expect to keep him only five or six days at most, and perhaps I shall send him back to you the next day, for I have too much vanity to wait until his impatience to return overtakes him and too good an eye to delude myself.

Do not fail, then, as soon as he is well again, to send him to me, that is to say, to allow him to come, or I shall not intend to joke anymore. You know very well that if I laugh when I weep and yet am not the less afflicted, I laugh also when I scold and am not the less angry. If you are quite wise and do things with good grace, I promise to send you with him a pretty little present which will give you pleasure, and very great pleasure. But if you keep me waiting impatiently, I warn you you will have nothing.

P.S. By the way, tell me does our sailor smoke? Does he swear? Does he drink brandy? Does he carry a large cutlass? Does he really have

the look of a buccaneer? Good heavens, how curious I am to see
the manner a man has upon returning from the other side of the
earth!

✤ LETTER IX ✤

From Claire to Julie

WELL, COUSIN, here is your slave I am sending back to you. I made
him mine during this week, and he wore his fetters with such good
grace that one sees he is completely formed for captivity. Thank me
for not having kept him still another week; do not be annoyed, but
if I had kept him until he began to be tired of me, I should not
have sent him back so soon. I kept him, therefore, unscrupulously,
but I did scruple not to dare lodge him in my house. Sometimes I
am conscious of my proud soul which disdains servile decorum
and is so consistent with virtue. But in this case I was more reserved, without knowing why, and all that is certain is that I am
more inclined to reproach than to applaud myself for this reserve.

But do you know why our friend stayed here so peaceably? First,
he was with me, and I maintain that is already enough cause to
make him patient. He spared me some worries and was of service
to me in my business; a friend does not weary of that. A third
reason that you have already guessed, although you pretend not
to perceive it, is that he spoke to me of you, and if we took the
time that this conversation lasted from all that which he spent
here, you would see that very little is left to place to my account.
But what a curious whim, to leave you in order to have the pleasure
of speaking of you! Not so curious as one would readily say. In
your presence he is constrained; he must watch himself incessantly.
The slightest indiscretion could become a crime, and in these dangerous moments, honest hearts permit duty alone to be heard. But
when we are far from that which was dear to us, we permit ourselves
to dream of it again. If we stifle a sentiment which has become
criminal, why should we reproach ourselves for having had it while
it was not so? Can the sweet memory of a legitimate happiness ever
be a crime? This, I think, is reasoning which would ill suit you but

in which, after all, he may indulge himself. He began, as it were, to run over the course of his former love. His early youth passed by a second time in our conversations. He told me all his secrets again; he recalled those happy times when he was permitted to love you; he painted to my heart the delights of an innocent passion . . . no doubt he embellished them!

He spoke very little of his present state in regard to you, and what he did say to me about it contained more respect and admiration than love, so that I see him returning much more reassured about his heart than he was when he arrived. It is not that as soon as you are concerned, one cannot perceive in the bottom of his overly sensitive heart a certain tenderness which friendship alone, though not less affected, still expresses in another manner; but for a long time I have observed that no one can see you or think of you coolly, and if to the general sentiment which the sight of you inspires we add the sweeter sentiment that an ineradicable memory must have left in him, we will find it difficult and perhaps impossible that, even with the most severe virtue, he should be otherwise than he is. I have questioned, observed, watched him well; I have examined him as much as possible. I cannot read his soul; he himself reads it no better, but I can answer to you at least that he is penetrated by the force of his duties and of yours, and that to conceive the idea of Julie contemptible and corrupted would be more horrible for him than that of his own annihilation. Cousin, I have only one bit of advice to give you, and I beg you to pay attention to it: avoid details about the past, and I answer to you for the future.

As for the restitution you mentioned to me, you must think no more of it. After having exhausted all imaginable reasons, I begged, urged, conjured, pouted, kissed; I took his hands, I would have fallen on my knees if he had let me do so, but he did not even listen to me. He carried his ill-humor and stubbornness to the point of swearing that he would sooner consent to seeing you no more than part with your portrait. Finally, in a fit of indignation, making me touch it where it was fastened over his heart, he said to me with such emotion that he could hardly breathe, "Here it is, here is this portrait, the only comfort I have left, which you desire from me yet. You may be sure that it will never be torn from me except with my life."

Believe me, cousin, let us be prudent and allow him to keep the portrait. What does it basically matter to you if it stays with him? So much the worse for him if he is obstinate about keeping it.

After having well opened and eased his heart, he seemed to me tranquil enough for me to speak to him of his affairs. I found that time and reason had not changed his plan and that he confined all his ambition to spending his life in the service of Lord Bomston. I could only approve a project so honorable, so suited to his character, and so becoming the gratitude he owes to his Lordship's unparalleled kindness. He told me you had been of the same opinion, but that Monsieur de Wolmar had remained silent. An idea comes into my head. From the rather singular conduct of your husband, and from other indications, I suspect that he has some secret plan for our friend which he is not disclosing. Let us leave him to himself and trust in his prudence. The way in which he is going about it sufficiently proves that if my conjecture is correct, he is meditating nothing which is not advantageous to the one for whom he is taking so much trouble. [51]

Admire my discretion. I have yet said nothing to you of the present I am sending you and which promises you another soon. But you have received it before opening my letter, and you who know how much I idolize it and how much reason I have to do so, you whose avarice was so anxious for this present, you will agree that I give more than I had promised. Ah, the poor little one! At the moment you read this, she is already in your arms. She is more fortunate than her mother, but in two months I shall be more fortunate than she, for I shall be more sensible of my happiness. Alas! Dear cousin, do you not already have me entirely? Where you are, where my daughter is, what part of me is still missing? There she is, that charming child. Accept her as your own. I yield her to you, I give her to you, I resign maternal authority into your hands. Correct my failings, charge yourself with the duties which to your thinking I fulfill so poorly. From today be the mother of the girl who is to be your daughter-in-law, and to make her still more dear to me, make another Julie of her if possible. [52]

Adieu, my beloved friend. Adieu, my dear inseparable one. You may be sure that the time is drawing near and that the grapes will not be gathered without me.

❧ LETTER X ❧

To Lord Bomston

WHAT PLEASURES, known too late, I have enjoyed these past three weeks! How sweet it is to pass one's days in the midst of a tranquil friendship, sheltered from the storm of impetuous passions! My Lord, what a pleasant and affecting sight is that of a simple and well regulated house in which order, peace, and innocence prevail, in which without show, without pomp, everything is assembled which is in conformity with the true end of man! The country, the seclusion, the tranquillity, the season, the vast body of water which is offered to my eyes, the wild aspect of the mountains—everything here reminds me of my delightful Isle of Tinian. I see fulfilled the ardent desires which I conceived so many times there. Here I lead a life according to my inclinations; here I find a society agreeable to my heart. Only two persons are wanting in this place for all my happiness to be centered here, and I have hopes of seeing them in it soon. [53]

Since the master and mistress of this house have fixed it as their residence, they have put to use all that formerly served only for ornament; it is no longer a house made to be seen but to be lived in. They have shut up long series of rooms to change the inconvenient situation of the doors; they have cut up excessively large rooms to have better distributed apartments. For old and rich furniture they have substituted simple and comfortable things. Everything here is pleasant and cheerful. Everything breathes an air of plenty and propriety; nothing savors of pomp and luxury. There is not a single room in which one may not recognize that he is in the country and yet in which he may not find all the conveniences of the city. The same changes are to be observed outside. The yard has been enlarged at the expense of the coach houses. In the place of an old, ramshackled billiard room, Monsieur and Madame de Wolmar have put a fine wine press, and a dairy room where the clamorous peacocks, which they have disposed of, used to stay. The garden was too small for the needs of the kitchen; they have made a second one out of the flower bed, but one so neat and so well arranged that the

flower bed thus transformed pleases the eye more than before. For
the mournful yews which used to cover the walls, they have substituted fine fruit trees. Instead of the useless horse chestnuts, young
black mulberry trees are beginning to give shade to the yard, and
they have planted two rows of walnut trees up to the road in place
of the old lindens which used to border the avenue. Everywhere
they have substituted the useful for the agreeable, and yet the agreeable has almost always prevailed. For myself, at least, I find that the
noises of the yard, the crowing of the cocks, the lowing of the cattle,
the harnessing of the wagons, the meals in the fields, the return of
the workers, and the whole aspect of rural economy give this house
an appearance more rustic, more lively, more animated, more gay
than it had before in its gloomy dignity, and it has something indefinable which savors of joy and well being. [54]

All idle subtleties are unknown in this house, and the great art
by which the master and mistress make their servants such as they
desire them to be is to appear to their people such as they are. Their
conduct is always frank and open because they have no fear that
their actions may belie their words. Since they do not have for themselves a set of morals different from that which they want to incul-
cate in others, they have no need of circumspection in their speech.
One word thoughtlessly let slip does not overturn the principles
they have striven to establish. They do not indiscreetly tell all their
affairs, but they openly proclaim all their maxims. At the table,
while strolling, in private, or before everyone, their language is always the same. Artlessly, they say what they think on every subject,
and without their having any individual in mind, each servant always finds some instruction in their discourse. Since the servants
never see their master do anything which is not upright, just, and
equitable, they do not consider justice as the tax upon the poor, as
the yoke of the wretched, as one of the miseries of their condition.
The care the master and mistress take never to let the workers come
in vain and lose days in order to beg payment for their work ac-
customs the servants to perceiving the value of time. Seeing the solicitude of the master and mistress to husband that of others, each
concludes that his own is precious to him and makes idleness
a greater crime. The servants' confidence in their master's integrity
gives force to their regulations which makes them observed and prevents their being abused. They do not fear that in each week's
gratuities the mistress may always find that it is the youngest or the
best looking who has been the most diligent. An old servant does
not fear that they may find some quibble to save increasing the

wages given him. No one hopes to profit from a disagreement between the master and the mistress to assert himself and obtain
from one what the other has refused. Those who are to be married
do not fear that there may be an obstacle placed in the way of their
settlement, in order to keep them longer, and that thus their good
service may do them injury. If some strange servant came to say to
the people of this house that masters and servants are in a veritable
state of war; that when the latter do the former all the injury that
they can they are only retaliating justly; that the masters being
usurpers, liars, and cheats, there is no wrong in treating them as
they treat the prince or the people or individuals and in secretly
returning them the injuries they do quite openly—he who would
speak in this way would not be understood by anyone. Here the master is not even minded to combat or prevent such talk; to be
obliged to refute it is the concern only of those who give rise to it.

There is never either sullenness or discontent in obedience because there is neither haughtiness nor capriciousness in the command, because nothing is demanded which is not reasonable or expedient, and because the master and mistress sufficiently respect the
dignity of a man, even though he is a servant, so as to employ him
only with things that do not debase him. Moreover, nothing here is
considered base except vice, and all that is useful and justifiable is
considered honest and proper.

Even if no outside intrigues are allowed, no one is tempted to
have any. The servants know well that their most assured fortune
is attached to that of their master and that they will never want for
anything as long as the house is seen to prosper. In serving it, therefore, they are taking care of their own patrimony and increasing
it by making their service agreeable; this is to their greatest self-interest. But this word is hardly in place in this case, for I have never
seen any establishment in which self-interest was so prudently directed and in which it nevertheless was of less influence than in this
house. All is done through affection. One would say that these mercenary souls are purified in entering this place of wisdom and harmony. One would say that a part of the intelligence of the master
and the sentiments of the mistress have passed into each of their
servants, so much does one find them judicious, kind, honest and
much above their station. To be esteemed, appreciated, wished well,
is their greatest ambition, and they consider the kind words said to
them as elsewhere others consider the presents given them.

There, my Lord, are my principal observations on the economy
of this house which concerns the servants and workers. As for the

manner in which Monsieur and Madame de Wolmar live and the direction of the children, each of these topics well deserves a separate letter. You know with what intention I began these observations, but in truth, the whole forms so enchanting a picture that to love to contemplate it I need no other reason than the pleasure I find in it.

❧ LETTER XI ❧

To Lord Bomston

NO, MY LORD, I do not contradict myself. One sees nothing in this household which does not combine the agreeable and the useful, but the useful occupations are not limited to pursuits which yield a profit; they comprise, furthermore, every innocent and simple amusement which nourishes the inclination for seclusion, work, and temperance, and which preserves, in whoever applies himself to them, a wholesome mind and a heart free from the disturbance of the passions. If indolent idleness engenders only melancholy and boredom, the delight of pleasant leisure is the result of a laborious life. We work only to enjoy ourselves; this alternating of labor and recreation is our true vocation. The repose which serves as relaxation from past labors and as encouragement to additional ones is no less necessary to man than the labor itself.

After having admired the effect of the vigilance and the attention of the most respectable mother in the ordering of her household, I saw that of her recreation in a secluded place where she takes her favorite walk and which she calls her Elysium.

For several days I had heard talk of this Elysium, about which they made a kind of mystery before me. Finally, after dinner yesterday, the extreme heat making the outdoors and the indoors almost equally unbearable, Monsieur de Wolmar proposed to his wife that she take a holiday that afternoon and, instead of withdrawing as usual into her children's room until evening, come with us to take the air in the orchard. She agreed to it, and we went there together.

This place, although quite close to the house, is so hidden by a shady walk which separates them that it is visible from no part of the house. The dense foliage which surrounds it makes it impervious to the eye, and it is always carefully locked. I was no sooner inside and turned around than, the door being hidden by alders and hazel trees which permit only two narrow passageways on the sides, I no longer saw by which way I had entered, and perceiving no door, I found myself there as if fallen from the sky.

Entering this so-called orchard, I was struck by an agreeable sensation of freshness which the thick foliage, the animated and vivid greenness, the flowers scattered about on all sides, the murmuring of a running brook, and the singing of a thousand birds brought to my imagination at least as much as to my senses; but at the same time I thought I saw the wildest, the most solitary place in nature, and it seemed I was the first mortal who had ever penetrated into this desert island. Surprised, impressed, ecstatic over a sight so little expected, I remained motionless for a moment, and cried out with involuntary enthusiasm, "Oh Tinian! Oh Juan Fernandez!* Julie, the world's end is at your threshold!"

"Many people think the same of it as you," she said with a smile, "but twenty paces more presently leads them back to Clarens. Let us see if the spell will last longer for you. This is the same orchard in which you formerly strolled and in which you have played with my cousin. You know that the vegetation here was rather dry, the trees rather sparse, affording insufficient shade, and that there was no water. Now here it is fresh, green, filled out, improved, embellished with flowers, and well watered. What do you think it cost me to put it into its present state? For you must know that I am superintendent of it and that my husband leaves its entire direction to me."

"In truth," I said to her, "it cost you only neglect. This place is charming, it is true, but uncultivated and wild. I see no marks of human work. You have locked the door, water has come I know not how, nature alone has done all the rest, and you yourself would never be able to do as well."

"It is true," she said, "that nature has done everything, but under my direction, and there is nothing here which I have not ordered. Guess again."

"First," I replied, "I do not understand how, even with trouble and money, you could supply the effects of time. The trees. . . ."

"As for those," said Monsieur de Wolmar, "you will observe that not many are very large, and those were already here. Besides, Julie

---

* Desert islands in the South Seas, celebrated in the voyage of Admiral Anson. [*Rousseau*]

had begun this long before her marriage, almost immediately after her mother's death, when she came here with her father to find solitude."

"Well," I said, "since you insist that all these massy bowers, these arbors, these sloping tufts, these well shaded thickets have grown in seven or eight years and that art had a hand in it, I estimate that if in an enclosure so vast you have done all this for two thousand crowns, you have indeed economized."

"You have guessed two thousand crowns too much," she said. "It cost me nothing."

"What, nothing?"

"No, nothing, unless you count a dozen days work each year from my gardener, as much from two or three of my servants, and some from Monsieur de Wolmar himself who has not disdained sometimes to be my apprentice gardener."

I understood nothing of this riddle, but Julie who until then had held me back, said to me as she let me go, "Go farther within, and you will understand. Adieu Tinian, adieu Juan Fernandez, adieu all enchantment! In a moment you will be on your way back from the world's end."

With ecstasy I began to wander through the orchard thus metamorphosed, and if I did not find any exotic plants or any of the fruits of the Indies, I found those natural to the country, laid out and combined in a way to produce a more cheerful and agreeable effect. The turf, green and thick but short and close, was interwoven with wild thyme, mint, sweet marjoram, and other fragrant herbs. I saw a thousand dazzling wild flowers, among which my eye with surprise distinguished some garden flowers, which seemed to grow naturally with the others. I encountered here and there some shady thickets, as impervious to the sun's rays as if they were in the densest forests; these thickets were composed of trees of the most flexible wood, the branches of which had been made to bend round, hang down to the ground, and take root, by a process similar to that which mangrove trees follow naturally in America. In the more open spots, here and there without order and without symmetry, I saw roses, raspberries, currants, lilac bushes, hazel trees, elders, syringa, broom, and trefoil, which embellished the ground by giving it the appearance of lying fallow. I followed winding and irregular walks bordered by these flowery thickets and covered with a thousand garlands of woody vines, wild grape, hops, convolvulus, bryony, clematis, and other plants of this kind, among which honeysuckle and jasmine condescended to twine. These garlands seemed as if negligently scattered from one tree to the next, as I had sometimes observed in forests, and formed above us a kind of drapery which sheltered us from the sunlight, while under foot we had smooth, comfortable, and dry walking upon a fine moss, with no sand, no grass, and no rough shoots. [55]

All these little paths were bordered and crossed by a limpid and clear stream, sometimes winding through the grass and the flowers in almost imperceptible rivulets, sometimes running in larger brooklets over a pure and speckled gravel which made the water more transparent. I observed springs bubbling and rising from the ground, and occasionally I saw deeper canals in which the calm and peaceful water reflected objects to my eye. [56] A layer of earth, covered with an inch of gravel from the lake and strewn with shells, forms the bed of the streams. These same streams, running at intervals under some large tiles recovered with earth and grass at ground level, form as many artificial springs where they issue forth. Some rivulets are lifted by siphons above rugged places and bubble as they cascade. The earth thus refreshed and moistened continually yields new flowers and keeps the grass always green and beautiful.

The more I wandered through this pleasant refuge, the more I felt increasing the delightful sensation which I had experienced upon entering. However, curiosity kept me pressing on. I was more eager to see the objects than to examine the impression they made on me, and I preferred to give myself up to that charming contemplation without taking the trouble to reflect about it. But Madame de Wolmar, drawing me from my reverie by taking me by the arm, said to me, "All that you see is nothing but vegetable and inanimate nature, and whatever we may do, it always leaves behind a melancholy idea of solitude. Come, see it animated and responsive. It is then that at every instant of the day you will find a new attraction."

"You anticipate me," I said to her. "I hear a noisy and confused chirping, and I perceive a few birds. I suppose you have an aviary."

"That is true," she said. "Let us go near it."

I did not yet dare say what I thought of the aviary, but there was something in this idea which displeased me and did not seem to correspond with the rest.

We descended by a thousand turns to the bottom of the orchard, where I found all the water collected in a pretty stream flowing gently between two rows of old willows that had often been trimmed. Their hollow and half bare tops formed a kind of vase from which came forth, by the process I have mentioned, some tufts of honeysuckle, of which one part entwined around the branches

and another dropped gracefully along the stream. Almost at the end
of the enclosure was a small pond, bordered with herbs, rushes, and
reeds, serving as a watering place for the aviary and as the last use
made of that water, so precious and so well husbanded.

Beyond this pond was a flat plot of ground which terminated, in
the angle of the enclosure, in a hillock covered with a multitude of
shrubby trees of all kinds; the smallest were toward the top, and they
increased in size as the ground sloped downward, which made the
tops almost on a level, or showed at least that one day they were to
be so. In front were a dozen trees still young but of a nature to become very large, such as the beech, the elm, the ash, and the acacia.
These made up a copse on this side which served as a refuge for
that flock of birds, whose chirping I had heard from afar, and it was
in the shade of this foliage, as under a huge parasol, that I saw them
flying about, hopping up and down, singing, provoking each other,
and fighting, as if they had not perceived us. They flew away so
little at our approach that according to the notion which I had
had before, I first thought them locked up by a wire lattice,
but when we had reached the edge of the pond, I saw several descend and approach us through a short passage which cut through
the flat part and connected the pond to the aviary. Then Monsieur
de Wolmar circled the pond and scattered on the passage two or
three handfuls of mixed seeds which he had in his pocket, and when
he had withdrawn, the birds flocked in and began to eat like
chickens, with such an air of familiarity that I plainly perceived that
they were trained to do this trick.

"That is charming!" I exclaimed. "Your use of the word aviary
had surprised me, but I understand now. I see that you mean
to have them as guests and not as prisoners."

"Whom are you calling guests?" Julie answered. "It is we who
are theirs. Here they are the masters, and we pay them a tribute in
order to be admitted sometimes."

"Very well," I replied, "but how do these masters get possession
of this place? How is it that so many voluntary inhabitants are
collected in it? I have never heard of anyone attempting something
of this kind, and I should not have thought it could succeed if I did
not have the proof before my eyes."

"Patience and time," said Monsieur de Wolmar, "have performed
this miracle. These are the expedients which rich people scarcely
think of in their pleasures. Always in a hurry to enjoy themselves,
force and money are the only means they know. They have birds
in cages and friends at so much a month. If the servants ever came

near this place, you would soon see the birds disappear, and if they are presently here in great numbers, it is because some have always been here. You cannot make them come when there are none in the first place, but it is easy when there are some to attract more, by anticipating all their needs, by never frightening them, by allowing them to make their nests with security, and by not disturbing the little ones in the nest, for by these means those who are here remain and those who arrive unexpectedly stay too. This copse existed before, although it was separate from the orchard. Julie has only had it enclosed by a quickset hedge, removed the one which separated it, enlarged and embellished it with new plans. To the right and left of the path which leads to it, you see two spaces filled with a confused mixture of grass, straw, and all sorts of plants. Each year she has sown here some corn, millet, sunflower seeds, hempseed, vetch, and all the grain that birds generally like, and nothing is ever reaped. Besides that, almost every day, summer and winter, she or I bring them something to eat, and when we fail, Fanchon usually supplies our place. They have water four steps away, as you see. Madame de Wolmar carries her attention so far as to provide them every spring with little heaps of horsehair, straw, wool, moss, and other materials suitable for making nests. With the proximity of materials, the abundance of provisions, and the great care which is taken to keep all their enemies away,* the uninterrupted tranquillity they enjoy induces them to lay their eggs in this convenient place, where they want for nothing and where no one disturbs them. That is how the habitation of the fathers becomes that of the children, and how the populace thrives and multiplies."

"Ah," said Julie, "you no longer see anything! Each no longer thinks beyond himself. But the inseparable mates, the zeal for domestic duties, paternal and maternal tenderness—you have missed all that. Two months ago you should have been here to give your eyes to the most charming spectacle and your heart to the sweetest sentiment of nature."

"Madame," I replied rather sadly, "you are a wife and mother. These are the pleasures which are your privilege to know."

Immediately Monsieur de Wolmar took me by the hand and said as he clasped it, "You have friends, and these friends have children. How could you be stranger to paternal affection?"

I looked at him; I looked at Julie. Both looked at each other and gave me such an affecting regard that, embracing one after the

* Mice, owls, and above all, children. [*Rousseau*]

other, I said to them with tenderness, "They are as dear to me as they are to you."

I do not know by what curious effect a single word can thus alter a mind, but since that moment, Monsieur de Wolmar has appeared to me to be another man, and I consider him less as the husband of her whom I loved so much than as the father of two children for whom I would give my life.

I wished to circle the pond in order to see this delightful refuge and its little inhabitants from close by, but Madame de Wolmar held me back. "No one," she told me, "disturbs them in their dwelling, and you are the very first of our guests whom I have brought up to this point. There are four keys to the orchard, of which my father and we each have one. Fanchon has the fourth, as superintendent, and in order to bring my children here sometimes, a favor the value of which is increased by the extreme circumspection required of them while they are here. Even Gustin never enters except with one of the four. Once the two spring months are past in which his work is useful, he hardly ever comes in anymore, and all the rest is done among us."

"Thus," I said to her, "for fear that your birds may become your slaves, you make yourselves theirs."

"Those," she replied, "are indeed the words of a tyrant who believes he is enjoying his liberty only while he is disturbing that of others."

As we were leaving in order to return to the house, Monsieur de Wolmar threw a handful of barley in the pond, and looking into it, I saw some small fish. "Ah, ah!" I said immediately, "there are some prisoners nevertheless."

"Yes," he said, "they are prisoners of war, whose lives have been spared."

"Without a doubt," his wife added. "Some time ago, Fanchon stole from the kitchen some little perch which she brought here without my knowledge. I leave them here for fear of killing them if I put them back into the lake, for it is better to confine some fish a little narrowly than to offend an honest person."

"You are right," I replied, "and the fish are not too much to be pitied for having escaped the pan at that price."

"Well, what do you think of it?" she said to me as we were returning. "Are you still at the world's end?"

"No," I said. "Here I am completely out of the world, and you have in fact transported me into Elysium."

"The pompous name she has given this orchard," Monsieur de

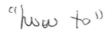
"how to"

Wolmar said, "truly deserves that raillery. Be modest in your praise of her childish games, and know that they have never entrenched in any way upon her duties as a mother."

"I know," I replied. "I am very sure of it, and yet her childish games please me more in this way than the labors of men. Yet there is one thing here," I continued, "which I cannot understand. It is that a place so different from what it was can become what it is only with cultivation and care, yet nowhere do I see the slightest trace of cultivation. All is green, fresh, vigorous, and the gardener's hand is nowhere to be seen. Nothing contradicts the notion of a desert island which came to me upon entering, and I see no human footsteps."

"Ah!" said Monsieur de Wolmar, "it is because we have taken great pains to efface them. I have often been witness to, sometimes the accomplice of, this roguery. We have hay sown over all the cultivated places, and the grass soon hides the traces of work. In winter we have the sparse and dry places covered with a few layers of manure. The manure eats up the moss, revives the grass and the plants. The trees themselves are not the worse for it, and in the summer it no longer shows. In regard to the moss which covers some of the paths, it was Lord Bomston who from England sent us the secret of making it take root.

"These two sides," he continued, "were closed in by walls. The walls have been hidden, not by trellises, but by thick shrubby trees which make the boundaries of the place seem to be the beginning of a wood. Strong quickset hedges grow on the two other sides, made with maples, hawthorns, holly, privet, and other shrubby trees mixed in, which take from them the appearance of hedges and give them that of a coppice wood. You see nothing laid out in a line, nothing made level. The carpenter's line never entered this place. Nature plants nothing by the line. The simulated irregularities of the winding paths are artfully managed in order to prolong the walk, hide the edges of the island, and enlarge its apparent size, without creating inconvenient and excessively frequent turnings." *

Considering all this, I found it rather curious that they should take so much trouble to hide that very trouble which they had taken. Would it not have been better to have taken none at all?

"In spite of all you have been told," Julie answered me, "you are judging the work by the effect, and you deceive yourself. All that

* Thus these are not like those of these small, fashionable groves, so ridiculously planned that one walks in zig-zag manner in them and at each step must make a pirouette. [*Rousseau*]

you see are wild or sturdy plants, which need only to be put into the ground and which then come up by themselves. Besides, nature seems to desire to hide from the eyes of men its real attractions, of which they are too little aware and which they disfigure when they are within reach. Nature flies from frequented places. It is on the summits of mountains, in the depths of forests, on desert islands that it displays its most affecting charms. Those who love nature and cannot go seek it so far away are reduced to doing it violence, to forcing it in some manner to come dwell with them, and all this cannot be effected without a little illusion."

At these words, a thought came to me which made them laugh. "I picture to myself," I said, "a rich man of Paris or London, master of this house, bringing with him an architect who is paid dearly to spoil nature. With what disdain he would enter this simple and rude place! With what contempt he would have all these worthless things torn out! The fine lines he would trace! The fine walks he would cut open! Fine goose foot plants, fine trees shaped like parasols or fans! Fine, well carved trellises! Fine hedges, well designed, well squared, well contoured! Beautiful grass plots of fine English grass—round, square, crescent-shaped, oval! Fine yew trees, trimmed in the shape of dragons, pagodas, grotesque figures, all sorts of monsters! Fine bronze vases, fine stone fruit with which he would adorn his garden! . . ." *

"When all that shall have been carried out," said Monsieur de Wolmar, "he shall have made a very fine place in which people will hardly ever walk and from which they will always leave eagerly in order to seek the country, a dismal place in which they will not stroll but use as a thoroughfare to go take a stroll, whereas during my rural excursions I often hurry to come back in order to walk here." [57]

"I have only a single objection to make in regard to your Elysium," I added, looking at Julie, "but one which will seem serious to you. It is that it is a superfluous amusement. For what good did you make a new place to walk, having on the other side of the house some groves, so charming and so neglected?"

"It is true," she said, a little embarrassed, "but I prefer this one."

"If you had well considered your question before posing it," Monsieur de Wolmar interrupted, "it would be more than indis-

---

* I am persuaded that the time is coming when people will no longer want anything which is found in the country in their gardens. They will allow there no more plants or shrubs. They will want in it only porcelain flowers, china figures, lattices, sand of all colors, and fine vases full of nothing. [*Rousseau*]

creet. Since her marriage, my wife has never set foot in the groves you speak of. I know the reason although she has always kept it secret from me. You who are not unaware of it, learn to respect the place where you are. It has been planted by virtuous hands."

I had scarcely received this just reprimand when the little family led by Fanchon entered as we were leaving. These three charming children embraced Monsieur and Madame de Wolmar. I had my share of their little caresses. Julie and I went back into the Elysium a few steps with them; then we went to rejoin Monsieur de Wolmar who was speaking to some workmen. On the way, she told me that after she had become a mother, an idea came to her with respect to this walk which had increased her zeal to embellish it.

"I had an eye," she said to me, "to the amusement of my children and to their health when they are older. The upkeep of this place requires more care than labor. It is more a matter of giving a certain contour to the branches of the plants than of digging and working the ground. I intend some day to make gardeners of my little ones. They will have as much exercise as is necessary to strengthen their constitution, but not enough to weary it. Besides, what is too much for their age will be done by others, and they will confine themselves to the work which amuses them.

"I cannot tell you," she added, "what pleasure I enjoy in imagining my children busied in returning to me the little attentions I bestow with such pleasure on them, and the joy of their tender hearts in seeing their mother strolling with delight along the shady walks formed by their hands.

"In truth, my friend," she said with emotion in her voice, "days spent this way suggest the happiness of the next life, and it is not without reason that in thinking of it I have given the name Elysium to this place."

My Lord, this incomparable woman is as dear a mother as she is a wife, as she is a friend, as she is a daughter, and, to the eternal torment of my heart, it is even thus that she was a mistress.

Enthusiastic about so delightful a place, I begged them that evening to think fit that during my stay with them Fanchon might confide me her key and the duty of feeding the birds. Immediately Julie sent a sack of grain to my room and gave me her own key. I do not know why I accepted it with a kind of reluctance. It seemed to me that I should have preferred to have Monsieur de Wolmar's.

This morning I arose early, and with childish eagerness I went to lock myself in the desert island. What agreeable thoughts I expected to carry into that solitary place where the sweet aspect of nature alone was to drive from my memory all that artificial order of society which has made me so unhappy. I was thinking that everything which is to surround me is the work of her who was so dear to me. I shall contemplate her all about me. I shall see nothing which her hand may not have touched. I shall kiss the flowers which her feet have pressed. With the dew I shall breathe an air that she has breathed. The taste she has displayed in her amusements will make all her charms present to me, and I shall find her everywhere as she is in my inmost heart.

Entering the Elysium with these intentions, I suddenly remembered the last word Monsieur de Wolmar said to me yesterday almost in the same place. The memory of that single word immediately changed the whole state of my mind. I thought I saw the image of virtue where I was seeking that of pleasure. This image was mingled in my mind with the features of Madame de Wolmar, and for the first time since my return I saw Julie in my imagination not such as she was for me and as I still like to picture her to myself, but such as she appears before my eyes every day. My Lord, I thought I beheld that woman, so charming, so chaste, and so virtuous, in the middle of that same group which surrounded her yesterday. I imagined around her those three amiable children, the honorable and precious pledge of conjugal union and tender friendship, giving her and receiving from her a thousand affecting caresses. I saw at her side the grave Wolmar, that husband so cherished, so fortunate, so worthy of being so. I thought I saw his penetrating and judicious eye pierce to the bottom of my heart and make me blush again. I thought I heard him utter reproaches too well deserved and lessons too poorly attended. Last I saw Fanchon Regard, the living proof of the triumph of virtue and humanitarianism over the most ardent love. Ah! What guilty sentiment could have reached Julie through this impervious guard? With what indignation I should have suppressed the base ecstasies of a criminal and poorly extinguished passion, and how contemptible I should be if with a single sigh I should sully such an enchanting picture of innocence and honesty! In my mind I went back over the conversation she had with me as we left; then my imagination, again with her, considering the future that she contemplates with such delight, I saw that tender mother wiping the perspiration from her children's brows, kissing their ruddy cheeks, and devoting that heart, made to love, to the sweetest sentiment of nature. There was nothing, even to that name Elysium, which might not rectify the faults of my imagination and bring a serenity to my soul preferable to the disturbance of the most seductive passions. The name Elysium was a symbol in some way of the soul of the one who had chosen it. I reflected that with a disturbed conscience she would not have selected that name. I said to myself that peace prevails in her inmost heart just as in the refuge she has named.

I had promised myself a pleasant reverie. I had dreamed there more agreeably than I had expected. I spent in the Elysium two hours to which I prefer no other time in my life. Observing with what charm and what rapidity they had slipped by, I found that there is in the meditation of honest thoughts a sort of happiness which wicked people have never known. It is that of being pleased with oneself. If we reflected on this without presuppositions, I do not know another pleasure which could equal that one. I feel at least that whoever loves solitude as much as I must fear to do anything which may make it a torment for him. Perhaps from the same principles we could derive the key to the false judgments of men in regard to the advantages of vice and of virtue. For the enjoyment of virtue is wholly internal and is perceived only by the one who feels it, but all the advantages of vice strike the eyes of others, and it is only he who has them who may know what they cost him. [58]

✤ LETTER XII ✤

From Madame de Wolmar to Madame d'Orbe

IT IS DECREED, dear friend, that you are to be at all times my protection against myself, and that after having delivered me with such difficulty from the snares laid by my heart, you will defend me again from those laid by my reason. After so many cruel ordeals, I am learning to distrust reason's errors as I do the passions which are so often the cause of them. Would that I had always taken the same precaution! If in the past I had relied less on my understanding, I should have had to be less ashamed of my sentiments.

Do not let this preamble alarm you. I should be unworthy of your friendship if I still had to consult it on this serious subject. Crime was always a stranger to my heart, and I dare believe it more distant than ever. Therefore, hear me calmly, my cousin, and believe that I shall never need advice about doubts which honor alone can resolve.

For the six years I have been living with Monsieur de Wolmar in the most perfect union which could ever exist between two partners, you know that he has never spoken to me either of his family or of himself, and that having received him from a father as solicitous for his daughter's happiness as for the honor of his family, I have shown no eagerness to know more of his affairs than he considered proper to tell me. Content to be indebted to him for my father's life, my honor, my repose, my reason, my children, and all that which can give me some value in my own eyes, I was convinced that what I did not know of him did not belie what I did know, and I had no need to know more in order to love, esteem, and honor him as much as possible.

This morning at breakfast, he proposed our taking a walk before the heat of the day; then, under the pretext, he said, of not gadding about in the country in our morning dress, he led us into the groves, and precisely, my dear, into the very grove where all the misfortunes of my life began. Approaching this fatal spot, I felt my heart throbbing frightfully, and I should have refused to go in if shame had not checked me and if the recollection of a word which was spoken the other day in the Elysium had not made me fear the interpretations of my refusal. I do not know whether the philosopher was more tranquil, but some time afterward, having by chance glanced at him, I found him pale and changed, and I cannot tell you what uneasiness all that caused me.

Entering the grove, I saw my husband cast a glance at me and smile. He sat down between us, and after a moment of silence, taking us both by the hand, he said to us, "My children, I am beginning to see that my plans will not be fruitless and that all three of us may be united in a lasting attachment, capable of constituting our common happiness and my consolation in the weariness of an approaching old age. But I know you both better than you know me. It is only fair to make things equal, and although I have nothing very interesting to impart to you, since you no longer keep any secret from me, I will keep no more from you."

Then he revealed to us the mystery of his birth which until now had been known only by my father. When you know it, you will comprehend just how far indifference and moderation can go in a man capable of keeping such a secret from his wife for six years. But this secret is nothing for him, and he thinks too little of it to exert a great effort to conceal it.

"I shall not detain you," he said to us, "over the events of my life. It is less important to you to know my adventures than my character. The former are simple, like the latter, and if you know what I am you will easily understand what I was able to do. I have a naturally tranquil mind and a cold heart. I am one of those men whom people think they are truly insulting when they call them insensible, that is, when they say they have no passion which diverts them from following the true direction of mankind. Little susceptible of pleasure and of grief, I even experience only very faintly that sentiment of self-interest and of humanitarianism which makes the affections of others our own. If I feel pain in seeing good people suffer, pity has no part in it, for I feel none in seeing the wicked suffer. My only active principle is a natural love of order, and the well contrived concurrence of the accidents of fortune and the action of men pleases me exactly like beautiful symmetry in a picture or like a well presented play in the theater. If I have any ruling passion, it is that of observation. I like to read the hearts of men. Since my own gives me few illusions, since I observe coolly and without self-interest, and since long experience has given me some insight, I hardly ever am mistaken in my judgments. This advantage is also the whole recompense my self-love receives from my constant studies, for I do not like to play a role but only to see others playing them. Society is agreeable to me for the sake of contemplation, not as a member of it. If I could alter the nature of my being and become a living eye, I willingly would make this exchange. Thus my indifference toward men does not make me at all independent of them. Without caring about being observed, I need to observe them, and though they are not dear to me they are necessary.

"The first two ranks of society which I had the opportunity to observe were courtiers and valets, two classes of men less different in essence than in appearance and so little worthy of being studied, so easy to read, that I was bored with them at first glance. Leaving the court where everything is immediately observable, I unknowingly escaped a dangerous rebellion which was threatening and which I should not have eluded otherwise. I changed my name and, wishing to become acquainted with military men, I went to seek a place in the service of a foreign prince. It was there that I had the good fortune of being useful to your father who was forced by despair over having killed his friend to expose himself rashly and above his duty. The sensitive and grateful heart of that brave officer began from then on to give me a better opinion of human nature. He attached himself to me with a friendship which it was

impossible for me not to return, and since that time we have not
ceased to form connections which become closer from day to day.
In my new state of mind, I learned that self-interest is not, as I had
believed, the only motive for human actions and that among the
multitude of prejudices which are opposed to virtue, there are also
some which are in favor of it. [59]

"Along with a true knowledge of men, of which idle philosophy
provides only the appearance, I found another advantage which I
had not expected. This was the opportunity to intensify, by an
active life, that love of order which I had received from nature and
to acquire a new relish for the good, by the pleasure of contributing
to it. This sentiment made me a little less contemplative, attached
me a little more to myself, and by a consequence rather natural to
this progress, I perceived that I was alone. Solitude, which was always tedious, became frightful for me, and I could hope no more
to avoid it for long. Without having lost my dispassionate nature,
I needed an attachment. The image of decrepitude without consolation afflicted me by anticipation, and, for the first time in my
life, I knew uneasiness and melancholy. I spoke of my anguish to
Baron d'Étange.

" 'You need not,' he told me, 'grow old as a bachelor. I myself,
after having lived almost independent even within the bonds of
marriage, feel that I need to become a husband and father again,
and I am going to retire into the bosom of my family. It only depends on you to make it your own and restore to me the son I have
lost. I have an only daughter to be married. She is not without merit. She has a sensitive heart, and love for her duty makes her
love all which is connected with it. She is neither a beauty nor a
prodigy of understanding, but come see her, and believe me, if you
feel nothing for her you will never feel anything for anyone in the
world.'

"I came, I saw you, Julie, and I found that your father had
spoken modestly of you. Your ecstasies, your joyful tears as you embraced him gave me the first, or rather, the only emotion I had ever
experienced in my life. If the impression was slight, it was unique,
and sentiments only need to be strong to produce a result in proportion to those which oppose them. Three years absence did not
change the state of my heart. The state of yours did not escape me
at my return, and I must here give you vengeance for the confession which has cost you so much."

Judge, my dear, with what extraordinary surprise I then learned
that all my secrets had been revealed to him before my wedding

and that he had married me without being unaware that I belonged to another.

"This conduct was inexcusable," Monsieur de Wolmar continued. "I offended delicacy, I sinned against prudence, I exposed your honor and mine. I ought to have feared plunging both of us irretrievably into misfortunes, but I loved you and loved only you. Everything else was a matter of indifference to me. How can one repress even the most feeble passion when it is without counterbalance? That is the disadvantage of cool and tranquil tempers. All goes well as long as their insensibility protects them from temptations, but if one happens to attain them, they are conquered as soon as attacked, and reason, which governs while it rules alone, never has the power to resist the slightest effort. I was tempted only once, and I succumbed. If the intoxication of any other passion had made me waver again, I should have fallen at every false step. It is only passionate souls who are capable of struggling and conquering. All great efforts, all sublime actions are their doing. Cold reason has never achieved anything illustrious, and we triumph over passions only by opposing one to another. When the passion of virtue comes to the fore, it alone dominates and keeps all the rest in a state of equilibrium. That is how the truly wise man is formed, who is not sheltered from passions any more than another man is but who alone is capable of subduing them with themselves, as a pilot sails by adverse winds.

"You see that I am not claiming to extenuate my fault. Had it been one, I should have infallibly committed it, but, Julie, I understood you and did not commit a crime when I married you. I felt that all the happiness I could enjoy depended on you alone and that if someone was capable of making you happy, it was I. I knew that innocence and peace were necessary to your heart, that the love with which it was preoccupied would never provide it with them, and that only the horror of crime could drive love from it. I saw that your soul was in an extreme dejection from which it would emerge only by a new struggle and that it would be by feeling how estimable you could still be that you would learn to become so.

"Your heart was exhausted by love. Therefore, I considered as nothing the disparity of our ages which took from me the right of pretending to a sentiment which he who was the object of it could not enjoy and which was impossible for any other to obtain completely. On the contrary, seeing in a life more than half elapsed that I had felt a single inclination, I concluded that it would be lasting and I pleased myself with the thought of preserving it for the rest of my days. In my long searches, I have never found anything which equalled you. I thought that what you would not effect, nothing else in the world could. I ventured to rely on your virtue, and I married you. The secret you kept from me did not surprise me. I knew your reasons, and I saw in your prudent conduct why you kept it so long. Out of regard for you, I copied your reserve and did not want to deprive you of the honor of one day freely making me a confession which every instant I saw on the tip of your tongue. I have been mistaken in nothing. You have given me all that I had promised myself from you. When I intended to choose a wife, I desired to have a companion who was amiable, prudent, and happy. The first two conditions are fulfilled. My child, I hope we shall not be disappointed in the third."

At these words, in spite of all my efforts to interrupt him only with my tears, I could not keep myself from embracing him as I cried out, "My dear husband! Oh, the best and most beloved of men! Tell me what my happiness lacks, if not to promote yours, and to be more deserving. . . ."

"You are as happy as you can be," he said, interrupting me. "You deserve to be so, but it is time to enjoy that happiness in peace which up to now has cost you much anxiety. If your faithfulness might have been enough for me, all would have been accomplished from the moment you promised it to me. I wanted it, moreover, to be easy and agreeable for you, and to make it so we have both worked together without speaking of it to each other. Julie, we have succeeded, better than you think, perhaps. The only fault I find in you is that you have not been able to regain the self-confidence you owe yourself and that you undervalue yourself. Extreme modesty has its dangers as well as pride. Just as a rashness which carries us beyond our moral forces makes them ineffectual, a fright which keeps us from relying on them makes them useless. True prudence consists in knowing them thoroughly and acting up to them. You have acquired new force by changing your position. You are no longer that unfortunate girl who deplored her frailty as she yielded to it. You are the most virtuous of women, who knows no other laws than those of duty and honor and in whom the excessively vivid memory of her faults is the only fault left to be reproached. Instead of taking injurious precautions against yourself again, you should learn, then, to have self-confidence, in order to be able to rely more upon yourself. Discard unfair mistrust, capable sometimes of reviving the sentiments which occasioned it. Congratulate yourself, rather, for having been able to choose an honorable man at an age when it is so easy to be deluded, and for having formerly taken a lover whom today you can have as a friend before your husband's very eyes. Your liaison was no sooner known to me than I judged you, one by the other. I saw what a delusive enthusiasm had led you both astray. It acts only on sensitive souls. It ruins them sometimes, but it is through an attraction that seduces only them. I judged that the same inclination which had formed your attachment would break it as soon as it became criminal, and that vice could enter hearts like yours but not take root there.

passion for virtue

"Since then, I have understood that the bonds which prevailed between you did not need to be broken, that your mutual attachment had so many praiseworthy things about it that it ought rather to be regulated than destroyed, and that neither of you could forget the other without losing much of his worth. I knew that great struggles only stir up strong passions, and that if violent efforts exercise the mind, they cost it torments, the duration of which is capable of destroying it. I used Julie's gentleness to temper their severity.

"I nourished her friendship for you," he said to Saint-Preux. "I took from it what was left but not wanted, and I think I have preserved you a greater share of her affections, perhaps, than she might have allowed you if I had left her to herself. My success encouraged me, and I determined to attempt your cure as I had brought about hers, for I esteem you, and in spite of vicious prejudices, I have always observed that there was nothing good which one cannot obtain from sensitive souls with confidence and sincerity. I have observed you, you have not deceived me, you will not deceive me, and although you are not yet what you ought to be, I see you better than you think you are and am more satisfied with you than you are with yourself. I know that my conduct has a curious appearance and is opposed to all ordinary maxims, but maxims become less general in proportion as we read hearts better, and Julie's husband is not to act like any other man.

"My children," he said to us in a tone all the more affecting as it came from a dispassionate man, "stay as you are, and we shall all be content. The danger consists only in opinion. Have no fear of yourselves and you will have nothing to fear. Think only of the present and I answer to you for the future. I cannot tell you more today, but if my plans are carried out and if my hope does not betray me, our destinies will be better fulfilled, and you will both be happier than if you had belonged to each other."

plans

Getting up, he embraced us and desired us to embrace each other too, in that place . . . in that very place where once before . . .

Claire, oh good Claire, how much you have always loved me! I made no resistance to it. Alas! How wrong I should have been to make any! This kiss was nothing like the one which had made the grove fearful for me. I congratulated myself sadly for it, and I knew that my heart was more altered than I had dared believe it until then.

As we returned to the road to the house, my husband took me by the hand and, pointing to that grove we had just left, he said, laughing, "Julie, fear that refuge no longer. It has just been profaned."

You will not believe me, cousin, but I swear to you that he has some supernatural gift for reading one's inmost heart. May Heaven allow him it forever! With so much cause to despise me, it is no doubt to this art that I am indebted for his indulgence.

You do not yet see in this any occasion for advice. Patience, my angel, I am coming to it, but the conversation I have just related to you was necessary for understanding the rest.

As we returned, my husband, who has been expected for a long time at Étange, told me that he proposed leaving tomorrow to go there, that he would see you on his way, and that he would stay there five or six days. Without saying all that I was thinking of such an ill-timed departure, I pointed out that it did not seem to me sufficiently necessary to oblige Monsieur de Wolmar to leave a guest whom he himself had invited into his house.

"Do you want me," he replied, "to use ceremony with him, to inform him that he is not in his own home? I like the hospitality of the people of the Valais. I hope that he finds their sincerity here and that he allows us to use their freedom."

Seeing that he would not listen to me, I took another course and tried to persuade our guest to make this trip with him. "You will find," I said to him, "a place which has its beauties, even those which you prefer. You will visit my patrimony and that of my ancestors. The interest you take in me does not permit me to believe that you may be indifferent to this sight."

I had my mouth open to add that this chateau resembled Lord Bomston's which . . . but fortunately I had time to bite my tongue. He answered quite simply that I was right and that he would do what would please me. But Monsieur de Wolmar, who seemed determined to drive me to the limit, replied that he was to do what pleased himself.

"Which do you prefer, to go or to stay?" he asked.

"To stay," he said without hesitating.

"Well, stay," my husband replied, clasping his hand. "You are an honest and true man. I am very content with that answer."

There was no way of disputing this point much before the third person who was listening to us. I kept silent but could not hide my concern well enough for my husband not to perceive it.

"What then," he resumed with an air of discontent, during a moment when Saint-Preux was at a distance from us, "shall I have pleaded your cause against yourself in vain, and will Madame de Wolmar be content with a virtue that needs to choose its opportunities? As for me, I am more demanding. I wish to owe my wife's fidelity to her heart and not to chance, and it is not enough for me if she keeps her faith. I am offended if she is in doubt about it."

Then he led us into his study where I all but fell in a faint to see him take from a drawer, along with copies of some of our friend's accounts that I had given him, the very originals of all the letters that I thought I had once seen Babi burn in my mother's room.

"Here," he said to me, showing them to us, "is the foundation of my security. If they deceive me, it would be foolish to rely on anything which concerns human nature. I consign my wife and my honor in trust to her who, unmarried and seduced, could prefer an act of beneficence to a single and sure tryst. I entrust Julie as wife and mother to the man who, at perfect liberty to satisfy his desires, was capable of respecting Julie as mistress and unmarried girl. If either of you despises himself enough to think I am wrong, say so, and I retract it immediately."

Cousin, do you think it was easy to dare answer these words? However, I found a moment in the afternoon to take my husband aside, and without entering into arguments which it was not permissible for me to urge very far, I confined myself to asking him to delay his departure two days. They were granted to me immediately; I am using them to send you this letter by express messenger and to wait for your answer, to know what I must do.

I know that I have only to beg my husband not to leave at all, and he who never refused me anything will not refuse me such a slight favor. But, my dear, I perceive that he takes pleasure in the confidence he puts in me, and I fear losing a part of his esteem, if he thinks that I have occasion for more reserve than he is allowing me. I know likewise that I have only to say a word to Saint-Preux and he will not hesitate to accompany him. But will my husband be thus misled, and can I take this step without preserving an air of authority over Saint-Preux, which might seem to allow him in turn some sort of privilege? Besides, I am afraid that he will infer from this precaution only that I feel it necessary, and this means, which seemed at first the best, is perhaps the most dangerous. After all, I am not unaware that no consideration can be weighed with a real danger, but does this danger in fact exist? That is precisely the doubt you must resolve.

The more I will probe the present state of my soul, the more I find in it to reassure myself. My heart is pure, my conscience is calm, I feel neither uneasiness nor fear, and for all that takes place within me, my sincerity toward my husband costs me no effort. Not that certain involuntary memories do not sometimes give me a tender feeling from which I had rather be exempt, but these memories are far indeed from being produced by the sight of him who caused them; they seem to me more infrequent since his return, and however sweet it is for me to see him, by what singularity I know not, it is sweeter for me to think of him. In short, I find that I do not have the same need for virtue's assistance to be composed in his presence, and that even if the horror of crime did not exist, it would be very difficult to revive the sentiments that it has destroyed.

But, my angel, is it enough that my heart reassures me when reason ought to alarm me? I have lost the right to rely upon myself. Who will guarantee me that my confidence is not another illusion of vice? How can I trust in sentiments which have so many times deceived me? Does not crime always spring from the pride that scorns temptation, and is not to defy the dangers to which we have succumbed to wish to succumb again?

Weigh all these considerations, my cousin. You will see that if they are trifling in themselves, they are serious enough in their object to deserve consideration. Deliver me, then, from the uncertainty in which they have thrown me. Indicate to me how I must behave in this delicate case, for my past errors have affected my judgment and made me fearful about deciding on anything. Whatever you think of yourself, your mind is calm and tranquil, I am sure. Objects present themselves to it such as they are, but mine, ever agitated like a moving wave, confounds and disfigures them. I no longer dare trust in anything I see or feel, and notwithstanding so many long years of repentance, I am experiencing with sorrow that the weight of an old fault is a burden we must carry all our life.

✤ LETTER XIII ✤

Response

POOR COUSIN! What torments you create for yourself continually when you have so many reasons to live in peace! All thy misfortunes come from thyself, oh Israel! If you followed your own rules, if in matters of sentiment you listened only to your inner voice, and if your heart silenced your reason, you would give yourself up without scruple to the security which it inspires in you, and you would not force yourself, against the testimony of your own heart, to fear a danger which can only arise from it.

I understand you, I understand you well, my Julie. Surer of yourself than you pretend to be, you wish to humiliate yourself with your past faults under the pretext of preventing new ones, and your scruples are much less precautions for the future than self-imposed punishment for the rashness which once ruined you. You are comparing the times, do you think? Compare also the situations, and remember that then I reproached you for your confidence as now I reproach you for your fright.

You are mistaken, my dear child. We do not thus mislead ourselves. If we can try to forget our situation by not thinking of it, we see it such as it is as soon as we will consider it, and we can no more conceal our virtues from ourselves than our vices. Your gentleness and your devotion have given you an inclination toward humility. Distrust this dangerous virtue which only excites self love by concentrating on it, and believe that the noble openness of an upright soul is preferable to the pride of humble ones. If moderation is necessary for prudence, it is necessary also in the precautions prudence inspires, lest the solicitude ignominious to virtue should debase the soul and make an imaginary danger a real one to it through alarming us. Do you not see that after having been raised from a fall, you must hold yourself upright, and that to lean to the side opposite that on which you fell is the way to fall again? Cousin, you loved as Eloise did. Now, like her, you are pious, may it please God with more success! In truth, if I were less acquainted with your natural timidity, your terrors would be capable of frightening me in my turn, and if I were as scrupulous as you, through my fears for you you would cause me to tremble for myself. [60]

Could you, without displeasing Monsieur de Wolmar, punish yourself for a vanity which you never had and prevent a danger which no longer exists? Stay alone with the philosopher, take against him all the superfluous precautions which formerly would have been so necessary, and impose upon yourself the same reserve that you would if even with your virtue you could still distrust your heart and his. Avoid too affectionate conversations, tender memories of the past; interrupt or forestall excessively long private talks; surround yourself constantly with your children; remain alone with him very seldom in your room, in the Elysium, or in the grove, despite its profanation. Above all, take these measures with so natural a manner that they seem a result of chance and that he may not imagine for a moment that you fear him. You like boat rides; you deprive yourself of them for the sake of your husband who fears the water and for your children whom you do not wish to hazard on it. Take advantage of the time of this absence to indulge yourself in this amusement, leaving your children in Fanchon's care. That is the way to give yourself up securely to the sweet effusions of friendship and peacefully to enjoy a long private talk under the protection of the boatmen, who see without hearing and from whom you cannot go far before you are aware of what you are doing.

Another idea comes to me which would make many people laugh but which will please you, I am sure. It is to keep a journal faithfully during your husband's absence, to be shown to him at his return, and to think of the journal during all the conversations which are to be set down in it. In truth, I do not believe that such an expedient would be useful to many women, but an open soul, incapable of bad faith, has many resources against vice which others always lack. Nothing is despicable which endeavors to safeguard purity, and it is the little precautions which secure great virtues.

Besides, since your husband is to see me on his way, he will tell me, I hope, the real reasons for his trip, and if I do not find them sound, either I shall dissuade him from finishing his journey, or at all events, I shall do what he has refused to do. You may count on that. Meanwhile, I think this is more than necessary to fortify you against a week's trial. Go, my Julie, I know you too well not to answer for you as much as and more than for myself. You will always be what you must and what you desire to be. If you would only trust yourself to the honesty of your soul, you would run no more risk whatever, for I have no faith in unforeseen defeats. Vainly we cover with the empty name of frailties the faults which are always voluntary. Never does a woman surrender when she has not desired to surrender, and if I thought such a fate might be awaiting you—believe me, believe in my tender friendship, believe in all the sentiments which can arise in your poor Claire's heart—I should take too lively an interest in protecting you to abandon you to yourself alone.

What Monsieur de Wolmar has declared to you about the knowledge he had before your marriage scarcely surprises me. You know that I always surmised it, and I shall tell you, moreover, that my suspicions were not confined to Babi's indiscretions. I have never been able to believe that an upright and true man like your father, who at the very least had suspicions himself, would resolve to deceive his son-in-law and his friend. If he compelled you so forcefully to secrecy, it was because the manner of revealing it would come from him very differently than from you, and because he doubtless wished to give it a turn less likely to repel Monsieur de Wolmar than the one he was assured you would not fail to give it yourself. But I must send you back your messenger. We shall talk of all this more leisurely in a month from now.

Adieu, little cousin. I have preached enough to the preacher. Resume your old occupation, and for good reason. I feel very uneasy over not yet being with you. I put all my affairs in disorder by hurrying to conclude them and hardly know what I am doing. Ah Chaillot, Chaillot! . . . If I were less foolish . . . but I hope always to be so.

P.S. By the way, I forgot to pay my respects to Your Highness. Tell me, I beg you, is my lord your husband *atteman, knes,* or *boyar?* As for me, I shall think I am swearing if I must call you Madame Boyar* Oh, poor child! You who have so often lamented being born a gentlewoman, here you are quite by chance the wife of a prince! Between us, however, for a lady of such high quality, I find your fears a little common. Do you not know that little scruples suit only mean persons, and that people laugh at a child of a fine family who pretends to be the son of his father?

---

* Madame d'Orbe is apparently unaware that the first two names are in fact distinguished titles, but a boyar is only a mere nobleman. [*Rousseau*]

✤ LETTER XIV ✤

From Monsieur de Wolmar to Madame d'Orbe

I AM LEAVING for Étange, little cousin. I had intended to come see you on the way, but a delay which you have caused forces me to make more haste, and I prefer to lay over at Lausanne on the way back, in order to spend a few hours more with you. Also, I have to consult you on several matters, which it is well to mention to you beforehand, so that you may have time to reflect on them before giving me your opinion.

I did not wish to explain to you my project with regard to the young man before his stay had confirmed the good opinion I had conceived of him. I already believe myself sufficiently assured about him to confide to you, between ourselves, that this project is to entrust him with the education of my children. I am not unaware that these important concerns are the principal duty of a father, but when it will be time to undertake it I shall be too old to fulfill it, and naturally tranquil and contemplative, I always had too little spirit to be able to govern that of youth. Besides, for the reason which is known to you,* Julie would not without uneasiness see me assume an office in which I should have difficulty acquitting myself to her liking. I have a thousand other reasons. Your sex is not suited for these duties, and their mother will busy herself wholly in rearing her Henriette properly. For your part, I allot you the management of the household, on the plan which you will find established and which you have approved. My part will be to behold three worthy people concur to promote the happiness of the house and to enjoy in my old age a repose for which I will be indebted to them.

I have always observed that my wife would have an extreme aversion to entrusting her children to mercenary hands, and I could not blame her scruples. The respectable capacity of tutor requires so many talents which one would not be able to remunerate, so many virtues which have no price, that it is useless to seek one with money. It is only from a man of genius that we may hope to find the talents

---

* The reader does not yet know this reason, but I beg him not to become impatient. [*Rousseau*]

of a teacher; it is only in a very tender friend that we may find a heart inspired with a father's zeal, and genius is hardly for sale, attachment still less.

Your friend has seemed to me to unite within him all the proper qualities, and if I have well understood his disposition, I do not imagine a greater happiness for him than that of making those cherished children contribute to that of their mother. The only obstacle which I can foresee is in his affection for Lord Bomston which will not easily permit him to detach himself from so dear a friend, to whom he has such great obligations, unless Edward himself requires it. We are expecting that extraordinary man soon, and as you have much influence over his mind, if he does not belie the idea you have given me of him, I may commit the business in regard to him to your management.

Now you have, little cousin, the key to my whole behavior, which can only appear very curious without this explanation, and which, I hope, will henceforth have Julie's approval and yours. The advantage of having a wife like mine has made me attempt expedients which would have been impracticable with another. Though I leave her in full confidence with her former lover, under the guard of her virtue only, I should be mad to establish that lover in my house before assuring myself that he had forever ceased to be one, and how could I be assured of it if I had a wife on whom I might depend any less? [61]

I think I am well acquainted with both their strength; I am exposing them only to trials which they can support, for prudence does not consist in taking all sorts of precautions indiscriminately but in choosing those which are useful and neglecting the superfluous ones. The week during which I am going to leave them together will perhaps be enough to teach them to distinguish their true sentiments and to recognize what they really are to each other. The more they see each other alone, the more they will easily find out their mistake by comparing what they will feel with what they formerly would have felt in a similar situation. Besides, it is important to them to accustom themselves safely to endure the familiarity in which they will necessarily live if my plans are fulfilled. I see by Julie's conduct that she has received advice from you that she could not refuse to follow without doing herself injury. What pleasure I should take in giving her this proof that I am sensible of her whole worth, if she were a woman with whom a husband might make a merit of her faith! But even if she had gained nothing over her heart, her virtue would still be the same. It would cost her dearer but would not be less triumphant. Instead, if now she has still some inward uneasiness left to endure, it can only arise from the tenderness of a conversation of reminiscence that she will be only too capable of anticipating and will always avoid. Thus you see that you must not judge my conduct in this by ordinary rules, but by the projects which inspire it in me, and by the unique character of her for whom I am anxious.

Adieu, little cousin, until my return. Although I have not made all these explanations to Julie, I do not demand that you keep them secret from her. I have a maxim not to interpose secrets between friends. Thus I commit these to your discretion; make such use of them as prudence and friendship direct you. I know that you will do nothing but what is best and most honorable.

❖ LETTER XV ❖

To Lord Bomston

MONSIEUR DE WOLMAR left yesterday for Étange, and I can scarcely believe the melancholy state his departure has left me in. I believe that the absence of his wife would afflict me less than his. I feel myself more constrained than in his very presence. A gloomy silence reigns in the bottom of my heart; a secret fright stifles its murmur, and less troubled by desires than by fears, I am experiencing the horrors of the crime without being exposed to its temptations.

Do you know, my Lord, where my mind is reassured and forsakes its unworthy fears? In the presence of Madame de Wolmar. As soon as I approach her, the sight of her calms my uneasiness; her looks purify my heart. Such is the influence of hers that it always seems to inspire others with a sense of her innocence and the tranquillity which is the result of it. Unfortunately for me, her system of life does not allow her to devote the whole day to the society of her friends, and in the moments that I am forced to spend out of her company, I should suffer less if I were farther from her.

What contributes even more to nourish the melancholy with which I feel myself oppressed is a word that she said to me yesterday after her husband's departure. Although until that instant she had kept up her spirits rather well, for a long time her eyes followed him with a tearful look that I first attributed only to the departure of that fortunate husband, but I understood by her conversation that these tears had still another cause which was unknown to me.

"You have seen how we live," she said to me, "and you know whether he is dear to me. Yet do not believe that the sentiment which unites me to him, as tender as and more forceful than love, may also have its weaknesses. If it pains us when the sweet habit of living together is interrupted, the firm hope of resuming it soon consoles us. So permanent a state leaves few vicissitudes to fear, and in an absence of a few days, we feel the pain of so short an interval less than the pleasure of envisaging the end of it. The sadness you read in my eyes comes from a more serious cause, and although it concerns Monsieur de Wolmar, it is not his departure which causes it.

"My dear friend," she added in an affecting tone, "there is no true happiness on earth. I have the most honest and the most gentle of men for a husband. A mutual inclination is joined to the duty which binds us together. He has no desires other than mine. I have children which give and promise only pleasure to their mother. There never was a friend more tender, more virtuous, or more amiable than the one my heart adores, and I am going to spend my days with her. You yourself help to make them dear to me by so well justifying my esteem and my sentiments for you. A long and troublesome law suit, nearly finished, will soon bring back the best of fathers into our arms. We are prosperous. Order and peace prevail in our house. Our servants are zealous and faithful, our neighbors show us every kind of affections, and we enjoy the goodwill of the public. Assisted in everything by heaven, by fortune, and by men, I see all things conspiring to my happiness. Yet, a secret sorrow, a single sorrow poisons it, and I am not happy."

She said these last words with a sigh which pierced my soul and in which, I saw only too well, I had no part. She is not happy, I said to myself, sighing in turn, and it is no longer I who am an obstacle to her happiness.

This gloomy idea instantly disordered all my thoughts and disturbed the tranquillity I was beginning to enjoy. Unable to endure the intolerable doubt in which these words had thrown me, I urged her so much to finish opening her heart to me that finally she poured that fatal secret into mine, and she permits me to reveal it to you. But here it is time for a walk. Madame de Wolmar is presently leaving the women's quarters to walk with her children; she has just sent word to me. I attend her, my Lord; I leave you for the present and will resume in another letter the subject broken off in this one.

❖ LETTER XVI ❖

From Madame de Wolmar to Her Husband

I AM EXPECTING YOU Tuesday as you informed me, and you will find everything disposed according to your desires. Call on Madame d'Orbe on your way back. She will tell you what has taken place during your absence; I prefer that you learn it from her rather than from me.

Wolmar, it is true that I believe myself worthy of your esteem, but your conduct is not the most proper, and you sport cruelly with your wife's virtue.

❖ LETTER XVII ❖

To Lord Bomston

I MUST GIVE YOU an account, my Lord, of a danger we incurred a few days ago and from which we fortunately were delivered with a good fright and a little fatigue. This indeed is worth a separate letter; in reading it you will feel what induces me to write you about it.

You know that Madame de Wolmar's house is not far from the lake and that she likes rides on the water. Three days ago, the idleness in which her husband's absence leaves us and the beauty of the evening made us plan one of these outings for the next day. At sunrise we betook ourselves to the shore. We took a boat with nets for fishing, three oarsmen, and a servant, and we set out with some provisions for dinner. I had taken a rifle to shoot at besolets,* but

* A bird of passage on the Lake of Geneva. The besolet is not good to eat. [Rousseau]

she made me ashamed to kill birds to no purpose and for the sole pleasure of doing mischief. I amused myself, therefore, from time to time in bringing in some whimbrels, greenshanks, curlews, and sandpipers,* and I only shot once from very far at a grebe, which I missed.

We spent an hour or two fishing five hundred feet from shore. The fishing was good, but with the exception of a trout which had received a blow from an oar, Julie had them all thrown back in the water. "These are animals," she said, "which are suffering. Let us free them and enjoy their pleasure in escaping the peril."

This freeing process was carried out slowly, reluctantly, and not without some protests, and I readily saw that our people would have enjoyed the fish they had taken better than the moral principle which saved their life.

Next we went out into the open water; then with the vivacity of a young man which it is time for me to check, having put myself at the master oar, I steered so much toward the middle of the lake that we soon found ourselves more than a league from shore.† There I explained to Julie all the parts of the superb horizon which surrounded us. [62]

While we were agreeably amusing ourselves in thus surveying the neighboring coasts, a rising gale, which pushed us obliquely toward the opposite shore, began to blow, and when we thought to tack about the resistance was so strong that it was no longer possible for our frail boat to overcome it. Soon the waves became terrible; we had to make for the Savoy shore and try to land at the village of Meillerie, which was opposite us and which is almost the only place on that side where the shore affords a convenient landing. But having changed, the wind gathered strength, made our boatmen's efforts useless, and made us drift lower along a line of steep rocks where there was no more shelter to be found.

We all took the oars, and almost at the same instant I had the grief of seeing Julie seized with sickness, weak and fainting at the edge of the boat. Fortunately, she was used to the water, and this condition did not last. Nevertheless, our efforts increased with our danger; the heat of the sun, the fatigue and perspiration put us all out of breath and exhausted us excessively. Then, recovering all her courage, Julie revived our spirits with her compassionate kindness. Indiscriminately, she wiped all our brows, and mixing some water

---

* Various kinds of Lake of Geneva birds, all very good to eat. [*Rousseau*]

† How is that? Opposite Clarens, the lake is hardly two leagues wide. [*Rousseau*]

in a jar of wine, for fear of intoxication, she presented it alternately
to the most exhausted. No, never did your lovely friend shine with
such a lively luster as in this moment when the heat and the activity
had given a greater glow to her complexion, and what added most
to her charms was that we saw so well by her tender behavior that
all her solicitude came less from fear for herself than from pity for
us. For an instant, two planks being partly opened in an impact
which wet us all, she thought the boat broken to pieces, and in an
exclamation from this tender mother, I distinctly heard these
words: "Oh my children, must I see you no more?"

As for myself, whose imagination always exceeds the peril, although I knew the real state of the danger, I expected to see the
boat swallowed up at any moment, that affecting beauty struggling
in the midst of the waves, and the pallor of death dulling the roses
of her cheeks.

Finally, by dint of labor we reached Meillerie, and after having
battled more than an hour at ten feet from shore, we succeeded in
getting to land. In landing, all fatigue was forgotten. Julie took
it upon herself to express gratitude for all the pains each one of us
had taken and, just as in the thick of the danger she had thought
only of us, on land she seemed to think that we had saved no one
but her.

We dined with the appetite one acquires from vigorous labor. The
trout was served. Julie, who likes trout very much, ate very little of
it, and I perceived that to make amends to the boatmen for the regret over their sacrifice, she did not desire me to eat much of it myself. My Lord, you have said it a thousand times: in little as well as
in great matters, that loving soul is always to be seen.

After dinner, the water still rough and the boat in need of re-
pair, I proposed taking a walk. Julie objected to the wind and the
sun and thought of my weariness. I had my views; thus I answered
all her objections. "I am," I told her, "accustomed since childhood to laborious exercises. Far from being harmful to my health,
they strengthen it, and my recent voyage has made me much more
robust still. As to the sun and the wind, you have your straw hat; we
shall have shelter from the woods. It is only a matter of climbing
between some rocks, and you who do not like flat country will willingly bear the fatigue of it."

She consented to what I wanted, and we left while our people
were at dinner.

You know that after my exile in the Valais ten years ago, I came back to Meillerie to wait for my permission to return. It was there that I spent such melancholy and such delightful days, preoccupied solely with her, and it is from there that I wrote her that letter with which she was so affected. I had always desired to revisit the isolated retreat which served me as a refuge in the middle of the ice, where my heart took pleasure in communing imaginatively with what it held most dear in the world. The opportunity to visit this cherished spot, in a more pleasant season and with her whose image formerly dwelled there with me, was the secret motive for my walk. I was pleased to show her the old memorials of such a constant and such an unfortunate passion.

We reached the place after an hour's walk over winding and cool paths which, ascending imperceptibly between the trees and the rocks, were not otherwise inconvenient except in their length. Approaching and recognizing my former signs, I was prepared to find myself ill, but I overcame it, I hid my distress, and we arrived.. This solitary place formed a retreat, wild and deserted but full of those kinds of beauties which please only sensitive souls and appear horrible to the others. A torrent caused by the thawing snows rolled in a muddy stream twenty feet from us and noisily carried along dirt, sand, and stones. Behind us a chain of inaccessible crags separated the flat place where we were from that part of the Alps called the glaciers, because of the enormous peaks of ice which, incessantly increasing, have covered them since the beginning of the world.* To the right, forests of black firs afforded us a gloomy shade. A large wood of oak was to the left beyond the torrent, below us that immense body of water that the lake forms in the midst of the Alps separated us from the rich shores of the Vaud region, and the peak of the majestic Jura crowned the landscape.

In the middle of these great and superb objects, the small piece of ground where we were displayed the charms of a cheerful and sylvan refuge; some streams filtered through the rocks and rolled over the green in crystal rivulets. Some wild fruit trees bent their heads over ours; the moist and fresh earth was covered with grass and flowers. As I compared such a pleasant place to the things which surrounded it, it seemed that this deserted spot should have been the refuge of two lovers who alone had escaped the general confusion of nature.

---

* These mountains are so high that a half hour after sunset their summits are still lit by the sun's rays, the red of which creates on these white peaks a beautiful rose color which is seen from very far away. [*Rousseau*]

When we had reached this refuge and I had contemplated it for some time, I said to Julie, looking at her with a moistened eye, "What! Does your heart say nothing to you here, and do you not feel some secret emotion at the sight of a place so full of you?"

Then, without waiting for her answer, I led her toward the rock and showed her her initials engraved in a thousand places and several verses from Petrarch and Tasso relative to my situation as I cut them. Observing them myself after such a long time, I felt how much the sight of things can powerfully rekindle the violent sentiments with which we were once shaken near those very things. I said to her, with a little vehemence, "Oh Julie, eternal delight of my heart! These are the spots where the most faithful lover in the world once sighed for you. This is the place where your dear image constituted his happiness and made way for that which he finally received from your person. Then, neither these fruits nor this shade was to be seen. The green grass and the flowers did not carpet these little fields. The courses of these streams did not divide them. The chirping of these birds was not to be heard. Only the fierce hawk, the ominous raven, and the terrible eagle of the Alps made these caverns resound with their shrieks. Great icicles hung from all these rocks; festoons of snow were the only ornament of these trees. Everything here betokened the rigors of winter and the horror of the frost. Only the fires of my heart made this place bearable for me, and I spent whole days here thinking of you. There is the stone on which I sat to contemplate your happy home in the distance. On that one I wrote the letter which touched your heart. These sharp pebbles served me as tools to engrave your initials. Here I crossed the frozen torrent to recover one of your letters that a burst of wind had carried away. There I came to reread and kiss a thousand times the last one you had written me. There is the brink where with an avid and gloomy eye I measured the depth of these abysses. Lastly, it was here that before my sad departure I came to grieve for you as you lay dying and to swear not to survive you. You, too constantly loved, oh you, for whom I was born! Must I find myself with you again in the same places and regret the time I spent there in sighing over your absence? . . ."

I was going to continue, but Julie, who, seeing me approach the edge, had been frightened and had seized my hand, clasped it without saying a word, looked at me tenderly, and with difficulty held back a sigh. Then suddenly averting her eyes and pulling me by the arm, she said in an emotional voice, "Let us go, my friend. The air of this place is not good for me."

Sighing, but without answering her, I went with her, and I left this retreat forever, as sadly as I should have left Julie herself. Slowly returning to the dock after a little wandering, we separated. She wanted to remain alone, and I continued to walk, not knowing too well where I was going. At my return, the boat was not yet ready nor the water calm; in a melancholy state, we ate supper, our eyes lowered, our looks pensive, eating little and speaking still less. After supper, we were seated on the beach waiting for the time to depart. The moon gradually rose, the water became calmer, and Julie proposed that we leave. I gave her my hand to get into the boat, and sitting beside her, I no longer thought of letting go of her hand. We kept a profound silence. The even and measured sound of the oars put me into a reverie. The rather gay song of the snipes,* recalling to me the pleasures of another time, saddened me instead of making me gay. Little by little I felt the melancholy with which I was overcome increasing. A serene sky, the soft rays of the moon, the silver shimmering of the glistening water around us, the concurrence of the most pleasant sensations, the very presence of that cherished person—nothing could turn my heart from a thousand sad reflections. I began by remembering a similar outing made once before with her during the rapture of our early love. All the delightful sentiments which then filled my soul were recalled to my mind, in order to afflict me; all the events of our youth, our studies, our conversations, our letters, our trysts, our pleasures,

> Et tanta fede, e si dolci memorie,
> Et si lungo costume!
> METASTASIO

> And so much trust, such sweet memories,
> And such long habit!

those hundreds of little things which brought back the image of my past happiness—all returned to take a place in my memory in order to increase my present sorrow. It is over, I said to myself; those times, those happy times are no more. They have disappeared forever. Alas, they will return no more, and yet we live, we are together, and our hearts are ever joined! It seemed to me that I should have borne

* The Lake of Geneva snipe is not the bird called in France by the same name. The more lively and animated song of ours on summer nights gives the lake an air of life and freshness which makes its shores even more delightful. [*Rousseau*]

her death or her absence more patiently, and that I had suffered less the whole time I had spent parted from her. When far away I was aggrieved, the hope of seeing her again solaced my heart; I flattered myself that an instant in her presence would efface all my miseries. At least I used to envisage, out of all possible situations, one less cruel than my own. But to find myself with her, to see her, to touch her, to speak to her, to love her, to adore her, and almost possessing her again, to feel her lost forever to me, that was what threw me into a fit of furor and rage which by degrees disturbed me to the point of despair. Soon I began to turn over deadly projects in my mind, and in a fit of passion, which I shudder to think of, I was violently tempted to hurl her with me into the waves and to end my life and my long torments in her arms. This horrible temptation finally became so strong that I was obliged to let go her hand suddenly and go to the bow of the boat.

There my lively agitation began to take another course. A gentler sentiment little by little wound its way into my soul; tenderness overcame despair. I began to shed copious tears, and this state, compared to the one I had emerged from, was not without some pleasures. I wept hard and long and was comforted. When I found myself composed, I returned near Julie. I took her hand again. She was holding her handkerchief; I felt it very damp. "Ah," I said to her softly, "I see that our hearts have never ceased to hear each other!"

"It is true," she said in a changed voice, "but let this be the last time that they will speak in this manner."

We began then to talk calmly, and at the end of an hour's rowing, we arrived without another accident. When we had come in, I perceived by the light that her eyes were red and quite swollen; she must not have found mine in better condition. After the fatigue of this day, she had great need of rest; she retired and I went to bed.

There, my friend, are the details of a day in which, without exception, I have felt the most lively emotions of my life. I hope that they will constitute the crisis which will restore me completely to myself. Moreover, I must tell you that this adventure has convinced me, more than all arguments, of man's free will and of the value of virtue. How many people succumb to feeble temptations? As for Julie—my eyes saw it and my heart felt it—that day she underwent the greatest struggle that a human soul could have sustained; yet she was victorious. But what have I done to be so different from her? Oh Edward! When seduced by your mistress you were capable of triumphing over both your desires and hers, were you only mortal? Without you, I would have been lost, perhaps. A hundred times during that dangerous day, the thought of your virtue restored my own to me.

PART V

✤ LETTER I ✤

From Lord Bomston*

EMERGE from childhood, friend. Awake. Do not give up your whole life to the long sleep of the reason. Time slips by; you have none left except in which to become wise. After thirty, it is time to think of oneself; begin, then, to reflect within yourself, and be a man once before you die. [63]   *1½ pp*

Your passions, by which you were enslaved for a long time, have left you virtuous. This is all your glory; it is great, without a doubt, but be less proud of it. Your very strength is the result of your frailty. Do you know what has always made you love virtue? In your eyes it has taken on the form of that lovely woman who typifies it so well, and so dear an image could hardly let you lose the inclination for it. But will you never love virtue for its own sake, and will you not court the good of your own accord, as Julie has done? Idly enthusiastic about her virtues, will you incessantly limit yourself to admiring them without ever imitating them? You speak warmly of the manner in which she fulfills her duties as a wife and mother, but when by her example will you fulfill your duties as a man and friend? A woman has triumphed over herself, and a philosopher has difficulty in conquering his passions! Do you wish, then, always to be a mere prater like the others and limit yourself to writing good books instead of doing good deeds? Take care, my friend; an air of softness and languor still prevails in your letters, which displeases me and which is much more a vestige of your passion than a result of your character. I hate weakness in anyone, and I do not like to find it in my friend. There is no virtue without fortitude, and the road to

* This letter seems to have been written before the preceding was received. [*Rousseau*]   *ℓ⅃*

vice is cowardice. Do you really dare rely upon yourself with a heart lacking courage? Wretch! If Julie were frail, you would succumb tomorrow and would be only a vile adulterer. But there you are, left alone with her; learn to understand her, and be ashamed of yourself.

I hope soon to be able to come join you. You know for what purpose this trip to Italy is designed. Twelve years of mistakes and troubles make me suspicious of myself. To resist marriage, my own abilities could suffice; to choose a wife I need a friend's eyes, and I take pleasure in making everything mutual between us, gratitude as well as affection. However, do not deceive yourself; before according you my confidence, I shall find out if you are worthy of it and if you deserve to return to me the services I have rendered you. I know your heart; I am satisfied with it. That is not enough. It is your judgment I need in a choice over which reason alone must preside and in which mine may deceive me. [64]

My affairs will keep me no longer than two weeks more in London. I shall set out for our army in Flanders with which I expect to stay again as long, so that you are hardly to expect me before the end of next month or the beginning of October. Write me no more at London but under the enclosed address in care of the army. Continue your descriptions; notwithstanding the sorry tone of your letters, they affect and instruct me. They inspire me with plans for retirement and peace agreeable to my maxims and my age. Above all, allay the uneasiness you have caused me concerning Madame de Wolmar. If she is dissatisfied, who is to dare aspire to happiness? After the detailed account she has given you, I cannot conceive what her happiness lacks.

⚜ LETTER II ⚜

To Lord Bomston

YES, MY LORD, I assure you with transports of joy that the scene at Meillerie has been the crisis of my folly and my misfortunes. Monsieur de Wolmar's explanations have wholly reassured me on the true state of my heart. This excessively feeble heart is cured, as completely as it can be, and I prefer the sadness of fancied regret to the fear of being continually tempted by the crime. Since the return of this worthy friend, I have no longer hesitated in giving him that dear title, the whole value of which you have made me feel so well. It is the least I owe to anyone who helps to restore me to virtue. Peace is in the bottom of my soul as in the place where I am living. I begin to find myself without uneasiness, to live here as if in my own home, and if I do not have the complete authority of a master in it, I feel even more pleasure in considering myself as a child of the house. The simplicity and the equality which I see reign here have an attraction which affects me and which I cannot help but respect. I spend serene days amid practical reason and sensitive virtue. In the company of this happy pair, their influence prevails over me and imperceptibly affects me, and my heart is put gradually into harmony with theirs, as one's voice insensibly takes on the tone of those with whom he is speaking. [65] Content with their lot, they enjoy it peacefully; content with their fortune, they do not labor to increase it for their children but to leave them, along with the inheritance they themselves have received, an estate in good condition, affectionate servants, the love of labor, order, moderation, and all that which can make sweet and charming for men of sense the enjoyment of a moderate wealth, as prudently conserved as it was honestly acquired.

✤ LETTER III ✤

To Lord Bomston

WE HAVE had guests these past few days. They left yesterday, and we renewed a society between us three, so much the more charming as there is nothing, even in the bottom of our hearts, which we wish to hide from each other. What pleasure I am enjoying in assuming a new character which makes me worthy of your confidence! I do not receive one mark of esteem from Julie and her husband that I do not say to myself with a certain pride in my soul: at last I shall dare appear before him. It is through your assistance, it is under your eyes that I hope to do honor to my present condition by means of my past faults. If extinguished passion hurls the mind into a state of dejection, subdued passion adds to the consciousness of its victory a new elevation and a more lively attachment to all that is great and fine. Should we wish to lose the fruit of a sacrifice which has cost us so dear? No, my Lord, I feel that by your example my heart will profit from all the ardent sentiments it has conquered. I feel that it was necessary to have been what I was in order to become what I wish to be. [66]

My Lord, we expect you from day to day, and this should be my last letter. But I understand what prolongs your stay with the army, and I tremble over it. Julie is no less uneasy; she begs you to send us news of yourself more often and implores you, as you expose your person, to consider how prodigal you are of your friends' tranquillity. As for me, I have nothing to say to you. Do your duty; advice of timidity can no more come from my heart than come near yours. My dear Bomston, I know too well that the only death worthy of your life would be to spill your blood for the glory of your country, but do you owe no account of your life to him who only preserved his for your sake?

❖ LETTER IV ❖

From Lord Bomston

I SEE by your last two letters that I have missed one preceding them, apparently the first you wrote me in care of the army, in which was the explanation of Madame de Wolmar's secret uneasiness. I have not received this letter, and I imagine it could be in the mail of a courier who has been taken. Repeat for me, then, what it contained; I am at a loss to imagine what it is, and my heart is uneasy, for again I say, if happiness and peace are not in Julie's soul, where will their haven be on this earth?

Reassure her about the risks to which she believes me exposed; we have to do with an enemy too skillful to let us pursue him. With a handful of men, he renders all our forces useless and everywhere deprives us of the means of attacking him. Yet, as we are confident, we could well raise difficulties which the best generals could not surmount and in the end force the French to fight us. I foresee that we shall pay dearly for our first success and that the battle won at Dettingen will cause us to lose one in Flanders. [67]

Be that as it may, I wish to see the maneuvers of the rest of this campaign, and I have resolved to remain with the army until it goes into winter quarters. We shall all gain by this delay. The season being too far advanced to cross the mountains, you and I shall spend the winter where you are, and we shall not go to Italy until the beginning of spring. Tell Monsieur and Madame de Wolmar that I am making this new arrangement to have more time to enjoy the affecting spectacle which you describe so well, and to see Madame d'Orbe established with them. Continue to write me, my dear friend, with the same solicitude, and you will give me more pleasure than ever. My equipment has been taken, and I have no books, but I read your letters.

✤ LETTER V ✤

To Lord Bomston

WHAT JOY you give me by announcing that we shall spend the winter at Clarens! But how dearly you make me pay for it by prolonging your stay with the army! What displeases me above all is to perceive clearly that even before our separation, your resolution to follow the campaign was already taken and that you did not wish to mention it to me. My Lord, I know the reason for this secrecy and cannot thank you for it. Did you despise me enough to believe that I might find it good to survive you, or have you known me so mean that I might prefer some attachments to the honor of dying with my friend? If it was not proper for me to follow you, you should have left me in London; that would have offended me less than sending me here.

It is clear from your last letter that one of mine was indeed lost, and this loss must have made the two succeeding letters quite obscure in many respects, but the explanations necessary to make them intelligible will come in time. What presently is most urgent is to extricate you from your uneasiness over the secret grief of Madame de Wolmar.

I shall not tell you again the exact conversation that I had with her after her husband's departure. Many things have happened since which have made me forget part of it, and we resumed it so many times during his absence that I shall content myself with a summary, in order to avoid repetitions.

She told me, therefore, that this very husband who did everything to make her happy was the sole author of all her grief, and the more sincere their mutual attachment was the more cause it gave her to suffer. Would you think so, my Lord? That man, so wise, so reasonable, so far from every kind of vice, so little subject to human passions, knows nothing of that faith which gives value to virtue and, in the innocence of an irreproachable life, he bears in the bottom of his heart the dreadful tranquillity of the unbeliever. The reflection which arises from this contrast increases Julie's sorrow, and it seems that she would sooner pardon him for disregarding his Creator if he had more reasons to fear Him or more pride to defy Him. If a guilty man were to appease his conscience at the expense of his reason, if the pride of thinking differently from the vulgar were to inspire a dogmatic person to disbelieve—those errors at least are conceivable, but, Julie maintains, sighing, for a man so honest and so little vain of his understanding to be an unbeliever is very difficult to understand!

You must be informed of the character of this pair, you must picture them taken up with their family and living for each other apart from the rest of the universe, you must know the harmony which prevails between them in everything else, in order to conceive how their difference on this single point is capable of troubling its charms. Monsieur de Wolmar, brought up in the Greek Church, was not able to bear the absurdity of such a ridiculous cult. His understanding, too superior to the silly yoke which people tried to impose on him, soon shook it off contemptuously, and at once rejecting all that came to him from so doubtful an authority, forced into impiety, he became an atheist.

Afterwards, having always lived in a Catholic country, he did not learn to conceive a better opinion of the Christian faith by that which is professed there. He saw no other religion than that which was in the interest of its ministers. He saw that even there religion consisted entirely of vain pretences, disguised a little more subtly by words which meant nothing; he perceived that all the honest people were unanimously of his opinion and scarcely hid the fact, that the clergy themselves, a little more discreet, mocked in private what they taught in public, and he has often assured me that, after much time and research, in his life he found only three priests who believed in God.* Wishing to be sincerely enlightened about these matters, he buried himself in the obscurity of metaphysics, in which a man has no other guides but the systems he brings to it, and saw everywhere only doubts and contradictions. When at last he came among Christians, he came too late; his faith had already been closed to the truth, and his reason was no longer open to conviction. All that which people proved to him destroyed rather than established any sentiment, and he ended by fighting every kind of dogma impartially, ceasing to be an atheist only to become a skeptic.

Such is the husband which Heaven destined for that Julie in whom you are acquainted with such a simple faith and such a sweet piety; but you must have lived as close to her as her cousin and I have to know how much her tender soul is naturally inclined to devotion. One would say that, nothing on earth being equal to the need to love with which she is devoured, her excess of sensibility is forced to ascend to its source. Hers is not a loving heart like Saint Theresa's, which deceives itself and will mistake its object. Hers is a truly inexhaustible heart which neither love nor friendship could consume and which carries its superabundant affections to the only Being worthy of accepting them. Love of God does not detach her from His creatures; it does not make her severe or sharp. All her attachments, proceeding from the same cause, one being enlivened by the other, become more charming and sweet, and for my part, I think she would be less devout if she loved her father, her husband, her children, her cousin, and myself less tenderly. [68]

Conceive, my Lord, what torment it is to live in seclusion with the one who shares our existence and not be able to share the hope which makes it dear to us! To be unable either to join him in blessing God's works or speak of the happy future which His goodness promises us! To see him, as he does good, insensible to all that

---

* God forbid that I should wish to approve these severe and rash assertions; I only affirm that there are people who make them and whose indiscretion is only too often sanctioned by the conduct of the clergy of all countries and all sects. But my purpose in this note is far from basely protecting myself; here, quite clearly, is my own feeling on this matter. It is that no true believer could be intolerant or a persecutor. If I were a magistrate, and if the law inflicted the death penalty upon atheists, I would begin by having those burnt as such who would come to denounce another. [Rousseau]

makes it pleasant, and, by the most curious inconsistency, think like an atheist and act like a Christian! Imagine Julie walking with her husband, one admiring in the rich and brilliant ornamentation that the earth displays the work and the gifts of the Creator of the universe, the other seeing in all that only a fortuitous combination in which nothing is connected except by a blind force. Imagine two partners sincerely united, not daring for fear of mutually troubling each other to indulge themselves, the one in the reflections, the other in the sentiments which the objects surrounding them inspire, and bound by their very attachment to the duty of restraining themselves incessantly. Julie and I almost never take a walk that some impressive and picturesque sight does not remind her of these grievous ideas.

"Alas!" she says tenderly, "the spectacle of nature, so lively, so animated for us, is dead in the eyes of the unfortunate Wolmar, and in this great harmony of creation, in which everything speaks of God with such a sweet voice, he perceives only an eternal silence."

You who know Julie, you who know how much this communicative soul loves to impart its sentiments, conceive what she would suffer from this constraint, even if it had no other ill consequence than such a sad division between those to whom everything ought to be common. But more dreary ideas are raised along with those she already has. In vain she tries to reject these involuntary terrors; they return to disturb her at every moment. What horror for a tender wife to think of the Supreme Being avenging His unacknowledged divinity, to think that the happiness of him who constitutes her own is to end with his life, and to behold merely a reprobate in the father of her children! At this frightful thought, all her sweetness barely protects her from despair, and religion, which makes her husband's unbelief bitter for her, alone gives her the strength to bear it. "If Heaven," she often says, "refuses me the conversion of this honest man, I have only one more favor to ask, that is, to die first."

Such, my Lord, is the extremely just cause of her secret sorrow; such is the inner affliction which seems to burden her conscience with the callousness of another and becomes only more cruel for her by the care she expends to conceal it. [69]

Whatever trouble his wife takes to disguise her sadness from him, Wolmar feels and shares it; one does not deceive an eye as sharp as his. He is only more aware of her grief when she stifles it. He told me he had been several times tempted to give in in appearance, and in order to calm her to feign sentiments which he did not have, but such baseness of soul is too far beneath him. Instead of imposing on Julie, that dissimulation would only have been a new torment for her. The sincerity, the openness, the union of hearts which is the consolation for so many misfortunes would be eclipsed between them. Is it by making his wife esteem him less that he could calm her fears? Instead of deceiving her, he tells her sincerely what he thinks, but he says it in so simple a manner, with such little contempt for common opinions and so little of that ironic pride of strong-minded men, that these melancholy confessions afflict Julie much more than they anger her, and that, unable to inspire her sentiments and her hopes in her husband, she tries more assiduously to gather around him those transitory delights to which he confines his happiness. "Ah!" she says sadly, "if the unfortunate man has his paradise in this world, let us at least make it as sweet for him as possible!"*

The veil of sadness with which this difference of sentiments covers their union proves Julie's invincible influence better than anything else, through the consolations with which this sadness is tempered and which she alone in the world perhaps would be capable of joining to it. All their arguments, all their discussions on this important matter, far from giving rise to bitterness, to contempt, or to quarrels, always end in some tender scene which only endears them more to each other.

Yesterday, the conversation having fixed on this subject, which often comes up when we three are alone, we lit upon the origin of evil, and I endeavored to point out not only that there was no absolute and general evil in the chain of being but that even particular evil was a great deal slighter than it seems at first glance, and that, on the whole, it was much surpassed by particular and individual good. I cited his own example to Monsieur de Wolmar, and penetrated with a sense of the happiness of his situation, I described it so justly that he himself seemed affected.

"Those," he said, interrupting me, "are Julie's delusive arguments. She always puts feeling in the place of reason and argues so affectingly that I must embrace her at every reply. Could it be from

---

* How much more natural is this humanitarian sentiment than the frightful zeal of persecutors, ever busy in tormenting unbelievers, as if to damn them even in this life and to become the precursors of hell's devils. I shall never cease repeating that these persecutors are not believers; they are impostors. [*Rousseau*]

her teacher of philosophy," he added, laughing, "that she has learned this way of arguing?"

Two months earlier, this pleasantry might have cruelly disconcerted me, but the time for embarrassment is past. I merely laughed in turn, and although Julie blushed a little, she did not seem any more embarrassed than I. We continued. Without contending about the quantity of evil, Wolmar contented himself with observing that we must recognize that, little or great, evil indeed exists, and from this existence alone he inferred the absence of power, intelligence, or goodness in the First Cause. On my part, I tried to point out the origin of physical evil in the nature of matter and of moral evil in man's free will. I maintained to him that God could do everything except create other substances as perfect as his own and as exempt from evil. We were in the heat of debate when I noticed that Julie had disappeared.

"Can you guess where she is?" her husband said, perceiving that my eyes were seeking her.

"No doubt," I said, "she has gone to give some order in the household."

"No," he said, "she would not have taken time from this matter for that. Everything of that kind is done without her leaving my side, and yet I never observe her doing it."

"Is she, then, in the children's room?"

"As little likely. Her children are not more dear to her than my salvation."

"Well," I replied, "I know nothing of what she is doing, but I am very sure that she is busy only in useful concerns."

"Still less," he said coldly. "Come, come. You will see if I guess well."

He began to step lightly; I followed him on tiptoe. We came to the door of the study; it was closed. He opened it suddenly. My Lord, what a sight! I saw Julie on her knees, her hands clasped together, her face in tears. She rose hurriedly, wiping her eyes, hiding her face, and trying to escape; I never saw similar confusion. Her husband did not allow her time to fly. He ran to her in a kind of ecstasy. "Dear wife!" he said as he embraced her, "the very ardor of your prayers betrays your cause. What do they lack to be efficacious? Go, if they were heard, they would soon be granted."

"They will be," she said to him in a firm and confident tone. "I do not know the time and occasion of it. Would that I could purchase it at the expense of my life! My last day would be the best employed."

Come, my Lord, leave your miserable fighting. Come to discharge a nobler duty. Does a wise man prefer the honor of killing men to the tasks which can save one?*

❖ LETTER VI ❖

To Lord Bomston

WHAT! Even after leaving the army, another trip to Paris! Have you completely forgotten Clarens, then, and her who lives here? Are you less dear to us than to Lord Hyde? Are you more necessary to that friend than to those who wait for you here? You oblige us to oppose our wishes to yours, and you make me wish I had some influence in the French court to prevent you from obtaining the passports you are waiting for. But, be satisfied; go see your worthy countryman. In spite of him, in spite of you, we shall be revenged for your preference, and whatever pleasure you might enjoy in his company, I know that when you are with us you will regret the time you had not spared us.

Receiving your letter, I had first suspected that you had a secret commission. . . . What mediator of peace more worthy? . . . But do kings put their trust in virtuous men? Do they dare listen to the truth? Do they even know how to respect real merit? . . . No, no, my dear Edward, you are not made to be a minister of state, and I think too well of you to believe that if you had not been born an English peer you might ever become one.

Come, my friend. You will be better off at Clarens than at the court. Oh, what a winter we shall all spend together, if the hope of our reunion does not deceive me! Each day makes way for it by bringing here some one of those privileged souls who are so dear to each other, who are so worthy of each other's love, and who seem only to wait for you to be able to do without the rest of the universe. Learning what a lucky accident brought here the adversary in Baron d'Étange's lawsuit, you foretold all that which

* There was here a long letter from Lord Bomston to Julie. In the sequel this letter will be mentioned, but for good reasons I have been forced to suppress it. [Rousseau]

was to happen from this meeting, which actually did happen.* The old litigant, although almost as inflexible and obstinate as his opponent, could not resist the influence which has subjugated us all. After having seen Julie, after having listened to her, after having spoken with her, he was ashamed to contend with her father. He left for Berne in such a good disposition and the settlement is now so well along that from the Baron's last letter we expect him to return in a few days.

This you already will have been told by Monsieur de Wolmar. But what you probably do not know yet is that Madame d'Orbe, having at last finished her business, has been here since Thursday and will no longer have another residence than that of her friend. As I had been informed of the day of her arrival, I went to meet her, unknown to Madame de Wolmar, whom she wished to surprise, and having met her this side of Lutri, I retraced my steps with her.

I found her more lively and more charming than ever, but absent-minded, distracted, not paying much attention, answering still less, speaking incoherently and by fits and starts—in short, given up to that restlessness we cannot resist when we are on the point of obtaining what we have desired very much. You would have said at every moment that she was afraid she would have to turn back. Her departure, although deferred for a long time, was undertaken so hastily that it turned the heads of the mistress and the servants. A whimsical disorder prevailed in the little baggage they brought along. As the maidservant expressed her fears that she had forgotten something, Claire was ever sure she had had it put in the trunk of the coach, and when they looked into it, joked about it although nothing at all was found.

Since she did not want Julie to hear her carriage, she got out in the avenue, went across the yard hurrying like a madwoman, and ran up the steps so precipitously that she had to stop for breath after the first flight before she could get up them all. Monsieur de Wolmar came to meet her; she could not speak a single word to him.

Opening the door of her room, I saw Julie seated near the window, holding little Henriette on her knees, as she often did. Claire had thought about a fine speech in her usual manner, a compound of sentiment and gaiety, but as she set her foot over the threshold, the speech, the gaiety, all was forgotten. She flew to her friend, cry-

---

* One sees that several intervening letters are missing here as well as in many other places. The reader will say that a writer gets out of difficulty quite easily with such omissions, and I am completely of his opinion. [*Rousseau*]

ing in an ecstasy impossible to describe, "Cousin, forever, forever,
until death!"

Henriette, seeing her mother, leaped up and ran to meet her, crying "Mama! Mama!" with all her might, and ran against her
with such force that the poor child fell backward. This sudden appearance of Claire, that fall, her joy, her agitation—all took hold
of Julie to such a point that, having stood as she extended her
arms, with a very piercing cry she let herself fall back and grew
faint. Wishing to raise up her daughter, Claire saw her friend turn
pale. She hesitated; she did not know to whom to run. Finally, seeing
me pick up Henriette, she rushed to aid the fainting Julie and fell
with her in the same condition.

Henriette, seeing them both motionless, began to weep and
utter cries which made Fanchon come running. The one ran to her
mother, the other to her mistress. As for me, seized, ecstatic, out of
my mind, I paced in long strides about the room without knowing
what I was doing, uttering broken exclamations and making con-
vulsive movements which I could not control. Wolmar himself, the
cold Wolmar felt himself affected. Oh sentiment, sentiment! Sweet
food of the soul! Where is the iron heart which you have never
affected? Where is the unfortunate mortal from whom you never
wrung tears? Instead of running to Julie, this happy husband
threw himself into a chair in order to contemplate this ravishing
sight eagerly. "Do not fear anything," he said, seeing our uneasiness
about him. "These scenes of pleasure and joy exhaust our nature
only to rekindle it with a new vigor. They are never dangerous. Let
me enjoy the happiness which I am savoring and which you share.
What must it be for you? I never felt anything like it, and I am the
least happy of the six."

My Lord, by this first moment you can judge the rest. This reunion has excited a sound of cheerfulness and a tumultuousness
through the whole house which is not yet subsided. Beside herself,
Julie was in a state of agitation such as I had never seen her in before; it was impossible for them to think of anything the whole day
long except to look at and embrace each other ceaselessly with fresh
ecstasies. The next day we had hardly enough composure to prepare a celebration. Without Wolmar, all would have gone awry.
Everyone dressed in his best. No work was permitted except that
which was necessary for the amusements. The feast was celebrated,
not with pomp but with delirium. A confusion prevailed in it which
made it affecting, and disorder constituted its finest embellishment.

The morning was spent in putting Madame d'Orbe in possession

of her post as intendant or housekeeper, and she made haste to take
on her duties with a childish eagerness that made us laugh. Entering the fine hall for dinner, on every side the two cousins saw their
initials formed with flowers and wound together. Julie guessed immediately the source of this solicitude; she embraced me in a fit of
joy. Contrary to her former custom, Claire hesitated to do as much.
Wolmar found fault with her for it; blushing, she decided to imitate
her cousin. This blush, which I noticed only too well, had an effect
on me which I could not explain, but I did not feel myself in her
arms without emotion.

In the afternoon there was fine tea in the women's quarters, into
which for once the master and I were admitted. [70] In the evening,
the whole house, increased by three persons, assembled to dance.
Claire seemed to be adorned by the hand of the graces; she had
never been so brilliant as she was that day. She danced, she chatted,
she laughed, she gave orders, she was equal to everything. She had
sworn to tire me out, and after five or six very brisk quadrilles all in
a breath, she did not neglect her usual reproach that I danced like a
philosopher. I told her that she danced like an imp, that she committed no less mischief, and that I was afraid she would not let me
rest day or night.

"On the contrary," she said. "Here is something to make you
sleep presently." And at once she led me again to the dance.

She was indefatigable, but it was not so with Julie. She had
difficulty in standing upright, her knees trembled as she danced,
and she was too affected to be gay. Often we saw tears of joy trickling
from her eyes; she regarded her cousin with a kind of rapture. She
took pleasure in thinking of herself as the stranger for whom the
celebration was made and looking upon Claire as the mistress of
the house who had ordered it. After supper I shot off fireworks which
I had brought from China and which had much effect. We sat up
well into the night; finally we had to leave each other. Madame
d'Orbe was tired, or ought to have been, and Julie wanted her to get
to bed early.

Gradually calm is being restored and order with it. Claire, as
playful as she is, is capable when she pleases of assuming an authoritative tone which commands respect. Besides, she has good sense,
exquisite discernment, the penetration of Wolmar, and the goodness
of Julie; and although she is extremely liberal, she nevertheless has
much prudence as well, so that although left a widow so young
and charged with the inheritance of her daughter, the fortunes of
both have only prospered in her hands. Thus, there is no reason

to fear that under her direction the house may be governed less well than before. This gives Julie the pleasure of giving herself up entirely to the pursuit which is the most to her liking—that is, the education of the children—and I doubt not but that Henriette will profit very much by one of her mothers having relieved the other from all those duties. I say her *mothers*, for to see the manner in which they act with her, it is difficult to distinguish the real one, and some strangers who arrived today are or seem to be still in doubt on the matter. In fact, both call her *Henriette* or *my daughter*, indifferently. She calls one *mama* and the other *little mama*. The same tenderness prevails on both sides. She obeys them equally. If the ladies are asked to whom she belongs, each answers, "To me." If Henriette is asked, it is found that she has two mothers. People would be puzzled over less. Yet the most discerning decide finally upon Julie. Henriette, whose father was blond, is blond like her and resembles her a great deal. A certain maternal tenderness appears in Julie's soft eyes even more than in Claire's more sprightly looks. Near Julie, the little one assumes a more respectful manner and is more attentive to herself. She automatically places herself more often at Julie's side because Julie more often has something to say to her. It must be confessed that all appearances are in favor of the little mama, and I have perceived that this deception is so agreeable to the two cousins that it could well be intended sometimes and become a contrivance which suits them.

My Lord, in two weeks, nothing will be wanting here but your presence. When you are here, we shall have to think ill of any man whose heart will search in the rest of the world for any virtues and pleasures that may not be found in this house.

❖ LETTER VII ❖

To Lord Bomston

FOR THREE DAYS I have tried each evening to write you. But after a day of labor, sleep wins over me as I come to my room. In the mornings at dawn I must return to the work. An intoxication sweeter than that from wine stirs my inmost soul delightfully, and I cannot take myself for a moment from these pleasures which are completely new for me. I cannot conceive what place could displease me with the company I find in this one, but do you know why Clarens pleases me in itself? It is because I feel myself truly in the country, and because this is almost the first time I have been able to say as much. [71]

2 pp or
country

For this month past, the autumn heat has been preparing a favorable vintage; the first frosts have induced us to begin it.* The parched vine branches, the leaves falling and exposing the grapes, spread before our eyes the gifts of Bacchus and seem to invite mortals to seize them. All the vines laden with that wholesome fruit which Heaven offers to the unfortunate to make them forget their misery; the noise of the casks, the vats, the tuns that are being hooped on all sides; the song of the grape gatherers with which these slopes reverberate; the continuous tread of those who carry the harvest to the press; the raucous sound of the rustic instruments that inspire them to work; the pleasant and affecting picture of a general cheerfulness which seems at this time spread over the face of the earth; finally, the veil of mist which the sunlight lifts in the mornings like a theater curtain in order to discover such a charming sight to the eye—all conspire to give it a festive air, and this festival becomes only more pleasing upon reflection, when one observes that it is the only one in which men have been able to combine the agreeable and the useful.

Monsieur de Wolmar, whose best land here consists of vineyards, made all the necessary preparations in advance. The vats, the press, the cellar, the casks await only the sweet liquor for which they are designed. Madame de Wolmar takes charge of the harvest; the selection of the workers and the order and distribution of the work are her concern also. Madame d'Orbe presides over the harvest dinners and over the wages of the day laborers, according to the established policy which the laws never infringe upon here. My task is to enforce Julie's commands at the press, for her head cannot bear the vapor from the vats, and Claire has not failed to recommend me to this occupation as being completely within the province of a toper.

The duties thus allotted, the common task with which we fill our free time is that of grape gatherer. Everyone is astir early in the morning; we assemble to go to the vineyards. Madame d'Orbe, who is never busy enough to suit her active nature, charges herself in

---

* The grape harvest is very late in the Vaud region because the principal crop is of white wines, and the frost is beneficial to them. [*Rousseau*]

addition with warning and scolding the lazy, and I can safely say
that in respect to me she fulfills this duty with a malicious vigilance.
As for the old Baron, while we are all working, he walks about
with a gun and comes from time to time to take me away from the
grape gathering to go with him thrush-shooting; they do not fail to
say that I have secretly engaged him to do this, so that I am little
by little losing the name of philosopher to get that of idler, titles
which at base are not much different.

You see by what I have just told you of the Baron that our recon-
ciliation is sincere and that Wolmar has reason to be satisfied with
his second test.* Shall I hate the father of my friend! No, if I had
been his son, I should not have respected him more perfectly. In
truth, I do not know a man more upright, more open, more generous, more honorable in every regard than this good gentleman. But
the singularity of his prejudices is odd. Since he has been certain
that I could not become a member of his family, there is no kind of
civility he does not show me, and provided that I may not be his
son-in-law, he would willingly put himself beneath me. The only
thing for which I cannot pardon him is that sometimes when we
are alone he rallies the would-be philosopher about his former
lessons. These pleasantries are bitter for me, and I always receive
them very badly, but he laughs at my anger and says, "Come, let's
shoot thrushes. That is enough argument." Then, as we pass by, he
shouts, "Claire, Claire! A good supper for your teacher, for I am going to make him get an appetite." Indeed, at his age, he runs along
the vineyards with his gun as vigorously as I and shoots incomparably better. What avenges me a little for his raillery is that before his daughter he no longer dares breathe a word, and the
little scholar awes her father himself hardly less than she does her
teacher. [72]

*This will be better understood by the following extract from one of Julie's
letters which is not in this collection:

" 'This,' Monsieur de Wolmar said to me, drawing me aside, 'is the second
test I determined for him. If he had not paid his respects to your father, I
should be distrustful of him.'

" 'But,' I said, 'how can you reconcile these respects and your test with the
antipathy you yourself have found between them?'

" 'It no longer exists,' he replied. 'Your father's prejudices have done Saint-
Preux all the harm they could do him. He no longer has anything to fear from
them; he hates them no more. He pities them. On his side, the Baron no longer
fears Saint-Preux. He has a good heart, he feels he has done him much harm,
and he has pity on him. I see that they will get along very well together and
will meet with pleasure. Also from this moment, I rely upon Saint-Preux completely.' " [Rousseau]

❧ LETTER VIII ❧

To Monsieur de Wolmar

ENJOY, MY DEAR WOLMAR, the fruit of your labor. Accept the homage of a purified heart, which you have taken so many pains to make worthy of being offered to you. Never did a man undertake what you have undertaken; never did a man attempt what you have executed. Nor did ever a grateful and sensitive soul feel what you have inspired in me. Mine had lost its force, its vigor, its being; you have restored them all. I was dead to virtue as well as to happiness; I owe you this moral life to which I feel myself reborn. Oh my benefactor! Oh my father! In giving myself up wholly to you, I can only offer you, as to God Himself, the gifts which I have received from you.

Must I confess to you my weakness and my fears? Hitherto I have always distrusted myself. Not a week ago I blushed for my heart and thought all your pains wasted. That moment was cruel and discouraging for virtue; thanks to Heaven, thanks to you, it has passed, no more to return. I no longer believe myself cured only because you tell me so but because I feel it. I have no more need for you to answer for me. You have put me in a state to answer for myself. I had to go away from you and from her in order to know what I could be without your support. Far from the place where she dwells, I am learning no longer to fear to approach it.

I have written a detailed account of our journey to Madame d'Orbe. I shall not repeat it for you here. I want you to be acquainted with all my weaknesses, but I do not have the courage to confess them to you. My dear Wolmar, that is my last fault; I feel myself already at such a distance from it that I cannot think of it without pride, but it is still so little a while since that I cannot confess it painlessly. You who were able to pardon my errors, how could you not pardon the shame which has brought forth my repentance?

My happiness lacks nothing further. His Lordship has told me everything. My dear friend, am I then yours? Shall I educate your children? Will the eldest of the three educate the other two? With what ardor I have desired it! How my hope of being found worthy of such employment has doubled my assiduity to satisfy yours! How many times I dared to show my eagerness in this matter to Julie! With what pleasure I often interpreted both your remarks in my favor! But although she was aware of my zeal and although she seemed to approve its object, I did not see her enter explicitly enough into my designs to dare speak more openly of them. I felt that I had to merit that honor and not ask for it. I expected this proof of your confidence and your esteem from you both. I have not been deceived in my expectation; my friends, believe me, you will not be deceived in yours.

You know that following our conversations on the education of your children, I had thrown on paper some ideas they furnished me with, which you approved. Since my departure some new thoughts have occurred to me on the same subject, and I have reduced the whole into a kind of plan with which I shall acquaint you when I have digested it better, so that you may examine it in turn. It is only after our arrival in Rome that I hope to have time to put it in a state fit to show you. This plan begins where Julie's ends, or rather, it is only the sequel and the development of hers, for the whole consists in not spoiling the natural man by subjecting him to society.

I have recovered my reason through your solicitude. Once again my heart is free and sound, and I feel myself beloved by all whose love is dear to me. The most charming future is presented to me; my situation should be delightful, but it is decreed that my soul will never be at rest. As the end of our journey draws near, I see in it the crisis of my illustrious friend's destiny; it is I who must determine it, so to speak. Shall I be able to do at least once for him what he has done so often for me? Shall I be able worthily to discharge the greatest, the most important duty of my life? My dear Wolmar, I have carried all your lessons away in the bottom of my heart, but to know how to render them useful, would that I could have carried away your wisdom as well! Ah! If one day I can see Edward happy, if, fulfilling his projects and yours, we will all rejoin each other to part no more, what wish will be left for me to have? Only one, the realization of which depends neither on you, nor on me, nor on anyone in the world, but on Him who has a reward in store for your wife's virtues and secretly counts up your good deeds.

❧ LETTER IX ❧

To Madame d'Orbe

WHERE ARE YOU, charming cousin? Where are you, amiable friend of this frail heart which you share for so many reasons and which you have consoled so many times? Come, let it now pour out into yours the confession of its last error. Is it not your province to purify it, and can it still reproach itself for errors that it has confessed to you? No, I am no longer the same, and this change is owed to you. You have given me a new heart, which offers you its first fruits, but I shall believe myself freed from the one I am abandoning only after I have deposited it in your hands. Oh you who have seen it born, receive its last sighs!

Would you ever have thought it? The moment of my life in which I was most content with myself was that in which I left you. Recovered from my long bewilderment, I looked upon that instant as the tardy beginning of my return to my duty. I began finally to pay the immense debts of friendship by tearing myself from such a cherished place in order to follow a benefactor, a philosopher who, pretending to need my services, was putting the success of his own to the test. The sadder this departure was for me, the more I prided myself on making such a sacrifice. After having spent half my life in nourishing an unfortunate passion, I was devoting the other half to justify it, to pay with my virtues a more worthy homage to her who for so long received all that of my heart. I proudly observed the first day of my life in which I put myself to shame before neither you, nor her, nor anyone dear to me.

Lord Bomston had feared the tenderness of the farewells, and we wanted to leave without being perceived, but though everyone else was still sleeping, we could not elude your vigilant friendship. Seeing your door half open and your maid on the watch, seeing you come to meet us, entering and finding a tea table prepared, I thought, from the resemblances of the circumstances, of another time, and comparing this departure to the one it called to mind, I felt myself so different from what I was then that, pleased to have Edward as a witness to these differences, I hoped to make him for-

get in Milan the shameful scene in Besançon. Never did I feel my
courage so much. I prided myself on displaying it to you; before you
I made a show of that resolution which you had never seen in me,
and I gloried as I left you in appearing in your eyes such as I was
going to be ever afterwards.

This idea added to my courage, I fortified myself with your esteem, and I perhaps would have said good-bye to you with a dry
eye, if your tears trickling over my cheek had not forced my own
to mingle with them.

I left with my heart full of all my duty, penetrated above all with
that which your friendship has imposed upon me, and very determined to use the rest of my life in deserving it. Edward, reviewing
all my faults, set before my eyes again a picture which was not flattering, and I knew by his just severity in censuring so many weaknesses
that he was hardly afraid of imitating them. Yet he pretended to
be afraid of it; he spoke to me uneasily of his trip to Rome and the
unworthy attachments which recalled him there in spite of himself, but I readily judged that he was exaggerating his own dangers
the more to engage my attention and put it further from those to
which I myself was exposed.

As we were coming to Villeneuve, a servant who was riding a bad
horse was thrown and got a slight bruise on the head. His master
had him bled and determined to spend the night there. Having had
an early dinner, we took the horses and went to Bex to see the salt
mine, and his Lordship having some particular reasons which made
this examination interesting for him, I took the measurements
and sketched the design of the graduation house. We did not get
back to Villeneuve before night. After supper, we chatted, drinking punch, and sat up rather late. It was then that he informed me
what duties had been entrusted to me and what had been done to
make the arrangement possible. You can judge the effect that this
news had on me; such a conversation did not incline me to sleep.
Yet I finally had to go to bed.

Entering the room which was prepared for me, I recognized it
as the same which I had formerly occupied when I went to Sion.
The sight of it made an impression on me which I should have
difficulty in conveying to you. I was so vividly struck by it that I immediately imagined myself again the same man as I was then. Ten
years were effaced from my life and all my misfortunes were forgotten. Alas! This mistake was short-lived, and the next moment made
the weight of all my former sorrows more oppressive for me. What
melancholy reflections succeeded that first enchantment! What

dreadful comparisons offered themselves to my mind! Pleasures of early youth, delights of first love, why recall them again to this heart, overwhelmed with troubles and burdened with itself? Oh time, happy time, it is no more! I loved, I was loved. In peaceful innocence, I used to indulge myself in the ecstasies of a mutual passion. In long draughts I used to drink in the delightful sentiment which gave me life. The sweet vapor of hope used to intoxicate my heart. An ecstasy, a rapture, a delirium absorbed all my faculties. Ah! On the rocks of Meillerie, in the midst of snow and ice, frightful abysses before my eyes, what creature in the world enjoyed a happiness comparable to mine? . . . And I wept! And I found myself pitiable! And sorrow dared approach me! . . . What should I be today, then, now that I have possessed everything, lost everything? . . . I have indeed deserved my misery because I felt my happiness so little! . . . Did I weep then? . . . You wept? . . . Wretch, you weep no more. . . . You do not even have the right to weep. . . . Would that she were dead! I dared cry that out in a fit of rage; yes, I should be less unhappy if she were. I should dare indulge myself in my griefs. Without remorse I should embrace her cold tomb; my laments would be worthy of her. I could say that she is hearing my cries, she is seeing my tears, she is affected by my sobs, she approves and receives my pure homage. . . . At least I should have the hope of rejoining her. . . . But she lives; she is happy! . . . She lives, her life is my death, and her happiness is my torment. After having torn her from me, Heaven has taken from me even the pleasure of regretting her loss! . . . She lives, but not for me; she lives for my despair. I am a hundred times farther from her than if she were dead.

I went to bed with these melancholy thoughts. They pursued me during my sleep and filled it with dismal visions. Bitter sorrows, laments, death composed my dreams, and all the misfortunes I had suffered assumed a hundred new forms in my imagination in order to torment me a second time. One dream in particular, the most cruel of all, persisted in pursuing me, and all the confused apparitions of phantom after phantom ended always in this one.

I thought I saw your friend's worthy mother on her death bed, her daughter on her knees before her, bathed in tears, kissing her hands and receiving her last breath. I saw again that scene which you once described to me and which will never leave my memory.

"Oh my mother," said Julie, in a manner to rend my soul, "she who owes her life to you is taking yours from you! Ah! Take back your favor. Without you, life is but a dreary gift for me."

"My child," her tender mother replied, ". . . we must fulfill our destiny. . . . God is just. . . . You will be a mother in your turn. . . ."

She could not finish. . . . I tried to raise my eyes and look at her; I saw her no more. In her place I saw Julie. I saw her; I recognized her although her face was covered with a veil. I gave a shriek, I rushed forward to put aside the veil, I could not reach it, I stretched forth my arms, I tormented myself, but I touched nothing.

"Friend, be calm," she said to me in a faint voice. "The terrible veil covers me. No hand can put it aside."

At these words, I struggled and made a new effort; this effort woke me up. I found myself in my bed, overwhelmed by fatigue and soaked with perspiration and tears.

Soon my fright was dissipated; exhaustion put me to sleep again. The same dream disturbed me the same way. I woke and went to sleep a third time. Always the mournful sight, always that same appearance of death, always that impenetrable veil eluding my hands and hiding from my eyes the dying person it covered.

As I awoke the last time, my terror was so great that I could not conquer it even though awake. I threw myself at the foot of my bed, without knowing what I was doing. I began to wander through the room, frightened like a child by the shadows of the night, believing I saw myself surrounded by phantoms, my ear still hearing that plaintive voice, the sound of which I never heard without emotion. Beginning to cast light on things, the dawn only transformed them according to my troubled imagination. My fright doubled and deprived me of my judgment. After having with difficulty found my door, I fled from my room. I bolted into Edward's; I opened his curtain and let myself fall on his bed, breathlessly crying, "It is over. I shall see her no more!"

He woke up with a start; he jumped for his weapons, believing himself surprised by a thief. Presently he recognized me; I recollected myself, and for the second time in my life I saw myself before him in a confusion which you can conceive.

He made me sit down, compose myself and speak. As soon as he knew what the matter was, he tried to turn the thing to ridicule, but seeing that I was violently affected, and that the impression it had made would not be easy to destroy, he changed his tone.

"You do not deserve either my friendship or my esteem," he said to me rather harshly. "If I had taken for my servant a quarter of the trouble that I have taken for you, I should have made a man of him, but you are worthless."

"Ah!" I said to him, "that is only too true. All the good I had in me came from her. I shall never see her again. I am now worthless."

He smiled and embraced me. "Calm yourself today," he said, "and tomorrow you will be rational. I shall undertake to make you so."

After that, changing the subject, he proposed to me that we leave. I agreed to it, the horses were put to, and we got dressed. Getting into the carriage, his Lordship said a word in the postilion's ear, and we left.

We traveled along without saying anything. I was so preoccupied with my gloomy dream that I heard and saw nothing. I did not even notice that the lake, which the day before was on my right, was now on my left. It was only the clatter of the carriage on paving stones which awoke me from my lethargy and made me perceive, with an astonishment easy to understand, that we had returned to Clarens. Three hundred feet from the gate, his Lordship had the carriage stopped and drawing me aside, he said, "You see my project. It needs no explanation. Go, visionary," he added, clasping my hand, "go see her again. You are fortunate in exposing your follies only to people who love you! Hurry up, I will wait for you, but above all, come back only after you have torn away that fatal veil which is woven in your mind."

What could I have said? I left without answering. I walked with a quick pace which reflection slowed as I approached the house. What sort of a part was I going to act? How could I dare show myself? What pretext could I use for this unexpected return? With what countenance should I go to plead my ridiculous terrors and bear the scornful look of the generous Wolmar? The closer I came, the more childish my fright seemed to me, and my extravagant behavior made me pitiable. Yet, a dark presentiment still disturbed me, and I did not feel myself at all reassured. I went on, although slowly, and I was already near the courtyard when I heard the door of the Elysium open and close again. Seeing no one leave, I circled it on the outside, and I went along the water to come as close to the aviary as possible. I did not wait long until someone approached. Then listening, I heard you both speaking, and though it was impossible for me to distinguish a single word, I found in the sound of your voice something indefinably languishing and tender which I heard with emotion, and in hers not only her usual affecting and sweet accent but also one that was peaceful and serene, which immediately restored me and truly woke me from my dream.

Immediately, I felt myself so changed that I laughed at myself and my foolish alarms. Reflecting that I had only a hedge and some bushes to cross through in order to see full of life and health her whom I had believed I would never see again, I renounced my fears, my fright, and my dreams forever, and I decided without further ado to leave again, even without seeing her. Claire, I swear to you not only that I did not see her but that I turned back proud of not having seen her, of not having been weak and credulous to the end, and of having at least done the honor to myself as Edward's friend of getting the better of a dream.

This, dear cousin, is what I had to tell you and the last confession left for me to make to you. The details of the rest of our journey are no longer interesting. It is enough for me to assure you that since then not only has his Lordship been satisfied with me, but I am still more satisfied with myself, I who feel my entire recovery much better than he can see it. For fear of giving him a needless distrust, I hid from him the fact that I had not seen you. When he asked me if the veil had been lifted, I answered without hesitating in the affirmative, and we have spoken of it no more. Yes, cousin, it has lifted forever, this veil with which my reason was obscured for a long time. All my unruly passions are extinguished. I see my whole duty and I respect it. You are both more dear to me than ever, but my heart no longer distinguishes between you and does not separate the inseparables.

We arrived at Milan the day before yesterday. We are leaving again the day after tomorrow. In a week we expect to be in Rome, and I hope to find news from you there upon our arrival. How anxious I am to see those two surprising women who have disturbed for so long the repose of the greatest of men. Oh Julie! Oh Claire! They would have to equal you to deserve to make him happy.

❧ LETTER X ❧

Madame d'Orbe's Response

WE ALL WAITED impatiently for news of you, and I do not need to tell you how much pleasure your letters have given to our little community, but what you will not imagine so readily is that of all the household I am perhaps the one whom they have least cheered. Everyone learned that you had happily passed over the Alps; as for me, I reflected only that you were too far away beyond them.

In respect to the detailed account you made me, we said nothing of it to the Baron, and I skipped over some very needless parts in reading it to everyone. Monsieur de Wolmar had the ingeniousness only to laugh at you, but Julie was not able to remember the last moments of her mother without fresh regrets and new tears. She noticed in your dream only that which rekindled her griefs.

As for me, I shall tell you, my dear teacher, that I am no longer surprised to see you in constant astonishment at yourself, always committing some folly and always beginning to become prudent, because for a long time you have spent your life in self-reproach the night before and in self-approval the next morning.

I confess to you also that this great courageous effort which, though you were so near to us, made you return as you had come does not appear so wonderful to me as it does to you. I find it more vain than prudent, and I think that on the whole I should prefer much less fortitude with a little more reason. From this manner of running away, could one not ask you for what purpose you had come? You were ashamed to show yourself, and it is for not daring to show yourself that you ought to be ashamed, as if the delight of seeing one's friends did not a hundred times efface the petty chagrin over their raillery! Should you not have been only too happy to come offer us your distracted air in order to make us laugh? Well then, I did not laugh at you then, but I laugh at you so much the more today, although since I do not have the pleasure of angering you, I cannot laugh with such good will.

Unfortunately, there is worse yet. It is that I have caught all your fears without, like you, being reassured. That dream has something frightening about it which disturbs me and saddens me despite myself. As I read your letter, I censured your agitation; when I finished it, I censured your security. It is impossible to see both why you were so affected and why you have become so tranquil. Through what capriciousness your dreariest presentiments prevailed up to the moment when you were able to destroy them, and then you did not try to do so. Another step, a gesture, a word would have done it. You alarmed yourself without reason; you reassured yourself in the same way, but you have infected me with the fright you no longer have, and it appears that, having had fortitude for once in your life, you have had it at my expense. Since I received your fatal letter, my heart has been constantly oppressed; I do not come near

Julie without trembling over losing her. At every moment I think I see the pallor of death on her face, and this morning, pressing her in my arms, I felt myself in tears without knowing why. That veil! That veil! . . . There is something indefinably sinister in it which disturbs me each time I think of it. No, I cannot pardon you for having had the chance to put it aside and not having done so, and I am indeed afraid of henceforth having no more peaceful moments until I see you again in her company. Admit also that after having spoken so long of philosophy, you have in the end shown yourself a philosopher very unseasonably. Ah! Dream again and come see your friends; that is better than fleeing them and being a philosopher.

It seems by his Lordship's letter to Monsieur de Wolmar that he is seriously thinking of coming to settle with us. As soon as he has made up his mind down there and as soon as his heart has made its choice, may you both come back happy and settled; that is the desire of the little community, and above all, of your friend,

Claire d'Orbe

P.S. As for the rest, if it is true that you heard nothing of our conversation in the Elysium, it is perhaps so much the better for you, for you know me sufficiently vigilant to see people without their perceiving me and sufficiently severe to speak maliciously of eavesdroppers.

❖ LETTER XI ❖

Monsieur de Wolmar's Response

I WROTE to Lord Bomston and spoke to him of you at such length that writing to you I have hardly anything left to say except to refer you to his letter. Yours would perhaps require on my part a return of civilities, but to call you into my family, to treat you as a brother, as a friend, to make a sister of her who was your mistress, to give you paternal authority over my children, to entrust you with my rights after having usurped yours—those are the compliments of which I have believed you worthy. On your part, if you justify my conduct and my solicitude, you will have praised me sufficiently. I have tried to do you honor through my esteem; do me honor through your virtues. All other encomiums must be banished between us.

So far am I from being surprised to see you affected by a dream that I see no very good reason why you reproach yourself for having been so. Yet, it seems to me that for a man like you one dream more or less in not of such great importance.

But what I readily reproach you for is less the effect of your dream than its kind, and I have a reason quite different from the one you could imagine. Once a tyrant put a man to death for dreaming that he stabbed his master. Remember the reason he gave for this murder, and make the application of it for yourself.* What! You are going to decide your friend's fate and you are thinking of your former love! Had it not been for the conversations of the preceding evening, I would never forgive you for that dream. During the day think of what you are going to do in Rome; you will dream less at night of what is taking place at Vevey.

Fanchon is ill; that keeps my wife busy and deprives her of the time to write you. Somebody here will willingly take on this task. Fortunate young man! Everything conspires to your happiness; all the rewards of virtue seek you to force you to deserve them. As to the reward for my good deeds, do not charge anyone but yourself with it; it is from you alone that I expect it.

❧ LETTER XII ❧

To Monsieur de Wolmar

LET THIS LETTER be kept between you and me. Let a deep secrecy forever conceal the errors of the most virtuous of men. In what dangerous task do I find myself engaged? Oh, my wise and gen-

---

* According to Mornet, Rousseau could have read this story in either Plutarch or Montesquieu; the tyrant's motive in having the man executed was that if he dreamed of stabbing his master at night, he must have thought of it during the day. Saint-Preux's dream, as it will be seen, assumes considerable importance in Part Six. [*Translator's note*]

erous friend! Would that I had a mind full of your counsel, just as I have a heart full of your kindness! Never had I such great need of prudence, and never did the fear of failing in it present such an obstacle to the little that I have. Ah! Where is your paternal advice? Where is your instruction, your insight? What will become of me without you? At this critical moment, I should give all the hopeful prospects of my life to have you here for one week.

I was mistaken in all my conjectures. I have done nothing but blunder until now. I was afraid only of the Marquise. After having seen her, struck by her beauty and her manner, I endeavored to detach the noble soul of her former lover completely from her. Charmed with the thought of bringing him back to the side where I saw no danger, I spoke to him of Laura with the esteem and the admiration with which she had inspired me. In weakening his strongest attachment by praising the other, I hoped eventually to destroy both.

He gave in to my project at first; he even overdid his obligingness, and wishing perhaps to punish my importunities by alarming me somewhat, he pretended even more ardor for Laura than he believed he had. What shall I tell you now? His ardor is ever the same, but he no longer pretends. His heart, exhausted by so many trials, is in a state of weakness which she has taken advantage of. It would be difficult for anyone to pretend love for her for a long time; consider the case of the very object·of the passion which consumes her. In truth, one cannot look at this unfortunate woman without being affected by her manner and by her face; an expression of languor and despondency, which does not leave her charming face, makes her features more interesting by extinguishing their vivacity, and as the sun's rays dart through the clouds, her eyes shoot forth more piercing looks when dulled by sorrow. Her very humiliation has all the grace of modesty. Seeing her, one pities her; listening to her, one respects her. In short, I must say in my friend's justification that I know only two men in the world who may remain near her without danger.

He is going astray, oh Wolmar! I see it, I feel it, I confess it to you with bitterness in my heart. I shudder to think to what point his extravagant passion can make him forget what he is and what his duty is to himself. I tremble to think that his fearless love of virtue, which makes him scorn public opinion, may carry him to the other extremity and make him defy even the sacred laws of decency and honor. Edward Bomston to make such a marriage! . . . You understand! . . . Under the eyes of his friend! . . . Who

permits it! . . . Who allows it! And who owes him everything!
. . . He will have to tear out my heart with his hand before thus
profaning it.

Yet, what shall I do? How shall I act? You know his violent nature. One gains nothing over him through argument, and for some
time his conversation has not been the sort to calm my fears. I first
pretended not to understand him. I reasoned indirectly in general
maxims; in his turn he pretends not to understand me. If I try to
touch him a little more to the quick, he answers sententiously and
thinks he has refuted me. If I am insistent, he flies into a passion;
he assumes a tone that a friend should not hear and to which friendship cannot answer. You may believe that on this occasion I
am neither fearful nor timid; when we are doing our duty, we are
only too tempted to be proud, but pride has nothing to do with this.
It is a matter of succeeding, and unsuccessful attempts can be injurious to the best means. I hardly dare enter into any argument
with him, for every day I feel the truth of the warning you gave me:
that he is a better reasoner than I and that I must not irritate him
by dispute.

He seems, besides, a little cool toward me. One would say that I
make him uneasy. Even with such superiority in all respects, how
diminished the man is by one moment of weakness! The great,
the sublime Edward fears his friend, his creature, his pupil! He
even seems, from a few words he let fall on the choice of his residence if he does not marry, to wish to test my faithfulness by opposing it to my interest. He knows very well that I neither must nor
wish to leave him. Oh Wolmar, I shall do my duty and shall follow
my benefactor everywhere. If I were cowardly and base, what would
I gain by my perfidy? Would Julie and her worthy husband confide
their children to a traitor?

You have often said to me that inferior passions never are
diverted and always go on to their end, but that one can fortify
great ones against themselves. I thought I could make use of this
maxim in this affair. Indeed, compassion, scorn for prejudices,
habit—all which determines Edward in this case is of that inferior
nature and becomes almost unassailable. However, true love is
inseparable from generosity, and through generosity one always
has some hold over him. I have tried this indirect way, and I do not
despair of success. This means seems cruel; I have undertaken it
only with repugnance. Yet, everything well considered, I think I am
rendering a service to Laura herself. What would she do in the place
to which she can rise by marriage except to expose her former ig-

nominy? But how great she can be by remaining what she is! If I know this extraordinary girl well, her constitution will make her enjoy her sacrifice more than the rank which she must refuse.

If this resource fails me, there is one left through the government, on account of their difference of religion, but this means must not be employed except as a last resort and for want of all others. Whatever happens, I will not spare any means to prevent an unworthy and dishonorable alliance. Oh respectable Wolmar! I am desirous of your esteem to the last moment of my life. Whatever Edward may write you, whatever you might understand him to say, remember that, at no matter what cost, as long as my heart will beat in my breast, Laura Pisana will never be Lady Bomston.

If you approve my measures, this letter needs no answer. If I am mistaken, instruct me. But hurry, for there is not a moment to lose. I shall have my letter addressed by an unfamiliar hand. Do the same in answering me. After having considered what I must do, burn my letter and forget what it contains. This is the first and the only secret that I have ever in my life had to hide from the two cousins. If I dared rely more on my understanding, you yourself should never know anything of it.*

❧ LETTER XIII ❧

From Madame de Wolmar to Madame d'Orbe

THE COURIER from Italy seemed only to wait for the moment of your departure for his own arrival, as if to punish you for having deferred it only for him. It was not I who made this pretty discovery; it was my husband who noticed that, having had the horses put to at eight o'clock, you delayed leaving until eleven, not out of love for us but after having twenty times asked if it was ten, because that ordinarily is the hour at which the mail comes by.

You are caught, poor cousin; you can no longer deny it. In spite

---

* In order to understand this letter and the third one of Part Six completely, the reader would need to know the adventures of Lord Bomston, and I had at first decided to add them to this collection. Reconsidering it, I could not resolve myself to spoil the simplicity of the story of the two lovers by the romance of his. It is better to leave something for the reader to guess. [*Rousseau*]

of Chaillot's prediction, this Claire, so foolish, or rather so prudent, could not be so to the end. Here you are in the same toils from which you took so much trouble to extricate me, and you have not been able to preserve for yourself the liberty which you restored to me. Has my turn come to laugh, then? Dear friend, I should have to have your charm and your graces to know how to laugh like you and give to raillery itself the tender and affecting manner of kindness. And then, what a difference between us! With what countenance should I laugh at a disorder of which I am the cause and which you took upon yourself in order to free me from it? There is no sentiment in your heart which does not offer mine some reason for gratitude, and all, even to your weakness, is in you the effect of your virtue. It is even this which consoles me and makes me cheerful. I had to lament and weep for my faults, but I can laugh at the false modesty which makes you blush for an attachment as pure as yourself.

Let us return to the courier from Italy, and leave moralizing for a moment. Otherwise I should excessively misuse my former role of preacher, for it is permissible to put one's congregation to sleep but not to put it out of patience. Well, then, what has this courier brought which has been so long in arriving? Nothing but good news of our friends and, moreover, a long letter for you. Ah good! I see you already smiling and breathing once more; since the letter has arrived, you will wait more patiently to know what it contains.

It may nevertheless be of value, even though it did not come when expected, for it breathes such an air . . . but I wish to tell you news only, and surely what I was going to say is none.

With this letter came another from Lord Bomston for my husband, with a great many compliments for us. This one contains veritable news, which is so much the more unexpected as the first was silent on the subject. Our friends were to leave the next day for Naples, where his Lordship has some business, and from there they will go to see Vesuvius. . . . Can you conceive, my dear, what this sight has which is so attractive? Back in Rome, Claire, think, imagine . . . Edward is on the point of marrying . . . not, thank Heaven, that unworthy Marquise. He indicates, on the contrary, that she is very ill. Who then? . . .Laura, the charming Laura, who . . . but yet . . . what a marriage! . . . Our friend has not said a word about it. Immediately afterwards, they will all three set out and come here to make their final arrangements. My husband has not told me what those are, but he ever expects that Saint-Preux will stay with us. [73]

I must, therefore, give you my opinion again on your present state. Our teacher's long absence has not changed your regard for him. Your restored liberty and his return have given rise to a new opportunity from which love has profited. A new sentiment was not kindled in your heart; the one hidden there for such a long time has only been put more at ease. Proud of daring to confess it to yourself, you made haste to tell me of it. This confession seemed almost necessary to you to make the sentiment completely innocent; by becoming a crime for your cousin, it ceased being one for yourself, and perhaps you have yielded to the disorder which you contended against for so many years only to cure me of it more effectively.

I have felt all this, my dear; I was little alarmed at an inclination which served me as a safeguard, and for which you did not have to reproach yourself. The winter we spent all together in the bosom of peace and friendship gave me even more confidence, as I saw that, far from losing any of your gaiety, you seemed to have augmented it. I saw you tender, eager, attentive, but frank in your affectionateness, ingenuous in your raillery, open and guileless in everything, and in your most lively coquetry, the joy of innocence atoned for everything.

Since our conversation in the Elysium, I have not been so content with you. I find you sad and pensive. You take pleasure in being alone as much as with your friend; you have not changed your language but you have your tone. Your pleasantries are more cautious; you no longer dare speak of him so often; one would say that you are always afraid he is listening to you, and one sees by your disquietude that you wait for news of him rather than ask for it.

I am afraid, good cousin, that you are not wholly aware of your disorder, and that the shaft may have pierced deep sooner than you seemed to fear. Believe me, probe your disordered heart well. Ask yourself, I repeat, if however prudent you may be, you can remain for long with the one you love without risk, and if the confidence which ruined me is completely harmless for you. You are both free; that is precisely what makes opportunities more suspicious. In a virtuous heart, there is no frailty which gives way to remorse, and I agree with you that one is always sufficiently strong against crime. But alas! Who can keep himself from being weak? However, consider the consequences; think of the effects of shame. We must honor ourselves in order to be honored. How can we deserve another's respect without showing any for ourselves, and where in the road of vice shall she stop herself who fearlessly makes the first step? That is what I should say to women of society for whom morality and religion are nothing, and who have only society's opinion of you. But you, virtuous and Christian woman, you who see your duty and respect it, you who know and follow rules other than public opinion, your foremost honor is that which your conscience gives you, and it is that which it is important to preserve.

Do you wish to know what your mistake in this whole affair is? It is, I say again to you, to be ashamed of an honest sentiment which you have only to declare to make innocent.* But with all your cheerful humor, no one is so timid as you. You jest in order to show your courage, and I see your poor heart trembling all the while. In the matter of love, at which you pretend to laugh, you act like those children who sing in the dark when they are afraid. Oh dear friend! Remember you have said a thousand times that it is false shame which leads to true, and virtue puts to shame only what is evil. Is love in itself a crime? Is it not the purest as well as the sweetest natural inclination? Does it not have a good and praiseworthy end? Does it not disdain base and groveling hearts? Does it not inspire great and strong hearts? Does it not ennoble all their sentiments? Does it not double their being? Does it not raise them above themselves? Ah! If to be honest and prudent, one has to be insensible to love's shafts, tell me who are left for virtue on this earth? The outcasts of nature and the vilest of mortals. [74]

Ah cousin! What delight for me to unite forever two hearts so well formed for each other, who have been joined for so long in my own. Let them be even more closely joined in it, if possible. Let there be but one heart for you and for me. Yes, my Claire, you will still serve your friend by indulging your love, and I shall be surer of my own sentiments when I shall no longer be able to distinguish between him and you.

But if, in spite of my reasons, this project does not suit you, my opinion is that no matter what the cost we send away that dangerous man, always formidable for one of us or the other, for whatever happens, the education of our children is even less important to us than the virtue of their mothers. I leave you time to reflect on all this during your journey. We shall speak of it after your return.

* Why does the editor leave in the continual repetitions with which this letter is full, as well as a great many others? For a very simple reason. It is that he is not at all worried that these letters may please those who will pose this question. [Rousseau]

I decided to send you this letter directly to Geneva, because you were to spend only one night in Lausanne, and it should no longer find you there. Be sure to send me some detailed accounts of the little republic. On the basis of all the good things that are said about that charming city, I should think you fortunate to see it, if I could set store by pleasures one buys at the expense of his friends. I have never loved luxuries, and I hate them now for having taken you from me for I know not how many years.* My dear, neither of us went to Geneva to do our wedding shopping; but however deserving your brother may be, I doubt that your sister-in-law may be more happy with her Flanders lace and her Indian cloth than we with our simplicity. Yet, I charge you, in spite of my malice, to engage him to come celebrate the wedding at Clarens. My father is writing to yours, and my husband to the bride's mother in order to invite them. Here are the letters. Deliver them, and enforce the invitations with your new influence. This is all I can do so that the festivities may not take place without me, for I declare to you that no matter what the cost I will not leave my family. Adieu cousin. Send me one word of news of you, and let me know at least when I am to expect you. This is the second day since your departure, and no more can I live so long without you. [75]

* Claire is gone from Clarens only for a few weeks. Julie's hyperbolic calculation of the time is apparently meant to show her impatience for her cousin's return. [*Translator's note*]

PART VI

✤ LETTER I ✤

From Madame d'Orbe to Madame de Wolmar

BEFORE LEAVING Lausanne, I must write you a note to inform you of my arrival here, not, however, so joyous as I hoped. I looked forward with pleasure to this little journey which has tempted you yourself so often; but by refusing to come along, you have made it almost troublesome for me, for how could I find it otherwise? If it is tedious, I shall have the tedium to myself, and if it is agreeable, I shall regret being pleased without you. If I have nothing to say against your reasons for staying home, do you think, therefore, that I am satisfied with them? In truth, cousin, you are very much mistaken, and what angers me more is that I do not even have the right to be angry. Tell me, wicked one, are you not ashamed to be always in the right with your friend and to oppose what gives her pleasure without even allowing her the right to complain? If you had slipped away from your husband, your house, and your little urchins for a week, all would have gone to wrack and ruin, wouldn't it? You would have committed a rash act, to be sure, but I should have liked you a hundred times better for it, whereas by troubling yourself to be perfect, you will be good for nothing now and will have to seek your company among the angels.

In spite of past disagreements, I could not find myself again among my family without tender feelings; I have been received with pleasure, or at least with many kisses. I will wait to give you an account of my brother until I have made his acquaintance. With a rather fine form, he has the rigid manner of the country he comes from. He is serious and cold; I find him even a little arrogant. I am greatly apprehensive for his wife that, instead of being as good a husband as ours, he may lord it above her a little.

My father was so delighted to see me that in order to embrace me he left off the account of the great battle that the French have just won in Flanders, as if to verify our friend's prediction.* What good fortune that he was not there! Can you imagine the brave Edward watching the English flee, or fleeing himself? . . . Never, never! . . . He would sooner have been killed a hundred times.

But with respect to our friends, it has been a long time since they have written us. Was not yesterday, I believe, the day for the postman? If you receive any letters, I hope you will not forget the interest which I take in them.

Adieu, cousin, I must leave. I shall expect news from you at Geneva, where we hope to arrive tomorrow for dinner. As for the rest, I warn you that somehow or other the wedding will not take place without you and that if you will not come to Lausanne, I shall come with all my family to pillage Clarens and drink all the wine you have made.

❧ LETTER II ❧

From Madame d'Orbe to Madame de Wolmar

ADMIRABLY DONE, my preaching sister! But you rely a little too much, it seems to me, on the salutary effect of your sermons. Without considering whether they once put your friend to sleep, I assure you that they do not bore your cousin now, and the one which I received last night, far from prompting me to sleep, kept me awake the whole night long. Disregard the remarks of your husband, my argus, if he sees this letter! But I shall see to that, for I protest to you that you had better burn your fingers than show it to him.

If I were going to recapitulate you point by point, I would encroach upon your privilege; it is better to follow my inclination. And then, in order to affect a more modest manner and not give you too much advantage over me, I will not speak first of our travellers and of the mail from Italy. If I should happen to do so, as

---

* An allusion to the French victory at Fontenoy, May 11, 1745. Lord Bomston predicted an English defeat in Flanders in Part Five, Letter IV. [*Translator's note*]

a last shift I shall only have to rewrite my letter and put the beginning at the end. Let us speak of the would-be Lady Bomston.

I am indignant at that very title. I should not pardon Saint-Preux more for letting that girl assume it than Edward for conferring it on her and you for recognizing it. Julie de Wolmar to receive Laura Pisana in her house! To tolerate her near her! Ah, my child, what are you thinking? What cruel kindness would that be? Do you not know that the air which surrounds you is fatal to infamy? Would the poor unfortunate dare mingle her breath with yours? Would she dare respire in your presence? There she would be more ill at ease than a creature possessed, touched by relics. Your looks alone would make her sink into the earth; your shadow alone would kill her. [76]

Let us not lose ourselves in idle conjectures. If you had not been Julie, if your friend had not been your lover, I do not know what business he might have had with you; I do not know what I myself should have had to do with him. All I am sure of is that if his evil influence had reached me first, it had been all over with his poor head, for whether I am a fool or not, I should infallibly have made him one. But what does it matter what I might have been? Let us speak of what I am. The first thing that I did was to become attached to you. From our earliest years, my heart has been absorbed in yours. As tender and sensitive as I might have been, I was of myself incapable of loving or feeling. All my sentiments came to me from you; you alone took the place of everything for me, and I lived only to be your friend. That is what Chaillot saw; that is upon what she judged me. Answer me, cousin, was she mistaken? [77]

Yes, dear friend, I am as tender and sensitive as you, but I am so in another way. My affections are more lively; yours are more penetrating. Perhaps with senses more animated, I am less able to direct them, and that very gaiety which costs so many others their innocence has always preserved mine. This has not always been easy, I must confess. How can one remain a widow at my age and not feel sometimes that the daytime is only half of life? But as you have said and as you prove, prudence is a great means of being prudent; for with all your serious countenance, I do not believe your case very different from mine. Therefore, sprightliness comes to my aid and does more, perhaps, for virtue than serious lessons of reason might have done. How many times in the stillness of the night, in which we cannot escape ourselves, have I driven away importunate thoughts by thinking of pleasantries for the next day! How many times have I been saved from the dangers of a private conversation by an extravagant fancy? You see, my dear, when one is frail, there is always a time when gaiety becomes serious, but this moment will not come for me. That is what I feel, and with what I presume to answer you.

After that, I readily confirm to you all I said in the Elysium about the attachment that I have felt growing and about all the happiness I have enjoyed this winter. I indulged myself with the best of hearts in the charm of being in the company of the one I love, feeling that I should desire nothing more. If that winter might have lasted forever, I should never have wished for another. My gaiety came from contentment and not from artifice. I turned the pleasure of busying myself ceaselessly with him into frolic. I felt that by contenting myself with laughter, I was not paving the way for tears. [78]

If we are not master of our sentiments, at least we are of our conduct. Without doubt, I could ask Heaven for a heart more at ease, but would that I could offer to the Sovereign Judge at my last day a life as innocent as that which I have spent this winter! In truth, I have nothing with which to reproach myself concerning the only man who could make me guilty. My dear, it has not been the same since he has left. Being accustomed to think of him while he is gone, I think of him every instant of the day, and I find the thought of him more dangerous than his person. If he is far away, I am in love; if he is close by, I am only frolicsome. Let him return, and I shall fear him no more.

To my regret over his departure is joined my uneasiness over his dream. If you have laid all this to love's account, you are mistaken; friendship has had a part in my sadness. At our friends' departure, I saw you pale and altered; every moment I expected to see you falling ill. I am not credulous, but fearful. I am convinced that a dream does not bring about an event, but I am always afraid that the event may take place after it. That accursed dream hardly allowed me a tranquil night, until I saw you recovered and resuming your color. Could I have suspected the effect his anxiety would have had on me, unwittingly I would certainly have given the whole world that he might have shown himself when he returned from Villeneuve like a madman. At last my vain fear vanished, with your suspicious looks. Your health, your appetite have done more than your pleasantries, and I saw you argue so well at the table against my fears that they were completely dissipated. To make it better, he is returning, and I am delighted in every respect. His return does not alarm me, it reassures me; and as soon as we shall see him, I shall no longer fear for your life or for my tranquillity. Cousin, be careful of my friend for me, and do not be uneasy about yours. I answer for her as long as she will have you. . . . But, good heavens, what then is the matter with me that still makes me uneasy and rends my heart without my knowing why? Ah, my child, must there be a day when one of us two will survive the other? Woe to her on whom so cruel a fate is to fall! She will remain behind, little suited for living or lifeless before her death.

Could you tell me for what reason I am exhausting myself in foolish lamentations? I don't care a fig for these terrors which are not in accord with common sense! Instead of speaking of death, let us speak of marriage; that will be more pleasant. A long time ago that idea came to your husband, and if he had never spoken to me of it, perhaps it would not have come to me at all. Since then, I have thought of it sometimes, and always with disdain. Fie! Marriage makes a young widow look old. If I had children from a second bed, I should think myself the grandmother of those from the first. [79]

That is my whole confession, cousin. I have made it to set you right, and not to contradict you. It remains for me to declare to you my resolution in this matter. At present, you know my heart as well as and perhaps better than I myself. My honor and my happiness are dear to you as much as to myself, and in the present tranquillity of your passions, reason will make you see better than I where I am to find both of them. Charge yourself, therefore, with my conduct; I submit its entire direction to you. Let us return to our natural state and exchange occupations; we will both be the better for it. You govern; I shall be docile. It is for you to decide what I am to do, for me to do what you will decide. Hold my heart secure in yours; what use have inseparables for two of them? [80]

❖ LETTER III ❖

From Lord Bomston to Monsieur de Wolmar

NO, DEAR WOLMAR, you are not at all mistaken; the young man is dependable, but I am hardly so, and I have well nigh paid dear for the experience which has convinced me of it. Without him, I would have myself succumbed to the test which I had destined for him. You know that, in order to satisfy his gratitude and divert his heart with new objects, I pretended to give this journey more importance than it really had. To gratify some former inclinations, to indulge in an old habit one more time—this, along with that which concerned Saint-Preux, was all that induced me to undertake it. To bid a final adieu to the attachments of my youth, to bring back a friend perfectly cured of his—that was all the fruit I hoped to gather from it.

I informed you that the dream at Villeneuve had left me uneasy. That dream made me suspicious of the transports of joy in which he indulged himself when I announced to him that he was to be tutor to your children and to spend his life with you. The better to observe the effusion of his heart, I had first removed the obstacles to it; by declaring to him that I would establish myself with you, I prevented any further objections for his friendship to make to me. But some new resolutions made me change my story.

He had not seen the Marquise three times before we were in agreement on that score. Unfortunately for her, she wanted to win him over and thus showed him only her artifices. Wretched woman! What great qualities, but without virtue! What love, but without honor! Her ardent and sincere love affected me, engaged me, nourished my own; but it became tinged with the blackness of her soul and ended by horrifying me. She was no longer a concern of mine.

When he had seen Laura, when he knew her heart, her beauty, her spirit and her unparalleled attachment, only too well suited to make me happy, I resolved to make use of her to acquire a perfect knowledge of Saint-Preux's state of mind.

"If I marry Laura," I said to him, "my plan is not to take her to London where someone could recognize her, but to a place where people are capable of honoring virtue in whomever it is found. You will fulfill your duty as tutor, and we will not cease living together. If I do not marry her, it is time for me to retire to a contemplative life. You know my house in Oxfordshire, and you will choose between educating the children of one of your friends or accompanying the other into his retirement."

He answered me as I could have expected, but I wished to observe him by his conduct. For, if in order to live at Clarens, he promoted a marriage which he ought to have opposed, or if in this delicate situation he preferred the honor of his friend to his own happiness —in either case the experiment was made and his heart was judged.

I first found him such as I desired him: firmly set against the
project I pretended to have and armed with all the arguments
which were to prevent me from marrying Laura. I was more
sensible of these arguments than he, but I was seeing her constantly, and I saw her afflicted and tender. My heart, completely
disengaged from the Marquise, settled upon Laura through these
regular visits. Laura's sentiments doubled the affection she had inspired in me. I was ashamed to sacrifice the esteem which I owed
her merit to the public opinion which I scorned. Did I have no obligations also to the hope I had given her, if not by my words at least
by my attentions? Though I had promised nothing, to do nothing
was to deceive her. This deceit was cruel. Finally, joining a kind of
duty to my inclination and thinking more of my happiness than my
reputation, I ended by reconciling my passion to my reason. I resolved to carry the pretended scheme as far as it could go, and
even to its very execution, if I could not otherwise extricate myself
from it without injustice.

However, I felt my uneasiness increasing on account of the young
man, seeing that he was not fulfilling with all his might the role
with which he had charged himself. He opposed my plans, he dis-
approved of the bond I wished to form, but he fought weakly
against my growing inclination and praised Laura so much to me
that, in appearing to turn me from marrying her, he was increasing
my penchant for her. This inconsistency alarmed me. I did not find
him so resolute as he should have been. He seemed not to dare oppose my sentiment directly; he gave way against my resistance, he
feared to make me angry, and, to my way of thinking, in doing his
duty he did not have the intrepidity which it inspires in those who
love it.

Other observations increased my distrust. I knew that he was seeing Laura secretly; I noticed signs of mutual understanding between
them. The hope of marrying the one whom she had loved so much
did not make her seem happy. I read the same tenderness in her
looks, indeed, but this tenderness was no longer mingled with joy
at my approach; sadness perpetually dominated it. Often in the
sweetest effusions of her heart, I saw her cast a side-glance at the
young man, and this glance was followed by a few tears which she
tried to hide from me. Finally, the mystery was carried to the point
that I was alarmed by it. Consider my surprise. What could I think?
Had I cherished but a serpent in my bosom? How far did I dare
carry my suspicions and return those he once unjustly entertained
of me? Frail and wretched creatures that we are, it is we who create

our own misfortunes! Why do we complain that the wicked torment us when even the good torment each other?

All this only ended by making me determined. Although I was ignorant of the basis of this intrigue, I saw that Laura's heart was ever the same, and this proof of her affection only endeared her more to me. I proposed to have an explanation from her before the conclusion of their intrigue, but I wanted to wait until the last moment in order to get all the light I possibly could beforehand. As for him, I was resolved to do justice to myself, to do justice to him—in short, to get to the truth of the matter before either saying anything or taking measures in regard to him, foreseeing an infallible rupture and being unwilling to place a good character and twenty years' honorable reputation into the balance with a few suspicions.

The Marquise was not ignorant of anything which took place between us. She had spies in Laura's convent and succeeded in finding out that it was a question of marriage. She needed nothing more to rekindle her rage; she wrote me menacing letters. She went further, but since it was not the first time and since we were on our guard, her attempts were vain. The only pleasure I had on this occasion was to see that Saint-Preux was capable of risking his life and did not hesitate to expose it in order to save that of a friend.

Overcome by her fits of rage, the Marquise fell ill and was soon past recovery. That was the end of her torments and of her crimes.* I could not learn of her condition without being afflicted by it. I sent Doctor Eswin to her; Saint-Preux was with her on my behalf. She wished to see neither of them; she did not even wish to hear about me and heaped horrible imprecations upon me each time she heard my name mentioned. I was grieved for her and felt my wounds ready to reopen; reason was again victorious, but I should have been the basest of men to think of marriage while a woman who was so dear to me was at her extremity. Saint-Preux, fearing that at last I might not be able to resist the desire to see her, proposed the journey to Naples, and I consented to it.

Two days after our arrival, I saw him enter my room with a resolute and serious countenance, holding a letter in his hand.

"The Marquise is dead!" I cried out.

"Would to God!" he replied coldly. "It were better to live no more than to exist only to do evil, but it is not of her that I have come to speak to you. Hear me."

* In a suppressed letter by his Lordship, one sees that he thought that the souls of the wicked were annihilated at their death. [*Rousseau*]

I waited in silence.

"My Lord," he said, "in giving me the sacred name of friend, you taught me how to bear it. I have acquitted myself of the charge with which you have entrusted me, and seeing you ready to forget yourself, I have had to make you remember who you are. You have been able to break one bond only by entering into another. Both were unworthy of you. If it had been a matter only of an unequal marriage, I should have said to you, 'Remember that you are an English Peer and either renounce all claims to public honors or respect opinion.' But a scandalous marriage! . . . You! . . . Choose your wife more carefully. It is not enough that she be virtuous; she must be without taint. . . . A wife for Edward Bomston is not easy to find. See what I have done."

Then he gave me the letter. It was from Laura. I did not open it without emotion.

"Love has been victorious," she wrote. "You have wished to marry me; I am content. Your friend has prescribed my duty to me; I am doing it without regret. In dishonoring you, I should have lived unhappily; in leaving you your reputation, it seems to me I am sharing it. The sacrifice of all my happiness to so cruel a duty makes me forget the shame of my youth. Adieu. From this instant I cease to be within your power, or within my own. Adieu forever. Oh Edward! Do not bring despair into my seclusion; hear my last wish. Do not give to any other the place that I have not been able to fill. There was one heart in the world for you, and it was that of

Laura."

Distress kept me from speaking. He profited from my silence to tell me that after my departure she had taken the veil in the convent where she was lodging; that the court of Rome, informed she was going to marry a Lutheran, had given orders to prevent me from seeing her again. And he confessed openly that he had taken all these measures with her consent.

"I did not oppose your plans," he continued, "as vigorously as I might have, fearing your return to the Marquise and wishing to distract that former passion with the one you entertained for Laura. Seeing you go further than necessary, I first appealed to reason; but having through my own faults acquired but too just cause to distrust it, I sounded Laura's heart, and, finding in it all the generosity that is inseparable from true love, I took advantage of it to bring her to the sacrifice which she has just made. The assurance of being no longer the object of your contempt restored her courage and made her more worthy of your esteem. She has done her duty; you must do yours."

Then approaching ecstatically, he said to me, clasping me against his breast, "My friend, I read in our common destiny sent us by Heaven those laws which are prescribed for us both. The reign of love is past; let that of friendship begin. My heart now hears only its sacred voice; it knows no other tie than that which binds me to you. Select the place you wish to live. Clarens, Oxford, London, Paris, or Rome—all suit me, provided that we live there together. Go where you will, seek seclusion wherever you may, I will follow you forever. I make a solemn vow before the living God: I will never leave you until death."

I was affected. The zeal and the emotion of this ardent young man shone in his eyes. I forgot the Marquise and Laura. What in the world can one regret when he has preserved such a friend? I saw also, by the resolution he unhesitatingly took in this case, that he was truly cured of his former passion and that you have not wasted the pains you took with him. At last I dare believe, by the vow that he made with such good heart to remain attached to me, that he was controlled more by virtue than by his former inclinations. I can send him back to you, then, in full confidence. Yes, my dear Wolmar, he is worthy of educating youth, and what is more, of living in your house.

A few days after, I learned of the death of the Marquise. She had been dead for me for a long time; this loss no longer affected me. Up to this point, I had considered marriage as a debt that everyone contracts at his birth with his race and with his country, and I had resolved to marry, less through inclination than through duty. I changed my mind. The obligation to marry is not universal; for each man it depends upon the rank into which fate has placed him. For the common people, for the artisans, for villagers, for really useful men, celibacy is wrong; for the classes which govern the others, to which everyone ceaselessly aspires and which are always only too full, celibacy is permissible and even proper. Otherwise, the State may only depopulate itself by the increase of subjects which are its dead weight. Men shall always have enough masters, and England will lack laborers sooner than peers.

I believe myself free, therefore, and master of myself in the rank in which Heaven caused me to be born. At my age, I can no longer repair the losses my heart has sustained. I shall devote it to cultivating that which I have left and cannot put it back together better than at Clarens. I accept all your offers, therefore, under the conditions that my fortune must add to yours, so that it may not be useless to me. After the vow that Saint-Preux has made, I no longer have any other means of keeping him with you than by dwelling there myself, and if ever he is troublesome, that will be sufficient reason for me to leave. The only problem left for me concerns my journeys to England, for although I no longer have any interest in Parliament, while I am a member that is enough for me to do my duty until the last. But I have a faithful colleague and friend, whom I can empower to answer for me in current affairs. On the occasions when I shall think it my duty to be there myself, our pupil will be able to accompany me, even with his own pupils when they are a little bigger and you wish to confide them to us. These journeys could only be useful to them and will not be long enough to afflict their mother a great deal.

I have not shown this letter to Saint-Preux. Do not show all of it to your ladies. It is fitting that the purpose of this experiment be ever known only by you and me. However, hide from them nothing of that which does honor to my worthy friend, even at my expense. Adieu, my dear Wolmar. I am sending you the designs for my pavilion. Amend them, change them as you please, but have the work begun now if possible. I wanted to remove the music room, for all my enjoyments are lost and I no longer care about anything. But I am leaving it in at the request of Saint-Preux, who proposed to exercise your children in that room. You will also receive a few books for the enlargement of your library. But what will you find that is new in the books? Oh Wolmar, you need only to learn to read the book of nature in order to be the wisest of mortals.

❖ LETTER IV ❖

Response

I HAVE BEEN WAITING, my dear Bomston, for the denouement of your lengthy adventures. It would indeed have seemed strange if, having resisted your inclinations so long, you had waited to give way to them only until a friend had come to sustain you; although, to tell the truth, one may often be more weak while leaning on another than when he relies only upon himself. Yet, I confess that I was alarmed by your last letter in which you announced your marriage to Laura as absolutely determined. I doubted the event despite your assurance, and if my expectation had been deceived, I should never have seen Saint-Preux again. You have both done what I had hoped from each of you, and you have only too well justified the opinion I had entertained of you, so that I shall be delighted to see you settle here, according to our first arrangements. Come, uncommon men, increase and share the happiness of this house. Whatever may be the hopes of those who believe in a future life, I like to spend this one in their company, and I feel that you all are more agreeable to me such as you are than if you had the misfortune to think as I do.

Besides, you know what I said to you on Saint-Preux's account at your departure. I had no need to pass judgment upon him after your experiment, for my own was completed, and I believe I know him as much as one man can know another. I have, moreover, more than one reason to rely upon his heart and am much more sure of him than he is himself. Although he may seem to wish to imitate you in renouncing marriage, perhaps you will find cause here to persuade him to change his mind. I shall explain further after your return. [81]

Our little cousin has been in Geneva for eight or ten days with her family, to shop and for other business. We expect her return daily. I have told my wife all that she ought to know of your letter. We had learned through Monsieur Miol that the marriage was broken off, but she was ignorant of the part that Saint-Preux had in that affair. Be sure that she learns only with the greatest pleasure all that he has done to merit your generosity and justify your esteem. I have shown her the designs for your pavilion. She finds them in very good taste; nevertheless we shall make some changes in them that the location necessitates which will make your lodging more comfortable. You will surely approve of them. We are waiting for Claire's opinion before touching them, for you know that we can do nothing without her. Meanwhile, I have already put everyone to work, and I hope that before winter the masonry will be well along.

Thank you for your books, but I no longer read those which I understand, and it is too late to learn to read those I do not understand. Yet I am less ignorant than you accuse me of being. The true book of nature is for me the heart of man, and the proof that I know how to read it is in my friendship for you. [82]

[handwritten margin note: letter from Claire on Genevans]

✤ LETTER VI ✤

From Madame de Wolmar

WHAT A DELIGHTFUL SENTIMENT I am experiencing as I begin this letter! This is the first time in my life that I have been able to write you without fear and without shame. I pride myself in the friendship which unites us, for it is the result of an unparalleled victory. People stifle great passions; rarely do they purify them. To forget a dear one when honor requires it is the effort of an honorable and ordinary soul; but after having been what we were, to be what we are today—that is a real triumph of virtue. The reason for ceasing to love can be a vicious one; that which changes a tender love into a friendship no less vigorous could not be equivocal.

Should we ever have made this progress by our own strength alone? Never, never my good friend. To attempt it even would have been rash. To avoid each other was for us the first article of our duty that nothing should have permitted us to violate. We might always have esteemed each other, no doubt, but we would have ceased to see each other, to write each other. We would have striven to think no longer of each other, and the greatest honor we could have reciprocally shown each other would have been to break off all communication between us.

See, instead of that, what is our present situation. Is there in the world one more pleasant, and do we not enjoy a thousand times a day the reward of the struggles it cost us? To see each other, to love each other, to be sensible of our love, to be satisfied with it, to spend our life together in fraternal familiarity and peaceful innocence, to attend to each other, to think of each other without remorse, to speak of each other without shame, and to acquire honor in our own eyes from the very attachment with which we reproached ourselves for so long—that is the point we have reached. Oh my friend! What a career of honor we have already traversed! Let us presume to boast of it in order to keep ourselves in it and finish it as we have begun it.

To whom do we owe such extraordinary good fortune? You know. I have seen your sensitive heart overflowing at the generosity of the best of men, pleased and impressed by it. And how could his goodness be a burden to us, to you and to me? It does not impose new obligations upon us; it only makes those more dear to us which already were so sacred. The only way of showing gratitude for his good deeds is to be worthy of them, for all their value for him is in their success. Therefore, let us consider that in the effusion of our zeal. With our virtues, let us recompense those of our benefactor—that is all that we owe him. He has done enough for us and for himself if he has restored us to ourselves. Apart or together, living or dead, we shall everywhere make manifest the proof of our love which will never be a dishonor for any of the three. [83]

According to what Lord Bomston informs us, I am expecting you both toward the end of next month. You will not recognize your rooms, but in the changes that have been made, you will recognize the attentions and the love of a good friend who has taken pleasure in decorating it. You will also find in it a small assortment of books which she has chosen for you in Geneva, better and in better taste than *L'Adone,** although that one may also be there as a joke. Yet, be discreet, for as she does not wish you to know that all this is her doing, I hasten to tell you before she forbids me to speak of it to you.

Adieu, my friend. Our excursion to the castle of Chillon, which we used to make all together, will take place tomorrow without you. Although it may be made with pleasure, it will not be the better for that. The bailiff has invited us with our children, which has left me no excuse, but I know not why I wish we had already returned.†

---

* By Marino. In a deleted portion, Saint-Preux has scoffed at this work. [*Translator's note*]

† The castle of Chillon, former seat of the bailiffs of Vevey, is situated on the lake upon a rock cliff which forms a peninsula, around which I have seen people sound the lake at more than 150 fathoms, which is almost 800 feet, without finding bottom. In this rock cliff, caves and cellars have been scooped beneath the level of the water, which is let in when desired through watercocks. It was there that for six years François Bonnivard, Prior of Saint Victor, was held prisoner, a man of unusual merit, with integrity and courage proof against everything, a friend of liberty although a Savoyard and tolerant although a priest. However, in the year when these last letters seem to have been written, it had been a long time since the bailiffs of Vevey had dwelled in the castle of Chillon. One may suppose, if he wishes, that the one there at that time had gone there to spend a few days. [*Rousseau*]

✤ LETTER IX ✤

From Fanchon Anet

OH MONSIEUR! Oh my benefactor! What am I ordered to inform you?
. . . Madame! . . . my poor mistress . . . oh God! I can see
your fright already . . . but you cannot see our desolation. . . . I
have not a moment to lose; I must tell you . . . I must hurry . . .
I wish I had already told you all. . . . Ah, what will become of you
when you know of our misfortune?

The whole family went yesterday to dine at Chillon. The Baron,
who was going to Savoy to spend a few days at the castle of Blonay,
left after dinner. The company went with him for a little way;
then they took a walk along the embankment. Madame d'Orbe
and the bailiff's wife walked ahead with Monsieur. Madame was
following, holding Henriette with one hand and Marcellin with
the other. I was behind with the elder boy. The bailiff, who had
stopped to speak to someone, came to rejoin the group and offered
his arm to Madame. To take it, she sent Marcellin back to me. He
ran to me; I hurried to him. Running, the child tripped, his foot
slipped, and he fell into the water. I uttered a piercing cry; Madame
turned round, saw her son fall, flew back like an arrow, and
threw herself in after him. . . .

Ah! Wretch, that I did not do as much! Would that I had not
stood there! . . . Alas! I held back the elder son who wanted to
jump after his mother . . . she was struggling, clasping the other
in her arms . . . we had neither servants nor a boat there; it took
time to get them out . . . the child is recovered, but the mother
. . . the shock, the fall, the condition she was in . . . who knows
better than I the dangers of such a fall! . . . She remained unconscious for a very long time. Hardly had she revived when she
asked for her son . . . with what transports of joy she embraced
him! I thought she was saved, but her spirits lasted only a moment.
She wished to be brought back here; on the way she fainted several
times. From some orders she has given me, I see that she does not
believe she will recover. I am too unhappy; she will not recover.
Madame d'Orbe is more altered than she. Everyone is in distress

. . . I am the calmest of all the household . . . why should I be uneasy? . . . My good mistress! Ah, if I lose you, I shall have no need for anyone. . . . Oh my dear Monsieur, may the good Lord sustain you in this ordeal . . . Adieu . . . the doctor is leaving her room. I shall hurry to meet him . . . if he gives us some hope, I shall inform you. If I say nothing . . .

✤ LETTER X ✤

Begun by Madame d'Orbe and Finished by Monsieur de Wolmar

IT IS OVER. Imprudent, unfortunate man, unhappy dreamer! You shall never see her again . . . the veil . . . Julie is no more . . .

She has written to you. Wait for her letter. Respect her last wishes. There are great obligations left for you to fulfill on this earth.

✤ LETTER XI ✤

From Monsieur de Wolmar

I HAVE ALLOWED your first grief to pass in silence; my letter might only have aggravated it. You were no more in a condition to bear these details than I was to write of them. Now perhaps they will be agreeable to both of us. I have only memories left of her; my heart takes pleasure in recalling them! You now have only tears to show to my heart; you shall have the consolation of shedding them into it for her. This pleasure of unfortunates is refused me in my misery; I am more unhappy than you.

It is not of her illness, it is of her that I wish to speak. Other mothers could throw themselves into the water after their children.

Accidents, fever, death are natural; it is the ordinary lot of mortals. But the employment of her last moments, her conversation, her sentiments, her spirit—all that belongs only to Julie. She did not live like any other; no one, to my knowledge, died like her. That is what I alone was witness to and what you will learn only from me.

You know that the fright, the distress, the fall, and the extraction from the water left her in a lengthy faint from which she recovered completely only at home. Upon arriving, she asked again for her son. He came, and no sooner did she see him walk in and respond to her caresses than she became completely tranquil and consented to take a little rest. Her sleep was brief, and since the doctor had not yet arrived, while waiting for him she had us sit around her bed—Fanchon, her cousin, and me. She spoke to us of her children, of the diligent care in regard to them that the plan of education she had undertaken required, and of the danger of neglecting them for a moment. Without giving great importance to her illness, she predicted that it would keep her for some time from discharging her part of those very duties and exhorted us all to divide that part among us.

She dwelled upon all her projects, on yours, on the means most apt to make them succeed, on the observations she had made as to what could promote or injure them—in short, upon all which might enable us to take her place as mother as long as she would be forced to suspend her duties. These were, I thought, a great many precautions for someone who thought herself prevented for only a few days from so dear an occupation, but what completely frightened me was to see that in regard to Henriette she entered into even greater detail. As to her sons, she had limited herself to that which concerned their early childhood, as if she was shifting the responsibility of their youth to someone else; for the daughter she extended her remarks to her coming of age, and sensible that on this point nothing could take the place of the reflections that her own experience had caused her to make, she exposed to us briefly but with force and clarity the plan of education which she had formulated for her, setting out for her mother the most lively reasons and the most affecting exhortations to engage her to follow it.

All these ideas on the education of young people and on the duties of mothers, mixed with frequent reflections upon her own life, could not fail to inject some warmth into the conversation. I saw that it was becoming too animated. Claire held one of her cousin's hands and pressed it every moment to her lips, sobbing at every reply. Fanchon was no calmer, and as for Julie, I observed that tears were also swelling in her eyes but that she did not dare weep, for fear of alarming us all the more. Forthwith I said to myself: she sees herself dead. The only hope left for me was that her fears might be deceiving her about her condition and representing the danger greater than it perhaps was. Unhappily I knew her too well to rely a great deal on this deception. Several times I tried to calm her; I begged her again not to disturb herself to no purpose by conversations which we could resume at our leisure.

"Ah," she said, "nothing disturbs women so much as silence! And since I feel a little feverish, it is so much the better to employ the chattering that it causes for useful matters than to talk unreasonable nonsense."

The doctor's arrival caused a confusion in the house impossible to describe. All the servants, one after the other with anxious looks and folded arms, were waiting at the door of the room for his pronouncement on the condition of their mistress, as if their own destiny were depending on it. This sight threw poor Claire into a distraction which made me fear for her reason. It was necessary to send them away under different pretexts to take from her sight that cause for alarm. The doctor vaguely gave a little hope but in a tone suited to take it from me. Nor did Julie say what she was thinking; the presence of her cousin restrained her. When the doctor left, I followed him; Claire wanted to follow too, but Julie held her back and gave me a sign with her eyes that I understood. I hastened to warn the doctor that if there were any danger, it was necessary to conceal it from Madame d'Orbe as carefully as and even more carefully than from the sick woman, lest despair might finally discompose her and make her unable to attend to her friend. He declared that there was indeed some danger, but that, twenty-four hours being hardly elapsed since the accident, he needed more time to form a certain opinion; that the next night would determine the course of the illness; and that he could not make a pronouncement until the third day. Fanchon alone was a witness to these words, and after having prevailed upon her, not without difficulty, to control herself, we agreed upon what would be told Madame d'Orbe and the rest of the household.

Toward the evening Julie compelled her cousin, who had spent the preceding night with her and who wanted to spend the next one there too, to go get a few hours rest. During this time, the sick woman, knowing that she was to be bled in the foot and that the doctor was making the arrangements, sent for him and spoke these words:

"Monsieur du Bosson, when you think you must deceive a timid patient about his case, this is a humanitarian precaution of which I approve. But it is cruel to lavish on all alike these superfluous and disagreeable treatments of which many have no need. Prescribe for me all that you consider truly useful to me, and I will obey promptly. As for treatments which are only for the imagination, spare me those. It is my body and not my mind which is suffering, and I have no fear of ending my life but of spending the remainder of it poorly. The last moments of life are too precious for it to be permissible to make ill use of them. If you cannot prolong mine, at least do not cut it short by taking from me the use of the few moments which nature has left me. The fewer I have, the more you must respect them. Make me recover, or leave me; I shall surely be able to die alone."

That is how that woman, so timid and so gentle in ordinary matters, could assume a resolute and serious tone upon important occasions.

The night was cruel and decisive. Suffocation, oppression, fainting fits, her skin dry and burning. A high fever, during which we frequently heard her call aloud for Marcellin, as if to get hold of him again, and sometimes pronounce another name as well, formerly much repeated on a similar occasion. The next day the doctor declared to me straightforwardly that he did not think she had three days to live.[84] I hurriedly ran to Julie's bed. I dismissed everyone, and I sat down, you can guess with what a countenance! With her I did not take precautions necessary for frail spirits. I said nothing, but she looked at me and understood me immediately.

"Do you think you bring me news?" she said, holding out her hand to me. "No, my friend, I am well aware of it. Death presses upon me. We must take leave of each other."

Then she held a long conversation with me of which some day I shall have to give you an account and during which she wrote her testament into my heart. If I had known hers any less, her last will would have sufficed to acquaint me with it. She asked me if her condition was known in the household. I told her that apprehension reigned in it, but that they knew nothing positive and that du Bosson had confided in me alone. She implored me to keep the secret carefully for the rest of the day.

"Claire," she added, "will never bear this blow except from my hand. She will die of it if it comes to her from another. I shall destine tonight to this sad task. It is for that reason above all that I wished to have the doctor's opinion, in order not to subject that unhappy woman unnecessarily, on the basis of my feeling alone, to so cruel a blow. Make sure that she may not suspect anything beforehand, or you run the risk of remaining without a friend and of leaving your children without a mother."

She spoke to me of her father. I confessed to have sent him an express letter, but I kept myself from adding that the messenger, instead of contenting himself with simply delivering my letter as I had ordered him, hastened to speak so loudly that my old friend, believing his daughter drowned, fell with fright upon the staircase and did himself an injury which kept him at Blonay in his bed. The hope of seeing her father again affected her sensibly, and the certainty that this hope was vain was not the least of the anguish which I had to stifle.

The fever of the preceding night had made her extremely weak. This long conversation had not helped to strengthen her; in her prostrate state, she tried to get a little rest during the day. I learned only two days later that she had not spent it entirely in sleeping.[85]

Madame d'Orbe had sat up the two preceding nights; she had not removed her clothing for three days. Julie proposed that she go to bed; she wished to do nothing of the kind.

"Well, then," said Julie, "let a little bed be made for her in my room, unless," she added reflectively, "she wishes to share mine. What say you, cousin? My sickness is not contagious; you have no objection to me. Sleep in my bed."

The proposal was accepted. As for me, I was sent away, and truly I had need of rest.

I rose early. Uneasy about what had taken place during the night, at the first sound I heard I entered the room. On the basis of the state Madame d'Orbe was in the night before, I expected I would find her in despair and witness her furors. Upon entering, I saw her seated in an armchair, wan and pale, ghastly rather, her eyes glazed and almost dead, but gentle, calm, speaking little and doing all that was told her without responding. As for Julie, she seemed less weak than the night before. Her voice was more steady, her gestures more animated. She seemed to have assumed her cousin's vivacity. I knew readily by her color that this visible improvement was the effect of the fever, but I also saw shining in her eyes an indescribable secret joy which contributed to it, the cause of which I did not discern. The doctor nonetheless confirmed his opinion of the night before; the sick woman nonetheless continued to think the same as he, and there remained no more hope for me.

Having been obliged to leave her for a little while, I noticed upon returning that her rooms had been carefully ordered. Neatness and elegance reigned there. She had had bowls of flowers put on her mantel; her curtains were half-opened and fastened back. The bedroom had been aired, and a pleasant scent was apparent. No one might have ever believed himself in a sick room. She had dressed with the same care. Grace and taste showed themselves even in her dishabille. All this gave her the air of a society woman who is expecting company rather than that of a country woman who is awaiting her last hour. She saw my surprise, she smiled at it, and reading my thoughts she was about to answer me when the children were brought in. Then they alone were her concern, and you may judge whether, sensing herself ready to part from them, her caresses were cool and moderate! I even observed that she turned more often and with embraces even more ardent to the one who had cost her her life, as if he had become more dear to her at that price.

All these embraces, these sighs, these raptures were mysteries for those poor children. They loved her tenderly, but it was with the tenderness of their age. They understood nothing of her condition, of the repetition of her caresses, of her regrets over seeing them no more. They saw us sorrowful, and they wept. They knew nothing more. Although we teach children the word death, they have no idea of it; they fear it neither for themselves nor for others. They fear suffering but not dying. When grief tore some lament from their mother, they pierced the air with their cries; when we spoke to them of losing her, one would have thought them stupid. Only Henriette, a little older and of a sex in which sentiment and understanding develop earlier, seemed disturbed and alarmed to see her little mama in bed, she who was always seen stirring about before her children were up.[86]

After having opened her heart with her children, after having taken each of them aside, especially Henriette, whom she kept apart very long and whom we heard lamenting and sobbing as she received her kisses, she called them all three, gave them her blessing, and said to them, pointing to Madame d'Orbe, "Go my children, go kneel at the feet of your mother. That is the one God gives you. He has deprived you of nothing."

At once they ran to her, threw themselves at her knees, took her hands, and called her their good mama, their second mother. Claire bent over them, but, clasping them in her arms, she tried in vain to speak; she could only sob, she could not utter a single word, she was choked up. Judge whether Julie was moved! This scene was beginning to become too animated; I stopped it.[87]

Then, sitting beside her and looking at her attentively, I said to her, "Julie, my dear Julie, you have broken my heart. Alas, you have waited quite late to do so!

"Yes," I continued, seeing that she was looking at me with surprise, "I have seen through you. You are rejoicing in death. You are glad to leave me. Remember your husband's conduct since we have lived together. Have I deserved so cruel a sentiment from you?"

Immediately she took my hands, and in that tone which was capable of piercing my soul, she said, "Who, I? I wish to leave you? Is it thus that you read my heart? Have you so soon forgotten our conversation of yesterday?"

"Yet," I replied, "you are dying content . . . I have seen it . . . I see it. . . ."

"Stop," she said. "It is true, I am dying content, but I am content to die as I have lived, worthy of being your wife. Do not ask me more. I shall tell you nothing more. But here," she continued, drawing a paper from under her pillow, "here is what will finally clarify this mystery for you."

This paper was a letter, and I saw that it was addressed to you.

"I am giving it to you open," she added, handing it to me, "so that after having read it you may decide to send it or suppress it, according as you find it most befitting your wisdom and my honor. I beg you to read it only when I am dead, and I am so sure of what you will do at my request that I do not even want you to promise me."

This letter, my dear Saint-Preux, is the one you will find enclosed. I can hardly realize that she who wrote it is dead; I can scarcely believe that she exists no more.[88]

"I feel weak," she said. "I foresee that this conversation could be the last we shall have together. In the name of our union, in the name of our dear children who are the pledge of it, be unjust toward your wife no more. I, to rejoice in leaving you! You who have lived only to make me happy and virtuous. You, of all men the one who was best for me, the only, perhaps, with whom I could establish a good household and become a deserving woman! Ah, believe me, if I set a value on life, it would be so that I might spend it with you!"

These words, pronounced with tenderness, affected me to the point where, frequently carrying to my lips her hands which I was holding in mine, I felt them moistened by my tears. I did not believe my eyes capable of shedding any. Those were the first since my birth; those will be the last until my death. After having wept for Julie, I can no longer weep for anything.

This day was fatiguing for her.[89] During the night I heard some movements which did not alarm me, but toward morning when all was calm, a muffled sound struck my ear. I listened; I thought I distinguished some moans. I hurried, I entered the room, I opened the curtain . . . Saint-Preux! . . . my dear Saint-Preux! . . . I saw the two friends motionless, locked in each other's arms, the one in a faint and the other expiring. I cried out, I wanted to hold back or to receive her last breath, and I rushed forward. She was no more.

Worshipper of God, Julie was no more. . . . I cannot tell you what took place for a few hours. I am unaware of what happened to myself. Recovered from my first shock, I asked after Madame d'Orbe. I learned that it had been necessary to carry her into her room, and even to confine her in it, for she would return each moment to Julie's, throw herself upon the body, warm it with her own, strive to revive it, importune it, press herself against it in a kind of frenzy, call it aloud a thousand passionate names, and feed her despair with all these useless efforts.

Upon entering, I found her completely out of her mind, seeing nothing, hearing nothing, knowing no one, rolling about the room wringing her hands and gnawing upon the legs of chairs, mumbling some wild words in a hollow voice, then at intervals uttering some sharp cries which made one shudder. At the foot of her bed, her chambermaid, dismayed, terrified, motionless, not daring to breathe, was trying to hide from her and trembling in every limb. Indeed, the convulsions with which Claire was seized were somewhat frightening. I made a sign to the chambermaid to withdraw, for I feared that a single ill-timed word of consolation might throw her into a furor.

I did not try to speak to her; she would not have listened to me nor even heard. But after a little while, seeing her spent with fatigue, I picked her up and carried her to a chair. I sat near her, holding her hands; I ordered that the children be brought and had them come stand around her. Unfortunately, the first one she perceived was precisely the innocent cause of her friend's death. The sight of him made her shudder. I saw her countenance change, her eyes turn aside with a kind of horror, and her bent arms stiffen in order to push him away. I drew the child to me.

"Unlucky boy!" I said to him. "For having been too precious to the one, you have become hateful to the other. Their hearts were not the same in everything."

These words irritated her violently and brought forth some very cutting ones for me. Nevertheless, they made an impression. She took the child in her arms and forced herself to caress him. It was in vain; she set him down almost immediately. She even continues to look upon him with less pleasure than upon the other, and I am very glad that it was not that one for whom her daughter was intended.[90]

The most pitiable task is to have still to console the others. That is what remains for me to do with respect to my father-in-law, Madame d'Orbe, friends, relatives, neighbors, and my own servants. The others are nothing, but my old friend, and Madame d'Orbe! You must see the affliction of the latter in order to judge what she adds to my own. Far from being grateful to me for my solicitude, she reproaches me for it. My attentions irritate her; the coldness of my sorrow aggravates her. She needs bitter grief similar to her own, and in her cruel sorrow she would like to see everyone in despair. What is most desolating is that we can depend upon nothing with her, for what comforts her one moment vexes her a moment later. All that she does, all that she says approaches madness and would be ridiculous to cold, unfeeling people. I have a great deal to put up with, but I shall never become discouraged. By serving her whom Julie loved, I believe I am honoring her memory better than with tears.[91]

This, my dear Saint-Preux, is about our present situation. Since the Baron's return, Claire goes up to him every morning, either while I am there or when I leave. They spend an hour or two together, and the care she takes of him somewhat facilitates that which we take of her. Moreover, she is beginning to become more diligent in regard to the children. One of the three has been ill, precisely the one whom she loves least. This incident has made her realize that she still has something to lose and has restored her zeal in her duties. With all that, she is not yet at the point of mere sorrow. Her tears do not yet flow. She waits for you in order to shed them. It is for you to dry them. You must understand me. Think of Julie's last counsel; it was first suggested by me, and I think it more useful and prudent than ever. Come rejoin all which remains of her. Her father, her friend, her husband, her children—everyone waits for you, everyone wants you back. You are needed by everyone. In short, without further explanation, come to share and cure my sorrows; I shall perhaps be more obligated to you than to anyone else.

❧ LETTER XII ❧

From Julie

(This letter was enclosed in the preceding.)

WE MUST give up our projects. All is changed, my good friend. Let us bear this change without a murmur; it comes from a Being more wise than we. We dreamed of rejoining each other. That reunion was not good. It is Heaven's blessing to have prevented it, thereby, without a doubt, preventing misfortune.

I have for a long time deluded myself. This delusion was advantageous to me; it vanishes the moment I no longer need it. You had thought me cured of my love for you, and I thought I was too. Let us give thanks to the One who made that delusion last as long as it was useful. Who knows whether, seeing that I was so close to the abyss, I might not have lost my head? Yes, I tried in vain to stifle the first sentiment which inspired me; it is concentrated in my heart. It reawakens at the moment when it is no longer to be feared; it sustains me while my strength is leaving me; it revives me while I am dying. My friend, I am making this confession without shame. This sentiment, nourished despite myself, was involuntary; it has cost my innocence nothing. Everything which was dependent upon my will was devoted to my duty. If my heart, which was not dependent upon it, was devoted to you, that was my torment and not my crime. I have done what I ought to have done; my virtue remains unblemished, and my love has remained without remorse.

I dare pride myself in the past, but who might have been able to answer for my future? One day more, perhaps, and I might be guilty! What danger might there be in a whole life spent with you? What risks I have run unknowingly! To what greater risks I was going to be exposed! Without a doubt, I felt for myself the fears that I thought I was feeling for you. Every trial has been made, but trials could be too often repeated. Have I not lived long enough for happiness and for virtue? What advantage was left for me to derive from life? By depriving me of it, Heaven no longer deprives me of anything regrettable and instead protects my honor. My friend, I am leaving at a favorable moment. Satisfied with you and with myself, I am leaving joyfully, and this departure is in no way cruel. After so many sacrifices, I consider as little the one left for me to make. It is only to die once more.

I foresee your grief; I feel it. You remain behind, to be pitied, I know it well. And the awareness of your sorrow is the greatest affliction I carry off with me. But see also what consolations I am leaving you! See how the duties you are to discharge for her who was dear to you put you under an obligation to preserve yourself for her! It remains for you to serve her in the better part of herself. You are losing of Julie only that which you have for a long time lost. The best of her remains for you. Come, rejoin her family. Let her heart dwell among you. Let all those she loved gather together to give her a new existence. Your duties, your pleasures, your friendship—all will be her work. The bond of your union formed by her will give her new life; she will expire only when the last one of all is dead.

Remember that you have left another Julie, and do not forget what you owe to her. Each of you is going to lose half of his life; join together in order to preserve each other. The only way left for you both to survive me is by serving my family and my children. Would that I could invent still stronger bonds in order to unite all who are dear to me! How dear you ought to be to each other! How this thought must strengthen your mutual attachment! Your former objections against this engagement are going to be new reasons for entering into it. How will you ever be able to speak of me without melting into tenderness together? No, Claire and Julie will be so united in your thoughts that it will no longer be possible for your heart to separate them. Hers will give you back all that yours has felt for her friend; she will be its confidante and its object. You will be happy with the one who is left for you, without ceasing to be faithful to the one whom you have lost; and after so many disappointments and misfortunes, before the age of living and loving is past, you will have burned with a legitimate passion and enjoyed an innocent happiness.

It is in this chaste union that without distraction and without fear you will be able to busy yourselves with the duties I am leaving you, after which you will no longer be at a loss to account for the good you have done on this earth. You know that there exists a man worthy of the happiness to which he is incapable of aspiring. This man is your liberator, the husband of the friend he restored to you. Alone, without interest in life, without expectation of the one which follows it, without pleasure, without consolation, without hope, he will soon be the most unfortunate of mortals. You owe him the same pains he has taken with you, and you know the way to make them beneficial. Remember my preceding letter. Spend your days with him. May none of those who loved me forsake him. He has restored your taste for virtue; show him the purpose and the value of it. Be a Christian in order to induce him to be one too. Success is closer than you think. He has done his duty; I shall do mine; do yours. God is just; my confidence will not deceive me.

I have but a word to say to you about my children. I know what trouble their education is going to be for you, but I also am convinced that these troubles will not be painful for you. In the fatiguing moments inseparable from this employment, say to yourself that they are Julie's children, and the moments will no longer be tiresome for you. Monsieur de Wolmar will deliver to you the observations I have made about your essay on education and on the character of my two sons. These observations are only begun. I do not give them to you as a rule; I submit them to your insight. Do not make scholars of them; make benevolent and just men of them. Speak to them sometimes of their mother . . . you know how dear they were to her . . . tell Marcellin that it has not pained me to die for him. Tell his brother that it was for him that I wished to live. Tell their . . . I feel tired. I must finish this letter. In leaving my children to you, I part from them with less pain. I think I thus am staying with them.

Adieu, adieu, my sweet friend. . . . Alas! I am ending my life as I began it. I have said too much, perhaps, in this moment when the heart no longer hides anything. . . . Ah, why should I be afraid of expressing all that I feel? It is no longer I who speak to you; I am already in the arms of death. When you see this letter, the worms will be preying upon your lover's features and upon her heart, where your image will exist no more. But could my soul exist without you? Without you, what happiness could I enjoy? No, I do not leave you; I go to wait for you. The virtue which separated us on earth will unite us in the eternal dwelling. I am dying in this sweet hope, only too happy to purchase at the price of my life the right of loving you forever without crime and of telling you so one more time.

❦ LETTER XIII ❦

From Madame d'Orbe

I LEARN that you are beginning to recover sufficiently so that we may hope to see you here soon. You must strive, my friend, to overcome your weakness; you must try to come over the mountains before winter finally closes them to you. You will find in this country the air which agrees with you; you will see here only grief and sorrow, and perhaps our common affliction will be a solace for your own. In order to be given vent, mine needs you. I alone can neither weep, nor cry out, nor make myself understood. Wolmar understands me but does not respond to me. The sorrow of the unhappy father is buried within himself. He does not imagine one more cruel; he causes it neither to be seen nor felt. Aged men no longer give vent to their griefs. My children affect me but are incapable of pitying me. I am alone amid everyone. In my stunned dejection, I have no further communication with anyone. I have only enough strength and life to feel the horrors of death. Oh come, you who share my loss! Come share my griefs. Come feed my heart with your sorrow. Come fill it with your tears. That is the only consolation which I may hope for; that is the only pleasure left for me to enjoy.

But before you arrive and I learn your opinion concerning a project which I know has been mentioned to you, it is well that you know mine first. I am ingenuous and frank; I will conceal nothing from you. I have loved you, I confess. Perhaps I do yet; perhaps I always shall. I do not know nor wish to know. It is suspected, I am aware; I neither am angry nor care. But here is what I have to tell you and what you must observe well. It is that a man who was loved by Julie d'Étange and who could resolve to marry another woman is in my eyes a merely unworthy and base creature whom I should consider a disgrace to have as a friend; and as for me, I protest to you that any man, whoever he may be, who will henceforward dare speak to me of love will never speak again to me in his life.

Think of the duties which are awaiting you, of the obligations which are imposed upon you, of her to whom you have promised them. Her children are in their formative years and are growing; her father is wasting insensibly. Her husband is uneasy and disturbed. In vain he strives, but he cannot believe her annihilated. His heart, in spite of himself, rebels against his empty reason. He speaks of her, he speaks of it, and he sighs. I believe I can already see the vows fulfilled that she has repeatedly made, and it is for you to finish this great work. What motives to draw you both here! It is indeed worthy of the generous Edward that our misfortunes have not made him change his decision.

Come, then, dear and respectable friends. Come rejoin all which remains of her. Let us gather together all who were dear to her. Let her spirit inspire us. Let her heart unite all of ours. Let us live always under her regard. I like to believe that from the place where she is dwelling, from the place of eternal peace, her soul, still loving and sensitive, takes pleasure in returning among us, in finding her friends again full of memories of her, in seeing them imitate her virtues, in hearing herself honored by them, in seeing them kiss her tomb and sigh while pronouncing her name. No, she has not forsaken this place, which she made so delightful for us. It is still full of her. I see her in every object; I perceive her at every step. At every instant of the day I hear the accents of her voice. It is here that she lived; it is here that her ashes repose . . . half her ashes. Twice a week, as I go to the church . . . I look at . . . I look at the sad and revered spot. . . . Beauty, there, then, is your last refuge! . . . Confidence, friendship, virtues, pleasures, cheerful joys—the earth has swallowed all. . . . I feel myself drawn along . . . I approach trembling . . . I am afraid to tread on this sacred ground . . . I think I feel it shake and tremble under my feet . . . I hear a plaintive voice murmuring! . . . Claire, oh my Claire, where are you? What are you doing far from your friend? . . . Her tomb does not contain her wholly . . . it awaits the remainder of its prey . . . it will not wait for long.*

* After having reread this collection of letters, I believe I see why the story, as weak as it is, is so agreeable to me and will be so, I think, to every well-disposed reader. It is that at least this weak story is pure and not mixed with unpleasantness; that it is not excited by baseness or by crimes, nor mixed with the disagreeable sensations of hatred. I cannot conceive what pleasure one can take in imagining and describing the character of a scoundrel, in putting oneself in his place while representing him, in lending him the most imposing brilliance. I greatly pity the authors of so many tragedies full of horrors, who spend their lives in making people act and speak whom one cannot hear nor see without suffering. It seems to me that one ought to sigh to be condemned to such cruel work; those who make an amusement of it must be indeed devoured by zeal for public usefulness. As for me, I sincerely admire their talent and their fine wit, but I thank God for not having given them to me. [*Rousseau*]

END OF *LA NOUVELLE HÉLOÏSE*

❦ APPENDIX ❦

Subjects of deleted portions, marked in the text by [1], [2], . . . *etc.*

[1] A method of study for Julie (five pages). Saint-Preux, dismissing all ostentatious displays of erudition as artificial, recommends that a genuine student of knowledge read very little but reflect a great deal on what he has read, thus finding in himself rather than in books the source of wisdom, virtue, and good taste. Cf. *Emile.*

[2] Further description of the wild beauties of the mountains (one page).

[3] Continuation of the above (one-half page).

[4] A description of the peasants of the High Valais region (four pages). Saint-Preux praises the sincerity, generosity, and hospitality of the Swiss mountain people. He comments upon their spontaneous and gratuitous kindness, their disdain of crass commerce, their simple and democratic table manners, and their robust physiques. Cf. *Letter to d'Alembert.*

[5] A reference to Saint-Preux's description of the women of the Valais (one-third page).

[6] A comparison of French and Italian music (four pages). Saint-Preux explains how harmony, the distinctive feature of French music, is an artificial invention of civilization, contrary to all the natural laws of the musical art. Italian music, on the other hand, understands well the importance of melody, which is truly natural and expressive of the deepest emotions of the passionate soul. Cf. *Letter on French Music.*

[7] A description of Julie's lessons in Italian music (one page).

[8] An argument against dueling (seven pages). Julie recalls to Saint-Preux a distinction he had once made between genuine and apparent honor and insists that his fighting a duel with Lord Bomston would serve only the latter. She argues further against dueling: the custom is barbarous and

inhumane; the moral stain of killing a man in such a way is greater than that of bearing his insult; honor resides within oneself, not in the opinions of others, and the way to defend it is not by dueling but by living an irreproachable life; a courageous man disdains dueling, and a good man abhors it. Cf. *Letter to d'Alembert.*

[9] An attack on nobility (one page). Lord Bomston denies the claims of the nobility to have done honor to Switzerland and insists to the Baron d'Étange that none of his country's true heroes has been an aristocrat. Cf. *Social Contract.*

[10] An attack upon the evils of the social conventions which permit a father to force a marriage partner upon his daughter (one page). Lord Bomston insists that a father's only duty is to advise his daughter about the character of the man she has chosen.

[11] A comparison of the appearances and temperaments of Claire and Julie (one-half page).

[12] Advice on happiness (three pages). Julie recalls to Saint-Preux the examples of Socrates, Brutus, Regulus, and Cato and reminds him that the only happiness in the world is found by the good man. She warns him against imitating the evil examples to be found in society and of then justifying his vice with the sophistic precepts of the world. Cf. *Emile.*

[13] An analysis of Saint-Preux's love (one page). Julie insists that even though Saint-Preux may be physically attracted by coquettish women, he will never be able to efface her image from his heart.

[14] A discussion of the falseness of Parisian society (four pages). Saint-Preux complains of the artificial terms of politeness one encounters in society which mask real emotions (cf. *Emile*), of the superficial wisdom of Parisian sages which is used only to justify society's current prejudices (cf. *Discourse on the Arts and Sciences*), and of the pressures of conformity which force men to hide their true natures.

[15] A criticism of Saint-Preux's comments on Parisian society (two pages). Julie claims that Saint-Preux has not been in society long enough to reflect so profoundly on it and warns him against developing a superficial style of expression.

[16] A brief reference to the above, in which Julie insists that Claire had dictated the critical remarks (one-fourth page).

[17] Saint-Preux's defense against Claire's criticism (four pages). Saint-Preux justifies his superficial style by maintaining that with it he has captured the tone of the fashionable Parisian society. He further insists to Julie that he is not really attempting to observe the true character of the French. To do that he would have to travel to the provinces and observe the people of the small towns and villages. Cf. *Letter to d'Alembert.*

[18] **Further comments** on the difficulty of observing society (one page). Saint-Preux gives up the idea of observing it truly either as a philosopher or as a simple spectator.

[19] An observation of Parisian society (eight pages). Saint-Preux comments on techniques of satire and ridicule among fashionable society (cf. *Letter to d'Alembert*); on Parisian conversations, both frivolous and serious; on the discussions he has heard about sentiment, the true meaning of which has escaped the fashionable people of the world; on the conformity among the affected Parisians; on the artificiality of the French theater (cf. *Letter to d'Alembert*).

[20] A brief comment on the virtues of the French people (one-half page). Julie cites especially Catinat and Fénelon as modern examples of virtue.

[21] A request from Julie to hear about the Parisian opera (one-fourth page).

[22] A reference to a French work of literary criticism on Pope's *Epistles*, by M. de Crouzas (one-fourth page).

[23] A description of the physical features of Parisian women (one-half page).

[24] Further observations on Parisian women (14 pages). Saint-Preux comments on the absurd dress of fashionable women, on their hair styles, on their lack of modesty, on their harsh speech and excessively frank manner of address, on the differences between them and Swiss women in their preference for male company, on their fondness for the theater, on their immoral liaisons, and on their scornful attitude toward love and marriage. Saint-Preux then tells Julie of a party in the countryside to which he was invited and at which he had the opportunity to observe several women very closely. Here he began to revise his estimate of French women and to see them as good and kind-hearted. But on the whole they are tyrannical and all of society's activities depend upon their tastes and whims. Cf. *Letter to d'Alembert*.

[25] A letter to Claire on the Parisian opera (11 pages). Saint-Preux discusses the reputation of the Parisian opera for magnificence, a reputation which he scorns as extravagant; he attacks the Royal Academy of Music for having false tastes; he describes the physical appearance of the theater and the disagreeable manner in which the performers sing and play French music; and he concludes with a description of the ballets, which he considers the best part of the opera. Cf. *Letter on French Music*.

[26] A letter to Julie in which Saint-Preux criticizes her portrait as not being sufficiently accurate to convey her beauty (four pages).

[27] A reprimand to Saint-Preux (two pages). Julie reminds him that she had warned him earlier not to take on the tone and style of a man of the world.

[28] Moral advice for Saint-Preux (one page). Julie suggests that, in order to avoid a repetition of his offense, he try to anticipate the quality of his remorse beforehand.

[29] Further moral advice (three pages). Commenting on how contact with the fashionable world has tended to make Saint-Preux flippant, Julie advises him to frequent only the homes of grave and studious people, to neglect the aristocracy, to visit with the honest and respectable bourgeoisie, and even to continue his observations in the homes of the poor.

[30] A postscript (one page). Julie reveals to Saint-Preux that she has seen his letters to Lord Bomston and compliments him on his astute insights into political matters.

[31] An analysis of love (two pages). Claire insists to Saint-Preux that a frustrated and unhappy love is preferable to an extinguished love.

[32] A description of the last days of the life of the Baroness d'Étange (one page).

[33] Saint-Preux's irrational lament over losing Julie (one page).

[34] Continuation of the above (one page).

[35] A recapitulation of past events and a description of Julie's marriage to Wolmar (28 pages). Julie reminds Saint-Preux of all the passionate moments of the past six years but insists to him that during the marriage ceremony when she promised to be faithful to her husband, the vow came from her heart. Immediately afterward, she claims, she felt herself cured of her passion for Saint-Preux and perfectly resolved to live as a chaste wife. Telling Saint-Preux of her horror of adultery, she urges him to follow her example in sacrificing his love to virtue.

[36] Further advice to Julie to keep her former affair secret from her husband (one page).

[37] Further description of Wolmar's character as a moderate man (one page).

[38] A comment on the possibility that passionate lovers may make insupportable husbands (one page).

[39] A restatement of the arguments both for and against Julie's telling Wolmar of her love affair (one page).

[40] Another statement of Julie's horror of adultery (one page). Julie once again urges Saint-Preux to subdue his love for her in the name of virtue.

[41] A reference to a 1736 publication in Latin by Johannis Robeck (one-fourth page). Robeck argues in favor of suicide.

[42] An argument in favor of suicide (nine pages). Saint-Preux claims that God permits men to take their lives for the following reasons: just as one

may cut off a diseased limb to save the body, so may one destroy the body to save the soul; it is no crime against God to wish to leave one's mortal life for immortality. Citing Socrates and numerous Romans who committed suicide as examples of courageous men, Saint-Preux insists that to kill one-self is not an immoral or a cowardly act. To be sure, there are responsi-bilities toward others which one must not shirk, but once these are ful-filled it is permissible to relieve oneself of life's miseries; and when those miseries are incurable, the only relief is through suicide. When God makes one's life so painful that death is desirable, then He is, in effect, inviting that person to kill himself. The Bible, after all, contains no injunction against that act.

[43] An argument against suicide (eight pages). Lord Bomston refutes Saint-Preux's arguments by insisting that God has put man on earth for a purpose, namely, to do good. He advises Saint-Preux to examine his conscience to see if he has done enough in his life to permit him to cut it short. If a man suffers from incurable physical ills which deprive him of his will and his reason, suicide is permissible, but as long as he has these faculties, a man of honor must live out his life and devote it to virtue, despite the personal suffering he experiences. Moreover, Saint-Preux would cause his friends to suffer if he committed suicide, sufficient reason in itself for abandoning the project. Finally, Lord Bomston dismisses Saint-Preux's examples: the noble Romans killed themselves not for per-sonal reasons but in the cause of their country.

[44] Julie's lament over growing old (one-half page).

[45] A statement of Claire's love for Julie (one-half page).

[46] A recapitulation of past events in Claire's life (four pages). Claire discloses to Julie that she has talked much to Wolmar and she knows he is confident of Julie's virtue. She gives a résumé of her life with Monsieur d'Orbe and expresses her aversion to a second marriage.

[47] A comparison of the characters of Claire and Julie (one page).

[48] A summary of the places visited and the trials undergone by Saint-Preux on his world voyage (two and one-half pages).

[49] A further statement of Wolmar's confidence in Julie (two pages).

[50] An analysis of Wolmar's trust in Julie's virtue (two pages). Claire warns Julie that her husband, though he is confident of her virtue, might be somewhat disturbed by the language she uses when she talks about Saint-Preux.

[51] A comment on the naturally easy manners of Saint-Preux (one and one-half pages). Claire compares his manners to those of the affected men of Parisian society. Cf. *Emile*.

[52] An anecdote concerning the child Henriette (one and one-half pages). Claire tells of a conversation in which her daughter revealed her fondness for Julie's son.

[53] A statement of Saint-Preux's intent to describe for Lord Bomston the conduct and economy of the Wolmar household at Clarens (one-half page).

[54] A description of the conduct and economy of the Wolmar household (32 pages). Saint-Preux tells Lord Bomston about the vineyards of Clarens and Wolmar's methods of cultivation; his fair treatment of his agricultural workers; the way he and Julie select and train their domestic help; the duties of the house servants and the easy, natural way in which they live together, as contrasted with the constrained manners in Parisian society (cf. *Letter to d'Alembert*); Julie's habit of spending Sunday evenings in a social hour with her women domestics; Julie's preferences in food and drink; the games of the men servants; the social gatherings for both the men and the women where dancing is permitted, despite the proscription of it by the Swiss Protestant church, because Julie feels that such public gatherings of both sexes are pleasurable and actually more innocent and more conducive to morality than private meetings (cf. *Letter to d'Alembert*); the contrast between the strife among the perfidious domestic servants in Paris, a result of wicked habits contracted from their masters and mistresses, and the concord which reigns in the Wolmar household; the ways in which Julie and her husband set examples for their servants; and the just discipline to which the servants are subjected.

[55] Further description of the foliage in Julie's Elysium (one-half page).

[56] Further description of the water passages in Julie's garden (one-half page).

[57] A comment on false tastes in gardens (five pages). Wolmar ridicules the artificiality of formal flower gardens. Flowers, he argues, were made to please the eye, not to be curiously arranged by man. A man of true taste does not try to improve on nature by making it orderly; he simply enjoys natural beauty. Saint-Preux then describes some gardens he has seen in China and in England which would please a man of Wolmar's tastes.

[58] A record of a brief conversation between Julie and Saint-Preux over the household routine (one page).

[59] Further details of Wolmar's self-analysis (one-half page).

[60] A statement of Claire's confidence in Julie's virtue (five pages). Claire believes that Julie's extreme circumspection is harmful, that she ought to have more self-confidence since all those around her have no fear for her virtue. Claire knows and shares Julie's horror of adultery, but she feels that Wolmar's trust in his wife proves that Julie is truly incapable of committing that crime.

[61] A comment on love and virtue (three pages). Wolmar indicates that he is aware that Julie and Saint-Preux still love each other profoundly, but he knows Julie's virtue as a wife and intends, by throwing the two together, to force Saint-Preux to abandon completely his former image of Julie.

[62] A description of the sights along the shores of the Lake of Geneva (one page).

[63] An analysis of the character of Saint-Preux (one and one-half pages). Reviewing the past twelve years, Lord Bomston maintains that Saint-Preux has passed his youth, which he had dedicated to sentiment and experience; now he is mature and must dedicate his life to reflection and thought.

[64] A statement on the usefulness of friends in helping one choose a course of action (one-half page).

[65] A description of life with the Wolmars (37 pages). Saint-Preux praises the harmony and happiness which reigns in the Wolmar household; comments on the fortune of the Wolmars and their manner of using and increasing it; explains Julie's simple tastes in furniture and decoration; describes Julie's care for the people of the villages around Clarens, the principles by which she dispenses her charity, the help she gives the villagers in developing their talents, and her attitudes toward beggars; comments on the moderation Julie displays in her amusements; describes the food and the dining habits of the household; describes Julie's simple tastes in clothes and her aversion to any ostentatious display of wealth; explains Wolmar's economic theories; describes the small economies of the household; describes Wolmar's work among the peasants; tells of the affection displayed among the members of the family and of the sentimental evening routine; and concludes with praise for Julie's beauty, grace, and virtue.

[66] A summary of the Wolmars' ideas on education (35 pages). Saint-Preux tells Lord Bomston of Julie's calm and loving manner with her children and of her mild and firm discipline. He then summarizes the Wolmars' educational theories: one must remember first of all that children are not rational beings; reason is acquired at a much later age. Therefore one must be patient with children and not expect them to act like adults; moreover, one should not try to teach them intellectual subjects before they are ready. Each child has his unique genius and character. One must not try to change or restrain it but to allow it to perfect itself, for all human beings are originally good and all vices observable in human character come from the false forms society tries to impose on their natural geniuses. Education, then, is a matter of allowing natural penchants to develop fully. Instead of disciplining a child rigidly, one should allow him freedom and provide him with examples of good conduct in an orderly, harmonious environment. However, one should not be over-indul-

gent. Children should not be urged to read at an early age, for their knowledge comes primarily from experience. Cf. *Emile*.

[67] A brief account of the war between the English and the French (one-half page).

[68] An explanation of Julie's natural religion (one page). Saint-Preux reports further on the quality of Julie's belief in and love of God, which stem from her sentimental response to the immensity of the universe. Cf. *Emile*.

[69] A comment on Wolmar's atheism (two pages). Saint-Preux attacks the open atheism to be found in papist countries (cf. *Emile*). Wolmar, however, for the sake of his wife and children, does not outwardly show his lack of faith. He attends church and conforms to established religious usage. Saint-Preux insists that Wolmar's atheism does not spring from any vice in his character but from the coldness of his heart.

[70] A reference to country games held in Claire's honor (one-quarter page).

[71] Saint-Preux's lyrical praise of life in the country (two pages).

[72] A description of the activities of the grape harvest (six pages). Saint-Preux tells Lord Bomston of the work, of the gaiety which accompanies it, and of the pleasurable musical gatherings during leisure moments.

[73] A comment on Lord Bomston's love affairs and on Claire's attitude toward love and marriage (five pages). Julie expresses her fears and doubts over Lord Bomston's decision and then, analyzing Claire's character, urges her to consider a second marriage.

[74] A suggestion that Claire and Saint-Preux marry (one and one-half pages).

[75] An anecdote told by Julie concerning Claire's child, and a letter from Henriette to her mother begging Claire to return to Clarens soon (one and one-half pages).

[76] Further assertions that Laura would be unsuitable as a wife to Lord Bomston (one page).

[77] A résumé of Claire's sentiments of the past twelve years in regard to Saint-Preux (two pages).

[78] Claire's confession of her growing fondness for Saint-Preux (one and one-half pages).

[79] Further arguments against a second marriage for Claire (two pages). Claire insists first that the memory of her first husband prevents her from marrying again; she also admits that she is not sure that Saint-Preux really is fond of her in the way that would make their marriage feasible.

[80] Claire's acknowledgment of her letters from Italy and from Clarens and her promise to write Julie a long letter from Geneva (one and one-half pages).

[81] An argument against celibacy (one-half page). Wolmar insists that men have a duty to propagate the race.

[82] A letter from Claire on the character of the citizens of Geneva (eight pages). Claire praises the Genevans for their smoothly functioning republican government and for their openness, generosity, good sense and insight. But she criticizes their love of money and their insufficient pride in their former simplicity and long-standing liberty. She discusses the Genevans' love for and skill in conversation, their pronunciation, the learning displayed by both men and women, their dress and manners, the harmony of their domestic life, and their courage. Cf. *Letter to d'Alembert*.

[83] Correspondence between Julie and Saint-Preux on matters of virtue and morality (45 pages). Julie insists that a wise and virtuous soul is a pure one (cf. *Emile*) and is the source of one's morality. She reminds Saint-Preux of the times in the past when he was tempted to act immorally and warns him that eternal vigilance is necessary. When he comes to live at Clarens, he will find temptation all around him. Subtly she suggests to him that his wisest course would be to marry Claire. She asks him to examine his conscience and pray to God for guidance rather than turn, like a philosopher, to general laws and merely human judgment for rules to live by (cf. *Emile*). Saint-Preux replies by insisting that Julie has nothing to fear, for both of them are changed persons and both are incapable of immoral acts. He assures her that he now loves only her virtues, not her person. He confesses that he has great affection for Claire, but of a totally different kind from that which he felt for Julie; he knows he cannot marry Claire, because she would know his heart too well to believe it could ever be totally hers, and because he has no desire to supplant Monsieur d'Orbe in her heart. He claims that he is happy simply living near her and enjoying her company; he wants no further union. Aware of Claire's growing love for him, he knows too that once having been Julie's lover he can never be another's. Saint-Preux then warns Julie against thinking too much about temptations and immorality, especially since he is convinced of his victory over his passions. Answering Julie's advice to trust in God, he defines divine grace: God has given us reason in order to know what is good, conscience to love it, and freedom to choose it; therefore one can safely trust oneself to decide upon a virtuous and moral course of conduct (cf. *Emile*). Like a Deist, Saint-Preux does not believe that God gives any individual extraordinary assistance as a result of prayer, for such preference is not in accord with divine justice; this is not to say that prayer is useless, but we must not believe that we have the power to make God perform miracles just for us (cf. *Emile*). Saint-Preux urges Julie not to send him away or make him marry Claire just

because of her fears for his virtue. Julie responds that she had no such intention. By urging his marriage to Claire she had simply hoped to unite them all more closely. She assures him that she is happier and more self-confident now than ever; her advice to him had not been meant to indicate any insecurity on her part. Yet, despite all her present happiness, she still has a secret regret, a secret longing which leads her to religious meditations. It is not that she is a mystic, nor that she subscribes to any creed which insists upon devotion to God at the expense of one's duty to one's fellow man. The God she worships is not a vengeful but a just and merciful God (cf. *Emile*). She cannot believe, therefore, that God would punish the good Wolmar, despite his atheism. Hoping by her true Christian example to convert her husband, she once again invites Saint-Preux to return and help her in this task.

[84] A self-analysis in which Wolmar reveals his initial suspicions of the truth of Julie's religious faith (one and one-half pages).

[85] A description of Claire's anxiety (one page).

[86] A brief reference to the death of the Emperor Vespasian (one-fourth page).

[87] A description of one of Julie's last dinners with her family and a résumé of a conversation with a minister (ten pages). Wolmar again confesses his inquietude over his atheism, and the beginning of his conversion as he listened to Julie's statement of her faith in a just and merciful God. Since her heart tells her that she is dying as a virtuous woman, she has no fears but instead rejoices as she draws nearer to God's throne (cf. *Emile, Reveries of a Solitary Stroller*). The minister compares Julie's joyous attitudes toward death with the fears and terrors of most Christians as they approach their last hour.

[88] An expression of Julie's concern for her father (one-half page).

[89] A description of Julie's last day (15 pages). Early in the day Claude Anet returns and there is a sentimental scene around Julie's bed as she recognizes him. In the afternoon Wolmar and Claire listen to Julie's last conversation. She recapitulates the events of her life and expresses her love for all those who were dear to her. When the minister joins them, the conversation turns to the subject of the immortality of the soul, a doctrine which Julie believes implicitly, for, as she says, God speaks to us not through our mortal organs but through the intangible sentiments of our hearts. Contrary to the belief of the minister that eternity will be spent in enjoying the sublimity of the Creator, Julie's hope is that she will meet her loved ones again in the next world (cf. *Emile*). During the evening, Julie experiences a momentary rally which raises Claire's hopes.

[90] A description of the return of the Baron d'Étange, of his grief and

anguish over his daughter's death, and of Claire's placing a veil over Julie's face (three pages).

[91] An account of Wolmar's attempt to restore Claire to her reason (two pages). Wolmar dresses Henriette to look like Julie; the resemblance is enough to touch Claire's heart and encourage her to continue living.

(2 years)

I. 1. St P declares love
2. St P wants a response
3. St P sees she's affected, bids adieu
   series of notes
4. J declares love
5. St P's joy – will be honorable
6. J–Claire: governess corrupted us, reform!
7. C–J (addressed to St P) – understands all.
8. St P– 2 months later – important → why is she so calm?
9. J – because sees love can be guiltless
10. St P praises her virtue, accuses her of killing him
11. J – sees thru St P, to take leadership
12. St P praises artless style, proposes books, will obey
13. J in country, to invite St P to arbor
14. St P passionate after kiss, J faints
15. J sends St P to the Valais
16. St P to obey, but refuses money
17. J insists he take money
18. St P in Sion
19. St P: did my letter go astray?
20. J explains postal system. father home.
21. St P's joy at receiving mail
22. J: parents discuss St P. come closer.
23. St P on mountains, villagers
24. St P refuses to consider salary
25. J's response
    note – St P across lake
26. St P's despair   (note on sentiment)
27. C–St P, J ill – come at once
28. J–C, St P wild. father has chosen husband
29. J–C, I am ruined.
30. C–J, she knew J would either love or die. one error & ruin
31. St P – sees her torment.
32. J – miserable because no longer virtuous, but has schemes.
33. J – uncomfortable meeting St P in public. has secret.
34. St P's pov of social gathering.
35. Jon jealousy & honesty
36. J: parents away, w/ uncle + C + chalet
37. J sad that dishonest w/ parents
38. St P gushes over last night's meeting
39. J – guilt of enclosed letter, St P must straighten out
40.   Fanchon's fiancé enlisted, almost driven to prostitution
41. J sends money
42. St P to obey
43. St P got Claude released, feels benevolence
44. J: parents back early, ok. intro Lord Bomston.
45. St P describes Bomston, a sensitive soul
46. J on gender
47. St P jealous of Lord B.

48. StP on Italian music
49. J on Lord B
50. J upset abt something StP said
51. StP prostrate, swears off wine
52. J forbids him to " " "
53. J sets up meeting
54. StP writes in J's room - "to the moment"
55. StP gushes abt night together
56. C's warnings: StP + Lord B to duel, affair to be found out (nb-2 years)
57. J against duelling
58. J-Lord B: admits has lover - relies on his sensitive soul
59. M. d'Orbe-J: Lord B still insists on code of honor
60. StP, Lord B's apology
61. J praises Lord B
62. C-J. Lord B suggested J-StP match - StP has noble heart, warns abt gossip (mis-carries)
63. J-parents argue - father beats her, forbids her to see StP - puts in C's hands
64. C-M. d'Orbe - friendship over passion. plans to handle J.
65. C-J. describes StP's departure

II. 1. StP still loves. what went wrong?
2. Lord B-C. on true love vs prejudice.
      encl: fragments by StP
3. Lord B-J. offers estate if she will elope w/ StP.
4. J-C. needs advice. eloping tempting but would hurt parents
5. C-J. J's power (elite) - C won't give advice - will follow J (mention Wolmar)
   note: J will do duty
6. J-Lord B. must not hurt parents.
7. J scolds StP, where is honor?
8. C scolds StP, takes credit for J's decision
9. Lord B-C. StP has submitted, will go to Paris, then London.
10. StP-C, reiterates.
11. J wants StP to use talents, fare well, won't marry w/o his permission.
12. StP loves her virtue. promises not to marry another.
13. StP in Paris, will copy all J's letters. Lord B has given pension
14. StP finds Paris society empty.
15. J - hearts still united, C to marry d'Orbe, is gay
16. StP on J's letters, finds pleasure in suffering
17. StP on Paris society, must lock up sentiments
18. J: C married, new role, now send letters via Regianino, mother ill
19. StP still down on Paris
20. J sends trinket
21. StP down on Parisian women
22. StP - rapture at receiving portrait
(23. StP on opera)
24. J on portrait
(25. StP on portrait)
26. StP tricked into going to whorehouse
27. J's response - forgives, but points out errors
28. J in a tizzy. letters gone!

III. 1. C–StP: J destraught, her mother ill. you must renounce

  2. StP–Mme d'E– renounces

  3. StP–C – angry

  4. C–StP –sees virtue. even Mme d'E sees love.

  5. J: mother dead, angry adieu to StP

  6. StP–C –wretched

  7. C–StP– esteems, but as child. Mme d'E died of illness, not grief, J still loves

  8. Lord B–StP – am I forgotten?

  9. StP–Lord B – no
   note from J: demands pledge back

  10. Baron d'E–StP – knows all–furious, insults StP

  11. StP–d'E– injured, but encloses note of release for J.

  12. J – forced into marriage

  13. J–C. has been ill, disfigured. dreamed StP visited

  14. C–J. he did visit. –J caught your smallpox. J not disfigured

  15. J still loves, but will obey father

  16. StP will return every year

  17. C–StP – J is married

  ⚹ 18. J– converted to virtue at wedding   (now 6 years!)

  19. StP doesn't want her to tell W. abt him. adieu forever.

  20. J praises W's moderation. love not nec. for marriage. thus best. adieu forever.

  21. StP–Lord B. contemplating suicide, arguments in favor.

  22. Lord B–StP – argues against suicide

  23. Lord B offers StP secret mission

  24. StP–Lord B – yes

  25. Lord B–StP– mission is 3-yr voyage

  26. StP–C– tells of voyage   (J has baby ⚹)

IV. 1. J–C. married (4 yrs since?) 6 yrs, C widowed, motherhood, debates telling Wolmar, worries abt StP. wants (to live w/her)

  2. C–J. grateful. StP on way home,

  3. StP– is back, wants to visit

  4. W–StP – knows all, invites w/ friendship

  5. C–StP – invites

  6. StP–Lord B. first meeting at Clarens

  7. J–C– POV of meeting, Wolmar's forgiveness.

  8. C–J. can't come now. send StP here.

  9. C–J. (later)–sends back StP + daughter

  10. StP–Lord B. long letter on management of Wolmar household

  11. StP–Lord B. natural garden Elysium

  12. J–C. Wolmar gave history, had originals of letters. J not sure can trust self.

  13. C–J. must trust self. (w. a prince)

  14. W–C. must test J & StP, wants StP to educate children

  15. StP–Lord B. J not happy – has secret ...

  16. J–W– miffed.

  17. StP–Lord B. boat outing, storm. visit Meillerie, still love, but virtue wins.

V.

1. Lord B - St P - grow up
2. St P - Lord B. content of Wolmars; their life
3. St P - Lord B. Wolmars' ed. theories
4. Lord B - St P. - missed letter - worried abt J.
5. St P - Lord B - her grief is that w. a skeptic
6. St P - Lord B - staying away. joyful reunion w/ Claire
7. St P - Lord B - grape harvest, reconciled of J's father
8. St P - Wolmar. travelling w/ Lord B. accepts role of children's tutor
9. St P - C. travels w/ B - dreams J dying - returns to see her - feels recovered. (loves C)
10. C - St P - is spooked by St P's dream
11. W - St P - dream means you think too much abt J
12. St P - W - Lord B at risk of marrying fallen woman
13. J - C - wants C to marry St P

VI.

1. C - J. in Lausanne w/ family
2. C - J. on love for St P. reluctant to remarry
3. Lord B - Wolmar. - St P extricated him from Laura, mutual loyalty.
4. ~~to~~ Lord B - approves
(5 - Claire on Genevans)
6. J - St P - gives credit to W. for virtue
   §
9. Fanchon - St P - J jumped in water when son fell - now very ill
10. C, W to St P - J dead, left instructions.
11. W - St P - describe J's virtue in dying, C's grief/madness
12. J - St P - still loves. wants him to marry C, educate her children
13. C - St P. come back but don't be unfaithful to J

Vevey
Clarens - country home
Sion - in the Valais
Meillerie - opposite shore to Clarens
Lausanne - Claire's house